When Colour
Became Grey

When Colour Became Grey (When Colour Became Grey series, Book 1)

Published by A C Lorenzen

® 2019 by A C Lorenzen

ISBN: 978-1-9161836-0-5

dedicated to Simon

I kicked wildly at them, but they were too strong and my kicks were ineffective. The one with the oily hair roared again and I could see its teeth in the streetlight; the razor-sharp corner teeth glistened dangerously. Holding up my arms to protect my face, the creature sank its teeth into my forearm while I screamed in horror. The other sunk its teeth into my leg. I could feel them draining me of my blood; the pain paralysed me. My body was set on fire. Was this how I would die? Or... die again?

PREMONITIONS

It was dark. No matter how much I ran, I couldn't escape them. Distorted creatures were following me, always just on my heel. They were trying to hurt me, their claws reaching for me. My feet became lead and I couldn't run anymore. The creatures encircled me in a deadly trap, yapping at me and flashing their sharp teeth. My heart was racing. I raised my arms to protect myself, but I was sure it was useless. Any moment now they would tear me apart, ripping my limbs off one by one.

Someone was touching my arms, pulling them slowly down from my face. It felt like ice sticking to my skin.

All I could see now was him. A man. A strong jaw line, blond hair and ocean blue eyes. The typical surfer. But he was not free-spirited and life-embracing; he was bleak and full of darkness. All the scary creatures that had hunted me before were gone. It was just him and me, in a lightless room.

'Ameerah, this is not a dream', he spoke, his voice resonating in my head.

His steel-blue eyes fixated on mine. It felt strangely real. The man's face leant further towards me. His face felt cold, like an ice statue the air prickled against my skin. I noticed I couldn't feel my arms anymore. 'I'm Blake. You can trust me. When they ask you, say yes and everything will be alright.'

'What do you mean?' I tried to turn away from him, but I couldn't. His hands pulled me closer to him. There was a feeling of imminent doom in my stomach.

'Trust me and everything will be ok,' he said as a draft crawled up my spine. He pushed me away brutally and suddenly I was falling, falling from up high into complete blackness. I screamed for dear life.

I opened my eyes and lay soaking in sweat, breathing erratically. I had been haunted by Blake – whoever he was – for the last many nights, so many I had lost count. Every night it was the same. He was becoming so real to me I feared I might one day wake up with him in my bedroom.

The radio turned itself on, and whether I liked it or not, it was time to start the day. I shook the unpleasant memories from my head and walked over to my bathroom. Only once I was sure the water was piping hot did I get into the shower, washing away the nightmare, and with it, the lingering torment.

The radio station announced another sunny day with temperatures near 38°C. With a towel wrapped around my hair I walked into the kitchen and turned on the coffee machine. My dog Bruce came rushing from the living room to greet me. He could barely contain himself. The moment I reached down he jumped up to cuddle with me, his tail wiggling happily against my leg.

I poured the coffee into my battered blue travel mug. Bruce sat by the terrace door, eyeing me with anticipation. Without any breakfast in me, I grabbed the keys and unlocked the terrace door. Bruce raced outside and made a loop in the garden.

We started our usual walk behind the house along a dusty sand road between the empty fields of long dry grass and patches of shrubbery. The sun was climbing the sky and warmed my skin. Crickets had already started their concerts and birds were eagerly swooping into the brush, ferreting out insects. The coffee sips slowly woke me up.

Bruce ran forward, following trails, stopping, sniffing in the wind, looking back to make sure I was still there, then he continued racing around the fields. Every now and again he ran back towards me, circled around me before speeding off once again. I could see how happy he was rushing through the grass and looking at me with his big goofy smile. I could still remember the day I found him in those very fields, abandoned. A small wincing beige-coloured ball of fur had tumbled onto the road in front of me; I had sat down and let him come closer, patting and caressing him. When I had walked home, he had followed me the whole way. I was sure my parents would be against adopting him, but my brother and I begged like we had never wanted anything else. That night my brother and the dog had fallen asleep together on the floor, and my mother had not had the heart to separate them. My brother was only six, so he was mostly my dog and I took care of him. The daily walks were my time to reflect and make sense of life, not that I wasn't still confused about the meaning of life at twenty-four.

I checked my watch. It was time to get back; I couldn't be late for class. With a sharp whistle I caught his attention; he stopped, looked up at me frozen in place. I turned around and just a few seconds later he raced past me back towards the house.

My mother was in the kitchen making breakfast. The chopping of fruit was audible and the smell of fresh ground coffee was lingering in the air. My younger brother Liam sat by the table playing with two toy cars. From the gentle sound of running water inside the pipes in the walls I knew my stepfather was upstairs in the shower.

'Good morning!' I shouted passing the kitchen and hurrying to my bedroom to pick up my backpack.

'Hun, get ready! You're gonna be late for class!' my mother shouted, her head sticking out of the door frame.

'I'm about to leave. Can you make me the usual milkshake?'

'Already done, here!' She came into my room and held the large black travel mug towards me. I stashed it into my backpack and was out the door just minutes later. With the helmet on my head I pushed my scooter out of the garage and turned on the engine. A loud puffing sound boomed and it awoke. The stony driveway leading up to the road made me vibrate uncomfortably on my small scooter.

As I approached the city, traffic became denser. The commuters caused a daily gridlock in the city and my campus was on the opposite side of town.

The morning lecture had just begun when I thought I suddenly saw out of the corner of my eye a Blake-persona standing in the corner of the classroom by the door. When I looked over, he was gone. A chill went down my spine.

I tried to concentrate on the professor in front of the blackboard and forget about Blake, but during the whole lecture I had the impression he was just behind me. Every now and again I could feel a cold breath on my neck, making me jerk up.

Luckily, I only had class in the morning and hoped I could rid myself of him on my way home. The hot air brushed against my skin and made my t-shirt swim in the air on my drive home.

When I finally arrived at home the thick air and intense sunrays baked me before I had locked my scooter.

'There you are!' Mum came out of the house as I emerged from the open garage. She planted a kiss on my cheek. 'Can you watch Liam for a bit? I'll just get some shopping done.'

I nodded and she left in her deep blue Mercedes.

Liam announced he wanted to go swimming in the pool, so I took my homework out on the terrace and studied while he splashed around in the water. Bruce followed me faithfully and settled in the shade under the patio table, his fury back resting against my shin.

Liam looked so small with just his head sticking out of the water and his floats around his two chicken-arms. For such a small person however, he did make a lot of noise, splashing around and paddling after his floating ducks.

From the terrace I could hear the entrance door being opened and heavy steps followed.

'Hey honey, how was your day?' said my stepfather, David, as he came out onto the terrace and kissed me on the forehead.

'Good, good, nothing special to report. I have a lot of stuff to study this weekend.' I said smiling at him from my chair.

'I'm sure you can do it. Is your mother home?'

'No, she left. She had to do some errands so I'm watching the sea monster.' I responded, nodding towards Liam and the torrent of splashes he was whipping up.

'Well, in a minute you'll be watching us both,' David smiled and disappeared into the house. A few minutes later he reappeared in a pair of swimming trunks. Liam tried to swim towards his father, but he had trouble moving around in the water and mostly ended up just splashing around in circles.

David let himself fall into the pool and swam in two strokes to his son. He pulled him high up out of the water and kissed him on the cheek. No one could mistake them for anything but father and son; both had light blond hair, identical brown eyes, and the same large forehead.

I didn't have many memories of my biological father. All I knew was that he had left us and started a new family. I had chosen to forget about him, as I presumed, he had done the same to my mother and I. David was a great man who treated my mother well and I had come to see him as my father. He had offered to adopt me shortly after their marriage. Since then we had grown very close and we regularly went to dinner together just the two of us.

Eventually, mum came out on the terrace, dressed in her bikini, ready to join them in the pool. I had been so deep in my thoughts I had not even heard her come back from her shopping.

'How is the homework going?' she asked and looked at my open folders and books on the table.

I grunted in response.

'Leave your notes in my bedroom and I'll take a look at it while you're at dinner with Dad,' she said, smiling and brushing my hair behind my ear.

'Leah, come! The water is perfect!' David shouted from the pool over Liam's shrieks. My mother walked over to the pool and gracefully stepped in.

'Mummy, mummy, look at me!' Liam screamed delighted and tried to paddle over to her. His movements made the water spill over and wet the terrace.

They looked so happy together, the three of them. Liam was still young; I wasn't sure he understood his father was not my father. Or he simply didn't care. Even if they hadn't treated me any differently, I always felt like an outsider. Like something didn't quite fit.

All three of them came out of the pool dripping with chlorine-saturated water.

'What time is it?' Mum came to me and looked at my phone, 'Oh honey you better get ready.' She turned to David and kissed him quickly.

'Right, Meerah, you ready?' David asked me.

'Just need ten minutes.' I got up and walked into my room with my books and notes. Bruce awoke from under the table and raced into the house ahead of me. I checked my scarce makeup and put on a loose blue top and short blue jeans and tied my hair back in a high ponytail.

Bruce gave a tortured sound and I bent down to scratch him behind the ears, 'You'll have to wait until I get back.'

The staff at the restaurant showed us to our table. The orange and beige décor and quiet music made me feel comfortable. The chef waved at us as we came in.

'How is work?' I asked David, picking at the slices of Baguette the waiter had placed on the table.

David took a sip from his glass of red wine and started talking. He was running his own company, but recently had thought about selling the company and start something new.

We then proceeded to talking about my studies and how I imagined my life after college.

We left the restaurant not too late; Bruce was waiting for his walk. At home, my parents went up to their bedroom to watch a movie together. Before they did, mum handed me back the draft of my history paper with her own notes. I took a look into Liam's room and kissed him on the forehead. He was already asleep and had twisted his duvet in all directions, so it only covered his back. I rearranged it and stood a while at his door watching him sleep. He was such a sweet boy.

Bruce was sitting by the terrace door in my room, anticipating his evening walk. I opened the door and let Bruce run out while I gathered my mobile phone and a torch light.

There was a thump.

When I turned around, a book had shifted on the shelf. It was an edition of the Good Omen. I walked over to it and put it back in place. There was a sound of something bumping into my desk. I spun around, but the room was empty. The door to the rest of the house was closed, the stack of books on my desk were untouched, my bed was made, the poster of Canada on the wall above my bed hadn't changed. It had to have been my imagination going wild with all those stupid nightmares.

I turned away and walked out to catch up with Bruce.

The sun was low, but it was still light enough outside. The smell of lavender swirled in the air. The typical smells of Provence were carried by the Mistral wind through the landscape and out towards the Mediterranean Sea. Even with this fresh breeze, I wasn't cold.

My thoughts drifted around just like the wind, until they were disturbed by a sudden bark.

Bruce only barked when he felt threatened, and that was a rarity. I followed him away from the road into the tall grass. He stared into the air and showed his teeth.

'Bruce!' I scolded him and he stopped. He seemed fixated on something in the middle of the air. With the torch light I scanned around us, but there was nothing but the swaying of the dried long grass. The sun had dipped below the horizon and the night was quickly rolling over us; I didn't feel comfortable staying out longer.

I turned around and headed back home. Bruce followed me even though he stopped a few times to look back and growl. He acted as though there was someone with us. I found myself sweeping the grounds more often with the torchlight, suddenly feeling paranoid. All I saw was the sea of grass moving with the wind.

It was dark. After being chased by distorted figures with long claws and sharp teeth, he was there. The ocean blue eyes, staring right at me, burning my skin with his icy hands. Again.

'Ameerah, this is not a dream.' Blake haunted me again in my sleep. I wanted to wake up and escape him. He always brought those dangerous creatures with him, and then he pushed me off the edge. I willed myself but was unable to move.

'It is time now. You will have to crossover. Don't be afraid. Trust me.'

His eyes stared into mine and I could feel his hands on my face. This time they felt warm, there was no burning from the coldness. Then, he let go, disappearing into thin air and I gently resurfaced into consciousness.

This time, I was not frantic; I was calm. With a strange feeling in my stomach I started my daily routine. The feeling in my stomach grew stronger with every passing hour of the day.

A stormy shower started in the late afternoon and it was pouring in streams by the time I got on my scooter to head home. I could barely see in front of me. The roads were slippery, and I was not confident riding my scooter in even a light drizzle. The condensed air settled on the inside of my visor transforming into fog. The heavy rain drew a grey curtain over the Earth. Blake's face kept appearing in front of me, distracting me.

Eventually, I made it out of the city and only a few more miles separated me from home. I switched on the high beam lights, though on the scooter there was not much difference. The rain had not calmed down; the cars overtook me too closely as always.

Finally, I saw a group of houses appear in the distance to my left; my house was at the bottom of that street. I slowed down. Only a few more minutes and I would be home. Lights from an oncoming vehicle appeared in front of me, but I had enough time to turn off the road before the car would be close.

A flash caught my eye. I looked in the rear-view mirror, but I had no time to act. Someone came up behind me, speeding out of the curve, way over the speed limit.

I had no time. I turned the gas dial hoping to clear the way, but the road was slippery. A deep honk echoed. The scooter slipped on the road just as the car made impact.

I closed my eyes.

When I opened them again, only a few seconds had passed. The pain struck me like lightning. I could still hear the honking; a deep horn from a truck driving by. I lay on the concrete ground in the middle of the road. I couldn't breathe. I couldn't move. The rain drummed down on me. Warm liquid filled my jacket.

Then it was quiet. There was just the sound of the rain on my helmet. It was growing dark around me. I was cold, so cold. Everything slowed down. Someone appeared above me, but I could already tell it was too late. I couldn't see who it was. My brain wasn't getting enough oxygen. It quietly shut down. Everything was so quick. The excruciating pain faded. It was all over now. I was relieved of my aches. And I let go…

BEHIND THE CURTAIN

With one big gasp I woke.

There was light around me. It was warm. I sat up and looked down at myself. Nothing was broken. All seemed fine. I wasn't hurting.

I got up and looked around. Everything was blurry, I couldn't recognise anything. I was surrounded by whiteness. There were no contours, no shades, nothing. Everything was white. What had happened? Where was I?

A strong current dragged me forward, where the whiteness seemed to be emanating light from, intensifying by the second.

I tried to remember how I got there but there was nothing. It was like a blank page.

I gave in to the current and stepped closer towards the light, shading my eyes with my arm. There was no one around, but I had a strange sensation I was not alone. With every step I took the light got brighter and brighter around me. The dragging current grew stronger, grabbing me with its invisible hands, pulling me inwards like a black hole.

Something ran down my forehead. I reached for it and looked at my hand; it was wet and clear. I touched my hair and it was wet. What had happened? I found I had trouble breathing. I looked down at myself again. Something was not right. I was both warm and cold. I opened my jacket and thick hot blood poured out of a wound by my stomach into the white surrounding. The blood immediately dissipated into thin air like smoke mixing into the air.

The accident.

The pain.

It all came back to me.

The car had crashed into me. It all came rushing back in powerful flashes. I tried to cover up the wound across my stomach, but the blood kept seeping through my fingers and disappearing into the nothing.

What had happened? Was I dead? *Dead?!*

Blake…

Was this real?! Had he warned me I would die? Was this what he talked about? Was this part of the decision I had to make?

The force pulling me into the brightness increased in painful waves with each memory of the accident that came back to me.

Black shapes appeared amidst the whiteness. They floated towards me somehow without moving. Their bodies were pale as dead corpses and their long robes were black and moved around them as if they were underwater. Their dark clothes were an extreme contrast to the surrounding whiteness. It was painful to look at.

'Ameerah…' I could hear my name, but it didn't come from the shapes approaching me; it came from everywhere, from inside my head.

'You will be judged now,' the voices announced. The shapes stopped in front of me and I could see there were five of them, looking at me. Their eyes were gone and grotesque black holes replaced them. A thin layer of skin stretched over their heads. So thin I could clearly see their skulls underneath the leathery skin. Where there should have been mouths, there was just leathery pale skin. The sight made me want to throw up.

I remembered what Blake had said. He had given me instructions.

'I want to cross,' I eagerly tried to say but no words would leave my lips. My mouth was sown shut.

'Everything has a price.' Five voices echoed perfectly synchronized in my head, 'Will you pay the price?'

'Yes! Please, just let me go! I will pay!' I pleaded in my mind.

'It is agreed. You will serve sixty-seven years-'

I was confused. 'Sixty-seven years?!'
'As a ghost.'

Somewhere a gong sounded. The echoing noise invaded the white space and the black shapes dissolved in the air like the blood from my stomach had. The strong current pulling me towards the light abruptly stopped and reversed. A cold rough wind knocked me over, only I did not hit the ground. I felt like I was falling down an elevator shaft. It would not end. I screamed in terror. It was suddenly very dark. The wind gushed past me.

My body smashed into something cold. I grunted in anguish and tried to move. The sky was above me, my back on the hard ground. It was grey and lightly raining; twilight was approaching. In agony I raised myself up. My clothes were soaked in blood; when I pulled up my sweater, I saw an ugly scar stretching over my abdomen, it appeared to have been sown shut by an apprentice embalmer. It was horrible. I quickly covered it up again before my stomach contracted to empty itself.

I walked into a busy shopping street with pedestrians crossing in all directions, pushing each other to get more quickly to their destinations.

Where was I? An empty sensation passed through me. It disappeared as quickly as it had risen inside me, leaving me disoriented. I looked at the crowd zigzagging. The shops around me looked to be closing up and this was the rush of commuters hurrying home.

'Excuse me,' I tried to catch a man's attention. He passed by me without even granting me a mere glance.

Before I had turned to ask another person for help, a second empty sensation hit me, disappearing just as quickly as the first one had. The dizzying feeling afterwards made my stomach turn. Across the street I saw a bar. They would surely give me a glass of water.

As I stepped into the crowd, the sensation of desolation repeated itself every few seconds, leaving me more and more drained. My feet stumbled backwards and I hit the wall with my back. The sensation stopped. I took a couple of breaths before attempting to cross the street once more, but the sensation returned. Every few seconds I was hit with this wave of dread and loneliness. Pushing as quickly as I could through the crowd, I reached the other side, exhausted. My hands held on to the door frame of the pub while I steadied myself. A burly man opened the door to the pub without glancing my way and walked through me. The feeling repeated itself.

A thought passed my mind.

That could not be.

Terrified, I stretched my arm out slowly towards the rushing commuters. The moment someone passed through it, the sensation struck me. I retracted my arm and glued myself to the wall. Could they even see me?

'Hello?' I asked hesitantly but no one took notice.

A couple of girls tumbled out of the pub on high heels, holding on to each other. I stepped in front of them. 'Ladies can I-' before I had finished my sentence, the brunette to the right had already passed through me. Literally.

I *was* a ghost! An actual ghost! Where was I? What had happened to me? Was I dead? Was this what it felt like to be dead?

Hugging myself I crumbled to the ground, motionless, letting the rain pelt down. What was going on? Was I dreaming? I had to be! This was not the afterlife! This *couldn't* be!

The rain had wet my clothes to my skin and made me shiver. The rush of people had dwindled down as time had passed and now the streets were empty. Twilight had gone and it was evening now.

I wanted to go home. Immediately. Desperately. I jumped to my feet and ran up and down the streets, randomly. I tried to recognise any buildings, landmarks... but everything was different. There were buildings but nothing I recognised. Tears ran down my cheeks. I was lost and people were blind to my very existence. Was I being punished? What had I done to deserve this? *Was this hell?*

The night air filled my lungs; I was too cold to stay outside. With nowhere to go and no idea where I was, I could only hope to locate Blake from my dreams. Only he seemed to have seen this coming. But how would I find him?

I could hear rumbling noises not too far away coming from what looked like a rundown restaurant.

When I came closer, I didn't see anyone outside and the windows were taped shut from the inside with newspapers. Something tingled in my system and told me to proceed, so I opened the door and stepped into the restaurant. The only source of light was from a naked bulb dangling from the ceiling. The walls were scratched and beaten up to the point that I worried about the foundations. There were yaps and high-pitched noises coming from further inside. Something in my stomach made me keep going. There was something I had to see.

I spied around a corner and saw three Bonobo-sized creatures crouched on the floor. They appeared to be animals, but I could not tell what kind. They were gathered around a person lying on the ground. I risked a step closer. The man lying on the floor was motionless. One creature was crouched by the man's upper leg, the other two on his upper body.

It hit me; the person on the ground was dead and the animals... were eating the corpse of a man!

I was mortified. Being invisible was terrifying enough, but this was too much. The floor under me creaked; the three creatures turned their blood-covered faces simultaneously. The dead man had bite marks on his body and blood oozing out of them.

Their skin was a mixture of light brown and green, with blood-coloured eyes and a long tail. Their claws were much longer than human fingers, their noses and mouths stuck out of their faces. Two of them were bald while the third one had thin black oily hair on its scalp. They looked to be a cross of dogs and bats without any fur on their bodies. The creatures hissed in my direction, bearing their sabretooth-like teeth.

I took another step backwards and they turned their bodies toward me, intrigued. Of course! This was hell so normal people couldn't see me, but sabretooth-creatures could! Lucky me.

Without wasting anymore time, I turned on my heels and ran as fast as I could out of the building and back into the misty rain. They followed roaring and hissing after me. I was too terrified to think of blocking the door behind me, but later wished I had. I ran faster than I ever had, but they were still catching up to me.

My mind wasn't thinking. After just a few minutes I sprinted down a street that turned out to be a dead-end. By the time I realised, the three creatures were already behind me, approaching on all fours with their tails raised high, blocking my exit. There was no other way out. Panic mounted inside me. I had to defend myself.

There was nothing around me but a dumpster and some long dirty pieces of wood, probably from a construction site. Completely desperate, I picked up one of the wooden planks and held it like a baseball bat. The timber beam was heavy and long; I could barely hold it upright.

This was a nightmare. I would die here... or die again! The adrenaline made me shiver. I prayed this was another nightmare and I would wake up, *now!*

One of the creatures ran at me and jumped up, reaching with its claws for my face. I swung the wooden beam like I had seen in so many movies. To my surprise, I managed to make contact with its face. It crashed into the dumpster as the two others approached. I clubbed the second one in the same way, but the third swung out with its claws and scratched my shoulder. With another swipe it hit the arm that was holding my weapon and I lost hold of it. It splintered into pieces as it crashed into the corner of the dumpster. I kicked the beast with my foot in its stomach as hard as I could. The first creature had recovered and lunged towards me as I ducked to pick up a splintered piece of wood.

Screaming and running only on hope, I rammed the piece of wood into its heart through its underbelly. The bright red eyes stared at me, its skin stretched thinly over its bones and the long teeth barely contained by its mouth. I slammed the piece of wood further into it and the creature slumped and fell to the ground. It terrified me to be so close to one.

What was going on here? Had all monster tales been true? Was this hell? *Wake up!*

The remaining two creatures threw themselves at me, overpowering me and smashing me onto the cold concrete. I kicked wildly at them, but they were too strong and my kicks were ineffective. The one with the oily hair roared again and I could see its teeth in the streetlight; the razor-sharp corner teeth glistened dangerously. Holding up my arms to protect my face, the creature sank its teeth into my forearm while I screamed in horror. The other sunk its teeth into my leg. I could feel them draining me of my blood; the pain paralysed me. My body was set on fire. Was this how I would die? Or… die again?

The burning sensation continued to spread. The pain dulled all my senses bit by bit. I hoped it would be over soon.

Amidst the pain, the sound of gunfire ripped the air apart. The hairy monster close to my face dropped to the side; the other let out a tortured howl before falling limply to the ground as well.

Determined steps approached me. I closed my eyes in despair and waited for the last shot. At least the nightmare would be over.

'Come on, get up,' the voice spoke in a firm tone. Someone grabbed me by my right arm and pulled me up in one quick motion. I opened my eyes.

'Blake?!' I asked baffled when I recognised his face. He was real! *WAKE UP!* I closed my eyes and wished to wake up in my bed, but as I opened them again, I was still in a dark alley held upright by Blake.

'We have to get out of here, the others will smell the blood,' he stated and laid my left arm around his shoulder. The deep scratches on my left shoulder and bites on my forearm and leg made every movement horrendous. Blake supported part of my weight and dragged me rapidly away from the bloody scene. I looked back and saw the three corpses lying on the floor; they looked tiny and inoffensive now.

Blake hurried through the streets before aiming for an old blue truck. Opening the passenger door, he shoved me inside and rushed to the driver's seat.

The pain intensified and I started feeling lightheaded. The two places I had been bitten burnt horribly.

'Where are you taking me?' I slurred.

'My place. We'll be safe there.' He took a look at me. 'How badly are you hurt?'

'I don't... I was bitten twice and my shoulder-' I shivered uncontrollably and the burning from the bites slowly spread. My hands started tingling.

'We're almost there, just hold on, ok?' Blake said; his voice sounded far away.

'What's happening to me?' I asked with clattering teeth, sweat pearling down my forehead.

'Don't worry, you're safe with me,' he answered.

We came to an abrupt stop and he turned off the engine. We were in front of a three-story high white house with a flat roof in a suburban area.

Blake pulled me through the front door and up the stairs. There, he laid me on a large wooden table in the middle of the living room. I was shivering from the wet rain and adrenaline cursing in my veins. My wounds burned so intensely, it made me dizzy and my brain fuzzy. Maybe I would die now and it would all stop.

'Hold on, Ameerah.' Blake fumbled around in the kitchen and rushed back towards me, 'Where were you bitten?'

I lay my hand on my leg and held my forearm up. He took out a giant needle and filled it with some liquid from a large clear bottle.

'This is going to hurt,' he said. Giving me no time to react, he had slammed the needle into my leg. I screamed in pain, and struggled and twisted, but Blake held me down easily with his muscled arms. Again, he filled the needle. I tried to wriggle away, but Blake had put one arm across my chest and pinned me down. The needle pierced through the flesh of my forearm. The two bite wounds sizzled like steaks on a hot grill. Blake pulled out a plastic bag filled with what I assumed was blood. For a third time, he inserted a needle into my arm, this time however it was connected to the blood bag.

'You'll be fine. You only have scratch wounds,' he stated and disappeared again.

I could see a strange clear liquid bubbling out of the bite in my forearm and the smell of rotten meat coming from it. There was a vaporizing sound whistling past my ear.

On my left shoulder my torn clothes revealed deep gashes, nearly to the bone. Four long open crevasses stretched over my shoulder and arm. Who had done that to me? No, *what* had done that to me? What were those creatures from the alley?

A numbing feeling spread from the back of my head all the way to my forehead as it began to dawn on me what I had agreed to by being here. This was not Earth. This was not normal.

An irritating tinnitus sound manifested itself, becoming louder and louder in my head. What the hell had I agreed to? What was this place? Finally, I admitted to myself I might not be stuck in a nightmare, but in something much, much worse...

'How are you feeling?' Blake shouted from somewhere to my left. When I turned my head, I saw him putting the bottle with the clear liquid away.

'Better,' I answered, wrestling myself up into a sitting position. The burning sensation had pulsed down; I had stopped sweating and I was more aware of my surroundings. I healed fast, I noticed, too fast…

Blake came back into the room and sat down on a chair not far away from me, leaning his arms on the armrests. He had a glass in his right hand containing some sort of whisky from the looks of it. His deep blue eyes lurked at me from under his blond hair.

'You must have a lot of questions,' he said. His head leaned against the back of the chair. Though his body was in shape, there was a look in his eyes that made me think he was tired and worn out.

'Where am I?' I asked the most urgent question.

'You died and chose to come here instead of going to heaven.'

'So… is this hell?' I whispered, fearing his answer.

Blake took another sip without breaking eye contact. 'No, you're on Idolon. We are still on Earth, but this is a sort of parallel world to Earth.'

'But… how does this place exist?' My mind tried to comprehend what I was being told.

'It was created a long time ago. Imagine a curtain between this world and where you used to live with your family and friends. Now you're on this side, and the only way to get back to the human side is to finish your time here.' Blake took another sip.

Even if he had saved my life, I didn't like it here. I didn't like being around Blake, whoever he was. How could I trust him? This guy had haunted me for weeks and now I was taking every word he said for granted? No.

I jumped off the table. The tube connecting the blood bag to my arm tugged at my veins. I reached for the bag and carried it with me in my right hand.

'I don't know what kind of games you're playing but I'm not staying here. I didn't die, I'm not in some weird Idolon parallel world and I am *certainly* not staying here! This doesn't make any sense! I'm going home...' I aimed for the staircase leading to the front door.

'Ameerah I know it's confusing, but you have to trust me.' His tone was suddenly filled with authority and I stopped at the top of the stairs.

'Why? Why should I trust you?' I fired back at him.

He gulped down the rest of his whisky and wandered towards the kitchen. 'If it wasn't for me, you'd be dead right now.' He called out from the kitchen. I could hear him opening and closing cabinets, moving glass bottles around. 'Do you want a drink?'

'No thank you!' I shouted back. There was no Idolon! What the hell was he talking about?

A few moments later he emerged from the kitchen with two identical tall glasses. Blake walked over to me and stretched his right arm towards me. 'It's a gin and tonic.'

When I didn't take the glass, he rolled his eyes and took a sip from it. 'There, you see? No poison!' With those words he pressed the glass into my hand and returned to his seat in the living room.

Hesitantly, I approached him. 'Who are you?'

Blake stared at me, scanning me up and down. Eventually, he put down his gin and tonic and approached me. He got uncomfortably close to me.

'I think you've had enough,' Blake stated. I didn't understand what he meant until he lifted my right arm and carefully removed the needle. He laid the needle, the tube, and the bag on the table behind me. 'You've healed,' he said pointing at my shoulder.

I looked down and sure enough the wounds on my shoulder and arm were gone. There was not even a scar. When I looked at my leg, I found two small patches of whiter skin where the teeth of the monster had punctured my skin. It was the same on my forearm. My fingers carefully trailed along the white marks making sure they were not an illusion.

How could this be?

'I'm a ghost, and so are you,' he began matter-of-factly, 'I appeared in your dreams to prepare you for your death. Fate or God or whoever you want had already decided you would die. When you died the council appeared and challenged you to pay the necessary price. By accepting that price you have become a ghost and will serve a sentence here, after which you will go back to your human life. Instead of dying in that accident, you will survive and continue living your life. It's like getting a second chance. Right now, you're just in between life and death. A ghost.'

Inadvertently, I found myself reaching for my chest. My heart was still beating. I was alive as far as I was concerned. 'How long will I stay here?'

'The council announced your sentence to you when you agreed.'

I tried to remember. So much had happened since then. 'I think... it was sixty-seven years... but-hold on, so I'm... I'm a "ghost" for the next sixty-seven years?!' I raised my hands and made quotation marks in the air.

'Correct. And once you've served your years here, you can return to the exact moment you died and survive from that accident.'

'Will I have sixty-seven years when I'm human again?'

'No. Your sentence here just means you will get another shot at living. You will recover from your accident and live on until you die. But, no one knows how long that is for. I hope for you it will be many decades.'

I looked out through the window into the pitch-black night. Was I safer in here with a stranger, or alone in the dark out there? Without any possible way of finding my way home and monsters lurking around ready to bite me again, staying here seemed the better option.

What had I gotten myself into? I raised the glass to my lips and took a long gulp of the gin and tonic.

'So, what happens now? What do I do here?' I tried to play along.

'Your job is to kill demons, mostly molochs. Those were the creatures in the alley. I will teach you how. I'm your trainer and I'm responsible for your well-being here. You are my recruit.'

I raised my eyebrows. Molochs? Demons? Could this get any more surreal?

Blake had wandered back to his chair and sipped on his drink. 'If you get wounded you need blood from your master to heal- oh speaking of which, I better let him know you're here.' He fumbled his phone out of his pocket.

'What's... what's a master?'

'He's a sort of spiritual guide. But you'll meet him later. First, I need to train you.' Blake typed on his phone for a minute or two, before he eventually looked at me again. 'Right. You need blood from your master to heal. Don't ask me why; I don't know. That's just how it works. But he is not a blood bank, so you have to be careful. You should also know you can only die in the line of duty or by decision of the council. You cannot kill yourself or bypass your sentence here in any other way. The whole point is to eventually get back to your human life and if you get killed you don't get that second chance, so... don't get killed.' He emphasised the last part. Blake finished his glass.

'Why do we have to kill molochs? What are they?' I asked.

'Molochs are distant relatives of vampires but they evolved separately. They kill and drain humans of their blood. We kill them so they can't harm humans,' he said looking into his empty glass.

'How many ghosts are there? And how many molochs?'

'There are a lot more molochs than us, so we're always outnumbered. I don't know how many ghosts there are, I know of around sixty. The city is divided in districts and the ghosts are assigned a district by the council. Not sure how big the city is, but you will be able to socialise with other ghosts when you're a bit more advanced in your training.'

I reflected on everything I had heard so far and a sinking feeling came over me. 'If I'm here all this time, won't my friends and relatives all have died by the time I get back?' I asked.

Blake shook his head. 'Time is distorted around your death. Essentially, you are in a time loop. When you go back, you'll get back to the exact moment where you would have died, no time will have passed. You will only have the memories of your time here.'

My head spun trying to grasp my new reality. I stared out the window into the blackness.

Blake cleared his throat, 'I think I've thrown enough information at you for the time being. Don't worry, you will be able to ask many more questions. But before you get some rest, there are a few rules. These are absolute musts. One; you have to obey me. I am responsible for your survival and cannot do that if you do stupid things. If I tell you not to do something, you don't. If I tell you to run, you run. It's very dangerous here and you're extremely vulnerable as a new ghost. Two; you need to trust me. Everything I do and teach you is to ensure your survival. If you die, I'll have to train a new ghost and start again so it's in my interest you get to the end of your sentence as much as it is in yours. Third and final point, and this one will be the hardest; I know you will be thinking about your family, your friends, and your human life, but you need to put that behind you and concentrate on your life here. If you commit, you will cope more easily. You'll see them again, in a few years' time.'

I nodded. As he was the only person I knew that wasn't trying to kill me, I would have to obey his rules. At least until I could figure out a way back, if that was at all possible…

'It has been a long night. Your bedroom is there,' he pointed at the door furthest to the left under the second staircase.

I shuffled to the room and peered inside. It was small with just a bed and a cupboard with a window at the back looking into the neighbours' garden. The walls were white and it looked all together gloomy. If I had to stay here for sixty-seven years I would have to decorate.

I went back to the living room to search for the bathroom. My gaze fell on Blake and I froze. He had stripped down to a pair of baggy shorts and was doing push-ups at the far-end of the living room. Having never been inside a gym in all my life, this was the first time I saw a man doing push-ups that wasn't on TV. I stayed rooted in place and gawked at him.

When he was done with his push-ups, Blake reached for metal bars above his head that stretched across the ceiling from one wall to the other, around ten feet above the ground. First, he did a series of pull-ups; then moved along one metal bar hand over hand.

He was incredibly strong and agile. His blond hair soon stuck to his forehead and droplets of sweat pearled down the middle of his chest and back. He didn't stop as he dropped to the ground for another set of push-ups; he barely seemed to be breathing hard.

I realised I had been staring for quite a while and darted off into the bathroom before he caught me. I splashed cold water in my face. Gazing in the mirror I inspected my neck and shoulder again. Apart from the two small spots of white skin where I had been bitten, my body was free of scars. There was just the one ugly scar from the car accident that stretched from my left hip all the way across my stomach to the rib cage on my right side. How could someone butcher me this way? It was too terrible to look at, so I let my top fall over it again.

The accident replayed in my head; I could still feel the pain, hear the honking echoing in my head. I had *died!* Actually died! Now I wished I had just stayed in bed that day...

I turned away from the mirror, heading back to my bedroom. I jumped backwards. Blake stood in the door frame, eyeing me with crossed arms, still only clad in a pair of shorts.

'How are you doing?' he asked dripping with sweat.

'Fine,' I answered tonelessly. I did not know where to look. His bare torso screamed for attention. I may not be alive, but I was clearly not that dead. But this was not the time nor the place.

'You know, this is not as terrible as it seems,' he started, coming into the bathroom. I had no place to escape.

'How long have you been here?' I asked, trying to make my voice sound casual.

'I have been here for years and I still have thirty to go, so I'll be here a while,' he chuckled. His abs tensing up with his laughter.

I didn't know what to say. I stayed quiet, trying not to look at his glistening body.

'Ok, it's late.' With that, he walked abruptly out of the bathroom.

I rushed into my bedroom and sighed, but Blake followed me. He was holding a gun in his hand.

'Here.' He held the gun out towards me. Hesitantly, I took it and held it up with as few fingers as possible.

It was heavy and black, a typical handgun as far as I could tell. Blake laughed at my attempt to not touch the weapon. He took my hands and showed me how to hold the gun properly, his warm strong hands wrapping around mine.

'Here is the safety. You need to take it off before shooting.' He showed me the small latch on the side that locked the trigger. I stretched my arms away, trying to keep the gun as far away from me as possible.

Blake laughed again. He took my shoulders and guided me to face away from him. He stood close behind me. I could feel the warmth coming off his bare chest and his breath tickled the back of my neck.

'Hold it like that,' he whispered into my ear. His hands tentatively glided along my arms, directing my movements.

'And now,' his voice murmured, 'you aim.' He lifted my arms, bringing the weapon's sight to eye level. His face was right next to mine. I could feel the heat and sweat from his body.

'Good!' he said as he moved away from me and walked out of my room. I let out a breath. How long had I been holding it?

'Always keep the gun in reach and don't hesitate to use it,' he shouted from the bathroom as he shut the door. Shortly after, I heard the water running.

I closed my eyes in relief. Finally! Alone. I looked in the cupboard and found a few T-shirts close enough to my size. I closed the door to my bedroom, undressed, and lay down in the bed. I wished, not for the last time, that I would find myself waking up from this bad dream. I missed my family and friends. I missed Bruce and the warm sun on my skin. Here, everything was cold and dark. I prayed I would wake up in my bed and this would all turn out to be a bad dream...

RULES OF THE GAME

I opened my eyes and looked around. It was blurry for a few moments until my eyes adapted. My prayers had not been heard; nothing looked like my room in France.

When I walked out of my bedroom, Blake was sitting in the chair he had lectured me from last night. The bright morning sun shone through the nearby window as he observed me. Outside it looked just like Earth. The sun, the sky, the houses along the suburban street. Nothing out of the ordinary.

'I'll teach you about the molochs first. Then I'll take you into town to get some essentials and maybe something to brighten up that room. When we get back, we will start your training.' Blake stood up in one energetic move and strolled past me towards the back of the living room where he had exercised the night before. He pulled something along with him back to where I was standing. It was a large chalkboard. When he had positioned it, he gestured me to sit down.

'Molochs are animal-like creatures with primitive brains. Their red eyes allow them to see at night. When they bite, they inject their prey with poison which makes you feel like you're burning. It slows you down and can give you fever.' Blake had started drawing with his left hand some rough sketches of the features of molochs.

'They prefer to be in groups and feed together, but they still fight among each other all the time, constantly re-establishing dominance between one another. They can move between Earth and Idolon. Once they have killed in the human world, they linger here in Idolon, so we have to make sure to kill them while they're here before they return to the human world.' Blake stopped.

I took it all in without responding.

'I'll train you to face them. You should know that since they live in groups, you need to be prepared to kill several of them in one go. You need to watch your back.'

'So, I just... I shoot them... with my-my gun?' I stuttered.

Blake nodded in acknowledgement. 'We'll go to the gun range later. Aim for the heart or the head. I'm not much for theory and prefer a practical approach so let's go. We have a lot to cover today.'

Without waiting for me he hopped down the stairs to the entrance, and I hesitantly followed him.

His old blue truck was waiting for him in the driveway. I got in the passenger seat and sat quietly. As we drove through the city, I scanned the horizon and the cityscape longing to see anything familiar. Even with the sun high in the sky I felt cold and pulled the sweater tighter around myself.

'You won't recognise the city, if that's what you're thinking,' Blake stated. He had only his left hand on the steering wheel.

I tried to imagine Blake's first day here, but it was inconceivable to me that this confident, posed, watchful individual could have been a scared, frantic, insecure person like I was right now.

'Why not?' I asked.

'I guess it's to keep us from trying to search for the people in our human life,' Blake sighed deeply.

'Where are we then? What city is this?'

'This universe consists of an endless city. It's just buildings, houses, shopping centres and streets. There are no landmarks either because anything too real that could reconnect you to your human life has been... let's say erased. It's like opening your eyes underwater; you can see things, but it's all blurry and you can't really make out what's in front of you.'

We came to a stop in front of a department store with a blue banner around it. The name was unfamiliar to me, but Blake explained it was the same as the fact that you couldn't see any landmarks.

When we walked into the shop, it seemed we were the only customers.

'You can take and use anything you want in this world. One of the benefits of being a ghost is everything is at your disposal.' He gestured towards the mountains of goods staked in the aisles.

Grabbing things here and there, I soon had my hands full and walked out with as much as my arms would carry. At least this bit of Idolon wasn't so bad; I would just have to make shopping my new hobby. My mother would be so proud.

I convinced Blake to follow me around with a trolley which I filled with bed linens, candles, posters, several lamps, books and motivational picture frames.

Next, he took me to a clothing store, where I took everything from jeans and tops to winter jackets.

While I had never been interested that much in shopping as a human, it was a welcome distraction now.

The sun was low in the sky by the time we got back to the house. I realised I hadn't eaten at all since arriving on Idolon. 'Is it normal I'm not hungry?'

'You don't need to eat' Blake explained. 'You can eat if you want but it doesn't taste of anything. Alcohol is the only thing that still affects you. All you really need is blood from your master whenever you're wounded. And that is injected, you don't even drink that.'

'Do I still have all my senses?' I feared I wouldn't like the answer.

Blake shifted uncomfortably. 'Most of them yes. You still have smell, sight and sound. But you can only partly feel. You can feel a table with your hands, but you can't feel the sun on your skin.'

'Why?' I felt like a five-year old asking question upon question.

'I assume it's again, so ghosts don't spend their time lying in the sun waiting for their sentences to run out. Their duty is to kill demons. Anything else is a distraction.'

All sense of satisfaction from shopping flew right out the window.

'What about the humans? Where are they? I saw them when I got here.' I felt a deep chill as I relived the feeling of someone walking through me.

'The humans are most of the times not visible. It's just sometimes there's a… a sort of glitch in the walls between this world and the human world and we see them, but normally we don't so you won't have to feel the emptiness when they pass through you.'

I was literally a ghost. The fact that I wouldn't be seeing many living humans was only a mild comfort.

Blake was eager to teach me how to use a gun, so he took me to a gun range after my shopping spree. My stomach was nervous at the thought of actually pulling the trigger on a gun. My stepfather had once taken me to a gun range to try out clay pigeon shooting, and I had not liked it. I didn't see the point in learning to handle a gun when we were not at war.

We drove towards the south as far as I could tell from the position of the sun. He stopped the car in front of a building that reminded me of a dodgy night club. The whole façade was painted in black paint.

I followed Blake towards the glass door. Suddenly, it opened and a tall man with black hair exited. He was on the phone and determinedly walked to a red Ferrari parked on the opposite side of Blake's truck. He waved with his keys in his left hand at Blake, who waved back. I slowed in my steps and stared at the mysterious man as he passed us. He winked at me and unlocked his Ferrari with his key. He had seen me!

'That's Dominic. He's another ghost from our district. Come on,' Blake called me. The Ferrari raced off and I shuffled to Blake, who was holding the door open.

The inside of this gun range looked just as rundown on the inside as you were led to believe from its exterior. At the bottom of the stairs, it looked pretty much like a bowling alley except that there were no oiled wooden aisles leading to the pins; instead there was grey carpet leading to mannequins and drawings of human shapes on large papers in the back. At the start of the lanes were high tables and between each lane a separating wall. We were alone in the basement.

Blake stopped at the first lane with a mannequin at the end of it. The white mannequin had two bullet holes in its left shoulder and one under the left ribcage.

'Take your gun and shoot the dummy,' he pointed towards the end of the lane.

Blake handed me protective headphones and positioned himself to my right. I pulled the gun out of my jacket pocket and put it on the table. The nervousness in my stomach made me sweat, so I took off my jacket and sweater before lifting the gun to my eyesight and pointing at the dummy.

Blake helped me with my stance before he let me shoot. It made me nervous that he was eyeing me, more so that I could *see* him eyeing me.

I aimed the gun at the dummy, closed my eyes, and squeezed the trigger. The backfire forced my hands back and the gun flew out of my grip. It fell clicking and clattering to the ground. Only when it was silent again did I open my eyes. Blake was scratching his chin with his left hand.

'Could be worse,' he picked up my gun.

'First, *never* close your eyes. Look at the enemy.' He put two fingers under my chin and lifted my gaze to meet his steel-blue eyes.

'Second, *never* let go of your gun.' I felt the uncomfortably familiar weight in my hands as Blake placed the gun in them. I could feel the heat coming off the weapon and a smell like cheap fireworks.

Blake moved to stand closely behind and guided my hands to adjust my aim. I had missed the dummy and it was impossible to see where the bullet had hit on the grey wall.

'Aim for the head or the heart,' he said, 'anything else will at best slow them down, and definitely make them angry.'

I felt his hands move from my arms down to my hips. That was too much for me. I wriggled out of his grip and backed to the table, holding the gun up in the air. 'Stop doing that! Just because you're my trainer now doesn't mean you can just touch me everywhere!' I exclaimed.

'Careful with that gun, please!' Blake stepped back, eyeing the gun in my right hand. 'I was just correcting your stance. I didn't mean anything by it. You're the first female I'm training; I didn't know the way I teach would be a problem.'

A few seconds passed while I let his response sink in. 'You haven't trained a girl before?' I asked dubious.

'No. Not many girls are selected to be here.' Blake still kept an eye on the gun in my hand.

'Fine.' I reluctantly agreed, turning back to the dummy.

Blake approached me again. He readjusted my shoulders and repositioned my hips. 'Now try again.'

Once more the gun backfired violently, but Blake put his hands on my shoulder to steady me and I was able to keep a grip on the gun.

After the gun range, he forced me to do exercises back at his house and then he took me jogging. I tried my best, but after fifteen minutes, I was out of breath and tortured by side stitches.

'Don't slow down or we will run twice as long!' Blake warned me. I schlepped behind him as best I could, dragging my feet, rasping like a chain smoker.

It was night-time now and a slow drizzle started. The streets were illuminated by yellow streetlights.

When we arrived at the house, I was so exhausted I barely managed to shower. Blake was still working out when I came out of the bathroom. I couldn't believe his endurance.

'How was the day for you?' Blake stopped and walked over to me.

'Intense.'

'Too intense?' he asked in a soft tone eyeing me.

I nodded tiredly. Tomorrow I wouldn't be able to walk. On top of that, my head was buzzing.

Blake sighed deeply. 'You have to get good fast, or you get killed. Whoever you were before, you're not anymore. Now you're a ghost, a soldier whose job it is to kill demons. And they're not waiting for you to get up to speed. And from what I've seen today, your shooting is alright for a beginner, but you're far behind in your physical shape.'

'Why do I need to get in shape if I can kill them with a gun?'

'What if you lose your gun? Or you run out of ammunition? You'll need to run after them or carry a ghost to safety. You can't neglect the physical aspect of it. Unfortunately, we need to be ready for anything.' Blake brushed his blond hair back. His eyes rested on me for a while.

'Alright' I approached my bedroom. 'I'll do what I can.' This was depressing me already, but there was no way back. And if I ever wanted to see my family again, I would just have to do as I was told.

Days passed. Training continued. Improvements were scarce. Blake did not lighten up and I was exhausted. I couldn't keep up with him in any way, but he expected me to. There was no special beginner training plan for me. More than once I completely fell to pieces and was unable to move. Blake would put his hands on his hips and sigh annoyed. Then, he would shake his head and sit in his chair strumming on his guitar until he had calmed down. I tried my best but deep down I was convinced I was not cut out to be a ghost.

After a few weeks, my shooting had improved somewhat, and Blake steadily increased the distance to the mannequin. I couldn't help but feel flustered when he corrected my stance and touched my skin. But I was sure this was more related to my need for reassurance and comfort than anything else. He was a strong man, confident and good-looking. My hormones were just spiking.

'You need to stop being so tense,' Blake said as he moved in front of me and I lowered the gun. 'I can see you don't like holding the gun, but that piece of metal is the thing that will save you.'

'I get that, but it's still a weapon!'

'You need to start thinking of it as your saviour. Now keep shooting.'

Blake moved to the side. I held the gun up again and discharged a full magazine into the dummies he had positioned at the back of the range.

My dad would be so proud to see me use a gun. He had hoped I would like clay pigeon shooting and it could be an activity we could do together. I wondered if he would also be proud to know I was training to kill demons. It made me think about how much this world would change me before I made it back to my human life. Would my family and friends even recognise me?

BOND OF SISTERHOOD

'Kim,' she introduced herself and stretched out her right hand. She had a round face, full lips, and long black hair that curled at the ends. She was my height and had a radiant smile. Her tan and facial traits indicated she had Asian roots in her family.

'Ameerah.' I met her hand with mine. We looked at each other with curiosity.

'Kim has been a ghost for a little longer than you and has been field approved. We thought she might help you... acclimatise,' Blake said. He looked over to Dominic, who was Kim's trainer. He was the man we had run into the first day at the gun range. Now he was much closer and I could see he had olive-skin and a strong jawline. He looked like he had come straight out of a coffee advertisement.

Blake had explained that I would be submitted to a field test supervised by the council in a few months. Once approved, I would be deemed able to defend myself and allowed to move freely, without Blake or another approved supervisor. It also meant that I would then officially be deemed combatant and would have to kill demons regularly.

'Kim can help you prepare for the test,' Dominic said.

The way Dominic and Blake stood together and eyed us; one could think they were brothers. They had the same hard stance, strong body, and watchful eyes.

Running around freely sounded nice, but I was unsure what would actually happen during my field test. Blake had always stayed vague about it. All he said was that I needed to be stronger, quicker, and better at handling guns. Personally, I was amazed I had improved at all!

'Can we go to Santa's pub?' Kim asked the men.

Dominic and Blake looked at each other. They seemed to be communicating telepathically.

'Ameerah is not ready to be outside without me. You can hang out together, but at our house, with one of us present,' Blake said, gesturing towards Dominic.

Predictable. He never let me out of his sight. Kim seemed just as annoyed at this decision.

'I'm field approved! I can watch over her!' she protested.

'Not yet,' Dominic countered with a tone that didn't allow any further protest.

Kim reached over and squeezed my forearm in support. She winked at me, a conspiratorial wink that told me to just be patient.

Kim and I called each other at night. Our trainers demanded our undivided attention during the day, but once we had retreated to our bedrooms, we could speak on the phone in low voices. Whenever she could, Kim would come over. We liked each other's company and escaping our responsibilities and trainers. Our trainers had intended for her to encourage me to invest myself more in my training, but they had not taken into account that we both craved an escape from this world and spent our time drinking, watching tv shows and talking.

Blake was never far and I sometimes wondered if he was eavesdropping on our conversations. But if he did, he wouldn't find out anything useful. We had no desire to talk about the dark and grim things our trainers seemed to be so interested in.

Kim was a happy person and found positive sides to every situation. The first time I noticed this about her was when I claimed there was nothing fun to do here. She pointed out one could indulge in alcohol, cigarettes, and drugs without any lasting damage. All it did was give you a buzz and after a good night's sleep it disappeared again. Blake had said only alcohol could affect us, but it had turned out to be a lie to keep me away from drugs. Not that I was into drugs, but who knew, after a few years here, I might have to take more drastic measures to survive the emotional turmoil.

For her the biggest advantage of being here on Idolon was not having to eat and that she could have everything materialistic her heart desired without paying for it. When she was a human she had lived in L.A. and had barely had enough money to survive. She was putting herself through school by waitressing in several restaurants and selling clothes she designed herself. After dying from smoke inhalation, she landed here and understood quickly she could learn from this world and bring her knowledge back to her human life once she had finished her term. In contrast to me, she was eager to progress and had been field approved early on, much to Dominic's delight.

Even though we were not allowed out together, she would bring me clothes and we would pretend to have fashion shows in my room. I laughed a lot with her and I felt much better since I had become friends with her.

* * *

At the end of yet another training day, Blake asked me to sit with him. He had pulled the chalkboard out and looked more on edge than usual.

'Dominic and I need to hunt a creature tonight that is a lot worse than molochs. So I'm taking the opportunity to teach you about vampires.'

I shuddered to think what could be worse than the monstrosities that had nearly killed me several times already. The times we had encountered molochs I still felt unprepared and Blake often ended up saving my life.

'Vampires have the same roots as molochs but evolved separately and are much closer in appearance to humans than molochs. Like molochs, they can move between this world and the human one.'

'How can these demons move between the worlds when we can't?'

'The separation between Idolon and the human world only applies to us. They on the other hand are not restricted. The more we kill here, the less damage they can do to humans on the other side.' Blake explained.

'Why would they come here to Idolon if they're hunted here?'

'Molochs are not intelligent enough and they most likely don't know there are different worlds. Vampires are so powerful they don't care. They enjoy killing ghosts and humans, they see it as a game.'

'How do they travel between the worlds?'

'They have portals. And no, we cannot use them or even see them,' Blake said, anticipating my next question. He then started sketching on the board. 'The fingers of vampires are longer and they have sharp nails. They have longer canine teeth and their skin is white. They also inject their victims with poison. While molochs' venom only makes you slow, vampire venom triggers an allergic reaction in ghosts, suffocating them so it is imperative that you don't get bitten.'

He paused and emphasised, 'If you ever come across one, *do not fight it.* Do everything possible to escape, got it?'

Blake stared intensely into my eyes.

'Why can't I fight them?'

Blake inhaled and pumped up his chest. 'Because molochs are primitive and easily killed if you know how. Vampires are intelligent and hundreds of times more deadly. You stand no chance against a vampire.'

I rolled my eyes. 'I don't even have a chance against a moloch-'

'Exactly!' Blake raised his voice. 'You have a very slim chance of defeating a moloch right now, and a vampire is so fast you won't even see him coming.'

'What about you? Aren't you hunting one with Dominic tonight?'

He crossed his arms over his chest. 'Yes, but Dom and I are advanced trainers and we know how to kill one. You're not even field approved. I hope for your sake you won't have to face one for a long time, but unfortunately, they exist… Kim will come over later and you two will stay here while Dom and I take care of that vampire.'

'You're leaving me alone?' I was surprised at my own words. Was I so dependent on him?

'I'm not keen on leaving you, but this vampire can't wait. You won't leave the house so nothing should happen to you.'

Blake came towards me and laid a hand on my shoulder and squeezed it lightly as if to reassure me. 'I need to prepare. Kim should be here in an hour.'

He walked towards the training section of the living room and started moving guns and ammunition around.

The thought of vampires scared me, but we had never encountered one and I had been here for months now. To me it was like worrying about being eaten by a shark when I never left the boat. It was just another threat. Another being trying to kill me. What else was new? There was nothing I could do anyway. I couldn't hide in the house for the next sixty-seven years; at some point I was bound to run into one, and hopefully by then I would be a seasoned fighter.

Within twenty minutes Kim knocked at the door. She was accompanied by Dominic. Blake and Dominic confined themselves to the back of the living room, talking in low voices and manipulating weapons. Kim and I mixed ourselves some drinks in the kitchen and then retreated into my bedroom.

I was applying a deep green nail polish to Kim's nails when Blake knocked at my open door. He had changed into dark combat gear. There were handguns strapped to both his thighs, the tip of a machine gun was poking behind his back on his right side, and two blades were strapped on the front of his chest.

'We're going now. We should be back within three hours. Ameerah you listen to Kim. And Kim, don't take her outside.' Blake had a stern look on his face.

I heard heavy footsteps down the stairs and the door close. A rumbling of a car was audible and then it was dead quiet.

'So,' Kim said taking a big gulp from her gin and tonic, 'Should we do masks tonight?'

I nodded in agreement, 'And then we have to catch up on all the latest Cosmo quizzes.' My free hand pointed towards the bedside table where a pile of magazines took up all the space.

Kim had her fingers sprawled out and waved them in the air to let the nail polish dry. I walked over the to the bedside table and threw all the magazines onto the bed.

'How's training with Blake going?' Kim asked while blowing on her nails.

'He's so hard on me. I always feel out of depth,' I sighed deeply.

'He just wants you to progress. Don't worry, once you're approved it will be a lot better.'

'I don't know if I'll ever be approved. I don't feel strong enough to face molochs alone and I can never keep up with Blake.'

Kim tilted her head. 'That comes with time. Just keep pushing. Have your eyes set on the prize and keep going.'

My thoughts immediately went to my family in France. That was my ultimate goal. I didn't care about some approval or killing demons. All I wanted was to go back to my family and forget this whole nightmare.

My emotions unexpectedly overwhelmed me and I couldn't keep the tears in. I missed them so much.

'Oh honey, I'm sorry!' Kim threw her arms around me and hugged me tightly.

The tears kept coming and I let myself sob in Kim's arms. She caressed my hair and back. How I hated being here. How I missed my innocent human life, my family, my Bruce, school, friends...

'You will see them again,' Kim whispered and swayed me gently. 'If it's that painful to you, you should say something to Blake. When are you meeting your master?'

'I don't know... Blake mentioned him in the beginning but didn't say when I would meet him. All he said was that he would be a spiritual guide to me.' I stuttered.

Kim's eyes opened wide. 'A master is much more than that honey! Your master can make you feel so protected and loved, it's crazy the connection you can have! It's like a super-parent that knows exactly how you feel and what to say to make you feel better and motivate you!'

I dried my tears and grabbed a tissue from the wardrobe to blow my nose.

'Since your master isn't coming by tonight, we're going to go to the next best thing. Come on, get yourself ready!' Kim jumped off the bed and smiled at me.

'What are we doing?'

'We're going to Santa's pub. It's not far from here and you will meet other ghosts. It will take your mind off of your sorrow.'

I had heard her speak of Santa's pub before, when I had first met her. 'But Blake told us not to leave the house...'

Kim tilted her head as she threw her jacket on. 'He isn't going to find out we left in the first place. We're going for one hour and then we'll come back here. They will be out for hours! Trust me! And if they somehow come back and we aren't here, I'll take the blame for it. Come on, it will be good for you.'

Kim rummaged through my clothes and picked out a green sweater with sparkles along the sleeves and a pair of black ripped jeans for me to wear. She gave me her red lipstick and a pair of earrings to add to my outfit.

I was a bit nervous of going out without Blake but since we would stay in the pub or in the car, I told myself it would be ok.

We tiptoed out of the house, even if we knew no one was there, and ran to her car. It was freezing outside but no snow or frost was yet on the ground. We giggled and laughed as we raced south along the river.

'Here, have some alcohol,' she opened the glove compartment and pointed to a flask behind the car manual.

I took a long gulp and identified the mix to be gin and tonic. She reached over and took a sip herself.

'Are you sure you want to be drinking while driving?'

Kim shrugged. 'I can't die from a car accident and there are no cars driving here besides other ghosts so the streets are mostly empty.'

After around fifteen minutes she turned to the left onto a large pebbled parking lot in front of a shabby-looking old industrial building. Kim swung the car sharply around and came to an abrupt stop. There were quite a few cars parked.

Kim led me across the parking towards an old warehouse that looked to once have been used for fish packing. There was barely any noise when we stepped out of her sleek black SUV. The warehouse was dark with very few windows and only a few stories high.

She opened a heavy wooden door. We walked into a long corridor with round opaque white lights on the ceiling. The corridor was cold and it smelled of mould. At the end of the corridor there was a second door. I could faintly make out the sound of music from the other side. When Kim opened the door, the music overwhelmed us.

It was a cute pub lit with small bedside table lamps of all shapes and colours, mostly nailed to the walls. There were old pictures hanging everywhere as well as various objects on the shelves along the walls, or nailed directly on the walls such as guitars, plates, decorative containers, dried flowers, vintage cameras, books and posters of advertisements featuring pin-up girls. There was a main bar to the right by the entrance filled with liquors of all kinds, but bottles were dispersed all over the pub.

There were pool and ping pong tables, and seating areas with booths and couches. Though the pub was dimly lit, it looked cosy to me. People were having fun, drinking, playing, talking, laughing, exchanging.

'Welcome to paradise!' Kim shouted to me and walked to the bar on the right. There were no bartenders and everyone seemed to just take whatever they wanted and mix their drinks at the counter. With a drink in hand Kim took me towards the far end of the bar where people were playing board games. She turned around a corner and there I saw four dartboards. One was not being used and she immediately claimed it as ours.

I had never played darts in my life, and after a few minutes I realised Kim was just as terrible at it as I was. We ended up playing against two men who were playing on the neighbouring dartboard. We made complete fools of ourselves, but we laughed heartedly. I couldn't remember when I had last laughed this much.

When we had ended our game, I went to the bar to mix us new drinks. I felt quite tired this late in the night and after having trained all day. I was about to go join Kim again, when I saw a dark corner behind the counter. There were two comfortable chairs with a small round table between them. On the table was a long candle that had been stuck on top of a bottle. Over the years of usage, the wax had dripped down along the bottle and given it an antique look. On the walls were old-fashioned posters of famous women. I sat down in one of the dark green chairs and observed the pub from my comfy corner. On the other side of the bar two men were having a discussion over a few drinks and looked pretty drunk, another played pool by himself; the rest of the pub was hidden behind the corner of the wall.

The alcohol had dulled the anxieties of the world. I closed my eyes and leaned back, letting my head rest on the green velvet. The music was quieter here too. There was something calming about this particular spot. All I wanted was to stay here, with my eyes shut and only open them once I was back in my human life, back with my family and friends...

I could feel someone watching me. Annoyed, I emerged from my beautiful dreams only to find a handsome man standing in front of me, holding a tall glass in his right hand.

'I see you've discovered my secret spot,' he had a deep voice.

'I didn't know these were assigned seats,' I responded playfully.

The man smirked and sat down in the other chair next to me. He put his glass down on the little table separating us. The flame of the candle slightly flickered when his glass touched the surface of the table.

'I haven't seen you here before, are you new?' he asked.

'Yes, I'm actually not supposed to be out tonight,' I explained. 'What about you?'

The man took a sip from his drink. 'Oh, I've been here for many, many years. But still so many left before it's finally over'

'I'm guessing you're not a fan of his place then?' I smiled. His green eyes looked into mine. He was attractive and I could feel my stomach tingling when he looked at me.

'Of this shithole? No, not a fan!' he laughed, taking another sip. He was so relaxed. 'I'm Ben by the way.'

'Ameerah.'

I stretched out my hand to meet his. To my surprise he took my hand and led it up to his lips, planting a soft kiss on the top of my hand. He was definitely flirting, and he did it so gallantly. We were both silent for a moment.

'Usually this is the part where I would ask what you do but ... I have a feeling we do the same thing,' Ben said.

I burst out in laughter. Indeed, flirting here was a bit different. 'Ok then, what about when you were human?' I asked.

'I worked at a garage in Vancouver. I used to race as well but, well I guess that's how I ended up here.'

It was weird for me to hear about his death. I didn't think of myself as dead.

'I studied in France and was hit by a car.'

He smiled and I was sure I was blushing.

'What do you do in your spare time?' Ben picked up his glass again. He rested both his elbows on the table. He had broad shoulders and big arms like most men did here. But it was his eyes that really drew me in. There was something… intriguing about him, something calming.

'I don't really have much spare time,' I answered. 'I spend most of my time with Kim.'

Another one of Kim's laughs echoed through the bar. I pointed at the ceiling and nodded.

'I'm not yet field approved,' I added.

'Really? I'm surprised. I'm sure you can handle a moloch or two,' he said with a wink.

I chuckled. 'I wouldn't be so sure. My trainer thinks I still need to improve.'

'Who is it?'

'Blake.'

I saw Ben's facial expression immediately change; clearly, he was not fond of Blake. He sighed and turned his eyes down to his drink.

'He's alright.' Ben shrugged his shoulders.

Kim came around the corner. 'There you are! Oh hello, I'm Kim, her best friend.' She approached Ben and eyed him up and down.

Ben got up and introduced himself, flashing a smile at her. 'I'm sorry, I didn't mean to come in between best friends,' Ben turned towards me and smirked.

Kim threw me a not so subtle look, indicating she was impressed with him. 'I hate to interrupt but my alarm went off, Meerah we have to go. We've been here already an hour and a half. It was nice meeting you, Ben.' Kim patted his bicep and headed towards the bar, leaving us alone.

I got up and approached Ben. 'I guess this is goodbye.'

'Don't think you're getting out of here without giving me your number.' Ben reached into his back pocket and held his phone towards me.

I couldn't help but smile. Once my number was in his phone he leaned down and kissed me on my cheek. He smelled of... comfort and strength. 'I'll send you a text'

With one last look at him, I walked past the bar and Kim hooked her arm around mine.

Before Kim started driving, she sent a text message to Dom. 'I just told him we're going to bed.'

'Do you think we'll make it?' I clicked my seatbelt in.

Kim nodded confidently and turned up the radio. With the music blasting and us singing along, we drove back to Blake's house.

We went to bed and fell asleep and didn't hear Blake come home. We had successfully managed to have a night out in secret.

FRICTIONS

'Again.' Blake returned to his position.

I tried to steady my breathing and drank some more water. My hair was sticking to my neck and face from the sweat. Taking one last deep breath I returned to the end of the mat, looking straight at Blake. In one swift movement, I lunged towards him. He easily pushed me to the side, but I got close enough to land a punch to his ribs. He moved away, but my jab had thrown him off guard. I kicked up with my left leg, aiming for the same spot. My heel plunged into Blake's ribs and he tumbled against the table.

Blake reached out and grabbed one of the many guns lying on the table. I jumped at him, reaching for the gun. He fired just as I pushed the barrel upwards. We were pressed up against each other, hot and sweaty, both holding on to the loaded gun in Blake's hand pointed at the ceiling. Our faces were so close, I could feel the heat emanating from his body.

'Good,' he whispered.

'Are you gonna let go of the gun?' I challenged. Previously he had tricked me into backing off only to shoot me afterwards.

Blake smirked and I could feel the tension in his arm slowly decrease until he let the gun slip from his grip. I mirrored his actions and relaxed my muscles. Eventually, I removed myself from his body.

'Next time you-' Blake started.

I didn't let him finish his sentence. 'Oh come on, I had you! You played dirty with that gun! You said we would do physical fighting and last time I checked, that means without guns!'

'Do you think this world plays fair?' he retorted.

I shook my head. 'I had you,' I reiterated.

After a cool shower, I mixed myself a cocktail to celebrate the end of another hard day. I had put on a pair of jeans and a white top paired with small earrings. Winter had finally passed and the temperatures were getting mild again.

After many nights of begging, Blake finally conceded to let me go to Santa's pub. He only agreed to one hour at the pub under his supervision. He still insisted it was not good for me to develop habits of drinking and socialising, but I explained I needed to be around other ghosts besides him to feel more at ease in my new world. My first night out with Kim still resonated in my mind as the best night since coming here.

I had thrown myself into training with all my heart to forget about Ben and to get field approved. Supposedly, Ben had to *take care of some things* and had not texted me much in the last months. He had been eager in the beginning and we had exchanged many messages, but then around January it had almost completely stopped. I kept asking myself what I had done wrong. Maybe it was all an excuse and he had simply lost interest... I tried to keep him off my mind by dedicating myself to training.

Blake stopped his old blue truck in front of the industrial building.

'You will not leave my sight,' Blake warned me, heading for the door.

'You want to hold my hand while I go to the bathroom as well?' I smirked at him.

He shook his head and rolled his eyes as we walked through the long corridor. It all came back to me. The deep rhythmic thumping of the bass was audible even before we reached the second door.

Blake headed for the bar. 'One drink only,' he announced and prepared me my usual gin and tonic that tasted like a glass of lemonade.

With my drink in one hand I walked to the first pool table. I wanted to meet new people and forget about Ben.

Blake stayed at the bar, his eyes scanning the crowd. I knew he was watching me and I had to be careful. Even though I was an adult, I didn't want him to find any reason to keep me away from this magical place. It annoyed me he had this much power over me, so I had to be a good girl and get field approved to become independent.

There were only a few balls left on the pool table and two guys were playing, both deeply concentrating. One of them was an older guy, mid-forties, grey untidied hair, unshaved short beard, brown eyes, and of average height. He was opposite me and leaned over the pool table to take his shot. He was clad in a white tank top and a checked shirt that he had left unbuttoned. His hands were thick from usage. I assumed he had done manual labour back in his human life. He pulled off a tricky shot to sink in the eighth ball. Spectators around celebrated or rumbled with annoyance; his gaze fell upon me.

'What's your name?' the man asked with a raspy voice that sounded like he smoked a few packs a day.

'Ameerah,' I replied. His skin was scraggly and made him look older than he probably was.

'Carl.' He stretched out his hand. I shook his warm abrasive hand.

'I'm Vladimir,' a guy to my right introduced himself with a heavy Eastern European accent. He had a pool stick in his left hand having just lost the match to Carl. He was incredibly tall and sturdy. He had short black hair and a potato-nose. His skin was pocked with acne scars.

'I'm Carl's recruit.' Vladimir pointed to Carl, who was now chalking his cue.

I looked to Blake. He was still scrutinising me.

'Blake's recruit?' Carl asked, 'Good man.'

'You want to play?' Vladimir asked and stretched the pool cue my way.

I nodded and took my jacket off while Carl reset the table. I had played a few times in my human life, but I was no match for Carl. He was incredibly focused. He seemed to only see the table. I on the other hand, was distracted by the people around us watching, most of all Blake, whose eyes I could feel burning on my back.

'Good game,' Carl said at the end with a warm smile. It had been over in just a few minutes.

'Vlad, play,' he handed Vladimir his cue and walked over to Blake. They started talking and Blake wasn't looking at me anymore.

'How long you been here?' Vladimir asked me as we started a new game. The crowd had turned to observe other games. The pub was full though and I had to be careful not to accidentally poke someone in the back with the end of the cue.

'A few months. You?' I didn't want to admit I had actually been here over six months and was still closely watched by my trainer.

'A few years. Have you met your master yet?' he inquired.

'No,' I answered, missing my ball and adjusting my position to observe Blake and Carl. They were talking calmly, not paying any attention to us.

'He watches you like a hawk,' Vladimir whispered in my ear. I was surprised to find Vlad right behind me and closer than I cared for.

'He just wants to make sure I'm ok.' I wished Blake would look over and see Vladimir. Normally, I was a no-bullshit kind of girl, but Vladimir was a large man and I didn't want to provoke him.

'I wish that wasn't the case,' he continued and moved past me to line up his next shot.

I knew exactly what he was implying but it took me so much by surprise I didn't know how to respond. Vladimir sunk his shot and approached me again. Next to him I felt ridiculously small and breakable.

'I bet you would do better with... my stick,' he leant closer to me.

'I'm not interested,' was all I said and I turned away from him. I was done. This was not what I had expected when I had begged Blake to take me to the pub.

Vladimir grabbed my wrist and pulled me towards him.

'I said no!' I tried to speak up, but the noise in the pub drowned me out.

'Come on, I know you want to,' he responded and pushed the hand he was still holding against his hard crotch.

What was wrong with this guy?!

'Leave me alone!' I shouted at him and tried to wriggle free.

'Where are you going?' he teased and tightened his grip on my wrist, crushing my bones.

A shot echoed. Immediately, the crowd panicked and guns were drawn everywhere. People pushed and shouted, trying to see where the gunshot had come from. Others charged towards the exit.

Someone grabbed me by the hip and pulled me backwards, out with the crowd. I tried to run but the movement of the people carried me outside. Desperate, I searched for Blake but he had disappeared in the mass. I called his name, but my voice was drowned out in the panic.

Outside of the pub, I was still being pulled by my hips. When I turned my head around, I saw that Vladimir had been the one pulling me.

'Let go of me!' I tried to unholster my gun and point it at him, but he ripped it out of my grip easily.

What was happening? Was *this* really happening? I wanted to kick him, but he hoisted me up over his shoulder and hurried away into the darkness, away from the large crowd gathering in front of the pub. I called for help, but the panic at the pub commanded everyone's attention within earshot. My screams went unheard.

With my hands and feet, I punched and kicked as much as I could. I swung myself back and forth to destabilise the massive body carrying me off. I knew exactly what he intended to do with me.

He had trouble keeping his balance and eventually let go of me. I fell to the ground onto the floor and hurt my back. Unable to get up I tried to crawl away from him. I could hear him unbuttoning his belt. Tears were streaming down my face. *This could not be happening!*

Vladimir pulled me by the leg towards him and twisted my body around, so I was facing him. His body weight made it impossible for me to get away. I pleaded for him to stop but he held my mouth shut with his massive meaty hand. He covered my mouth and nose. I could barely breathe. His massive torso pressed down on me, barely letting any air into my lungs.

My heart raced. I had to do something. With his other hand he fumbled with his pants.

I grabbed a handful of gravely dirt and threw it at his face. He just shook his head and spit in my face. It wasn't enough.

I forced my thumb into his left eye. Vladimir leaned back and pressed my mouth and nose completely closed, but I wasn't letting it go. I used my nail and forced it further into his eye starting to draw blood. He let go of my mouth and twisted my thumb out of his eye.

My right arm was now pinned under his weight. Vladimir grabbed my left arm trying to pin it down as well. He pulled my thumb back further than it should ever go. Any second, I was sure it would break.

I heard a noise in the distance. Vladimir looked up. Someone was calling my name and they were getting closer.

'Fuck!' I heard him breathe on top of me. He froze a few seconds, looking around.

My mouth was uncovered. This was my chance.

'Blake!' I screamed as loudly as I could. Vladimir punched me in the face, breaking my nose.

'Blake!' I screamed again, my voice shaking, blood bubbling in my mouth.

He called my name, this time much closer.

Vladimir held my mouth closed and pulled a knife out of his pocket and placed it under my chin, pushing the tip into my flesh. 'You say one word and you're dead!' he hushed and got off me.

Vladimir ran off, holding his pants up.

I lay bleeding, in shock, struggling to breathe, and to comprehend what had just happened. Tears streamed down my face. I couldn't let Blake see me like this. Rolling over, I clawed the wall to raise myself up, I tried to tell myself encouraging words. With the back of my hands I brushed over my face. I pulled up my jeans and took a few deep breaths.

I had been seconds away from rape. If Blake hadn't-

A new wave of tears overcame me.

'Ameerah!' I heard steps approaching.

'Blake' I mouthed relieved. He sprinted around the corner and I fell into his arms. I held on so tightly I didn't want to let him go.

* * *

Since that night at the pub, I had been even more motivated to excel. I promised myself I would train hard to be able to defend myself from more than just molochs. I was terrified he would try again...

Blake informed me my initial training was approaching its end. I would soon get to meet my master and take the test to be field approved. Once I had passed, I would graduate to a combating ghost and go on missions with Blake.

In the final stretch of my training, as long as it did not affect my physical condition, I was allowed to go out every now and then and have some fun. Blake chose to come along most of the time and truth be told, I wasn't against him watching over me. I never went to Santa's pub alone; I was too afraid.

The first few weeks after the incident I had been perfectly content to stay at home, but the more time passed, the more I hated *him* having control over my life. Whatever he had done, I had to try and live a normal life and enjoy it.

Whenever I saw Carl, I worried Vladimir would be there too. Later, I overheard they had had a falling out and Vladimir had taken off and hadn't been seen for a while. I hoped he had been killed by molochs, but considering all the things that had happened, this world would not be so kind to me.

Every now and again Blake would have an obsessive moment where he would suddenly not let me out of his sight. But those hiccups always passed, eventually. He quickly understood that trying to keep me away from Kim would just mean more trouble for him.

'You can have my truck for tonight,' Blake agreed.

'What about my own car?' I poked at him with a cheeky smile.

'Once you've passed your field test, then yes,' he conceded.

It wasn't exactly what I wanted to hear but it was better than I had expected. Any small step towards independence was a huge victory!

I smiled and took another sip from my wine. It had been a long training day focused entirely on hand-to-hand combat and I was looking forward to a night out.

I put on a little dress that was sexy, though not too revealing. Kim had picked it out for me, along with a whole new more feminine wardrobe. My mother would be so proud of my newfound identity…

A smile played across my lips. I hadn't thought about my mother in a while. What would we be doing if I was home right now? Watching a movie? Baking a cake for the family…

I took a deep breath and closed my eyes. It was so easy to fall down that dark hole. It snuck up on me without warning; and then it was there, this big gap of heartache. You couldn't escape your memories. That abyss was always there ready to swallow you without a second's notice.

Taking another deep breath, I turned my head upwards and let it fall back between my shoulders. I placed my hands on both sides of my hips.

Each time I accidentally stumbled into the memories of the life I had left behind, a crushing pain spread in my chest, suffocating me. Those memories served as a reminder that this was a prison. Why couldn't I just forget? Why couldn't the council or whoever controlled this entire world wipe away all this anguish? Why did we have to suffer?

I didn't want to cry. I was ready to go out and Kim was waiting for me; I couldn't break down now. Or ever. I had to keep going. Until this was done.

I took a few deep breaths before opening my eyes again. For a moment, I thought I saw Blake flash by the open bathroom door. Had he been watching me? Or maybe he had just walked by?

I pushed my memories back into a far-away pocket of my mind where they resided.

'I'm going,' I announced grabbing my phone and gun.

'Be careful. And remember to text me.' Blake sat in his chair by the window and had his guitar on his lap. He winked at me and started strumming a vaguely familiar tune.

I nodded and walked down the stairs, opened the door to the old truck, and put my heels on the passenger seat; I couldn't drive in heels, so I used moonboots instead.

It was a quick ride to Kim's place. Once I arrived at her door, I texted her. A few minutes later she came out and hurried towards the truck. Kim had put on a pair of tight blue jeans with high heels and a dark purple top with a plunging neckline. Her hair was loosely tied in the back. She had thrown on an old leather jacket to top off her look.

'Hey sweet thing,' she greeted me with a hug and a kiss, 'What's been happening with you?'

'Blake said I could get my own car after I get field approved,' I announced full of joy.

'That's great! Did he say when you would take the test?'

'No, but it should be soon. I've done exactly what he's told me and I've kept up my training. I'm doing alright in hand combat and I am definitely good with the guns now, so I hope it's soon.'

Kim nodded. 'If it were up to me, you'd take the test now. I think you're ready. And you need to move forward, once you pass your test you can be free and do what you like-'

I burst out laughing. 'Oh because Dominic lets *you* do what you want?'

Kim stuck her tongue out at me. 'Ok ok, you can do *more* stuff than you do now. You could hang with me, go on dates. Maybe this Ben will come back in the picture?'

I felt a sting at the mention of Ben's name, followed by a surge of anger and confusion. 'What makes you think he'll come back?'

'Because he would be fool to let a woman like you go,' Kim stated, shrugging her shoulders. I smiled at her flattery but feared he didn't see it that way.

We arrived at the usual parking lot. There were only a few cars parked in front of it. It was still early in the evening.

Kim went into the pub ahead of me. We mixed ourselves drinks at the counter and sat down in a corner with a chess set. Kim and I loved to play games in the pub, especially when it was a quiet night. My phone vibrated. I took it out and read the message.

'Blake?' Kim asked.

I nodded and confirmed I had safely arrived at Santa's and was now playing chess. As proof I sent him a selfie. Our game was not interrupted further. The evening continued and we played a few games of pool with some of Santa's regulars. Carl greeted us quickly and disappeared into the depth of the pub with a large bottle of whisky.

I was still paranoid whenever I saw him but once again, Vladimir was nowhere to be seen. I was too afraid to ask Carl about him, I prayed they were still not speaking. Or better yet, Vladimir was dead somewhere in a ditch.

As the time passed, the pub filled up and there were people everywhere. We didn't mind. It was great when there were more people; it almost felt normal and brought us back to our partying days as humans.

Kim flirted with a few guys but seemed to enjoy having them battle over her more than actually finding herself a boyfriend. Some tried to flirt with me and I responded dryly, without leading them on. None of them interested me and all they did was remind me of the disaster with Ben. I was not ready to repeat that just yet.

As the night wore on, Blake began texting more and more frequently asking when I would be home. Since the reception in the pub was bad, his messages would come through an hour late and all together, so my phone kept beeping. I couldn't hold him off any longer. I had dropped Kim off and was on my way home when I decided to drive to the riverfront and for a bit of fresh air before heading home. The night had gotten chilly and it was dead quiet, which was a welcome feeling after hours spent in a stuffy bar with loud music and lots of people around me. I leant against Blake's rusty truck and listened to the water. The river flowed uninterrupted. It was so peaceful.

The city was sleeping. My thoughts found their usual path and soon I was thinking of my family and friends from my old life. I reminded myself this passage on Idolon was only temporary and I would see them again soon. I kept repeating this to myself, before tears invaded my eyes and sorrow shook through me.

A quick movement, or maybe it was just a sound, snapped me out of my dreams. I turned around, scanning the vicinity for danger. My right hand was on my gun, ready, just like Blake had taught me. There was a rumbling sound in the distance.

Behind the truck was a huge square with a few trees and streetlights dispersed. The square was lined with four-story high buildings and narrow pedestrian walkways. Out of the far-right corner a metallic bin was tipped over and two figures appeared, sniffing around the garbage spilling from the bin. I ducked behind the truck. There was a tingling feeling spreading in my body into my extremities. The feeling was familiar and manifested itself whenever there were molochs close-by. I felt torn; should I kill them even though I wasn't field approved? Should I drive away and be safe? But could I really drive off when my duty was to kill them?

I observed the figures while I debated in my head. They hissed and snapped their teeth at each other, establishing dominance over the trash.

My phone vibrated, startling me. I took my eyes off the molochs, fumbling around with the damn thing. It was Blake calling. I silenced the call. When I looked back up, the molochs, were nowhere to be seen. Had they heard my phone? Were they close? Stalking me? I swirled around, swinging my gun, but pointing only at the air. There was no one here with me at the riverfront.

A chorus of roars broke the silence and I finally spotted them still on the square, but on the far-left side now, battling. A third moloch had appeared. No, it looked like the two molochs were attacking the third one, but he was larger than the other two... The way he defended himself, it could not be a third moloch. It had to be a ghost!

I had to do something! If I ran away now, I would always run. Blake would shoot me himself for taking the risk, but I had no choice. Whoever it was out there, they were going to be torn apart if I didn't help.

I ran swiftly towards the left building front and snuck up along the buildings so they would not see me unless they stared right in my direction. I had my gun in hand and was close enough to see the ghost was bleeding from his arm. My heart was drumming in my ears.

This was it.

I aimed but was unable to get a clean shot. Luckily, the ghost threw one of the molochs off himself and far enough away I could risk a shot. It resonated in my ears and the echo bounced off the buildings. The ghost was startled by the sudden loud bang; the last moloch took advantage of their hesitation and jumped onto the ghost, entangling them again before I could shoot. I approached the battling duo, leaving my hiding place.

My eyes were focused on the ghost. They were struggling, wrestling, falling to the ground, too close to each other. I couldn't risk a shot, but I couldn't jump on them and battle with them either!

I spotted something in the corner of my eye, but I wasn't quick enough to react. My gun flew out of my hands; a third moloch slammed me to the ground, bruising my hip. I rolled over and tried to get up. I was barely crouching when the moloch jumped at me again, dragging me down. My left shoulder hit the hard concrete and I felt something snap inside me. With trembling hands, I held the moloch's jaw away from my neck, as its claws lashed out, scratching every inch of skin it could reach. The pain from my left shoulder spread, sapping my strength. I shifted my weight and managed to push the moloch off me. I spotted my gun not too far away. I used my right arm to crawl forward. The moloch was back on me just as I had my fingertips on the gun. I turned on my back, leaving the gun, kicking the moloch with my naked legs several times before I made contact with its face. It howled in pain and laid its long claws on its face.

I reached for the gun behind me, turned around, and pulled the trigger. The dead moloch landed on my legs. I wriggled and pushed its wrinkly body away from me, trying to catch my breath.

The other ghost picked up his gun and hurried over to me as I was getting up.

'You alright?' he asked out of breath.

I recognised his deep voice immediately. 'Ben?!'

He froze and the light fell on his face. 'Ameerah?' he asked surprised. 'Where's Blake? Have you been approved?'

'No, no, no Blake, no approved. I was on my way home... and I stopped to look at the river when... when I heard the molochs and then I saw... someone and-' I explained, gasping for air.

'Are you hurt?' Ben asked.

'I think I broke something.' I winced as I tried to move my arm.

'Let me see.' Ben helped me take off my jacket.

The cold inched up my legs now that the adrenaline had stopped pumping through my body.

'Where were you tonight? Did you go out to Santa's?' Ben asked his eyes fixed on my shoulder.

'I was outaaAAAAAHHHH!' I screamed. Ben had pushed my shoulder and it had rolled back into its socket.

'Sorry. Don't move your arm. Here.' He carefully laid my jacket over my shoulder, pulling it closely over my body. I looked up into his eyes. His lips were so close, his breath on me. The electricity sparked between us, everything disappeared. I forgot the cold, I forgot my shoulder, all I saw were his lips...

My phone vibrated. Damn it. Ben backed away from me. It was Blake and for once I was grateful, he had interrupted.

'Where are you?! I have been trying to reach you-' Blake yelled.

'Yes... I'm sorry- I... no, I had- ok, I'm coming home now!'

'Did I get you into trouble?' Ben smiled apologetically.

'Yes, you did,' I stated annoyed and started walking towards Blake's truck.

'Can you drive?'

'I'll manage,' I snipped at him and I climbed up into the driver's seat. Ben laid my left arm into my lap so he could close the door. His hands were warm on my skin. I refused to meet his eyes.

'I'll follow you home in my car, ok?'

'No, it's really-'

'No discussion. At least let me explain to Blake what happened.'

I wanted to object, but he had already darted off, running along the lit buildings, and disappearing around a corner. The old truck roared to life with a steady thumping. Its vibrations travelled up my shoulder, making the pain double. A red Ford Mustang pulled up and Ben waved at me. I put the truck in drive and tapped the gas pedal.

The rusty old truck had trouble keeping up with Ben's sports car.

Why was he here? Where had he been? Why hadn't he gotten in contact with me? Did he not want to see me? And why on Earth did I have to run into him and save his ass? Things had been going so well and now Ben was back interrupting everything...

When I pulled up in the truck, Blake burst out the door before I had turned off the engine.

'Where the *hell* have you been?!'

Blake flung open the door to the truck. His expression immediately changed.

'What happened?'

'Molochs.'

'It's my fault.' Ben announced jogging up the driveway.

When Blake recognised him, I could sense the storm brewing.

'I was dealing with a pair of molochs when Ameerah saw me and stepped in,' Ben explained.

Blake's stare was ice-cold. His arms tensed and his jaw tightened. All colour vanished from his face. Maybe I was mad at Ben, but it was nothing compared to the storm that was about to erupt from Blake.

To my surprise I found myself defending Ben.

'Really it was my fault. I was not careful; I didn't see the third one-'

Blake's head swirled. 'There were three?!' he repeated, staring at me.

Before I could answer he had turned back to Ben. 'You missed the third one?'

'It must have followed the sound of the fighting and caught up with us,' Ben explained shrugging his shoulders.

'You put her in danger.' Blake pointed his finger at Ben. 'She's **not** field approved and she risked her life to save yours! I will report your complete incompetence and lack of proper assessment of the situation to *her* master and *yours!* This will not go without consequences!'

'Blake!' I shouted at his overreaction.

'Fine. Report me to Jesper. It was an unpredictable-'

Blake got into Ben's face, dug his finger into Ben's chest and hissed, 'She's *not* field approved!'

After a few tension-filled seconds, Ben finally backed away from Blake. He turned to me, his expression softening. 'Sorry for the trouble I caused you. Good night.'

Blake watched him carefully until we heard Ben's car squeal as he sped away.

'Let's go.'

Blake helped me out of my jacket and inserted a syringe filled with blood into my arm. It was not much, just enough to make the scratches disappear. He insisted on taking a look at my shoulder himself, even if Ben had put it back into its socket. Then he went on to be unusually smothering, asking me if I needed anything, even touching my arm and squeezing it lightly.

'I'm fine!' I jumped up, waving my arm to show I could move it again, 'But you could have been just a smidge less aggressive to Ben!'

Why was I poking the bear?! I knew this would only end in a fight. And why the hell was I defending Ben after he had left me high and dry all this time?!

Blake's face changed to anger when I mentioned Ben's name. 'He's a trainer. It is his responsibility to watch over new recruits.'

'But I'm not *his* recruit! And he was fighting with two molochs already, there was no way he could have looked around and seen the third one-'

'He doesn't have a recruit; did you know that?' Blake crossed his arms in front of his pumped-up chest.

'I didn't know he was a trainer, I only met him once before at Santa's.' I hoped it wasn't obvious to Blake that I was attracted to Ben.

'His last recruit had been here about six months, but while I watched you with eagle eyes and pushed you to train harder, he decided his recruit could handle himself. So, he went out drinking and left his recruit unsupervised. His young recruit didn't know better and went outside, where he was surprised by a gang of vampires. And *I* found him, or what was left of him.'

Blake took a moment, almost as if trying to compose himself.

'He was… tortured- I almost didn't… butchered beyond' Blake closed his eyes.

I stayed quiet. 'When was this?' I finally asked.

'Before you came here.'

Now I understood why Blake never left me out of his sight. Maybe vampires were more dangerous than I had first thought…

Blake exhaled deeply. 'It's late and I still need to talk to your master. Just… stay away from Ben, he's bad news.'

I nodded. Not that Ben wanted to see me anyway. It was a moot conversation.

Blake turned to walk up the stairs but stopped. He swung around again, a tired smile on his lips. 'I thought you might want to know; I think you're ready.'

'Ready? To meet my master? Be approved for field work?'

'Slow down. I will suggest to your master that you take the test. He will make the decision. And you will still have to *pass* the test.'

My swelling joy was stifled. 'Right...'

'But tonight, don't worry about it. Get some sleep,' Blake stated with half a smile. He brushed his left hand through his blond hair and took out his phone.

I trotted into my bedroom and let myself fall onto the bed. There was a soft mumbled voice coming from above me; Blake was on the phone right now to my master!

I reached for my phone to text Kim and saw a message from Ben. *'Sorry for everything. Can we get a drink?'*

Against my better judgment I replied. *'Why? You blew me off and now you want to see me? You're just feeling guilty!'*

I didn't want to see him. But I also did.

While I texted with Ben, I also informed Kim of his reappearance. It was unsettling knowing what had happened to his recruit, but there was a little voice in the back of my mind that didn't believe it was really Ben's fault. Or was it because I just didn't want to believe it was true? Was I refusing to see Ben for who he was? Or was Blake manipulating me? He had always been possessive...

Another message from Ben. *'I'm sorry for not calling please let me make it up to you'*

He added a kissing smiley face. I pondered what to say. He annoyed me. I left my phone on the nightstand and went to bed. No use losing sleep over it.

THE COVER-UP

The drive to Santa's pub was quiet. Kim had preferred meeting there instead of at her house. She had had a fight with Dominic and she needed a break from him.

'He is so exhausting sometimes,' she announced walking in and smacking her car keys on the bar counter next to me.

Startled at her sudden arrival, I leant back on the bar stool.

'That dude is impossible! I just went on a raid with him and killed six molochs. Now he wants me to go to some of the usual hide-outs tonight and take out some more! I've already been on a raid today and I fucking got bitten again!'

She poured herself a shot of tequila and downed it without taking a breath.

'If he wants to kill molochs he can just go do it himself!'

'Why doesn't he?' I asked carefully.

'Because,' she downed another shot, 'We are a team and the number of dead molochs and vampires are linked to the both of us, so he wants me to sweat while he goes out fucking girls or whatever.'

When she saw the question mark written on my face she explained, 'The council tracks the number of molochs and vampires you kill, but since you and your trainer are a team, they don't count your individual kills. Once you're field approved, you'll have to contribute as well. Dom has been riding me hard the past few months because he had been slacking off before and we had to get our numbers up. But I know him, now that we are back on track, he will be slacking off again while I am stuck keeping the numbers up.'

'Can't you tell your master?'

Kim sat down and pushed the bottle of tequila away. 'Gordon is in the human world for something and until he's back, he's impossible to reach. And Dom *knows* that!'

She exhaled deeply and relaxed her shoulders. Her hair fell in waves over her arms and played with the bar top.

'Masters can go into the human world?'

'Yes, there are portals that they can use, but they are monitored and you need to explain why you need to use one. Most of the time it's to look for a new recruit. I don't know what Gordon is doing over there now, but I guess the council agreed.'

I assumed there was a reason why masters returned to Idolon when they could just go stay in the human world with their families and friends. Were those the same portals that vampires and molochs used to travel between the two worlds? But if it was, why were they allowed to go through? And why hadn't they been sealed so the monsters would stay here and not harm the humans? No, vampires and molochs had to be a different thing. I doubted the council was letting those monsters travel freely into the human world to wreak havoc.

The pub was starting to fill with ghosts back from a night of hunting. It was getting loud.

I remembered Blake talking about districts before. He had explained that we were assigned one by the council and had to patrol it. The boundaries between districts were not strict but helped coordinate the overall ghost force.

'Why is it always so busy? I thought only you, me, Blake, Dominic and Carl guarded this area.'

'We are blessed with one of the best pubs, so many of the neighbouring ghosts travel here.'

'Tell me, what was all that with Ben you texted about?' she suddenly asked.

'Eeehh, well I ran into him and saved him from those molochs and now he's acting all apologetic and wants to make it up to me. And Blake doesn't like him at all. Ben took me home and Blake almost hit him.'

Should I tell her about his recruit? Probably not, at least not while I didn't understand everything.

'Blake is always so protective of you, it's almost suspicious…'

'What do you mean?'

Kim looked into my eyes for a few seconds. 'Nothing. I need to go to the ladies.' She left me alone at the bar.

There was a large group of men gathered around one of the pool tables, cheering and making all sorts of noise while watching two people play. Absentmindedly, I watched too, but couldn't really see much with all the people crammed around the table.

Then, I saw him.

All the blood drained from my limbs; my heart stopped. The horrible images of what he had done to me burned in front of my eyes and played back over and over.

I had to leave. I could not risk him seeing me. I left the bar stool and pushed people aside to get to the door and out of the pub as quickly as possible. My heart raced; my breathing was ragged. Paranoid that he might be following me, I ran across the parking lot to Blake's truck. In my haste, I tried to open the door without unlocking it. Annoyed, I scrambled for the key in my pockets and dropped them on the asphalt under the truck. Without any regard for my clothes, I threw myself on the ground looking for them. They were not far. I grabbed them and stood up. I could hear footsteps. Someone was approaching. Panic set in and I fumbled with the key. Finally, the door squeaked and I jumped inside, slamming the door closed behind me.

Out of the corner of my eye, I saw the person getting into another car. They quietly backed out of the parking spot and left.

Fuck.

My hands were shaking. It wasn't him! He probably hadn't even seen me and I completely lost it over some stranger just minding his own damn business. My whole body was drenched in sweat. I closed my eyes and tried to breathe in normally.

Nothing had happened. Everything was ok.

The door suddenly opened and someone grabbed me by the arm. I screamed and kicked at whoever was trying to pull me out of the truck, clinging to the driver's seat. The person was big and strong; within seconds he had gotten me out of the truck. With all my strength I fought him, trying to inflict pain on him in any way possible. The man spun me around and my head banged against the door of an adjacent car. My head was spinning and I couldn't see straight. I stopped struggling.

The man pulled me towards the hood of Blake's pick-up truck, further into the trees and bushes that lined the parking lot. I remembered I had a gun inside my jacket.

'I'm going to have you,' he announced in his Eastern European accent.

'No,' I pleaded with him, but I knew it was pointless. My right hand glided along my torso to my left side where I had the gun.

Vladimir dropped me on the hood of the truck and pushed my upper body against it, holding me in place. I heard him undo his belt and zipper.

I tried to reach the gun, but my arm was blocked by Vladimir's weight leaning against my back. My shoulder hurt as I tried pushing my arm further inwards to reach the gun. I couldn't reach it. Desperate, I screamed for help.

'Shut up bitch!'

Vladimir grabbed my jaw and nose and held my mouth shut, while he eagerly ripped my tights and pulled the dress up with his other hand. His grubby hand fumbled between my legs. I tried to move but he was so much bigger and heavier than me. Tears streamed down my face and sobs rattled through me.

A loud bang tore through my ears.

There was a moment of silence. Vladimir was still standing right behind me, his weight forcing me to remain bent over the hood, but he had stopped moving. Another bang pierced the silence.

A groan echoed behind me and then Vladimir's weight shifted. He fell to the ground to the side of Blake's truck, still alive and bleeding from his gut.

I heard my name being whispered. I blinked and saw Kim. Vladimir let out a moan; Kim shot twice more without so much as a glance. I pulled my dress down over my exposed bottom and looked down at Vladimir.

Kim drew me into her arms and hugged me tightly. We held the embrace for several minutes. I felt so relieved he was dead, relieved he had not succeeded in his second attempt. If she hadn't killed him, he would have kept trying.

'Did he…' Kim breathed in shakily. 'Was he…?'

I shook my head in response. A few seconds more and he would have. His hand had touched me.

'We need to get rid of the body,' Kim announced, slowly letting go of me.

I knew she was right; I just needed a moment to deal with the fact I would have to touch him. My eyes fell back onto his body. He was dead and could no longer hurt me. He was dead and could no longer hurt me. I repeated it several times.

'I don't know if I can.' My voice was shaking.

'I'm not strong enough to lift him by myself. I'm sorry, you have to help me.' Kim was crying. 'I can't do it alone'

He was dead. There was a dead body lying in front of us. A real corpse…

I turned away and threw up in the bushes.

'Ameerah we can't stay here. Someone might see us.'

'Let's just get this over with.' I brushed my hands over my face and pulled my hair back. What had we done?

We pulled him towards the back of the truck and hoisted him up into the open flatbed of Blake's truck.

'Where do we dump him?' I looked at Kim once the body was lying in the back.

She sighed deeply and gathered her thoughts. 'Outside of this district, in the river'

Kim drove us further downriver, until we reached the edge of district, by a large bridge. There were no lights on the bridge so we rolled up and stopped on the pedestrian walkway, hoping the darkness would keep us hidden from unwanted eyes. Even if it was dead silent and we were obscured, we couldn't help but feel paranoid.

'We need to do it quick.'

Kim jumped up into the back and rolled the corpse out until it plumped to the ground.

A new wave of dry heaves overtook me.

'We're so close, come on!' She grabbed my arm and squeezed it tightly.

We each took an arm and pulled him to the rail. We hoisted his chest up so his head dangled over the river. With a heave, we pushed the rest up until the weight on the other side was greater and his body toppled over the railing. There was a splash. The body disappeared under the dark surface of the water. Further downstream it emerged again and quietly floated at the surface.

'We should have weighted him down,' Kim stated dryly.

'It's done now. I want to leave.' I climbed into the passenger seat.

It was silent for a long time in the car.

'They will find the body at some point.' Kim said and turned to look at me. 'You need to be ready if this comes back to us.'

I nodded silently. I felt drained and disconnected from reality. It all felt so unreal, like the hazy memories of a bad movie, far away and out of focus, as if it had all happened to someone else.

'It wasn't the first time,' my mouth said but it didn't sound like my voice. With the least number of words possible, I told Kim everything. Reliving it was traumatising; I could barely bring myself to say it out loud.

Kim reached over and squeezed my hand tightly.

'He can't hurt you anymore,' she said, tears running down her face. Seeing her cry, just made me cry harder.

We were back at Santa's within two hours. Kim said we had to avoid any unusual or suspicious behaviour, so she would drive back in her car and we had to keep everything a secret.

'You need to get rid of the blood in the back. Does Blake have a hose at the house?' Kim asked me quietly when she had turned off the engine.

Everything had happened so fast. Only a few hours before I had pulled into this parking lot getting ready for a night out at Santa's with Kim...

'Probably in the garage.'

'Clean out the blood when you get home. I can't go with you, it's already late and Dominic will notice if I stay out all night.'

'I can't believe it happened to me.'

We tried to keep the tears in, but we were both unsuccessful.

'It will be ok, honey. I'm in it with you.' Kim hugged me tightly.

Eventually, she got out of the old truck and headed for her own car. I knew I had to muster the courage to clean the back. If I thought about it, I wouldn't be able to. I had to get it done. Climbing over to the gear stick I sat in driver's seat, I turned the engine on with trembling hands and headed home. The tears kept coming. I felt so dirty and used. Every mental image made me shudder. Every time I closed my eyes, I saw him, felt his breath on my neck, his fingers clamping over my mouth, between my legs. A new way of dry heaves made me gag. By now there was nothing left inside me. Only saliva drooled down my front onto my bare legs.

Exhausted, I arrived at home. I had never been inside the garage. My hand tried the knob, but the door was locked. I tried all the keys on my key chain before one finally unlocked the garage. It was filled with tactical gear of all sorts: weapons, ammunition, grenades, rocket launchers, goggles, clothes, hunting rifles. Along the wall on the left were a few tools you would usually find in a garage such as an axe, a chainsaw, ladders, hammers, screws, and a short hose at the very back.

The hose was too short for me to be able to get close enough to see what I was doing. I had to spray the flatbed from further away, switch off the water and walk to the back of the truck and check my progress. I used an old broom to scrub the metal clean and brush the excess water from the flatbed.

My limbs barely managed to carry me up the stairs and into my room. Exhausted, I pulled off my ripped, dirty clothes and stuffed them in a spare bag. Next time I went out I would have to get rid of them. I had already decided I would not tell Blake what had happened. If he knew what Vladimir had tried to do, he would want to kill him, and that impossibility would inevitably lead to more questions. From there, it would not be hard to put two and two together.

It was very late by now. But nothing mattered beside the fact that he was now dead. Vladimir would never be able to touch me again.

REVELATIONS

The days that followed were filled with nothing but preparation for my field test. According to Blake, my master was observing me closely, and would soon agree to meet. It was tradition for a master not to meet his recruits before they passed the field test. Maybe it was their way of not getting too attached in case their recruit didn't make it...

The summer was in full force and the temperatures high during the day. Blake often forced me to work out under the blazing sun. He wanted me to get used to unfavourable circumstances, since the council would usually create unusual environmental circumstances to increase the adversity I would be facing.

Ben and I texted every now and again and he was very keen on meeting up with me, but after my incident with Vladimir, I was nervous around men I didn't know. Even if he was dead now, there were predominantly male ghosts in this world and some, undoubtedly, would have the same ideas as Vladimir.

The fact that Ben had left his recruit out to die did nothing in his favour. Still, I had trouble believing he would do such a thing. Vladimir had shown his true intentions pretty quickly after meeting him for the first time. Ben had always been friendly and charming. I couldn't imagine Ben purposefully endangering anyone. But then again, I hardly knew him. I wanted him to be a good guy. No matter how much I turned and twisted the story, it came back to the same result; Ben was on my mind and I wanted to get to know him.

The sheer brutality those vampires had shown Ben's recruit weighed on me as well. To think that there were creatures out there capable of much worse than molochs, sent shivers down my spine. Molochs were just primitive beings, but vampires had to be able to think to want to torture someone. They had to be much more intelligent than molochs. Suddenly, I wasn't so afraid of molochs anymore. Vampires were the real evil. They were not those poor tortured souls portrayed in some romantic story of forbidden love that somehow always ended well.

Kim had been busy after our last night out. Dominic was on her more than ever to keep their numbers up.

Blake continued pushing me and was harsher than ever. His constant remarks about my performance fuelled my sense of self-preservation. Blake forced me to go out at night to hunt molochs. On several occasions he had to swoop in and stop the molochs from killing me.

He taught me more and more combat skills and I was fighting him physically more and more intensely. It was frustrating not being able to defeat him, even though I knew he had trained for decades before I came into this world. I couldn't help but be reminded of my inferiority against all men.

* * *

It had been another hot day. The air in the house was suffocating; the sun had shone into the windows all day trying to bake us inside.

Blake had just ended our training session. 'Don't beat yourself up. It will be a long time before you can defeat me. If you keep training this hard, it will be sooner rather than later.'

Blake took a towel and patted his sweat-covered body.

'Why do I even need to defeat you? As far as I know only ghosts fight like this,' I contested, annoyed at myself more than anything.

'Vampires fight like this,' Blake stated dryly.

I froze. 'Let's keep going.'

I threw my towel into the corner and got into a defensive position.

Blake chuckled. 'I'm pleased with your eagerness. But we have done enough for today.'

I opened my mouth to object. Blake's phone intercepted my attempt. As soon as he answered the phone, the happy Blake disappeared and the concerned one replaced him. He kept his eyes on me while debating on the phone.

'Now? … In a snowstorm?! … - yes, I know… fine. I'll prepare her.'

Blake hung up and looked very serious when his eyes met mine. 'It's time for your test.'

My nervousness bubbled in my stomach. I had just fought with Blake for hours and I was drained. Blake looked at me, his blue eyes piercing through me. My legs started quivering.

'What happens now?' I asked in a hushed tone.

An uneasy feeling spread in my stomach, warning me of something I would not like.

Blake went to the kitchen and came back with a pill and a glass of water in his hands. 'This will sedate you. When you wake up, your test begins.'

I quickly washed down the pill, trying not to think about it. This was it. It would happen now. The moment I had waited for so long.

'Are you sure I'm ready?' I could feel my speech slurring, my brain slowing down. That thing was powerful!

'Remember what I taught you, ok? And beware of traps.' Blake's voice accompanied me into the darkness. I could not feel my legs anymore; the warm black cloak draped itself around me and took me into unconsciousness…

I awoke to strange squeaking noises. I was lying on cold concrete. It was wet and vague shapes moved around me. When I pushed myself up to a sitting position the squeaking got louder and the movements accelerated. Water dripped down on my head. Everything smelled of damp and mould. There was barely any light.

As my eyes adjusted, I saw the rats running around me. In one quick motion I drew my legs closer and they darted off squealing. I was in a small dark space. The faint shaft of light came from my right. Leaning towards it, I saw the light emanated through the cracks of an old wooden door. The stony ceiling was low and I had to stay crouched on my knees. I peered through the cracks of the door trying to get a sense of where I was. A rat ran over my leg and I jumped up in surprise, bumping against the door, making it rattle loudly. I froze and listened, waiting for any response from beyond the door. But it stayed quiet.

I swung the door open, crawled out, and closed it again before the stinking rats could follow. There were a few bare light bulbs hanging from the ceiling, giving scarcely any light. The air was cold, wet, and heavy. An unpleasant smell lingered making me wriggle my nose.

My hand instinctively reached to my belt; no gun. Of course not. That would have been too easy. There was something in my back pocket, though: a folded piece of paper with a map drawn on it. I must have sat in a wet spot because part of the map was deformed and erased by a watermark.

There were two crosses on the map, presumably where I was and where I had to go. The one on the bottom right corner had to be where I was; there was a rat drawn next to it. A thin pencil line went straight up until it stopped in a mass of small dots making it look almost like a dandelion. Another line led out to the left and over some sort of bridge. Something was drawn on top of the bridge that looked to be a lamp. The line continued to the right along a river that was drawn right across the page. The line turned left next to the drawing of an eye. The end cross was clearly in a building with a roman numeral two next to it. On the right of that building was a fish.

I couldn't figure the whole thing out, but at least I had a few clues.

I commenced walking down the brick-layered hall and hoped that was the direction of the line on the map. Though it was dead silent around me, I walked as quietly as I could. There would surely be molochs hiding in the shadows of this tunnel system, leering at me, ready to pounce.

Everything was covered in a thick layer of dust and spider webs. I spotted hairy spiders as big as my hand and had to force myself not to shriek or jump.

Walking in the dead silence made me shiver. The cold clung on to me, cooling me to my very core. A few hours ago, I had been roasted by the sun, now it was freezing. I began wondering if that *was* the test, surviving in the cold, barely clothed.

I came to a point where the corridor parted. To my right I heard hissing and yapping. It was too dark to see anything. And I was unarmed.

I crept into the left one, as quickly as I could, and as silently as possible. The sparse light faded completely and in the darkness I crashed into a metal door. The sound echoed loudly and I could hear the pleased molochs behind me somewhere hissing in response. My hands slid along the door and grasped a thick handle covered in cobwebs. I managed to pull the door inwards and light flooded the passageway. A gust of wind blew snow through the door.

Snow! The clustered dots on the map! I had to be on the right path! But damn, snow! It was the middle of the summer! How did the council do this?!

I struggled to pull the door further open, but it wouldn't budge. There was a thick chain holding it in place.

The sound of approaching molochs amplified. I frantically searched around for anything that could help me get the chain off. I opened the door as far as I could and slid my shoulder and head through the gap. Snow bombarded my face, forcing me to squint. I sucked in my chest and stretched as much as I could. They were close. I squeezed my right leg through, trying to pull through the rest of my body.

Harder and harder I pushed, the terrible wind whipping snowflakes into my face. My ribs felt like they would shatter and collapse under the pressure from the door. Looking back into the pitch-black tunnel, I could now see the terrible glowing eyes of the approaching molochs.

I tried to pull myself out of the door jam. If this was the end, I wanted to go down fighting. But I was just as stuck as ever. Damn!

Then I felt a stabbing pain in my leg; one of the molochs had reached me. I kicked my leg around, trying to lose it. Its teeth were deep in my flesh and its weight slowing down my thrashing. There was only one way out; I placed my hands on either side of the freezing door and started pulling myself out as hard as possible. The monster was still tightly gripping my leg. Another one jumped on top of my leg and bit me in my upper thigh. Their combined weight made me drop onto my knees.

With one last pull I finally popped out, scraping the two off my leg and falling to the ground into the deep white snow. I had no time to breathe. The molochs slammed into the door, closing it momentarily. They would fit through the opening easily if they figured out how to open the door. I jumped to my feet and ran to the left like the map had told me. My left leg hurt with each step I took but I had to keep going.

There was snow everywhere. I couldn't see more than a few feet in front of me and had no idea where I was. The wind howled, completely drowning out any other sound.

I stumbled and fell. Or so I thought. I looked down to see a moloch tearing at my jeans to get a grip on my tender skin. I kicked it away and fumbled with my numb fingers through the snow, but there was nothing to help me fight it off. As the moloch circled back for another attack, I swung myself up onto my feet just as it launched against me, pulling me right back onto the wet cold snow. Its teeth grazed my left arm as I smacked it across the jaw. While it was dazed, I threw myself on top if it and smashed its head repeatedly into the ground until it stopped struggling.

I got to my feet and continued limping on, the poison now spreading.

A line of buildings appeared on my left. I slowed down and looked for a way in. My extremities were freezing and my head was growing foggy from the onset of hypothermia. My left leg and arm were burning from moloch poison.

All the doors were locked. Something grabbed me from behind. I swirled around, my hands protecting my face. It was another one. I punched its face with a right hook. It ran away screeching and was out of sight as quickly as it had appeared. I kept an eye on the perimeter in case it decided to try again, but the snowstorm made it impossible to see anything but distant grey shadows of buildings.

The cold was unbearable. The wind was tearing at my skin, hammering the snow onto my body. Desperately, I continued my search for an open door. My fingers were frozen solid; I wasn't sure they were capable of opening a door.

The next building in the row was a clothing shop. The front door was made of... glass! Without any other way to break the glass, I put my back to the window and used my left elbow. It took me several tries before I finally cracked the glass. A piece of glass got stuck in my skin when I punched through it. I unlocked the door and opened it with my right hand and let myself in. The heating was off but it was still warmer here than outside in the storm. I bent my elbow up to my eyes to inspect it. The piece of glass was lodged above my elbow in my upper arm. Carefully, I pulled it out. Blood poured out of it. Trying to hold the blood in with my hand I went towards the counter at the back. There had to be a medical kit somewhere.

Behind the counter were folders and loose papers. When I pulled those out, I found a medical kit stashed away behind a box of brown wrapping paper. I laid it out on the counter and started disinfecting my bleeding arm. With sweaty and blood-covered hands I laid a pad onto it and laid my arm across the counter to hold it in place. I used my free right hand to pull out a bandage and held one end between my teeth while I clumsily wrapping the wound up with my free hand, using the counter to put pressure on the wound as much as possible. When I was done, it looked quite amateurish, but I hoped it was enough to stop the bleeding.

I sprayed disinfectant on the bite wounds from the molochs but doubted it would have any effect. I needed the antidote for moloch bites, the clear liquid Blake had injected me with in the past whenever I had been bitten. Without it, the bite wound would keep burning and only very slowly dull down. The disinfectant would have to make do for now. Once I was done drenching the bite wound, I could feel the tiredness pulling me slowly into its arms.

With a blinding headache and trembling limbs, I barricaded the door using a desk from the back office and a few display racks. I had built such a huge mountain in front of the door I doubted I would even be able to get out again.

I put on two sweaters and two jackets and covered my legs with heavy coats. With my back against the wall, hiding behind the counter, out of sight from the street, I sank to the ground. My teeth clattered and my body trembled uncontrollably. Eventually, I calmed down and an overpowering drowsiness pulled me into a deep sleep.

My face was cold. But the rest of my body was pleasantly warm. I stretched my legs and bumped into the back of the counter. The mountain of coats avalanched off me, landing with a dull thump on the ground. The door was still barricaded. Outside the storm had calmed to a slow snowfall. Reluctantly, I left my comfortable cocoon. I pulled the sweater up and inspected my elbow. The bandages were soaked in blood, but I didn't have enough clean ones to restart. I used the leftovers and covered the bloody ones up as best as I could. The smell would attract unwanted attention.

I rearranged the newly acquired thick sweater and heavy jacket, threw on a pair of large sweatpants above my ripped jeans and approached the door.

It was night. The streetlights were on, giving a gloomy orange colour to the outside world. I padded for the map in my back pocket, but it wasn't there. When I checked all my pockets, I realised I didn't have it on me anymore. It must have slipped out while I was trying to fit through that metal door... or fighting off the molochs...

I had remembered it somewhat in my head. There was something about a bridge, an eye and then something with a number and a fish.

I stepped outside into winter wonderland. With the heavy jacket draped over my body, the temperature didn't seem unbearable anymore. It was dead quiet.

Was I still on Idolon? How could it be winter when I knew we were in August?

I looked back the way I had come; there were no bridges anywhere in sight. I hadn't accidentally passed it as I escaped the monsters. Forcing my way through the thick white cover, I continued down the orange-gleaming street.

After fighting my way through miles in the thick snow, two bridges appeared in the distance. One thin and high to my left and a broad battered one to my right. Which was the right one? I scrutinised the details of the bridges. Both were broad enough for cars and pedestrians to pass on, a flag on both sides, streetlights on top of them... I took a closer look at the lights. The map had specifically included the lights; they must be a clue. Both had five, all of them working. How would I know which one to take?

I stood in the snow, looking back and forth between the two bridges, undecided. Then I saw a flicker. One of the lights on the thinner bridge was flickering. It was the one on the top of the bridge, at the highest point.

A smile crossed my frozen face. I hurried over the bridge and turned right to walk along the river. The snow was not so deep here.

I kept a lookout for the 'eye' from the map. On the left side of the street were small houses pressed together. They puffed thin clouds of smoke from their chimneys. How warm and cosy it must be inside them… I imagined all the families sleeping inside, no cares on their minds. At the same time, I knew if I ran into the houses, I would find them empty, unable to see the humans peacefully sleeping.

When I was human, I had loved Christmas; all the present buying and wrapping, making people happy, baking cookies for my family, hanging out with my friends drinking Glühwein at the Christmas market, and telling Liam fairy tales about Santa and Rudolph…

I slammed into something and was painfully torn from my dreams. Now free of snow from my collision with it, I recognised a park meter.

I continued my walk, my hands inside the jacket pockets trying to rub some heat into them. The snowing had ceased, the silence still prevailed. Christmas lights illuminated the streets around me. It looked so magical. If I was not a ghost, if I was not trying to pass this stupid test, if I had not died, I could be happy. Even the cold would be tolerable.

It all reminded me how much I had lost; the feel of the sun on my skin, the taste of food… But, the coldness of winter was still there. It was like a cruel joke, laughing at me, making fun of my misery, torturing me with my remaining senses.

A shiver went down my spine. I had to keep moving; reminiscing like this slowed me down and made me stop paying attention to my surroundings.

As if they had heard my thoughts; two molochs appeared to my left, their heads sticking out of an open manhole. The smell of the sewers made my eyes water.

I looked around for anything to use as a weapon, but I was once again out of luck. One of them was missing an ear, while the other one had a gash across its skull. They approached me head-on. The one missing the ear leapt at me first; I punched it in the face, but it still managed to claw at my arm. The second jumped up. I ducked and swerved away just in time. It crashed into a bench behind me. I slammed my foot onto the body of the missing ear one several times until the scarred one ran towards me, reaching my upper right leg and digging its claws into it. I pulled at its arm while I pushed its chin backwards with my other hand. Missing ear threw itself at me again. We all fell backwards onto the broken bench. Missing ear skidded away, while scarred skull was firmly attached to my leg. My hand got a hold of a splintered piece of wood from the broken bench and I slammed it into scarred skull, killing it. Missing ear hurried back, but I had rolled on all fours and swung the piece of wood with both hands towards it, smacking it right into its chest. It sacked into the ground and stayed there wincing.

As I straightened up, I heard the roar of yet another moloch behind me. With the piece of wood still in my hands I turned around and swung but missed the moloch. Slippery from the blood and disturbed snow, I lost my balance and fell on my back. The moloch lunged at me and I held it away from my neck with the piece of wood between my hands. With my leg I pushed myself to the side and the monster off my face. Now I was on top of it, the piece of wood across its chest. I put all my weight on it and squeezed as hard as I could. The creature first panicked and tried to dislodge the piece of wood, until its movements slowed down and it eventually stayed still.

Before any other molochs got the jump on me I closed the manhole. Who had left it open?! Or... was this part of the test...?

I rested my hands on my knees, my upper body bent over, while I tried to regroup. There was a small gash on my right arm and deep lacerations and puncture wounds on my right leg, curtesy of the scarred moloch. Everything else was alright. The wounds on my leg made it painful for me to stand, but there was nothing I could do at the moment. Blake had not specified, but I was sure I would not have access to my master's blood until I finished the test, or the moloch bite antidote for that matter.

The night sky was no longer inky black, but instead a baby blue. Soon the sun would come up. Awkwardly running along the river front with my wounded leg, I kept a lookout for some sort of eye. When the sun pierced through the horizon, a scenic point appeared to my right, which I assumed was the 'eye'. I turned into the city again, looking for the building where it would finally end. I tried to picture the map in my mind. The final clue had been a number and a fish of some sort.

Business offices lined the streets. I read all the signs on the doors, looking for anything that might relate back to the clues I could remember. I hurried between buildings, hoping I would be done before the smell of my blood attracted more trouble.

It took me another hour before I finally found a newly added small paper label indicating a firm called 'Supreme Salmon' on the second floor. It had to be it; the fish and the roman numeral two for second floor.

The stairs were on the right and I climbed them solely with the help of the bannister that allowed me to take some of the weight off my injured leg. The second floor was an open-plan office packed with desks and computers. Apart from two humans it was empty. I wondered why I could see these two.

They were hunched over, looking at a computer screen to my right by a window. They remained unaware of my existence, so I ignored them and continued my search for the 'cross' and end to this test. I started to check the doors dispersed in the corners of the office floor. The first two were restrooms. I moved further to the back, towards the last door.

I entered a spacious private office. There was a wooden desk to the back, in front of floor-to-ceiling windows. Through the windows, I could see the street I had just crossed. There were bookcases filled with books and folders, and shelves on walls holding vases and several awards made out of glass. I walked slowly around the office, looking for any sign of danger. I wandered to the back of the desk and saw something.

There on the floor behind the desk was someone curled up. As I came closer, I could see it was a little boy crying.

'Hey, are you lost?' I asked him, kneeling beside him and patting him on the back. Stupid! Humans couldn't hear me!

To my surprise the boy raised his head.

I jumped backwards in shock, tripping over the desk chair.

No, it was an illusion. This was not happening! No!

'I want to go home,' he blubbered.

I *knew* that voice. No, no, no... He was not part of this! He had not died! He had not been recruited into this world! This *had* to be a trick!

'Liam?' I gasped.

'Ameerah? Where are Mummy and Daddy? I want to go home!'

'How did you get here?' I finally managed to ask.

'I followed you.' Liam got up and hugged my legs, clutching them tightly.

Tears ran down my face. This was not right. He was too young. I looked down at his hair. I wanted to touch his hair, hold him close, wake up with him from this nightmare in our house in the south of France and forget everything.

My palms caressed his hair... but it felt different. His hair had always been surprisingly crunchy, even if it looked smooth.

'Liam, what are you doing here?' I asked him and pushed him softly off my legs.

'I was looking for Mummy and Daddy,' he answered in the same voice.

'Liam, do you remember where I found Bruce?'

Liam looked surprised. His expression was odd.

'Bruce my dog, Liam. Where did I find him?' I stared into his eyes. I could see he had perfectly understood the question, but his expression was blank.

The office door suddenly burst open making us both shriek in surprise. In walked a tall sharply dressed man with blood-red eyes.

'Oh no,' said a voice that was not Liam's but came from his mouth. Liam's face had turned into the seriousness only an adult could express. His flesh turned to smoke and vanished into the air. My hands which had held on to his arms were suddenly grasping nothing.

I slowly got up, eyeing the man who had made Liam disappear. My stomach tingled just like it did when molochs were close-by.

'Well, well, well, what do we have here?' the man asked with a devilish smile on his pale face. He had thick brown curly hair and his skin was as white as if he had never seen the sun. What made me most uneasy, were his eyes.

'I thought I smelled a new ghost.' He inhaled deeply and smiled mischievously. His teeth were white as paper and looked sharp as knives.

'Is – is this part of the test?' I asked him nervously.

He roared a maniacal laugh and threw his head back. 'You're taking your field test now? This will be even sweeter.'

A cold draft clung to me. 'Who are you?'

In less than a heartbeat he was standing right before me. I didn't even see him move. His pupils were vertical like those of cats, and his irises were a deep red.

'I am Viktor,' he announced theatrically, showing off his razor-blade teeth. They were close to my cheek.

I could feel my breathing accelerating; Viktor smiled pleased at the reaction.

'Have you ever been in the presence of a vampire before?' Viktor asked, taking a step back. He turned and walked casually around the office. As he passed the wooden desk, his hand leisurely trailed along it, his nails leaving deep scratches in the wood.

'No,' I answered with a trembling voice. I wanted to be strong and fearless, but I didn't even have a gun on me! I looked around for anything I could use as a weapon if I got the chance.

'You see, I almost didn't believe it. Two recruits in such a short interval; it's almost too good to be true.'

Viktor walked around the desk and I mirrored his movements. If I could get to the door, maybe I could run just like Blake had instructed me to...

Somehow, I doubted I could outrun Viktor...

'What do you mean two recruits?' I asked trying to keep him talking.

'Oh you must have heard of my fun with the other one. He was carelessly wandering around when I surprised him with my companions. But that was not the only surprise; halfway through our playing, his trainer showed up.'

Viktor chuckled, his cat eyes staring at the ceiling. 'Oh what a night it was.'

He turned his head back down to look right at me. I could not hide my shock, and he looked very pleased about it. 'You *have* heard of it.'

'What did you do with the trainer?' I asked, fearing the answer.

'Too bad yours is not with us...' Viktor approached me, ignoring my question, his gaze cold and calculated. 'Don't worry... I will still have my fun...'

I turned to run but crashed into the wall behind me and fell to the ground. The air was ripped out of my lungs. I was paralysed with pain. I coughed and sputtered from the dried plaster drizzling down. Viktor knelt down, observing me with curiosity. I struggled up onto my hands and knees; I had a few broken ribs at the least. He had been so fast I had not seen him throw me into the wall.

'Get up, little girl. I'm not finished playing with you.' Viktor spoke in a low voice, drugged with pleasure.

He patiently waited for me to stand again, before smashing me once more into the wall, making the contents on the shelves next to me tremble. He caught me before I hit the ground and held me upright by the throat. His face was only inches away from mine. I could see his eyes had dilated into round crimson pupils. He looked completely high on the imminent thrill of the kill.

'Unfortunately, I cannot take as much time as I did with the last one' Viktor paused. 'But don't worry; I will enjoy this very much.'

The sunbeams hit his face and made his skin even whiter. He showed his teeth and a low hiss escaped the depth of his throat. The sound made my skin crawl.

With my right hand I had slowly reached over to the shelf and could feel something made of glass in my hand. It was heavy.

'Do it,' I whispered.

At first, he looked surprised by my words. I turned my head and stretched my neck, exposing the pulsing veins inside. It had the desired effect; Viktor's gaze was fixed on my throat. He was hypnotised and slowly leant in. I could see the saliva in his mouth and around his searing teeth. With one quick motion I smashed the object against the back of his head.

Caught off guard, he let go of me. I made a run for it. I was barely at the door when Viktor appeared in front of me, blocking my way. A playful smile decorated his face.

'I like it when they fight,' he hissed softly.

With a simple push from the vampire I crashed into the wooden desk. The impact crushed my arm. My head hit the floor and the desk broke into two. I was dizzy but managed to raise myself up onto my shaking legs. I floundered backwards, away from him.

He was too fast. I could not beat him at his game. And I had no way of defending myself. I could barely fend off molochs and I was trying to fight a vampire, an evolved beast that had been around for thousands of years that was faster than my eyes could see...

'I will have you,' Viktor assured me, playfully scratching anything his hands could get a grip on.

I wanted to run away, scream him away, close my eyes and wish him away...

'Please.' I gave in, tears pouring out of my eyes.

Viktor tilted his head to one side. 'Poor little girl, have I scared you now?'

He was still approaching and now I had my back to the office window.

'Please!' I sobbed again. I didn't want to fight anymore; I didn't want to feel any pain. My whole body ached and I was so scared. I just wanted it all to end. But there was no way out.

'Please let me go!' I pleaded.

Viktor now stood in front of me. There was nowhere to go. He let out a satisfied groan as he grabbed my throat with his left hand, lifting me from the floor. I could still breathe but not for long. With the other hand he trailed along my neck and shoulder, careful not to rip it open with his claws. Viktor bowed and licked my neck with his tongue. I could feel his sharp teeth touching my skin. He breathed in my scent and threw his head back with delight.

I tried to kick him, but he slammed my already throbbing head into the window in response. The glass cracked and I could feel warm blood flowing down the back of my neck. My vision started blurring as the oxygen didn't reach my brain anymore.

Viktor froze and sniffed at the smell of fresh blood in the air. He showcased his teeth in one last roar and approached my throat again. It was the end now. In a moment or two, I would be gone. My throat was closing, my vision disappearing. My strength was leaving me. At least I wouldn't have to feel him draining me of my blood. The darkness closed in on me and I welcomed it.

Loud noises tore at my ears. A tortured roar echoed. I fell to the ground. The bangs kept coming. Why wasn't it the end? Could it just... everything was blurry... I wanted to... I tried to open my eyes... get up... I gasped for air, but none would reach my lungs. The undercurrent was too strong. It pulled me back into the darkness.

* * *

I was thirsty... so incredibly thirsty. I opened my eyes. Softness surrounded me. My head turned to the right and there was the poster of Canada.

I raised myself into a sitting position. I felt sore and drained, but nothing specifically hurt. I stood up, letting out a sigh and rubbing my eyes. Slowly I started walking out of my room when Blake appeared in the door.

'How do you feel? Are you ok?' he asked, inspecting my face and checking my limbs.

'I'm thirsty,' I said in a croaky voice.

'I'll get you some water. Sit down,' he commanded and hurried to the kitchen.

I bowed to his will and sat back down onto my bed. The muscles in my legs were sore. Blake reappeared with a tall glass of water. His worried eyes followed my every move.

'What happened?' I asked him after emptying half the glass. Swallowing was painful. I remembered the test, the molochs, Liam and then Viktor, but my memories got blurry as I tried to understand how I was still alive. A ghost anyway...

'You should rest. We can talk about it later.'

'No, I want to know. Was that vampire part of my test? Tell me,' I insisted.

He sighed deeply and scrutinised my face.

'The council created an illusion of your brother to test your resilience towards loved ones. But before they had gotten into the details, the vampire interrupted. He was definitely *not* part of the plan,' Blake started, 'I was not far, but far enough to be too late. When I arrived, Carl, Dom and Kim were already there. We killed Viktor.'

Blake paused, looking at me with those blue piercing eyes. 'You were in a bad shape. I thought... I was afraid we... were too late. But we got you to your master just in time.'

Blake had to stop again. He closed his eyes and concentrated on breathing steadily. I had never seen him so emotional.

I reached out and squeezed his hand lightly.

Blake got up with a smile and placed his hands on his hips. 'We'll have to discuss what happened during your test. I have a lot of questions and so does your master.'

'Did I pass?'

Blake nodded. 'You survived so that's good. The council will give the final judgment, but you shouldn't have any problems with them. I'm going to call your master to tell him you're awake. You should call Kim. She's been worried about you.'

With these words Blake left with a smile across his lips. I reached for my phone that lay next to my computer. There were endless messages from Kim and some from Carl. The first number I dialled was hers. Kim unleashed her waterfall of words before I had even said hello.

'Ameerah! How are you? Are you ok? How did your test go before... you know... what happened? Tell me from the beginning, I want to know *everything!*'

I recounted everything that happened up until my unfortunate encounter with the vampire. I couldn't believe I was not dead. Viktor had been so strong and he had nearly suffocated me. My right hand reached up to my neck and gently massaged it.

Kim wanted to throw me a party at Santa's pub to celebrate my success and surviving a vampire attack. I was not really in the mood to be in a cramped place talking about almost dying, but I couldn't say no to her.

She had organised the party by the time we were done talking on the phone and I had had no chance to object. She needed it. I had almost died and she had almost lost me.

I slowly stepped out of my room, towards Blake. 'Kim planned a party at Santa's tonight. There was no talking her out of it.'

He nodded slightly. 'I guess it's alright. I'll come with you. You're still in a fragile state.'

I went back to my room to rest a little. All this talking had made me really tired. It was already getting darker outside again. Before I knew it, I had fallen asleep.

A few hours later I was in Santa's pub, surrounded by fellow ghosts. All I had wanted to do was stay in bed and sleep for a few more weeks. Blake let me sleep as long as he could. We showed up an hour late to my own party.

Ghosts I hadn't even met brought me drinks and congratulated me on passing my field test, even though technically speaking, I didn't know if I had. I politely declined the drinks and smiled and nodded at the congratulations. Kim had hung a huge sign at the entrance to make sure everyone knew why we were there. My head span and I had periodic flashbacks of Viktor's face. My throat hurt.

Not long after we had arrived, Kim stood on the bar table and called for attention. She had a speech prepared.

'Let's all toast to Ameerah!' she began, lifting her drink. 'Ameerah passed her test not only during a blizzard; she was surprised by a vampire!'

I could hear a whisper going through the crowd and eyes turning towards me. All I wanted was to crawl into a dark corner and be invisible!

Blake stood next to me but didn't move. His eyes scanned the crowd.

'Ameerah fought with a vampire and almost died!' Kim declared to the crowd, 'But she prevailed. And now, let's all lift our glass and toast to a great ghost. She will kill many more vampires. We can count on that!'

Kim whooped and the crowd cheered in agreement. Cups and glasses were lifted into the air with chants and screams. Drinks were spilled everywhere as the crowd rejoiced. They all hugged and cheered me, clapping me on the back. I toasted with my glass of water. I nodded, unsure of myself and smiled anxiously at the herd around me.

I looked around and realised Blake had disappeared on me. I was left alone to fend off all the unwanted admiration. I had tried to deny the story; I insisted I had barely stalled Viktor long enough to be rescued, but the real story got drowned out and Kim's version was all anyone wanted to hear.

Carl made his way through the crowd towards me. He was one of the few people I wanted to see and thank. Carl could see I was not well and took me aside from the beaming crowd. He inadvertently led me into the corner where I had first met Ben.

'How are you holding up?' Carl asked in his usual rough voice.

'Still a little shaky, but I will be ok,' I repeated once more my rehearsed response.

His brown eyes gazed at me through the strains of his grey hair. 'Are you sure?'

I nodded my head but failed to convince him.

'Have you talked to Blake or your master about what happened?'

'No, not yet.'

I glanced to where I had last seen Blake, but I couldn't see him anywhere.

Carl leaned closer and whispered in my ear. 'Don't worry, it will all be ok. You are strong and resilient, just like Kim. Makes me think the masters should choose more women to become ghosts.'

I had to chuckle.

Carl rubbed my arm. 'You will be alright, kid. Blake has trained you well.'

He nodded and a warm smile spread across his aged face. A warmth radiated from the seasoned trainer that made me feel safe.

'I'll do my best,' I said.

With one last smile he disappeared back into the crowd. I took a deep breath, but the air was stuffy. The music was loud, but somehow the crowd managed to be even louder. I smuggled myself through the masses, out of the yellow-lit party zone and into the cool night.

What a relief! I walked towards the waterfront across the massive parking lot. Carl's speech had triggered so many memories; I daydreamed about the great human life I had underappreciated all those years. The carelessness my life had had... I trailed off into memories of holidays together, walks with Bruce, concerts with my friends...

I could see Liam smiling at me. But he abruptly deserted me leaving Viktor and those violent red eyes. What if he *had* killed me that very moment? I had barely been here a year and it had almost all come to an end, long before my sixty-some years' sentence was up.

How would I survive this until the end? There were probably millions of vampires in this world. If they were all so powerful, which was a pretty safe bet, how *could* I survive? Another would come along soon enough, and then what?

I began to realise how valuable Blake's training had been... but also how utterly useless. I had no chance against any vampire, I couldn't even outrun one. The best way to stay alive was to avoid them altogether! How much stronger and faster would I have to be? How much more did I have to train?

I bent my upper body over the railing, my elbows resting on it. A fresh breeze played with my hair. This was worse than an uphill battle; this was like an ant trying to defeat a shark, in the water.

I couldn't help but feel tricked; this was not a fair fight! How could the council not give us a weapon to kill those blood-thirsty monsters? There had to be a way! How could I have been tricked into coming to this shit-hole parallel world?!

The more I thought about it, the more the logical part of my brain kicked in, trying to reason with me; if they were so invincible, they would have wiped the ghosts out a long time ago. They were intelligent enough to do it, so why were we still here?

My thoughts drifted in another direction. Viktor had mentioned another victim. He had insinuated that somehow a trainer had been involved too. Was he talking about Ben? And how had the trainer been involved? Could he have been part of it? No, that was out of the question.

Blake had said he had found the recruit and didn't mention anything about Ben. But... why would Viktor lie? Or did Viktor mean Blake discovered them?

Suddenly I thought I felt someone touching my shoulder. Instinctively, I pushed myself away from the railing, drew my gun and shot without thinking.

'DON'T TOUCH ME!' I screamed before I recognised the shadow.

The gun shook in my hands. My ears rang from the shot.

I could feel him, standing behind me, pressing me against Blake's truck...

'Ameerah it's me!'

He didn't move. It took me a few moments before it sank in that I had shot Ben.

'Are you... hurt? Did I get you?' I realised I had the gun still pointed at him. With shaking hands, I holstered it onto my right side.

'Doesn't matter, are you alright?'

He dared to come closer and the sparse light illuminated his face.

I closed my eyes and brushed through my hair.

He was gone, he would never hurt me again. Nobody would ever touch me again.

'You scared me. I didn't mean to shoot... Did I hit you?'

Ben glanced at his left shoulder. 'You grazed me.'

'Blake has a medical kit in his car.' I walked towards the parked truck away from the river.

My mind was racing. Why was I so jumpy when I knew he was dead?

I gestured for Ben to sit down in the driver's seat with the door open and placed the medical kit in his lap. He had taken off his jacket and t-shirt and I disinfected the wounds with sweating hands. I asked him to gently lift his arm so I could wrap the wound as best as I could. My fingers were numb and the bandages took forever. I used my left hand to hold the bandages in place as I wrapped his wound, inadvertently touching his warm skin. His strong muscles around his shoulders were visible even in this sparse light.

While I pretended to be a medical professional, Ben stayed quiet and looked at me with a soft expression.

'Ameerah?'

I made a sound indicating I was listening.

'Did someone hurt you?'

For a moment I froze. When the tears suddenly kept falling, I quickly finished up.

'There, all done' I tried to smile and zipped the kit closed. My eyes were looking down at his shoes. I couldn't look at him.

Ben didn't move.

'I... I don't want to talk about it,' I whispered. My face was covered in tears and the memories were playing in front of my eyes.

I could feel his weight on me.

He slowly raised himself up. In the dark and in a confined space between the parked cars he seemed so much taller and stronger than me. Ben quietly stretched his hand towards me and I let him touch my hand. He didn't squeeze it or close his hand around it, he only caressed my fingers very gently.

'Just tell me who and I'll take care of it,' Ben whispered in my ear as a promise.

He then turned away and quietly walked off to his car and drove off.

I sat down on the driver's seat of Blake's truck and calmed down while I let the tears dry. Vladimir was dead. His body had been carried away by the river, hopefully far away before it was found. No one would trace it back to Kim and me.

There was a sound of a door being opened. A man came out of the pub and lit a cigarette in front of the door, bringing me back to the present.

I texted Blake I wanted to go home. He appeared only a few minutes later and waved at the man smoking by the door as he walked towards the truck. I hoped I had wiped away the distress from my face.

'What's going on?'

I was in the passenger seat and looked at my phone, trying to hide my face. 'I have a bad headache and all those people- it's just making it worse.'

He nodded and drove us home. I apologised to Kim via text message.

'I hope you enjoyed your party at least,' Blake finally broke the silence. His eyes were on the road, but I could see him glancing over to me every now and again.

'Yeah, it was nice. It was just too soon…'

'What happened? In the office with Viktor?' Blake asked in a soft tone.

I looked over to him and our eyes locked in on each other. I couldn't hold long and quickly averted my eyes.

'I was with Liam when he… came in. I knew right away I couldn't escape him. Every time I tried to outrun him, he would… hit me or throw me against the wall.'

I was not enjoying talking about it. Yet another man that petrified me from the grave.

'Did he say anything to you?'

'No, he just mentioned he had... killed another recruit.' When I spoke the words, our gaze crossed again.

We drove in silence for a while. Eventually, we pulled up at the house.

'How do you kill one?'

Blake took the key out of the ignition. We both got out of the car.

'Burning them is the most effective way. They are so fast you usually can't get close enough to set them on fire. Shooting them from several angles holds them in place and eventually kills them. Generally, you need to be three or four ghosts to be on the safe side. Once they are down, you set them on fire.'

'But,' I replied as we went through the door, 'What if I'm alone?'

We went up the stairs and Blake took his jacket, sweater, and top off and got ready for a nightly workout. I waited, standing in the middle of the living room. Minutes passed before he eventually answered.

'If you're alone against one then yes, you'll probably die. All I can say is it's better to try to escape than to try to fight.'

'I guess I'm lucky you all came when you did.'

'You were. Now you understand why I'm so hard with you.' He smiled encouragingly. His voice was unusually quiet.

I managed a smile back and headed to my bedroom to put my purse away. My body was still hot from the crowd and I craved a shower. While soaping in the cool water, my thoughts drifted off to Ben. He had said he would protect me, but how could I trust another man? I barely knew him and the story with his recruit was appalling... and yet... I found myself wanting to be around him. There was something about him that made me feel safe. I longed to be close to someone, close to a loving man who would protect me even if I didn't want to need his protection.

Half an hour later I got out and Blake had finished training; he was now leaning against the table and looking at the chalk board, gently strumming his guitar. 'You took a long time in there.'

'I... I was really hot from the crowd and... just lost track of time.'

Even after the long shower I couldn't sleep. Only a few hours after lying down I found myself wandering around the house. Every time I closed my eyes, images of Viktor with his bright crimson eyes haunted me. When I wasn't seeing Viktor, I saw Vladimir pushing me and trying to force himself onto me. The clinging of his belt buckle continuously rang in my head.

I curled up on Blake's chair and looked outside. There were barely any streetlights, but I could still see everything in the dark. The sun was not up yet but the sky had started to turn blue.

SECRETS

I awoke to the sound of Blake playing his guitar.

'Good morning,' he said with his back towards me.

I rubbed my eyes and stretched my limbs as I approached him and looked at his charts lying on his desk. There were drawings of moloch nests.

'I didn't sleep much.'

'Tough life,' he responded and spun around, 'Get dressed, you're jogging in five.'

'I thought I was field approved now! Why are you giving me orders?' I grumbled.

Blake smiled his devilish smile, which meant he was about to reveal a loophole. I hated that smile. 'Technically speaking, you're not field approved until the council has said so. And secondly, just because you're field approved doesn't mean you can slack off, on the contrary!'

'What's the point of being field approved then?' I questioned, shaking my head.

'You can finally help me kill molochs and vampires on missions. I can't do it all by myself!' he chuckled and wrote some notes on the board.

I shivered at the mention of vampires. I would avoid them at any cost, whatever Blake said.

It was another excruciatingly hot morning. After resenting the council for making me pass the test in the freezing arctic, I now found myself wishing it was colder. The sun was intense, and the many windows and buildings attracted more of its heat.

Even after a long cool shower, I quickly started sweating again. When I opened the door to the bathroom, Blake was standing in the living room, his arms crossed across his chest, looking at me with a smile on his face.

'What?' I asked at his blank expression.

'Your master is here,' Blake quietly stated, his ocean eyes observing my reaction.

I could feel my heart speeding up, my breath accelerating and my hormones spiking. A feeling of peace spread through my cells, relaxing and exciting at the same time.

'I'll leave you two.' Blake nodded and as he stepped aside, a man was revealed sitting in Blake's chair. When I walked closer, I saw a black man dressed in a white shirt and black pants. He was bald and had a strong jaw line.

At first, I eyed the man suspiciously, until he smiled showing off a row of paper-white teeth. A fresh wave of positive emotions drowned my body. It made me sway backwards, almost losing my balance.

'Good afternoon, Ameerah,' he spoke with the renowned French accent. 'My name is Caleb.'

'Hello,' I responded shyly. His aura impressed me. He had a strong presence and it was impossible not to be attracted by his power, whatever it was.

'We finally meet, officially. I have observed you for a long time.'

After a few moments of silence, he continued, 'I am the one who watched you in the other world. Blake appeared in your dreams, but it was I who decided to open the door to this world to you.'

He rose with lightness off the chair and strolled to the window.

All my unanswered questions came rushing back to my consciousness. 'You were the one who brought me here?'

'Yes and no,' he grinned, 'I chose you, but Blake had to convince you to cross over.'

'Why Blake? Why didn't you appear in my dreams?' I inquired.

Caleb smiled and looked out the window. 'Because it is not my duty to bring ghosts into this world, I only choose.'

'Why me?' I restrained myself from adding *Why did you tear me away from my innocent life?*

'Your fate in the other world was sealed. I observed you for a long time before deciding you were worthy of... escaping your death. Our... connection formed before you were even aware.'

Caleb turned to me with his magnificent smile. I just stood there, startled by his very presence, dealing with all the positive emotions cascading inside me. With every step he took towards me, my breathing accelerated. Caleb opened his hands and offered them to me. I paused but he smiled encouragingly and I laid my hands in his. The moment our skin touched the connection overwhelmed me; the positive feelings were nothing compared to how I felt now. I was in ecstasy, surrendering to the gentle massage of happiness invading me. All worries were gone; I had no guilt, shame, reluctance, resentment, or any other remotely negative feeling in me. They had all been replaced by positive and loving feelings.

'Ameerah, follow my voice.'

I could hear a distant whisper calling me back. My head swam in happiness.

'Ameerah, come back to me,' someone softly called. I obeyed and felt no reluctance in leaving this heaven. I knew I could return here anytime I desired.

When I opened my eyes, I was standing in front of Caleb, our hands still touching. The heavenly feeling had dulled but it was still claiming most of my attention. It was hard to concentrate.

'I had not anticipated your reaction to be so strong,' Caleb stated, pleased. 'What you are experiencing is the master-protégé bond between us. You can feel my presence when I'm close and it gives you comfort.'

I clung to every word he uttered. He made me feel loved.

'Do you remember, before you crossed into this world? I was always around you.'

I remembered walking in the fields in the south of France with Bruce. He had been upset and acting strange. Then I remembered I thought someone was in my room, but it was empty.

'Yes, my child. That was me.'

'But why did you choose me?' I asked in a dreamy state.

'Because you have qualities I seek in my protégés. Blake used to be my protégé and I therefore knew you could counterbalance and complete him.'

So, I was just an addition to Blake? The only reason I had been chosen was to counter Blake's eccentricities?

'No Ameerah. You are not only a balance to Blake. After observing you, I saw you are intelligent, resilient, and able to question yourself. I needed someone who was strong and who could be a partner to Blake in his mission.'

I blushed at the compliments I was receiving from a completely foreign man.

Caleb let go of my hands. The positive flow was abruptly interrupted and I stumbled backwards, like one unexpectedly stepping off a moving walkway at an airport. I had to sit down in my chair to avoid fainting. I had experienced so many positive emotions in such a short time it made me dizzy.

Caleb smiled. 'As it is our first encounter, you are greatly overwhelmed by my presence. It is time for me to go.'

I couldn't help but feel hurt. He was going to leave me? Why? I wanted him to stay! He brought me comfort I so desperately needed. I got up and made a step towards him, wanting to hug him to experience again the ecstasy, but Caleb backed away. The hurt I felt was much stronger than I had anticipated; I went from euphoric to devastated in no time.

'Your need for me is accentuated. I have over-sensitised you to me. If you touch me now you will pass out from the feeling of comfort and reassurance I give you.'

I grunted in protest. Once more, I was surprised by my reaction. This was all so new to me. I nodded and backed away from him.

'I will see you soon again, Ameerah.' His voice caressed my name. I closed my eyes and enjoyed the echo of his voice in my head. When I opened my eyes again, I was standing alone in the living room. He had slipped out faster than I had thought possible.

The welcoming feeling slowly pulsed down. I was shaking from the feelings I had experienced. The bond with Caleb was a strong attachment that I tentatively compared to unconditional love, but the love I felt for Caleb was more of a craving of his presence, approval, and attention, rather than passion. He was a comfort in this harsh world that I wanted around me to protect me from its evils and to bring me back home.

I was sitting in my chair, staring into space, when Blake came home. The moment his eyes fell on me, he smirked knowingly.

'He's impressive, isn't he?' Blake teased.

He let himself fall into the chair next to mine and observed me. 'Did he answer some of your questions?'

I nodded.

Blake couldn't stop himself from grinning. 'A word of advice, don't think of anything you don't want him to know when he's around.'

I raised my eyebrows at Blake, waiting for him to explain further. He kept smiling with his I-know-something look. He leant forward, resting his elbows on his knees.

'Didn't you notice?'

My frown deepened and Blake's delight augmented.

'Caleb can read your emotions,' he said in an obvious tone.

I was startled. My horrified face brought Blake more pleasure. He leant back, laying his head on his left hand, enjoying my reaction.

'He knows what I'm thinking?!' I repeated carefully.

Blake did not make any sign of acknowledgement, but just kept smiling.

I had risen onto my legs, shocked by this revelation. Now it all came back to me. Caleb had answered my questions without me uttering a word. How could I not have notice before?

'I'll let you get used to this idea.' Blake got up and jogged up to his room, noisily fumbling with his drawers.

I tried to remember everything I had thought about while Caleb was here. Had I inadvertently told him things I didn't want him to know? No, nothing came to mind, but it was a lucky break; I would have to be careful in the future.

Blake came down the stairs, in a baggy pair of shorts ready for another workout session.

'Blake, Caleb said you used to be his protégé. Is that right?'

He came towards me while stretching his arms and back. 'Yes, and when my trainer had finished his sentence, I graduated to his trainer status. When I'm done here in twenty-nine years it will be your turn to train someone.'

'How did Caleb get here? Is he also here for a second chance in his human life?'

'No,' Blake had lowered his voice. 'Caleb did bad things when he was human and when he was close to his death, he was tormented with guilt and regret. When he died, he got a chance to redeem himself by serving here as a master. At the end of his sentence he will have absolution and can rest in peace.'

'What did he do that was so awful?'

Blake turned away and walked towards the back of the living room. 'That you will have to ask him yourself.'

My eyes wandered out the window. It was early afternoon and the sun was high in the sky and beating down on the grey structures of Idolon. The apartment would soon be as hot as an oven.

'I'm going out for a walk.' I swung myself out of the chair.

Blake let himself fall from the rails on the ceiling and landed on cat's feet.

'Alright, just be careful. Even if you'll be approved soon, it's better to be safe.'

His abs contracted as he jumped back up and started pulling himself up. His strength was infinite it seemed.

With a gun and my phone on me, I exited the house and started walking north. I reached a park after about twenty minutes. It was small with large willow and birch trees. The rustling of their leaves invited me closer and I sat in the shade under a smaller willow tree.

I was leaning against the tree with my eyes closed when my phone vibrated.

'How are you feeling? Are you doing better since the party? Ben.'

A shudder travelled through my body. It would still take me some time to put Vladimir behind me. But I wanted to get over it as quickly as possible. With the approaching council hearing I couldn't risk being distracted. And Caleb could read my emotions! He could possibly feel my distress! I had to get rid of all this.

I texted Ben my location and asked if he wanted to join me. He responded he would be there shortly.

A cool breeze blew through the park, playing with my hair and making the leaves and branches whirl. The shadow and light game that danced on the ground was soothing.

My butt cheeks were asleep. I opened my eyes and stretched to counter the tingling. Ben was sitting across from me, his legs stretched out, shades on his eyes and his head pointing towards the canopy of the trees above us. He was wearing dark shorts and a fitted blue t-shirt. The t-shirt was tight around his shoulders and pecks.

'How long was I out?' I croaked.

Ben smiled at me. 'About an hour. I didn't have the heart to wake you.'

I realised I had been completely defenceless lying in plain sight. An open target for any kind of assault. My hand glided to the weapon by my side.

The sun was further down the horizon. With the increased wind the temperature was pleasant.

'So how are you doing?'

I sat up and sighed deeply. 'Nervous. I still need to pass my hearing and my master can read my emotions. I can't hide things it seems, but I don't want to talk about them.'

'You feel under pressure. All these... men around you.'

My heartbeat accelerated and a hot wave flashed through my body.

'Are you afraid of me?'

Ben had not moved. He was still leaning back, a few feet away from me.

'I don't want to be... but I don't know you. Even Blake scares me and I've known him for a year. I trust him... to an extent. All of you can suddenly attack me. All of you are very strong.'

'Do you think Blake would hurt you?'

I pondered his question before answering. 'No, but I'm still scared.'

Ben stayed quiet for a few moments. 'Are you... still – in danger?'

'No.'

'Are you sure?'

A few tears fell from my eyes, but I quickly shook my head. 'He's dead.'

He nodded. 'Good. I don't want to ask more questions, but if someone hurts you, you let me know and I'll take care of it. I like you and I don't want anyone hurting you.'

Though he was perfectly calm, even I could sense the threat in his tone.

'Where did you go in January?'

'I told you, I had to take care of some things.' Ben became defensive.

'You say you like me and you'll take care of things, but you ghosted me for three months and now you're asking me to trust you.'

Ben took his sunglasses off and cleaned the lenses with the bottom of his t-shirt. He put them back on and adjusted them, before he finally responded.

'I know I've let you down. I... my master and I had a – disagreement, which led to him threatening to report me to the council. I couldn't stand it anymore, so I had to leave for a while to cool off. I didn't want to leave you, but I couldn't stay where Jesper would find me.'

It was strange to me that his relationship with his master was so explosive. I couldn't imagine disagreeing with Caleb. I wanted his approval, whatever it cost.

'Where did you go?'

'I went south, but I kept moving so Jesper wouldn't be able to sense me.'

'Why didn't you tell me before? Why didn't you text me or call me?' I couldn't quite hide the despair in my voice.

Ben bowed his upper body towards me as if to whisper something. He was at about an arm's distance from me.

'If we had talked and texted, I would have wanted to come back to spend time with you, but I needed to cool off. If I had returned earlier, I would have ended up in front of the council again.'

I tilted my head. 'So, you do like me?'

Ben smiled and my heart warmed. 'Of course I do. I think you're great.'

The butterflies in my stomach suddenly appeared, buzzing happily. My knees got weak and I was relieved I was sitting and not standing.

'If I'm supposed to trust you, I need to get to know you,' I suggested.

We continued talking for hours. He told me he had run away from home at fifteen. His mother was an alcoholic and he had not known his father. He had a brother but he had gone to jail and he had not seen any of his family for years. Ben loved to race cars as well as boxing. Even though he was eager to leave Idolon, there was not much waiting for him in his human life. He didn't speak much of his family and mostly talked about his life after he ran away.

We bonded over Canada. I had lived for a few years in Vancouver and he had lived there too. The butterflies in my stomach became a continuous humming. Even though I didn't feel in danger or in any way uneasy around Ben, there was a part of my brain that knew if he wanted to, he could overpower me and take advantage of me. No matter how many times I told myself he wouldn't, I couldn't shake the worried feeling that he still was capable.

My phone vibrated in my pocket, interrupting our conversation. The sun had now disappeared behind the buildings and it was starting to cool down. The blue of the sky was no longer light blue, but a deeper ocean blue. A few white clouds had appeared on the horizon.

'Where are you? You've been gone for hours now.' Blake had an angry tone.

'I'm almost field approved, what's the problem? I'm in a park not far from the house.'

'What are you doing?'

'I'm talking with a friend. What do you want?' My words were a bit too harsh, but I was growing tired of him.

'Who are you talking to?'

'None of your business!'

Blake breathed into the phone. 'Ameerah, I'm still your trainer so I need to know what you're doing and who you're with. It's starting to be late. Come home now. I'll expect you here within half an hour.'

Blake hung up on me.

I was fuming. What was he thinking? What did it matter to him who I was with?

'I'll take you back.' Ben got up and stretched his hand my way.

Hesitantly, I took it and let him pull me up. His hand was warm and the skin on his fingers rough. He held on to my hand a few seconds longer before letting go.

Ben brushed the grass and twigs off himself and guided me towards his car. It was a short drive back to Blake's house. He stopped the car three houses before Blake's.

'Do you want to get out here or should I drive up to the house?' Ben turned towards me.

'Here is better. The way Blake reacted last time I think it's better he doesn't get the chance to throw a punch.'

Ben smirked. 'Not that he has a chance, but I understand. Send me a message later on.'

I nodded and got out of the car. I wanted to kiss him, but I also wanted to wait. He was sweet but I couldn't shake the fear Vladimir had given me.

'Who were you with?' Blake stood at the top of the stairs as I walked up. He had stretched himself to his full length.

'It doesn't matter, stop asking me questions.' I tried to wave him off.

'It can't be Kim because you would have told me, so tell me!' He followed me as I tried to get to my bedroom. Blake positioned himself in front of the door and eyed me with his icy eyes.

'Fine! I was with Ben!' I threw my hands in the air.

Blake's face immediately changed. 'Ben? You were... you were with Ben? After I told you to stay away from him? After I told you about his recruit being butchered by vampires?'

'We were just sitting in the park talking, what's the big deal? And what does it matter to you anyway? I'm a grown woman and I can do whatever I want.'

'*No*, you *cannot* do what you want! We have to work together! I'm your trainer and he cannot be trusted! He's careless and I don't want you in any danger! That's the end of it.'

I took a step back. 'First of all, I'm always in danger! There are demons running around ready to kill me so don't tell me Ben will put me in more danger. And secondly, you can't tell me what to do. I can talk and socialise with anyone I want and you can't stop me!'

'Ameerah, I'm serious,' he warned me. There was a light in his eyes that I hadn't seen before. The veins on his neck started to show.

'So am I. Back off Blake.'

I pushed past him and closed the door behind me. My legs were shaking. I was proud of myself for finally taking a stand and not letting myself be manipulated and controlled, but this defiance would have consequences. Blake would find a way to make me pay. That, however, was a problem for tomorrow.

I breathed in deeply and let myself fall onto the bed. Another day gone. Another day closer to leaving.

TERRITORY INFRINGEMENTS

The day of my hearing, Blake and Caleb dropped me off on the steps of the courthouse building. I proceeded inside into a dark room. As instructed, I turned to the right and opened the heavy wooden door to the hall where I would present my case. The hinges creaked as I carefully opened it. It was a heavy door and a dozen feet tall.

Once I had slipped inside, the door closed loudly, making me jump. The hall was huge. It looked like it could have been a royal court. The ceiling was covered in frescos, reminding me of the Sistine Chapel. At the far end was a large table at which the five hideous creatures were sitting. They were deathly pale and draped in black robes. Even from this distance I could make out their empty sockets staring through my skin. My nerves instinctively spiked. I tried to recall the warm feeling Caleb's presence had given me just a few minutes ago and used it to stay composed.

I stopped when I was a few yards from their long wooden table; any further and I worried I would start to gag. The table was on a high podium, making me feel even smaller. It seemed ridiculously unnecessary to lift those creatures higher up; they had to know they scared the living crap out of every person having to stand so close to them.

'Do you know why you are here, Ameerah?' the familiar echoes resounded in my head. The white creatures in front of me did not move. With a loud gulp I took a deep breath. *I can do this.*

'To tell you about my field test…?' I hesitated. My voice was no louder than a whisper. Blake had warned me the council had heightened auditory capacities, so I had to hush my responses. Apparently, they were able to hear everything from my heartbeat to the electricity passing between the neurons in my brain. All in all, it enabled them to sense lies. Or at least that's what Blake and the other ghosts seemed to think. I didn't know for sure, but I could imagine they had some sort of X-ray vision into my mind. Back when I had first passed over to Idolon, I hadn't even spoken out loud. I had only thought of my responses and agreed to this visit in hell.

'Tell us how you defeated the vampire by the name of Viktor,' their voices echoed. It was spoken as a command. The empty sockets burnt holes in my eyes.

I took another deep breath to calm myself. *Take your time.* 'The illusion of my little brother Liam vanished, and I saw Viktor. He was tall. His eyes were red and his pupils vertical. I knew immediately he was dangerous. Viktor revealed himself as a vampire and said he wanted to play with me. I tried to fend him off, but he was too fast.' I paused to emphasise. 'So, I tricked him. I showed him my throat and Viktor let his guard down. I managed to smash a glass vase against the side of his head. He lost his temper and threw me around the office and into the walls. I tried to kick him, but he had his hand around my throat and I passed out.' I explained it all in one go. After Blake had prepped me, I was well versed.

'Did the vampire named Viktor bite you?'

'No,' I hushed under my breath.

'Did the vampire named Viktor mention another attack involving two other vampires named Tom and Jason?'

Those had to be the ones involved in torturing and killing Ben's recruit. 'No. Viktor only mentioned I was not the first ghost he would have the pleasure of killing.'

The white monsters leant closer towards me. It was the first movement they'd made since I had entered the hall. The sudden movement startled me.

'It seems you are celebrated for defeating the vampire named Viktor without help. Do you concur?' they stated.

'I did not defeat him, I only held him off until the other ghosts came to my rescue.'

'How did you keep yourself alive just in time to be rescued?'

I could feel heat rising in me. Their questioning made me more and more uneasy.

'Has your trainer named Blake instructed you in the art of combat of a vampire?'

I nodded.

'Tell us what your trainer named Blake taught you to do when faced with a vampire.' The white creatures sat motionless.

'Blake taught me to run away.'

'Why did you not follow his instructions when faced with the vampire named Viktor?'

'I… I tried, but Viktor was too fast!' I raised my voice ever so slightly, making the monsters hold up their right hands.

'Tell us again your encounter with the vampire named Viktor.'

I repeated my story, changing the words but keeping the same outline. The flow of questions continued, pointing to small inconsistencies. The more I said, the more questions arose. It seemed endless. My feet and back hurt from standing so long in front of those arrogant beings. My eyes were itchy. My brain had trouble forming complete sentences. I wanted to draw my gun and shoot them right in their empty sockets. The questions wouldn't stop. The more time passed, the less sense I made. Somehow, they managed to twist everything I said and use it against me.

Finally, they had heard enough. I let out a sigh of relief, but it was premature. 'Ameerah, your second hearing will take place tomorrow. We find your telling to be inconsistent. It is out of character for a vampire to let their prey live so long once trapped.'

That was all they said. In one movement they rose from their chairs and floated off the podium and disappeared through a backdoor, leaving me alone in the great hall.

All I could think of was how much I craved a drink.

When I exited the building, Caleb and Blake were waiting, leaning against the blue truck, having an intense conversation. They both looked up at the same time as I stepped down the marble stairs of the courthouse building. My heart accelerated at the sight of Caleb. I could feel the wave of comfort build inside me. Caleb stretched his dark hands out when I was close enough and I immediately reached for them. The moment I touched his hands the ecstasy transported me into heaven. It was better than smelling my mother's clothes. I got lost in the happiness.

'Ameerah,' his voice sung in my ears. 'Tell me what happened.'

I was pulled back to reality.

'I have a second hearing,' I stated simply, not wanting to show any distress.

Caleb squinted. 'I can feel your torment.'

Blake leant closer to me, his fierce blue eyes like lasers. That definitely ripped me out of my peaceful trance. 'They think I'm lying. They don't believe I could have fought off a vampire by myself, which I don't even claim! I kept saying I just tricked and distracted him until you all came, but they dismissed it, saying it's not normal the vampire didn't kill me straight away.'

'It is alright, child. Don't worry about the council.' Caleb let go of my hands to embrace me in a hug. The emotions enveloped me; I was swimming in peace. He erased all worries from my mind.

Caleb softly pushed me from him.

'Do you feel better?' I nodded, completely high. 'Get in the truck and let me speak to Blake for a moment.' He sat me on the passenger's seat and Blake and Caleb walked off towards a bench next to the marble steps.

My senses came back to me as the drug of Caleb's presence wore off. What were they discussing? Did they also not believe me? I reached for my phone and dialled Kim's number.

'Hey what's up?' she greeted me cheerfully.

I told her what had happened. Blake and Caleb were still debating.

Kim cursed under her breath. 'They are just testing you and seeing how you react under pressure. This is all part of their game. I'm sure of it, just stay calm and stick to your story. Nothing will happen to you,' Kim urged me in a soothing tone.

'You make it sound like I'm lying.'

'That's not what I meant. They are just trying to destabilise you, just keep calm and repeat what happened and they will leave you alone.'

Blake and Caleb had gotten up from the bench and were walking towards the car. 'I hope you're right. Blake and Caleb are coming back; I'll talk to you later.'

'Do you also not believe me?' I asked the moment Blake had opened the door.

Blake closed the door behind him. Caleb drove off in his own car. He sighed deeply and looked into my eyes for a while before answering. 'I do. Viktor was a vampire that enjoyed to toy with his victims. He got caught up in the game and didn't sense we were coming. The council probably just wants to go over the details again. If you remain consistent, they will grant you your approval.'

I nodded and leant back in the car seat. It was exhausting to think about facing them again.

'How are you going to celebrate? After tomorrow?'

'I'll probably go to the pub with Kim and have a quiet evening. I don't want another party.'

Blake kept his eyes on the road and drove us home. His arms were tense and gripped the wheel tightly, his knuckles becoming white.

We pulled up onto the parking in front of the white house we lived in. 'Are you going to see Ben again?'

I was surprised by this random question. 'Why... why are you bringing this up again?'

'I care about your safety and he is a dangerous man. I told you I don't want you near him.'

I turned towards him in my seat. 'Listen to me,' I started and had to hold my anger back. 'Approved or not, you cannot tell me who to see and what to do. Get that in your head.'

With those words I got out of the car and smacked the door closed too violently. The car swayed on its suspension.

Blake followed me into the house. 'I *can* tell you what to do! I'm your trainer and responsible for your survival here! You have to obey me!'

A sense of ease built inside me. My nerves calmed down and my worries disappeared. Caleb was sitting in Blake's chair by the window.

'Blake, Ameerah, what troubles you that you have to scream at each other?' His voice was sweet as honey.

'She has been seeing Ben and is lying about it! I told her to stay away but she keeps defying me!' Blake burst out.

My own emotions swelled and Caleb's effect was overpowered. 'I'm not "seeing" Ben. I spoke to him several times and Blake suddenly feels entitled to comment on who I spend time with! I'm not with Ben but if I were, it wouldn't be anybody's business!'

'Calm down, my child.' Caleb's magic increased and I found myself happy at the whole situation. 'Blake is concerned about your wellbeing. He is right to express his concerns.'

The knife in my heart bore all the way through my ribs and out my back. I had trouble breathing.

'Blake do not overstep your boundaries. Now, Ameerah why don't you go for a drive or see Kim while Blake and I speak.'

The pain of the knife slightly decreased when I heard Caleb address Blake. It was unbearable to hear Caleb criticise me.

'Car keys?' I stretched my hand out towards Blake. Reluctantly, he handed them to me, but not without giving me a warning look that followed me all the way down the stairs until I was out of his sight.

As I drove away from the house, Caleb's knife in my chest eased and I could almost forget it was there. His influence over me scared me. How could he impose and manipulate my emotions so strongly? And why did I have this unwavering desire for his approval?

I drove north and soon passed the park where I had talked with Ben. The truck climbed up a hill and I parked it when I could see the surrounding neighbourhood through the windshield. It was a small hill, so it didn't permit me to see far over the city. How I longed to be out in nature, by the sea, or in the mountains, or even in the tropical forest. I hated bugs, snakes and spiders, but now I would welcome them. It was depressing to be surrounded by concrete, glass and cobblestones.

I put my feet up on the dashboard, pushed the seat back and sat there quietly with the window open, letting my thoughts drift.

Somewhere further away, I could hear gunshots disturbing my peace. They were too far away for me to do anything and frankly, I didn't want to. I would have enough time and opportunity to kill molochs. No need to rush towards danger just yet.

After an hour or so, when the light in the sky was fading, I made my way back to the house. Caleb had gone and Blake was training intensely. He acknowledged my coming home but did not speak to me for the rest of the evening.

The council repeated most of the questions in the second hearing. They kept insisting on little details. But my answers were more consistent this time. When Caleb had driven me to the second hearing, I had let his warmth and support appease my anxiety, and I was more confident in my responses. Once the council was off my back, I could concentrate on getting Blake off my back.

After hours of pestering me with questions, the council finally decided to grant me my approval. They left without so much as an apology for their lengthy interrogation or congratulations on my successful passing of the probation period.

I had told Blake I was meeting up with Kim after the hearing, but it was Ben who picked me up. Blake probably suspected I was lying, but I didn't feel it was any of his business and he had no right to tell me what to do.

'I passed.' I got into his fiery red car, exhausted and relieved.

'I'm happy for you!' Ben responded, a warm smile on his face. Electricity sparked between us.

'Where would you like to go?'

I thought about Santa's pub, but there was a chance I might run into someone I knew, so I suggested his place. I was nervous at the thought of being alone with him, let alone in his apartment, but something in my gut told me it was alright.

We drove south and over the river to a part of town I wasn't familiar with. Ben took me to his apartment which was located on the top floor of a six-story building. His apartment was equipped with an open-plan kitchen and a large living room with a fireplace and wooden floors. The living room led towards bay windows and a terrace oriented towards the southwest with an impressive view of the city. Just like in Blake's house, Ben had a training section stuffed full of guns and weapons of all kinds. It was a room next to the kitchen. The door was slightly ajar and I could make out the extensive arsenal.

We sat down on his white leather couch in front of the fireplace and talked. He told me about his long years here and his different recruits. Ben had been a soldier here for eighteen years and had another thirty-three to go before he would be released. I felt a sting of jealousy at his thirty-three compared to my sixty-six years.

As time passed, I could feel myself relax. He had not tried to approach me, even though he was clearly flirting with me. There was a soft glimmer in his eyes when he looked at me. His face seemed to light up the more we spoke. As if he allowed himself to loosen up.

I guessed in this world there wasn't much downtime for us ghosts or moments where we could completely relax. There was always danger around us, even when you couldn't see the demons, you knew they were around each corner. And when they weren't, gunshots resonated around the city faint or near, reminding us of the constant and never-ending fight.

Suddenly Ben looked at the time and his expression changed. It was time for me to go home.

We got up from the couch at the same time and unexpectedly found ourselves standing close to one another. We both halted for a moment. My heart was pounding in my ribcage. I was sure he could hear it. Ben very slowly moved closer to me and bowed his head down towards my lips. The tingling in my stomach intensified.

I took a step back just before he reached me, breaking the moment.

'I'm sorry, I didn't mean to push you,' Ben whispered, leaning backwards.

'No, it – it was a reflex. Stay still.' I stepped forward.

Our faces were inches from each other. I breathed quietly and let myself get used to having him in my personal space. I closed my eyes and felt his breath down my neck. My hands trailed up his arms, feeling the hairs on his skin, the tendons and muscles underneath them. I let my hands brush over the crease of his elbows, up over his biceps and onto the cotton fabric of his t-shirt until I reached his neck. I could feel the gentle pulsing in the veins of his throat. The tips of my fingers reached further over his stubbly beard, across his jawline and to the back of his neck.

I opened my eyes again and looked deep into his forest-green eyes. Slowly I stretched up onto my toes and touched his lips with mine. They were hot and soft. Ben's tongue caressed mine; his hands were on my back, drawing me closer.

It didn't take long before Ben started kissing me along my jawline and trailing over my neck all the way to my left shoulder. The air between us grew heavy.

I wanted to, but I also didn't.

Gently, I pushed myself off him.

'Sorry, I got carried away,' Ben exhaled loudly and brushed his hand through his hair.

'I… let me get used to you.' I felt my cheeks blush.

Ben smiled and approached me hesitantly. 'I'm not going anywhere.'

I wrapped my arms around him and we swayed from side to side.

A few days later Kim and I made plans to meet up at her and Dominic's apartment. Ben and I texted often since the day we kissed. He was kind and I felt he understood me.

Blake was growing more and more annoyed and suspicious. Whenever we trained, he pretended to hurt me by accident. Lucky for him, we healed fast with Caleb's blood. I'd had enough of his passive aggressive tone. Caleb only always told us to be civil but never really put Blake back in his place. I suspected he hoped we would figure it out between us without him having to intervene.

Before driving to Kim's, I dropped Blake off in the middle of town. He had to go see Caleb, but I was not allowed to know where Caleb lived so I stopped at a deserted square.

'Call me if you need me,' Blake said before closing the door of his rusty truck.

I rolled my eyes at him and punched the gas pedal. Even though I had been promised my own car after I became approved, Blake had always found an excuse for why it wasn't the right time. I promised myself if he didn't budge within the next few days, I would go out by myself and organise my own car. There had to be dealership somewhere.

When I knocked on the front door, a shirtless Dominic opened the door and said Kim was still training, so I let myself fall heavily on the couch in the living room and observed them.

Kim was powerful and much more technical than I was. Every time she committed an error, Dominic hit her with a long wooden stick. It smacked on her skin and she suppressed a scream. I could see her usually full lips pressed together into a hard line and her eyebrows pulled towards one another. When she repeated an error too many times, Dominic made her stop and do sit-ups or pull-ups as punishment. There were bars fixed on the ceiling like at Blake's. At the end of the session, Dominic explained what she had to work on and showed her more techniques and moves she had to learn.

Afterwards, Dominic disappeared into the bathroom while Kim was condemned to do a series of pull-ups with additional weights attached to her legs. Dominic came out of the shower before Kim had finished her set. He was just as comfortable as Blake in his home, walking around only clad in a pair of sweatpants. Maybe it was common for trainers…

Kim planted a kiss on my cheek when she was finally done and rushed to the shower.

Dominic was in the open-plan kitchen mixing himself a post-workout drink with raw eggs and tabasco.

'Why are you drinking that?' I asked, pointing at the tall glass as he made his way towards me and sat on the opposite couch, his feet up on the coffee table.

'Just because I can't taste it, doesn't mean it has no effect.' He winked and swallowed the content in one go.

'You know, Kim thinks you're a really good trainer.' I buttered him up, even if Kim had never said anything.

'Thanks, same to Blake. I respect him and respect is earned with me.' He finished his drink.

'Hey, do you know Ben and his master… Jesper?'

'Ben was a good trainer. But he lost his last recruit. The circumstances were suspicious and now I'm not so sure about him.' He shrugged his tanned strong shoulders.

'What about his master?'

Dominic 'tssd' and waved his hands in annoyance. 'Jesper is a scared little man. He never shows up when his ghosts need him.'

'You mean he neglects Ben and the recruit?' I tried to sound interested but not overly eager.

'Worse. He has lost more protégés than any master. Word on the street is he's even lost ghosts because he just wouldn't show up.'

'What do you mean by "show up"?'

'When the wound of a ghost is too extensive, the master needs to be present along with the blood transfusion. Something about the emotional connection.' The door to the bathroom opened and Kim emerged. 'I'll leave you two.' Dominic trotted off to his room.

Kim hugged me tightly, her dark wet hair sticking to my skin. She showed a broad smile when Dominic had closed the door behind him. 'What did you two talk about?'

'Ben,' I said and couldn't help but grin sheepishly.

'This is a wine conversation!' Kim proclaimed and rushed off to the kitchen. She came back with two wine glasses and a bottle. Her eyes were sparkling. 'You can officially start!'

I told her about Blake's latest outburst after finding out I had met up with Ben again. I explained what had happened to Ben's recruit and how Viktor had insinuated things about his recruit that made me believe Ben was not all wolf in sheep's clothing.

'You know what I've noticed,' Kim started, finishing off the bottle of wine, 'Blake is always crazy possessive of you. Have you ever considered that he might be jealous… you know… as in, *he* wants to be in Ben's place?'

I was nothing but confused. He had never made a move or indicated he was interested in me in any way. I was sure it was because he had a wrong impression of Ben, coupled with the fact that after all this training I was slowly becoming independent and he couldn't control me so easily anymore.

'No, I can't imagine Blake likes me that way.'

'Whatever you say, but from the outside that's what it looks like.' Kim leaned back into the couch and crossed her hands behind her head.

'He's never made a pass at me!'

I looked into Kim's dark eyes. The alcohol had taken its effect on both of us. She would probably think differently in the morning.

DUI

Days passed with the usual training and suspicions from Blake. Ben and I texted every day and the butterflies in the stomach intensified. I wanted to see him again. But as long as I didn't have my own car, it was impossible. Whenever I said I would go to Kim's or Santa's pub, Blake would insist on driving me and I couldn't escape to meet Ben.

Eventually, two weeks after begging Caleb, I was allowed my own car, a matte black Dodge Challenger. Finally, I could sneak away. The first evening I had my new ride, I made plans to meet up with Ben at his apartment. I used Kim as a cover and ignored Blake's suspicious eyes as I headed out.

As I drove over to Ben's apartment, I thought about what Kim had said; was Blake jealous and acting out because he was interested? I couldn't understand why he would then not have showed it somehow. I was sure he needed to feel I wanted his protection and with time, I had proven to everyone, I was finally independent and able to defend myself. While I was grateful for his training, he was now unable to accept I didn't need to hide behind him anymore.

I pulled into the parking and walked towards the entrance glass door. The butterflies in my stomach buzzed happily around. I pressed the button number six in the elevator. The doors closed and the metal box started moving up. Typical elevator music played, contrasting with the fluttering in my body.

A 'ding' sounded and the door opened. My feet carried me out to the left towards his door. He was standing in the open door, smiling at me.

Time slowed down as I approached. His green eyes looked into mine, flaming with desire. I pushed myself onto my toes. He eagerly met my lips with his and closed his arms around me.

When we finally did detach from each other, Ben looked at me with his soothing green eyes. They were so mellow I could get lost in them.

He took my hand and led me into his apartment. I shed my jacket and shoes, following him into the bedroom across from the entrance. I took off my sweater and gestured him closer. Ben kissed me intensely, while we undressed each other. I could feel his hot breath on my neck. Teasingly, slowly, I took off his long-sleeved shirt. He had several large tattoos, inked over his chest and arms. Ben pulled me closer, holding me with his strong arms. Emerald eyes inspected my body as if to memorise each individual cell. He kissed me passionately and we fell into the bed…

With his hand he brushed a few strains of hair out of my face. With the tips of my fingers I outlined his numerous tattoos.

'Tell me about them,' I whispered.

Ben looked down at the art sprawled on his skin. 'Which one?'

I pointed to the one across his right shoulder and chest; four playing cards, all in black ink, spreading from his shoulder towards his heart.

'The first card is the Joker. He has two faces, one happy, one sad. Even if he gets you out of trouble, it always comes at a price. The second one is the Queen of Spades, represented by Medusa. She's a goddess from the ancient Greek mythology. To me it means there are always two sides to things; even a beautiful woman can have hair made of snakes. The third one is the Ace of Diamonds.' He pointed to the card with a skull topped by a burning candle. The letter 'A' was on the top left and bottom right corners. 'This means that people might be dead, but they're not really gone, so you should not speak ill of them. And the last one is the Jack of Clubs. It's a reminder to have fun in life because it could all be over unexpectedly.'

There was another colourful tattoo on his left arm stretching from the top of his shoulder to almost the crease of his elbow. It was a drawing of an owl looking straight at you. 'What about this one?' I traced along the outskirts.

'I saw this drawing one day. I decided it would make a great tattoo,' he chuckled to himself.

A vibrating sound interrupted us. It came from the floor somewhere. Kissing Ben once more I swung out of bed and picked up my buzzing jacket.

'Kim, this is not a good time,' I answered, falling back onto bed.

Ben rolled over, planting gentle kisses, hovering over my naked body.

'Are you still with Ben?' Kim whispered.

'Yes, why? Is there a problem? Why are you whispering?' I lowered my voice as well. With my free hand I surfed through Ben's hair and down his back. I had a hard time paying attention to Kim as Ben started kissing me more intensely using his tongue.

'I just overheard Dominic on the phone. He said that I was here and that I have been here the whole day by myself, so I'm guessing it was someone who wanted to know where my other half was, and since *you're* my other half I think you're in trouble!'

Ben looked up as my body tensed.

'It looks like even though you passed your test, someone wants to know where you are! Get your ass home and find a really good explanation to tell your warden!' I put the phone down, my lips pressed into a frown.

'Trouble?' Ben guessed, sitting up in the bed.

'Blake is being annoying again. I better get home.' I rolled my eyes, exasperated.

We both got dressed reluctantly, but not overly hurrying. We enjoyed being around each other too much. Anyway, Blake knew I had lied to him, no point in rushing towards an exploding volcano.

'What exactly was your cover story?' Ben asked when he escorted me out of his place to the elevator.

'That I was hanging out with Kim.' I shrugged my shoulders.

'I guess there is not much else Blake would have allowed anyway…'

Ben held my hand in the elevator. To think that just a few hours ago our time together was just beginning… and now it had come to a car-crashing-into-a-wall sudden stop.

'He doesn't understand he can't tell me what to do. He can't keep me away from you.'

Ben and I kissed several times as I stood by the open car door.

'Let me know when you're safe, ok?' He gave me one last hug before letting me get into my car.

I smiled sheepishly at him and was sure I was blushing.

When I opened the front door and took my shoes off, I overheard Blake arguing with Caleb. It could only be Caleb because I felt strangely at ease. At the same time, I was filled with dread; having lied and being found out by Blake was one thing, but Caleb's disappointment would be like knives in my chest again.

As I arrived at the top of the stairs, they both stood still. Caleb smiled at me while Blake quietly brewed, throwing darts at me with his eyes. Then Blake shifted to pacing up and down next to the two chairs close to the windows, eyes following me, breathing rigidly. The veins on his arms and neck were showing. This promised to be fun!

I sat down in my chair and waited. As Blake kept on pacing furiously around, Caleb sat in Blake's chair and folded his hands together. 'Ameerah, you told us you were with Kim, but when we called her, Dominic said she had not left the apartment.'

I could feel my throat closing up. It felt like I had swallowed sand. 'I didn't mean to worry you. I…' I stopped. It was impossible to lie to Caleb. But I didn't want to admit I had been with Ben. Blake would undoubtedly interject his opinion again and I was afraid Caleb would side with him. Why else had he not told Blake to leave me alone?

I looked up at Blake who had frozen in place and was staring me. A loud gulp was audible when I tried to swallow; the sand had transformed into jagged glass.

'Tell your master who you were with,' I heard Blake's voice, ramping up the pressure.

I drew in a shaky deep breath, but no air seemed to reach my lungs. I shook my head in all directions, resisting as best as I could.

Caleb reached over and held my arm. 'Who were you with my dear?'

The connection immediately numbed me to all sense of resistance and I immediately caved at his request.

'I was with Ben,' I answered in a dreamy state.

As soon as I answered, Caleb detached his hand and I was back in the living room, but much more relaxed than before. I was grinning, until my eyes met Blake's.

His steel-blue eyes tried to *kill* me.

'I told you to stay away from him!' Blake growled in a low yet deadly tone.

I sighed and rolled my eyes. Caleb's drug made me feel safe from Blake's wrath.

'Don't you dare roll your eyes at me! You do as I say! You will *not* see him again!' Blake exploded, pointing his finger at me.

Caleb glanced disapprovingly at Blake. 'Leave us,' was all he said, before Blake had time to unleash all his anger. He stormed down the stairs and smacked the door closed.

'My child, do you like Ben?' Caleb asked with a knowing wink.

I nodded without hesitation.

'If he makes you happy, you can see whomever you wish,' he encouraged me. But before I got too excited his face changed. I detected anxiety. 'Ben has a… dark past…'

'I know,' I hurried to say.

'Tell me what you know,' he commanded.

'His, eh… recruit was killed by vampires.'

'Did Ben tell you anything else?'

I shook my head.

Caleb leant back and placed his hands in his lap. 'I want you to do something for me. If Ben says anything to you about his recruit, I want you to tell me.'

'Oh, I don't know if he will want me to say-'

'My child, I do not wish to cause problems for Ben. He is a good man. What happened to his recruit was tragic, but I believe, like you, there is something we don't know. I have suspicions but I cannot be sure.' Caleb leant forward again and touched my forearm. 'Don't worry, my dear. I only have good intentions. Ben might need our help, but he is too stubborn to ask for it. So, if he tells you something, let me know. Do not tell Ben about our arrangement.'

Caleb enforced this last sentence looking intensely into my eyes. There was no denying him anything. He was my master, literally. I would not, no, *could* not lie to him or keep something from him. I was completely at his mercy.

Caleb let go of my arm and I felt relieved. His request had put a lot of weight on my shoulders and it was as if the air above me had become water, but when he finally let go of me, so did the feeling of responsibility.

Caleb raised himself up from the chair and waved from the window to Blake. Blake re-entered the house, still fuming. I was worried Caleb would tell him what we had discussed.

'Ameerah is a grown woman and she has been field approved. You will now work together and keep your killing numbers up. I do not want to have any issues with the council because you haven't killed enough. Have I made myself clear?' Caleb's sharp voice did not leave room for any protest.

'Ameerah my child, you will listen to Blake and obey his rules unconditionally.' His razorblade voice cut sharper than betrayal.

'Yes Caleb,' I stuttered, the muscles tightened around my lungs. I avoided Caleb's look.

'Blake.' Caleb finally took the stage light off me. The grip around my chest lightly decelerated. 'You will keep your inquiries only to relevant subjects. What Ameerah does in her free time is none of your business, as long as it does not endanger her or you.' Caleb was much softer with Blake, making me jealous. Blake was the one watching me like a hawk and sticking his nose in my private business!

As soon as I formed that thought, Caleb's eyes were on me. I was painfully reminded he could read my emotions. My face ran hot.

'I will leave you two. Blake, we can speak tomorrow on drawing up a schedule for Ameerah.' Caleb smiled at me. Immediately my mood lifted. He walked towards me, laid one hand on my arm, filling me with his drug. 'I'll speak to you later, my child.'

My eyes opened and he was gone.

'Does he always disappear when I have my eyes closed?' I wondered out loud.

'He makes you close your eyes and *then* disappears.' Blake said, although I had not asked him. Our gazes crossed again after the slapping we had received. We were both eager to please Caleb, so we would have to try. Neither of us liked the idea. And neither of us trusted the other.

* * *

It was very hot; so hot it was hard to breathe. Blake and I stood to the left of a front door to an apartment in a dark blue corridor. Kim and Dominic stood on the right side of the door. We were all geared up with heavy machine guns, handguns, knives, and ammunition. I felt like a soldier, but at the same time

I felt very much out of place. I never wanted to be a soldier. I didn't ask to go out and kill supernatural beings. And yet, here I was.

I took a deep breath and checked the safety. With a tiny nod of his head, Blake indicated it was time. We were all tense. A bead of sweat ran down my forehead.

Blake and Dominic blasted through the door first. Kim and I followed behind just half a second later. The two trainers were already shooting at the vampire. To my surprise when we stormed in, I saw two vampires instead of one. The anxiety in me rose immediately.

The entrance led into the kitchen with an island in the middle, providing some cover. Blake and Dominic were by the kitchen island and as soon as Kim and I had reached them, they ducked behind the island and reloaded their weapons. Kim and I fired continuously at the two creatures. The vampires were standing close to one another and tried to approach us, but their movements were slowed due to the impacts of the gunshots. One of the creatures started to tumble; the other tried to shield himself with his arms.

The moment I ran out of bullets I slid back behind the wall to my right and Blake emerged to keep firing. As quickly as I could, I reloaded and got back to firing at the creatures. One of the vampires was down; the second one tumbled out of sight, followed by a loud thump. Blake went down to reload. We ceased fire. My ears rang from the shots and I couldn't make out anything but muffled sounds.

'Stay here,' Dom shouted to Kim and me, and went towards the vampire sprawled on the floor. Blake got up and went after the one that was out of sight.

The trainers reappeared and were much more relaxed. Both vampires were dead. I sighed in relief and let my head fall back into my neck. I took off the band in my hair and let it unfurl over my shoulders.

'Can't you wait until we're at least in the car?' Blake scolded. The others were busy splashing alcohol onto the two vampires.

I made a face at him when he had his back turned. Kim saw it and chuckled. Dominic lit a match and let it fall to the floor. The noxious alcohol immediately caught fire and spread like wildfire. I had located the fire extinguisher in the hall and went to get it. We watched the dead bodies burn for several minutes before I put the fire out.

Kim and I left the apartment and made our way out to the cars while the two trainers discussed tactics further behind us. The sun was low and the air ripe for a thunderstorm. It had been so damn hot in that hallway; there were windows everywhere trapping the sunrays inside and heating up the building like a greenhouse.

'Any plans for tonight?' Kim asked me.

'Seeing Ben, you?'

'I think I'll go to the pub. I want to play pool and relax.'

'Do you want me to come with you for a bit?' I felt bad for leaving her on her own.

'No, no, go have fun with Ben, don't worry about me.' She kissed me on my cheek.

'See ya later,' Dominic called from behind us and walked towards his Ferrari. He sped off with squealing tyres.

Men. I rolled my eyes.

'I'll see you later.' Kim also disappeared into her car and only Blake and I were left in the parking lot.

'Caleb is waiting for us at home,' Blake told me.

'Fine,' I conceded and went around my Dodge Challenger and opened the boot. There I laid down my M-16 and started taking off my clothes. They were drenched in sweat.

'What are you doing? We need to go,' Blake asked perplexed, standing in front of the open driver's door of his truck.

'Just give me a minute. I'll be right behind you!' I answered trying to hide my annoyance.

Blake shook his head and drove off in his rusty rattle-machine. My car was much faster than his anyway. I would still arrive way before him!

The moment he was out of sight I took out my phone and dialled Ben's number. I held the telephone between my right shoulder and head while I took off my pants. 'Hey babe, just wanted to tell you we're done.'

'How many did you take down?' Ben asked. Hearing his voice immediately calmed my nerves.

'Two. It was supposed to be just one, but we got them both.'

'Are you on your way here then?'

'No, I have to talk to Caleb first and then I'll come over. Give me an hour or so, ok?' I had slipped into a pair of daisy dukes and a see-through top.

'Ok honey. I'll see you later then. Love you.'

'Love you too.'

With shades on my eyes, I closed the boot and got into the car. I rolled the windows down and blasted the stereo. It didn't take long for me to catch up with Blake. As I passed him, I winked and sped on, refraining from flipping him off. When he finally arrived at the house, I had already taken the gear out of the boot and was cleaning up my mess.

'You should really stop taking your clothes off right after we kill vampires, or molochs for that matter,' Blake said.

I grunted in acknowledgement.

'It's dangerous to linger around there with your scent spreading. Another vampire might surprise you!' he added.

'How many times have we done this now and nothing has happened?' I reminded him.

'You just need one single mistake to get killed by vampires… in your sleep,' Blake stated, taking a bottle of water and splashing some on his face.

'That's why I sleep with a gun under my pillow,' I stated putting the guns away in the designated part of the living room.

'I'm guessing you will be out with *him* again?' he asked without making any effort to hide his disgust.

The entrance door opened and a sense of ease announced him before he was visible.

'My child! How are you?' Caleb greeted me with a light hug. The intense feeling of happiness calmed me and I refrained from responding to Blake's insult. 'How was the raid?'

'There were two, but we killed them,' Blake said in a matter-of-fact tone.

Caleb looked at the both of us. 'Oh, have we been fighting again?' he teased us.

Blake and I threw looks at each other. 'No, everything is fine,' Blake responded.

'Meerah?' Caleb turned and I could feel his eyes on me. I nodded my head. This incessant bickering couldn't be qualified as fighting. We had had fights that ended in screams and gestures. We let our frustration out daily in our training. This was harmless.

'Good. My child I need to speak to Blake for a moment.'

I turned to Blake, annoyed. 'You told me he needed to see both of us!'

Blake remained cold. 'My mistake.'

Of course, as if it hadn't been on purpose. When I turned to leave, I saw out of the corner of my eye a look exchanged between Caleb and Blake.

'Talk to him, Caleb!'

Rolling the windows down, I tapped the accelerator and saw Blake from the corner of my eye standing by the living room window. I reached into the glove compartment and got out a pack of cigarettes. Lighting the cigarette, I inhaled the delicious poison. After all, I could not get cancer and die in this world, so why not take advantage of it? My right hand held the cigarette and the steering wheel, while my left elbow rested on the open window frame.

I remembered in the beginning thinking this would be like living in an action movie. And it was, in a way. Sometimes I could hear the audience holding its breath when I was fighting off molochs or an occasional vampire. When I managed to kill the bad guys, I could hear them cheering my name and applauding. The men in my life were hot enough to be in a movie. But an action movie lasted two hours at most. In the end the bad guys died and that was it: happy ending, big kiss from the two main characters, and drive off into the sunset.

It was not like that here. The bad guys so largely outnumbered us that it was a hopeless battle. My body was constantly tired. Nothing tasted of anything. Only alcohol, drugs, cigarettes, and human companionship moderated the depressive state I was in.

I didn't see Caleb much. He mostly asked to speak with Blake and only occasionally spent time with me. Blake was... Blake. He loved being in charge. At his whistle, I had to come running without complaining.

I took another deep drag between my thoughts. More than once I found myself enviously staring at the rare humans that sometimes appeared, wishing I had never died, wishing I was still living my boring student life.

I was not suicidal; I was just swimming in a sea of grey with the painful memories of what colours looked like. All the ghosts I had met felt the same way. I had the misfortune to have one of the longest sentences. Most other ghosts had between forty and fifty years of service before being released back into their human life. But even then, what would happen? I kept imagining what my return would be like, but I couldn't foresee anything positive. With all the memories of this world it was hard to believe I could just go back to living with my family and going to university as if nothing had happened. This world had changed me so much already in the two years I had been trapped here. I had killed molochs and vampires, suffered an endless number of wounds, learnt to fight and shoot, I was smoking and drinking excessively... there was no going back, definitely not back to the innocent twenty-four-year-old I had once been...

I turned the last corner on my way to Ben's. I threw my cigarette out the window along with my worries. I tried to keep my depressive thoughts to myself and only share them with Kim. I did not want to infect the time I had with Ben with the grey disease as well.

I chomped on some chewing gum, checked I had everything in my purse, and entered the tall apartment building. Inside, I walked into the tight elevator box and pressed the number 'six'. The doors closed and all I could hear was the slow upwards movement and the ridiculous elevator music.

'That was fast.' I could hear his voice coming from the terrace. I took my phone out of my purse and left the rest including my flip-flops in the entrance. There was the sound of the bay window being slid on its rails, steps, and then Ben appeared in front of me. He was only dressed in a pair of shorts, just the way I liked it.

'Caleb wanted to speak to him alone.' I put my arms around Ben, holding him tightly and inhaling his scent. When I loosened my arms, I kissed him on his warm sweet lips.

'So, tell me about this raid today.' Ben grinned.

He poured us each a large cocktail glass of freshly prepared margarita and we went out onto his terrace. I sat across from him with the sun on my back, putting my feet up into his lap.

'Blake had seen a vampire in town and followed him to a building in the east. After staking it out he figured out in which apartment he was in and we raided it with Dominic and Kim.'

'What about Carl?' Ben asked, his face lit by the sun.

I could still feel the sting of fear as distant memories echoed in my head.

'He is mostly in other districts helping out.'

I took a long sip from the cocktail and leaned my head back onto the chair.

After several minutes of silence Ben coughed and placed his margarita on the table. 'Have you heard anything about Vladimir?'

I inhaled before responding. 'No, they haven't found his body yet.'

After several months of dating, I had confessed to Ben everything that had happened with Vladimir, including Kim killing him and where we had dropped his body into the river.

'Seems odd that they haven't found his body after all this time. Unless they have and they've not told Carl about it. Maybe the council suspects Carl was involved.'

Ben massaged my left foot and switched to the right; the muscles across his chest tensed and relaxed with the movements. His tattoos were darker through my sunglasses; I could see Jack Skellington stretching over his right pectoral and part of the owl on his left arm.

'I hope they never find his remains. There is still a chance the council discovers the truth, and then Kim and I will get added more years onto our sentences, or worse…'

'His body will not carry any evidence anymore against either of you.' Ben got up and my feet fell to the ground. He returned with the rest of the margarita pitcher and a lit cigar clenched between his teeth. I placed my feet back in his lap.

'Someone could still have seen something or suspect something. If he tried it several times with me, he must have had other victims. But there are not many women in this world, and they will probably not be inclined to share their experiences. And frankly, I don't think the council would see it as a justified act.'

'Probably not, no.' Ben took a deep drag, laid his head back and blew the smoke out. 'Let's talk about nicer things. When are you next catching up with Caleb?'

Ben took the cigar out of his mouth and held it towards me. I reached for it and puffed a few times. 'Probably tomorrow. He always debriefs with Blake first.' I passed the cigar back to him.

'Good. Are you going to bring up what we discussed?' he added and topped up his glass.

'I've told him several times already I want to move out. There is no good reason why I should stay living with Blake in that depressing room. I just want to be around you all the time.'

I got up and came around the table to sit with Ben on his chair. Sunset was approaching and the alcohol almost made me believe I could feel warmth from the sun. I took off my top and leant my naked back onto Ben's naked torso. Then I put my feet up on the railing and just enjoyed the moment. I closed my eyes and rested my head against Ben's muscular arm around my shoulders. At least I could still feel his warm skin on mine and his heart beating lazily in his ribcage.

I was softly shaken awake. When I opened my eyes, the sun had disappeared under the horizon. 'You fell asleep, Meerah,' Ben whispered in my ear and kissed my forehead.

'Ok, I should go,' I moaned half asleep, half drunk.

'Can you drive?' Ben had gone inside and was cleaning up in the kitchen.

'Yeah, I'll be alright. If I stay Blake will use it somehow to get his way and since I'm speaking to Caleb about moving out, I don't want to give Blake more ammunition than he has.' I stuffed my phone into my jeans pocket.

'You sure you don't want me to follow you until you're at least back in your neighbourhood?' Ben asked hugging me and rubbing my back.

'Don't worry,' I muffled into his chest. I had to gently push him off me to get away.

In the elevator, I closed my eyes and only opened them again when I heard the bell of the ground floor. Tumbling across the parking lot I noticed how tired I actually was.

Blake's house was only twenty minutes away. It was doable, I told myself. Slowly, I drove out of the parking lot and onto the deserted streets. It was dark and even with the headlights on, I had trouble seeing straight. My nap had not cleared my mind from the alcohol. It must have gone straight to my head this time. I rubbed my eyes and tried to concentrate on the street. To keep myself from falling asleep I opened the windows. The cool wind made my heart pump more blood up to my brain and I could see better. But the effect only lasted a few minutes. More than once I slapped myself as my eyes fell closed.

I had to make it back.

Shaking my head made me swerve, so I stuck to slapping myself whenever I felt the exhaustion pulling at me.

But I was just so tired. I didn't want to keep my eyes open. Maybe this was all a dream... maybe if I closed them, I would realise I was already in bed, dreaming only...

VENGEANCE

With a sudden spasm I opened my eyes. I pulled my head up. A trickle of saliva dripped from my mouth. Something was cutting into my chest, restricting me. It was dark around me except for the big white cushion right in front of me.

My head fell back against the hard seat. Something vibrated close-by. I tried to recount where I was or what had happened. There was the ticking of hot metal cooling down and contracting in front of me. My head was torn apart from pain. When I touched my forehead, I felt something wet. Bringing my fingers close to my eyes I saw my own blood. The vibrating stopped. I looked around and realised I was in my car. The frontend was smashed into a wall. The metal was curled up on itself and the windshield had shattered into a million spiderwebs.

What time was it? How long had I been here?

The vibrating started again. I reached into my jeans and whined as I had to twist my body to get my phone out. Just as I was about to answer the call, I looked outside and saw them in the distance.

They must have followed my scent. The numbness dimmed as panic overtook my mind; my hands searched for my gun. Where was my purse? There! On the floor in front of the passenger seat. I couldn't reach it; the seatbelt kept me bolted to the seat. Annoyed I detached the sharp belt cutting into my chest and slithered out of the driver's seat. I could see them carefully approaching. The phone began vibrating again. I looked at it, trying to decipher who was calling, but my vision was blurred.

I couldn't find the gun in my purse; I opened the glove compartment and pulled out my back-up. The metal in my hand gave me a sense of security. My eyes were so heavy. The vibrating sound awoke again. This time I managed to answer the call after a couple of tries. 'Helloooo?' I slurred into the phone.

The molochs were barely fifty yards from me. I opened the passenger door and fell onto the cold concrete. The phone slipped from my grip and slid away along the ground.

'Shit!' My hand reached for the phone, but it was further away than I had thought.

They were coming closer; I could hear them hissing nearby. I got on all fours and moved towards the phone, following the glow of its screen. Finally, I felt the squared object in my hands and I forced myself onto my feet, but I could not stand still. I stumbled into the wall. The world was spinning around me and only the wall kept me from falling over. I pressed the phone to my ear.

'Helloo?' I repeated into the phone. My head hurt badly and a steady beeping noise plagued me.

'Where are you? Are you alright?' Ben's voice sounded far away. Emotions overwhelmed me. I wanted him by my side to keep me safe.

'Noo, akzident... molooochs...' I slurred and cried in the phone. 'Heeelp'

'Stay where you are. I'm coming right away!' Ben's voice was suddenly deadly serious. 'I'll be there in three minutes, ok? Stay where you are.' With those words he hung up.

One of the molochs roared and jumped upon my car. I turned around and fired once. Though I completely missed, the sound made the creature squirm and crawl back behind the car.

I held my head between my hands. It hurt so bad I thought my skull was about to burst open. The beeping paralysed my thoughts. Blood ran down my face and dripped from my lips and chin. The molochs snarled again and I could see the creatures hiding behind the car, their eyes hungrily staring at me.

The molochs crept further and more boldly out of the shadow of the car to inspect their prey. I moved along the wall down the street. I had to find a place to hide.

It was all foggy around me and I had trouble seeing and understanding where I was. With my gun in one hand and my phone in the other, I tried to wrestle my way along a brick wall towards safety, not knowing where safety was. The beeping in my ears intensified.

There was a hiss right behind me. I turned and shot the moloch, but a burning slicing sensation awoke on my other side along my leg. I screamed and turned back to see another moloch crouched right behind me. I shot it as well, but the damage was already done. There were so many of them, coming from every angle.

My leg was spouting blood. I could feel the hot liquid streaming down my leg and onto my flip-flops.

The rising adrenaline suddenly made it crystal clear the critical situation I was in. My right leg was losing blood rapidly. I couldn't put any weight on my right leg, making me schlepp it along behind me. I realised that this many molochs could attract a vampire and then I was definitely done.

The hissing intensified to a grotesque choir. One moloch dared to approach further than the masses. I pointed my gun and shot. Before I limped further along, another one risked a closer look and dug its claws into my left thigh, pulling my flesh to its mouth. The beast bit me before I had time to get it off.

My legs collapsed under me. The red pool under me spread. My head hurt and felt too light. Desperate, I raised my gun and started shooting in every direction. My eyelids lowered; the delicious darkness called me again. It was too easy to let go.

Seconds later, or minutes later, I was torn out of the darkness. Rough hands pulled me back to consciousness.

'Honey, wake up,' I could hear him softly whisper into my ear. His warm hands held my face. The pain was now distributed throughout my body, making me wish I was bathing in a field of lava instead of here in this moment.

'Ben,' I managed to say tonelessly.

'Yes, it's me Meerah.'

I wanted to open my eyes and see him, but it was all shadows and everything became blurry.

'Give me your phone honey, I'm calling Caleb.'

I realised my left hand was still clutching the piece of metal. I relaxed my fingers and let him take it.

There were a few moments of silence. All I could make out was Ben holding me tightly. I felt safe in his arms.

'Caleb, Ameerah had an accident. She needs blood and it's probably best you get here too.' I could dimly make out Ben's voice. His voice sounded far away and underwater.

'Ameerah, honey, Caleb will be here very soon. Do you have blood bags?' Ben addressed me, caressing my face. There was no tension or stress in his distant voice.

I pushed myself further out of the darkness. My eyes were open, but I couldn't see clearly. 'In the car,' I tore out of my mouth. The poison of the bites had inflamed my entire nervous system.

'Alright my love, I'll go get them, but I'll be back before you know it.'

I made a sound in response, unable to speak anymore. It cost me too much energy.

Ben moved and then all I felt was the cold concrete on my back, bringing a slight relief to my burning body. There was distant hissing and muffled noises. The darkness seduced me once more. This time, I let myself be swallowed by it.

* * *

It was nice here. My mind was detached from my body. There was no suffering here, only happiness and serenity. My senses tingled with pleasure. I drowned in hormones.

'Ameerah,' someone called from the distance. Was that my name? Did I have to listen to whoever was calling me?

'Ameerah, follow my voice,' the sweet bird sang in my ears.

Kidnapped by curiosity, I obeyed. Slowly the merry state dimmed down until I opened my eyes. When I turned my head to my right, I saw Caleb holding my hand. His smile showed a row of perfect white teeth.

'How are you feeling?' His voice wrapped me in comfort and security.

I swallowed. 'How long have I been out?' I rasped.

'One day. You sustained a dozen bites and lost a lot of blood.' Caleb caressed my arm, the motion radiated sunlight into my jaded body.

I pulled up my eyebrows. 'Only one day? Feels longer.' I raised myself up in my bed. My free hand brushed against my head. It was intact. My body was stiff but functioning.

Blake entered my bedroom. He smiled and nodded shortly, but then crossed his arms in front of his chest like he so often did when we fought. Caleb read my thoughts and gave my hand a brief squeeze. His eyes were gently looking upon me. 'Ameerah, we need to talk about your accident.'

'I told you, I told you he was dangerous!' Blake burst out in anger.

'Ben had nothing to do with the accident. I was tired and had too much to drink.'

'Why did you not stay at Ben's apartment?' Caleb asked. The gentle loving feeling from his presence ceased.

'Because Blake would have turned and twisted it around that Ben was keeping me away from my duties.'

'Oh please, like I would be so petty!'

I raised myself up onto my wobbly legs. 'You have done nothing but criticise Ben every single time you got the chance! I had an accident and you know what? He was there! He stayed with me and called Caleb!'

Even if I had only just awoken, the adrenaline was quickly building in my body and I was close to punching Blake in his stupid face.

'If he was so amazing, he should have never let you drive just like he should have never let his recruit-'

'That's enough!' Caleb's voice boomed and silenced us both instantly. 'Blake, let me talk to her.' Caleb said in a low voice.

I could see Blake was boiling with anger. He stormed out of my room.

Caleb tapped on the bed and I sat next to him. He folded his hands together, staring down at them. All I felt was coldness now. 'Ameerah, I told you, you could do whatever you desired with whomever you wished, *as long as it didn't endanger you or Blake.*' His voice cut to the bone.

'It wasn't his-'

Caleb turned his head to me and the harshness in his face silenced me immediately. I felt like a dog backed into a corner.

'You could have *died!* Do you realise that?!' he whispered intensely. I felt myself trembling at Caleb's wrath.

'I drove back because I didn't want to break any of Blake's ridiculous rules! I'm tired of this ping pong game! Blake will never let me be with Ben and I will never stay away from Ben just because Blake doesn't like him. I can't be around Blake anymore! I don't want to live with Blake anymore! I don't want to train with him!'

Caleb stayed silent for several moments before he exhaled deeply. He reached out to me and laid his hand on mine. I could feel a sense of peace spreading.

'I know, my child,' he whispered. 'Blake is... troubled and he cannot see reason when it comes to you.'

Was he implying the same thing that Kim had?

Caleb turned his head and looked at me with his dark eyes. 'Let me think about it today and I will speak to him tomorrow. In the meantime, go to Ben's and stay there. He must be worried about you.'

He sounded a hundred years old. While he sent loving feelings my way, I could detect his exhaustion underneath.

Slowly, he got up and let go of my hand. He walked out of my bedroom slowly and said a few words to Blake. I could hear Blake trying to protest. After several minutes, there were footsteps down the stairs and the sound of a car driving away. All the while the feeling of calmness diminished until it was completely gone.

I texted Ben I was on my way and packed a small bag. When I came out of my bedroom with the bag over my shoulder, Blake eyed me with deadly eyes, but did not say anything.

As always, the front door was unlocked. The moment I opened it Ben hurried to meet me. He closed his arms around me tightly.

'I was so scared.' Ben's rough voice was thin. 'You're staying over next time! Don't scare me like that again!'

'I definitely am staying.' I put the bag down on the floor.

Ben's face lit up when he saw what I was implying. He kissed me passionately and pulled my legs over his hips. Ben then carried me to our bedroom and ravaged me.

Ben was quietly snoring, occasionally mumbling indistinct words. I had woken up in the middle of the night and not been able to fall back asleep. After an hour of watching Ben sleep, I decided to try something else. I walked through the living room and sat outside on the balcony. Curled up on a chair, I gazed out over the dormant city. The lights of civilization twinkled against the dark sky.

More than ever, I missed my family. How I wished I could bring Ben home and we could go on holidays together and celebrate Christmas and birthdays.

Ben would leave Idolon years before me. I didn't know how it worked with the time loops, but I assumed when I got back to my human life, he would have long returned to his. There were thirty-three years of service separating us and he had been in his thirties when he had died. By simple math he would be in his sixties when I finally made it out, and I would still be twenty-four.

I didn't want to ask him about it and we had only been together for a year. Things were going well between us, but I didn't want to presume we would spend all our time here and on the other side together.

It had been two weeks since I had last heard from Caleb or Blake. Blake's radio silence was expected but not Caleb's. Was he still deliberating about our situation? Was he trying to reason with Blake? There was no way I would go back to living under the same roof as Blake.

I had not gone hunting molochs since. When Caleb had told me to stay with Ben, I had only a few bags of his blood in the car. I hadn't thought about taking more, and I was not interested in calling Blake and asking him for favours. I took it as an excuse to avoid molochs and vampires and take a well-deserved break from my duties.

The sky started getting lighter. It was specked with sombre clouds hanging low. Some touched the top of high skyscrapers and seemed to be held in place.

There was a buzzing sound from inside the apartment. I got up and walked over to the kitchen counter. When I looked at my phone, I saw Caleb's name flash. Had he sensed I had been thinking about him? After a quick exchange he asked me to meet with him at the shooting range in thirty minutes.

By the time I arrived the sun should have pierced through the horizon, but more clouds had rolled over the sky and the air smelled of rain.

Caleb was standing in the entrance looking at a shotgun hanging on the wall.

He turned and hugged me, a bright smile on his lips. The happiness warmed my soul. 'It is good to see you, sweet Meerah. I have been worried about you.'

'Don't worry about me. Ben takes good care of me.'

He guided me around the tall counter and we sat down on two grey metal stools. Our heads were at the height of the top of the black counter.

'I know he does, but the situation with Blake cannot be gentle on your mind.'

'The situation with Blake had been deteriorating for months; you know that. He just cannot accept I'm with Ben. He's so dead-set on hating Ben he can't be reasoned with!'

Caleb nodded his head several times, his eyes glancing over the counter towards the main entrance of the shooting range.

'I do not think it is a question of simply accepting your relationship. Blake is troubled by several issues and he is directing his anger towards you.'

'What issues? What's going on with him?'

'My child,' Caleb took my hand. 'Blake is very suspicious of Ben because of Ben's recruit. He is tormented by past memories and is fearful you will suffer the same fate. He is also stubborn and thinks no trainer can protect you as well as he can. His discipline is unparalleled, but he has lost himself. You know how he is; he cannot relax. To him, danger is omnipresent and you need to always be ready to fight. As you progressed, you started to build a life with Kim and then Ben, which he sees as a distraction. Kim he could handle, but Ben was too much for him.'

'Is he jealous of Ben?'

Caleb's eyes intensely looked at me. He knew that was not my actual questions. I could sense a stab of frost for a split second.

'I cannot discuss what his feelings are towards you. You will have to ask him yourself. But I don't think you are able to live under the same roof again just yet.'

'I want to stay with Ben. Please Caleb, don't make me go back,' I urged Caleb. My fingers desperately clung onto his forearms.

'No, my dear, I will not force you to go back. You both need more time before we can revisit the question. For now, you will remain at Ben's apartment.'

I felt love and sadness at the same time as Caleb's emotions washed over into mine. He was getting ready to leave. His eyes flickered over to the door and he stood up from the stool.

'When will I see you again?' I asked, even though I was afraid of the answer.

Caleb sighed. 'There are things I need to attend to, but I will try and see you very soon, my sweet Ameerah'. He tilted his head and smiled at me.

I was comforted and depressed at the same time.

'I hope with time we can all move on.' He kissed me on the forehead. I blinked. And he was gone.

* * *

I unlocked the door and listened. It was quiet. Relieved, I proceeded to let myself in. Caleb had promised me Blake would be out while I packed my belongings. I grabbed a large bag and started throwing everything that was of value to me in it. The longer I stayed here, the bigger the chance of Blake coming home. Pictures, make-up, candles, a mirror, a lamp, most of my clothes; the rest I left. I could get anything I wanted from the shops anyway.

Just as I put the bag into my car, he pulled up in his old truck. What a surprise…

I quickly closed the boot and walked towards my door, but Blake was faster. For a few moments, he stood undecidedly by my door. Finally, he started walking away, towards the house.

'You need to kill more molochs,' he announced, turning back to me.

I didn't know how to answer, so I stayed quiet.

'Our numbers… they're not looking good and if you want the council to stay away from us, we have to kill more,' he explained.

'Fine,' I agreed. 'Only if you give me some more of Caleb's blood.'

Blake thought about it a few seconds before nodding in agreement. 'Wait here.' He disappeared into the house. When he reappeared, he held out two plastic bags filled with the magical liquid. It was less than I had expected but more than I currently had. Reluctantly, I accepted them. Our hands inadvertently touched.

Blake turned away, but after two steps, he turned once more towards me. 'I'm sorry it came to this.'

'Me too.'

He placed his hands in his pockets. 'I hope with time, you and I can work and train together again.'

I nodded and got into my car. As I backed out of the driveway, I lit a cigarette and quietly made my way to Ben's. I found myself regretting my many outbursts with Blake.

When I arrived at home, Ben wasn't there. A piece of paper was left on the kitchen counter.

'I had to take care of something. Will be back soon. Xoxo'

I decided to go for a run to clear my mind. The clouds had turned the whole world grey and the temperatures were low. I ran a loop down the hill and reached the river taking in the fresh air, before I started the long road back home.

After one last sprint, I fell back into a walking pace as I reached the outskirts of the parking lot. As I approached the main door, I saw Ben's car parked in his usual spot. I was happy he was back. I missed him even when we were only separated for a few hours.

Someone was leaning against the door frame of the building, one leg raised up with the foot against the glass door. Coming closer, I saw he had a white t-shirt on with an open light blue shirt draped over his shoulders and a worn-out pair of jeans. The person was quietly talking on their phone. He stopped the conversation when I came within earshot.

'Carl, what a pleasure,' I said, hugging him with just my hands to avoid wiping my sweaty body on him.

'Likewise, it's been a long time.' He smiled at me grimly. 'I need to talk to you about Vladimir.'

Immediately my body tensed up. 'What about Vladimir?'

'He's dead. His body was found two districts south of here.' Carl watched me closely for a reaction.

'Oh! How awful! What happened to him?' Was I overplaying the shock?

'Nothing yet. The council has taken the body and is opening an investigation. But his body was in the river for a long time, so who knows if they'll find anything.'

'In the river? That's weird. Was he attacked?' I counted myself lucky I was already sweaty from the run, otherwise my sweaty palms and forehead would have been very obvious.

Carl shrugged. 'We will see.' I prayed that was the end of it, but I had no such luck. 'Did you notice anything unusual?'

'No, not really. I didn't speak to him other than that one time.' I remembered it clearly. It was the first time he had tried. He had pulled my hand onto his crotch, before tearing me away from the crowd. A cold shiver went down my spine.

'He mentioned you a few times afterwards,' Carl simply stated. 'He was quite fond of you.'

I couldn't help but shudder. It took all self-control not to gag. 'I'm sorry, I didn't speak to him other than that one time. It's really sad what happened to him, hopefully the council can figure out what killed him,' I said making a motion to open the door to the building.

'Who,' Carl said.

I stopped and frowned at him.

'*Who* killed him,' Carl corrected looking at me intensely.

'Hope they catch the killer then. Let me know when you hear back from the council.' I managed a smile.

I hurried into our apartment and immediately rushed to the bathroom to vomit. The images of him, touching me, overpowering me, ripping my clothes, beating me, the sound of his belt clicking…

Another wave of dry heaves shook through me.

It was over now. I had to keep calm. Vladimir would not hurt me ever again.

I heard a door open somewhere in the apartment. That was Ben. I didn't want him to see me like this. I brushed my teeth and splashed cold water on my face. When I stepped out of the bathroom, I saw Ben was fuming. He had laid out an arsenal of guns on the dining room table and was arming himself heavily.

'What's going on?'

'I have to take care of a vampire,' he growled.

'Alone?'

'Yes.'

'You can't go alone. Let me come with you,' I offered. The moment I had uttered the words, I regretted them. Facing a vampire again? Last time I had been forced to do so, we had been four ghosts and I had caved in to peer pressure. But I couldn't let him go alone.

'No. You're staying here,' he answered, walking past me into the bedroom.

'You're not going alone!'

Ben stopped in front of me and looked down into my eyes. I held onto his arms. 'You can't go alone, I'll come with you, please.'

He bent down and kissed me. 'I'll be ok.'

I felt a stinging sensation in my shoulder. When I turned my neck, I saw a needle protruding from the fleshiest bit. 'What's this?'

'You'll be ok my love.' His voice drifted. The tingling amplified as my brain grew numb. Ben caught me before I collapsed.

My back ached. I opened my eyes. The room was dark. I jumped up calling out for Ben, running through the apartment. He wasn't there. I looked at the clock. It had been hours since he had drugged me. Looking down from the balcony I saw Ben's car wasn't in the parking lot. I stumbled back into the armoury, looking for adrenaline shots. Blake had always had lots of them in the kitchen; Ben had to have some as well. I rummaged through the drawers and found a shoe box at the bottom of a drawer. It contained all kinds of syringes and doses of all kinds of liquids. Underneath some packages of band-aids I finally found them. I injected myself in my upper thigh and waited for it to take effect. A few minutes later my senses cleared and my heart accelerated.

I grabbed my keys, some ammunition and a rifle, and was out the door in seconds.

Since smashing my Dodge to pieces, I had procured myself a white Volvo SUV. Aimlessly, I sped down the block, having absolutely no clue where to look for Ben. Next chance I got I would make his phone share his location with me.

Anxiously, I fumbled with a cigarette. Where was he? I dialled his number. No answer. Why the hell would he confront a vampire by himself?!

Two hours passed before Ben finally answered his phone. He was back at home.

I slammed the front door behind me and glared at Ben. 'You *drugged* me! Then you went god knows where and wouldn't answer your fucking phone!' I pointed at him. 'I was terrified!'

Ben didn't respond. He sat on the white couch motionless. There was an empty blood bag next to him, the needle recently removed from his arm.

'Where were you?!' I asked, bending down to look him in the eyes.

He snapped out of his trance. 'I killed the dirtbag, ok? Nothing happened, I'm fine.' He brushed me aside and poured himself a tall glass of whisky.

'Why did you drug me and just take off like that?'

He finished his glass and filled it up again before answering. 'Because, I knew you didn't really want to fight a vampire.'

'I didn't want you to go alone! And, you could have used someone to watch your back!' I nodded towards the empty blood bag.

'I'm an experienced fighter. I don't need you to back me up.' He downed his whisky.

'What is that supposed to mean?! Just because I'm a woman I don't know what I'm talking about?!'

'You *don't!* I've killed vampires for *decades!* I know what I'm doing and I don't need you!'

Ben smashed his glass onto the kitchen counter, breaking it.

He was hiding something. I softened my tone. 'What's going on with you?'

'Nothing,' he moaned while cleaning up the mess.

I crossed my arms and waited for an explanation. Ben avoided my gaze, clearing up the broken glass and bandaging his hand. Eventually, he caved at my silent determination.

'I didn't leave my recruit,' Ben's mouth said. His eyes filled with tears. Those rough strong hands of his shook. 'Jesper said he was with him and I- I trusted... I should have never- they got a hold of him and...'

I could tell he was reliving the moment. He was blaming himself. 'Jesper left him alone. I went looking for him, but it was too late. When I found him, they were... they were there...' His breathing accelerated. 'I was too late... I tried everything but they were three and- and I was alone and- I couldn't... I wasn't strong enough... and then...' A tear left his right eye, but his gaze was so static I wondered if he could feel the wetness on his cheek.

'They forced me to watch,' he eventually stated, dryly, as if not aware of what he said. Ben's eyes focused on me. 'Jesper forced me to lie. When they were done with... they chained me up and left me to die. I was a toy to them. I escaped, but I needed blood... Jesper wouldn't... unless- unless I promised... to take the fall. They gave me twenty years more.'

'Why didn't you tell anyone?'

A hollow snort escaped his mouth. 'It would have been his word against mine! Who would ever believe he left his protégé?! Jesper has gotten away with it-' Ben's hands clenched into fists. The veins in his neck throbbed. 'But not them! They will **pay** for what they **DID!**' Ben's voice was scraped of all humanity and filled with fury.

I couldn't imagine what it must have felt like to watch his recruit be tortured and killed by vampires. And the blame he had endured for it afterwards! Blake had stumbled upon the remains of Ben's recruit and of course everyone assumed it was Ben who had been careless. No one even imagined it could have been his own master! Who would believe Jesper was capable of such cruelty? He was a master with an emotional connection to his protégé.

Ben had composed himself. His face was nothing but revenge and wrath. His fists were still clenched.

'Viktor was killed at your field test. The piece of shit I just sliced open?' Ben pointed backwards, 'That motherfucker gave me a lead on Jason. He's roaming west of our district. And then there is Tom who has not resurfaced since.'

'I'll come with you,' I blurted out.

'Have you forgotten I knocked you out before? I'm not taking you along with me for the next one.'

'You need someone to watch your back and you don't have anyone else.'

Ben shook his head. 'No. There's no way. I'm killing them out of revenge, if you get hurt in the crossfire- I will be blamed for it, again.' He downed a new shot of whisky and poured another. The bottle was almost empty. 'If that happens, I **will** be terminated by the council.'

I reached for his arm and waited until he finally looked me in the eyes. 'I understand why you want to keep me away. But if something happened to you, don't you think the council will figure out we lived together and ask why I didn't go with you? They will blame me and terminate me. I'm coming with you.'

Ben's expression was pained. He let go of his shot glass and swung his arms around me. We stayed locked together for a long time.

My anger against Jesper was brewing. Ben might have given up on punishing him, but I would try to find a way.

Sleep evaded me that night. I stared at the ceiling for hours, haunted by images of Ben's recruit being tortured, Viktor trying to kill me, and Ben being slaughtered.

Ben was asleep but tossed and turned. I wondered if he was tortured by the same images I was. I got up and retreated to the balcony with my pack of cigarettes. What now?

I lit the cigarette and dragged the first wave of nicotine into my lungs. As long as those two vampires were alive, Ben would not rest.

My thoughts drifted to Caleb. I was reminded of a conversation we had had a long time ago. I texted Caleb and sucked the last bit of life out my cigarette. When I walked towards the bedroom, my eyes fell upon Ben's phone lying on the kitchen counter. I unlocked his phone and turned on the location sharing. At least now if he stole away, I would be able to find him. Somehow, I had a bad feeling I would need it. I climbed back into bed and laid an arm over Ben's warm chest.

* * *

Caleb agreed to see me a week later at Santa's pub at midday.

The cold air and rain hit me when I opened the door. Water splashed under my boots as I ran across the gravel parking lot and into the long corridor leading to Santa's pub. I used my phone to light the way to the pub, and finally reached the warm and cosy bar. The yellow lights from the lamps eased my mind. Caleb was at the back. With every step I took, I could sense my mood mellowing. I slipped into my personal heaven. Caleb hugged me and the serenity overwhelmed me. Nothing could shake me. Nothing bad would ever befall me.

'I sense you are worried, my dear.' He dimmed down the happiness.

My brain returned from heaven back to Santa's pub. 'Yes, I'm worried about Ben. He... he told me what happened to his recruit and I'm worried.'

Caleb nodded, encouraging me to continue. 'His recruit was tortured by vampires and he was forced to watch. He somehow escaped but now he's out for revenge and I'm afraid he will end up dead!'

'Did he leave his recruit alone?'

'No, Jesper was supposed to be with him. When Jesper told Ben he wasn't with him, it was too late.'

Caleb reached for my hand and his power over me increased exponentially. 'I need you to tell me again; **who** was supposed to be with the recruit when he was captured by the vampires?' I could feel the weight of his authority weighing me down like wet bedsheets.

'Jesper,' I repeated.

'How many vampires were there?'

'Three. Viktor was killed. The other two are still out there.'

'Alright my child.' Caleb let go of my hand.

I was back in the pub. 'Can you help him?'

Caleb remained silent. Then, he leant forward and sighed, 'It will be difficult. It will be Jesper's word against Ben's. Our best shot will be to confront Jesper outside of the council's scope...'

'Caleb, we have to do something! I don't want to wait until it's too late. Ben won't want to go to the council. He's too afraid of being terminated! He was already punished with twenty years of additional service when they thought he caused the death of his recruit.'

'Meerah, you must be patient. I have to think about the best way to approach this. Jesper is sneaky and he won't let himself be trapped easily.'

'But I'm scared Ben is so blinded by revenge he may take unnecessary risks! We can't wait until it's too late. Let's get Jesper now!' I urged Caleb.

Caleb sighed and considered for what felt like an eternity. 'I'm very aware of that, Ameerah. But what can we do? Confront Jesper and imprison him, force a confession out of him? I have no access to a prison cell, nor do I wish to imprison Jesper, which would undoubtedly attract attention from the council. You have to let me think this through. I will find a way. Don't get upset, Meerah. I'm on your side.'

Somehow, I had trouble believing him. Just as I had finished my thought, I could feel my ribcage ceasing up. Caleb's eyes were on me and threw darts at me. But this wasn't like Blake throwing darts, these actually hurt me.

'Hurry,' I managed to say through clenched teeth.

Caleb loosened the chains around my chest and I could breathe again.

Ben's car was gone when I got home. My mind went to a dark place. I ran up to the apartment and checked but he was gone. Without wasting any time, I grabbed an M-16, several handguns and as much ammunition as I could carry. On my way out, I took my keys and phone and headed back out into the night. Once in my car I looked on my phone and saw with relief, he had not discovered what I had done. Now at least I knew where he was.

DECISIONS

I pressed the gas pedal to the floor, but the Volvo could not get there quick enough. I had too much time to think about the vampire. Was he facing one right now? Could he have fallen into a trap and now be facing both of them? Was he chasing down a lead or confronting one of the actual vampires involved?

I needed help. I dialled Kim's number. She finally answered after several calls. I shared Ben's location with her. Kim made me promise to wait until she got there before getting out of the car.

Shortly after, I arrived as close as I could at Ben's location. Kim was nowhere to be seen and while I had made a promise to her, I was too scared to stay in the car. I jumped out, strapped a handgun on each hip and held the M-16 in my hands.

A voice in my head tried to calm me, promising me Ben would be there, unharmed. Another answered telling me he was already dead...

I opened the gate and squinted through the darkness. The smell of wet fur and rubbish assaulted my nose. My steps echoed, announcing my arrival. Hissing and scratching sounds accompanied me deeper into the alley to a small courtyard. There were several open doors leading down into the basements of the surrounding buildings. A distant streetlight illuminated the night sky, but very little light reached the courtyard.

I stopped and swinging the M-16 onto my back, I reached for my phone. From the blinking dot on the screen I couldn't make out where exactly Ben was. I squinted into the alley; there were several basements and more archways with stairs leading up to the tall buildings around me. There was a medieval round tower on my left with vertical slits as windows.

I waited a few seconds for any movement or sign but all I could make out were molochs hissing close-by. My feet turned right and I carefully stepped down the stairs to my right, my trusted machine gun at the ready.

Three molochs lay dead within minutes. I heard something behind me and ran back up the stairs to see another two fleeing. The machine gun wouldn't be precise enough. I pulled out my handgun and shot them.

I cleared out the nests one basement at the time, hoping each time I would find Ben. There was absolutely no trace of him; no empty shells on the ground, no dead molochs. I started doubting the accuracy of the phone. Hissing and growling sounds escaped through the closed wooden door of the last basement I needed to clear. I kicked the door open and shot at the molochs reaching for me. The stench made my eyes water.

I took a step further into the basement and slipped on the wet slabs. I landed on my back and slid the remaining few steps down, hitting the back of my head on the concrete steps. Disoriented I tried to stop my vision from swimming. The shock rang in my ears. I took my left hand off the machine gun and applied pressure to my forehead. The pulsing in the back of my head slowly dulled down.

A hissing surprised me from above. Immediately, I tilted the machine gun up and shot the bastard. My ears rang from the shot. I couldn't hear anything besides the high-pitched screech of my damaged eardrums.

Several molochs lurked in the corners. I sat up and shot those I could make out. There was no time to dwell on my pain. I exited the basement and a wave of fresh air welcomed me. The absence of foulness helped clear my mind. There was a small trickle down my neck and I was convinced it was blood.

A rumbling from an engine approached and a flash of lights illuminated the square. A car door was slammed shut. 'Meerah!' I could hear someone calling.

'Yeah,' I responded.

'I told you to wait for me!' she scolded.

I gently pressed on my head to get the hammering to cease.

'Do you know where he is?' Kim had caught up to me now and was looking me up and down. 'Are you good?'

'I don't know where exactly. He's here somewhere.'

Suddenly, there was a muffled sound. It was like a scratching of wood on wood.

Kim looked up towards the tops of the buildings. 'Come on. Let's start with that tower.'

We made our way up the tight winding stairs. The steps were short and more than once I tripped and almost smacked my face onto the cold stone.

It took us several minutes to reach the top. By the end my quads were burning. At the top of the staircase was a wooden door with a latch. Kim stopped and listened. She looked down to me and made signs with her left fist to communicate soundlessly that when we stormed through the door, she would go left and I was to go right. Then she opened her hand and counted down. At the end of the countdown she pushed against the door and crashed into the room. I followed close behind her. It was dark and all I could see was a shape on the ground. It moved and flapped around in a weird way. My eyes fixated on the dark shadow as my eyes dilated and I recognised him.

'Ben!' I exclaimed and ran to him.

'Ameerah no!' I heard behind me, but it was too late.

Something grabbed me from behind and ripped the machine gun out of my hands. My foot was pulled backwards and I fell to the ground. As I fell, I rolled to my back and drew my gun, landing a few shots onto the large shadow with piercing red eyes.

Kim shot him from the door and we let the bullets rain. Only seconds later, I ran out of ammunition. While I reached for another magazine the vampire lunged at me and pulled me up across his upper body. He was dangerously close to me and I tried to push myself away from him. His mouth snapped at me and I could see his sharp teeth glistening.

The vampire grabbed hold of my jacket and pulled me down. I reached along the back of my belt and unsheathed a blade. As he pulled me down and opened his mouth, I stabbed him in between the ribs on his right side. The vampire let go of my jacket and barred my right arm as I tried to stab him again. With ease he twisted my wrist around and made me drop the blade onto the floor. He reached for it and sunk the blade deep into my liver. I had no chance to stop him. I fell backwards trying to hold in the blood that was pouring in between my fingers.

The vampire climbed on top of me but now that I was out of the line of fire, Kim resumed shooting. The bullets pierced holes in his body, but it didn't seem to slow him down. The vampire turned away from me and sprinted at Kim who was still shooting him.

Ben rolled onto all fours and tried to get up. He was heavily bleeding from his left arm and his left leg. I let go of my side and reached across my hips with my right hand and unholstered my handgun. The vampire had cornered Kim and she was taking a heavy beating.

Finally, the gun was securely in my hand and I pointed at the monster and shot. Ben got on his legs but stumbled onto the wall and crashed back onto the floor.

The vampire let go of Kim and turned back to me. I had now emptied my clip into him. I was out of bullets. As he moved in on me, I could see he was not walking straight anymore.

Ben mumbled my name but couldn't do more than wiggle.

Kim shot the vampire several times from the back, blood sprayed across me as the bullets pierced through his chest, and he fell on top of me. Some of the blood had sprayed into my mouth and I had accidentally swallowed it. It was more than just a drop or two.

Kim stashed the gun away and moved towards me.

'Get Ben! I'm right behind you!' I told her.

She nodded and tumbled towards Ben. She pulled him up and headed for the door. I could hear them making their way down the long staircase.

I breathed deeply and tried to wrestle with the vampire's body on top of me. My heartrate was quick and I could feel it pulse right up in my throat.

Suddenly I felt a sharp pain in my hip as I tried to move out from underneath the vampire. It paralysed me for a few seconds before I was able to function again. I boxed the body away from me and saw that the vampire was not dead. It was barely clinging to life and had bitten me in my hip. The bite wound burned horribly. The muscles around it contracted and spasmed, making me squirm on the floor uncontrollably.

The vampire gurgled as it started laughing and crawled towards me.

Frantically, I looked around and saw the blade that he had stabbed me with on my right. I reached for it, but my blood-covered fingers slipped. The vampire had gotten a hold of my left leg and was pulling me backwards. I managed to make the blade spin and got a hold of it on the sharp end. I twisted it around in my grip and swung around with it. My hand stabbed the blade into the vampire's stomach and it slipped from my grip as I did so. Finally, the vampire stopped moving and the murderous red eyes lost focus.

The burning from my hip spread up towards my intestines and down toward my hip joint. It was getting harder to breathe. I needed Caleb. And I was alone!

I pulled my phone out and looked for Caleb's speed dial on the foggy screen. My blood-covered fingers slipped around the screen. I pressed the phone to my ear and could feel the long beeps stretch out.

'I'm on my way, my child. I'm not far. Try to not panic or move too much.'

'Ok, hurry Caleb,' I managed to cough into the phone. Talking was exhausting.

With great difficulty I crawled and fought my way across the room to the wooden door. I reached up to the latch and pulled myself up. The door started swinging back and I swung with it, crashing into the wall. My head banged against the concrete and the ringing in my ears intensified. I prayed that Caleb could feel my distress. How long ago had Kim and Ben left? It felt like an eternity. My right hand reached down to my bleeding liver and tried to cover the stab wound up. With my left hand I pulled myself back up and made it through the door.

My vision was swimming. I aimed for the first step but missed it. I tried to stop myself, but my upper body was leaning too far out and I rolled down quite a few steps before I stopped. When I did, I was lying on my back with my head down and my knees against the outer wall of the stairs. My back slipped and I slid down a few more steps until my head hit something hard. I stretched my hand backwards to steady myself, pulling the muscles around my pierced liver and making me scream.

My breathing was fast and growing shallow. My throat had started swelling, black spots appeared in my vision. I managed to get my legs down from the wall and my head pointing towards the top of the stairs. Using the wall, I slithered down step by step.

I could feel my breathing unexpectedly easing. The burning at my hip was still just as strong and every time I moved, I could feel the pain travelling like lightning up my hip and across my ribcage. I wasn't quite sure what was going on, but I used my slight improvement to get down as many steps as I could.

There were steps audible rushing towards me. I reached down my right leg to my ankle and got my emergency blade out.

I could hear my name being called from somewhere beneath me.

'Kim!' I shouted in response.

Finally, she came around the corner and helped me up. 'We're almost there!'

As we made our way down, I could feel my windpipe closing again. Whatever had happened to slightly improve my state, had reversed. The wheezing intensified and the black spots in my vision came back.

'What's going on? Were you bitten?' Kim pulled me through the door at the bottom and out onto the courtyard.

It was now raining, making it even harder to see in the dark.

'Ameerah were you bitten?' I could hear Kim next to me.

I tried to answer but I had no more force. No air would reach my lungs. I got dizzy and tried to hold on to Kim. It felt like I was drowning and I couldn't get to the surface anymore.

'Did you call Caleb? Is he on his way?'

I grunted in response. I breathed in desperately, but it was useless. The burning in my hip had spread widely and was paralysing my stomach and my right leg. I could no longer walk with it and it had become a dead weight.

'Don't you dare give out on me!'

A sense of calmness came to me. My breathing slowed.

'I'm here my child,' I heard a voice sing in my ears.

His voice took my anxiety away and I could feel my body relax. I was lying on the cold floor with the rain pelting down on me.

'How is Ben?' I heard him ask quietly.

At the mention of his name I stirred. I wanted to see him. I wanted to be around him.

'He's fine. Meerah, relax. He's safe in the car and getting a transfusion. He'll be alright.' Someone held on to my hand.

'Hold her in place.'

Before I had time to think about what I had heard, I could feel something at my hip. The pain immediately cranked up and it was like the fire reignited in my veins and boiled my blood. I screamed out. My mouth was muffled.

The excruciating pain repeated like acid poured over my whole body. It was too much to bear.

I came to myself and was gently rocked. When I opened my eyes, I saw something grey above me. My eyes slowly focused and I realised I was in a car. I drew in a deep breath.

'She's waking up.' I heard Ben's voice above me. I could see him smiling down on me.

'Thank fucking god!' Kim said from the driver's seat.

My hand glided down my side. The stab wound in my liver had been bandaged. Gently, I travelled further down and could feel where the vampire had bitten me. The skin was burning but it wasn't searing anymore. I could breathe again.

Kim drove us home and helped us up into our apartment. I was surprised to see how quickly we had recovered. We were just exhausted now.

Ben and I made our way across the entrance and fell into our bed and fell asleep within minutes.

I raised myself up into a sitting position and realised I was still wearing my clothes from the previous night. I tried to remember the sequence of events. A moment came back to me that I couldn't explain. For a few minutes, the poison of the vampire bite had lessened. In the back of my mind I recalled the taste of blood in my mouth. I also remembered the vampire had stabbed me with the same blade I had stabbed him in between his ribs. His blood had entered my liver...

Had it been the vampire blood countering the poison?

No, it couldn't be. Otherwise every ghost would be using it.

Groggy and tired, I walked to the kitchen to make myself a cup of coffee. The movement helped to stretch my muscles back to life. Ben was sitting on the couch, looking out over the balcony. I joined him and we sat quietly next to each other for a while.

'How did you know where I was?' Ben finally asked me.

I took a sip from the coffee that tasted like hot water. 'Your phone shares your location with mine. I knew you would go out alone again.'

Ben's eyes looked dark and sunken from lack of sleep and his voice was strained. His hands were folded, resting in his lap. He was leaning forward and supported his upper body with his elbows on his legs.

'You shouldn't have come.'

'If I hadn't, that vampire would have finished you off.'

'And it almost took you out.' Ben's voice was no more than a whisper.

'I thought he was dead. If he hadn't bitten me, it would have been fine.'

I involuntarily shuddered. I remembered all too clearly the boiling pain of the poison in my veins slowly suffocating me.

'You cannot come with me again. If something had happened to you-' He stopped and closed his eyes.

'If something had happened to you, it would have ripped me apart. If you had told me from the beginning, we could have had a plan. And if you're thinking about not taking me with you next time, I'm going to throw myself at danger.'

Ben rolled his eyes at me.

'You don't think I'm serious? Fine. I'm going.' I slowly got up.

'No, please!' Ben reached for me and held my hands. 'I just don't want to lose you.'

'You won't.' I kissed him repeatedly.

Ben and I spent the day together. We were both drained from the vampire hunt and we gladly used it as an excuse to spend the day in bed together.

I texted with Kim. She had gotten home unscathed. Dominic had gone on a hunt with Blake two days earlier and they had not yet returned. She wanted to meet up with me and said she had some important news. Reluctantly, I left my love cocoon behind and dressed half-decent to meet with Kim at Santa's.

Once inside, I could feel the joy in the air. We were only a few months away from Christmas and no one had wasted any time in decorating the pub appropriately. There were large garlands and swags across the ceiling, twinkly lights of all colours blinking uncontrollably and capable of triggering an epileptic reaction and miniature elves on the tables. Most ghosts were wearing Christmas or party hats. Some even had festive sweaters on. Everyone was merry and celebrating, even if Christmas was still a good two months away.

I spotted Kim behind the counter mixing herself a drink. When she saw me come in, she waved me over and reached for a second glass. She poured me the same drink and we cheered. The music blasted and people danced.

'So, what's this big news that was so urgent?' I asked and clinked my glass with hers.

Kim smiled cheekily and looked down at her hands. 'I'm seeing someone.'

'Ooohh, who is it? Do I know him?'

She took a large gulp. 'No, I'm seeing... a girl.' Apprehension took over her face.

It took a few seconds for me to hear the words and understand what she was telling me. All this time I had not had a clue. There had never been a shred of doubt in my mind about her sexuality. I had seen her constantly flirt with men!

'Wooohh,' was the first sound I made. My brain needed a few more seconds to process the news. 'But... you've never even insinuated you were gay. Did you only find out now?' I asked.

'I have known for a long time but when I became a ghost, I realised I was surrounded by 99% men and I... I just wanted to protect myself. I didn't know how people would react, so I pretended I was straight,' she said whilst stirring her drink with a straw.

'Do you think people would treat you differently if you were honest?'

Kim's eyes grew big. 'Of course! There are almost no women here and you're surrounded by a herd of horny, strong men. I was afraid of being bullied, rejected, raped- sorry!' She had spoken the word before she could stop herself.

It took me a moment to regroup myself. 'It's ok.' I swung my arms around her and hugged her tightly, tears rolling down my cheeks. I could feel her wet tears on my arm. I gently detached myself from her and looked her in the eyes. 'I just wish you would have felt comfortable enough to tell me before.'

Kim sighed. 'I wanted to but you're my closest friend and I was terrified!' A new tear travelled from her eye down her cheek.

I shook my head. 'You have nothing to worry about, I'm so happy for you. Whether you're straight or gay, I don't care as long as you are with someone who makes you happy. And you and me, that's not going to change. We are always going to be friends. So,' I smiled at her. 'Who is the lucky girl?'

She brushed her index fingers under her eyes trying to wipe the tears away without destroying her make-up in the process. 'Her name is June. Here, I have a picture.' Kim reached into her pocket and scrolled through her phone. She showed me a picture of a woman with straight ginger hair, freckles on her face and dark blue, hypnotising eyes.

I pulled the phone closer. 'She is beautiful!'

Kim smiled sheepishly and stuck her phone back into her pocket. 'I met her a few weeks ago when I was out on a mission in another district. We've tried to meet a few times since but because she's far it's not always easy.'

'Maybe one of you can move closer?' I added, hopefully.

'I mentioned it to Dom, but he was not receptive. It's still early so I'll see how it goes.'

My face hurt from grinning, and I couldn't stop. 'I'm very happy for you. You deserve it!' I kissed her on the cheek.

Kim told me everything about June, how they had met, how she had asked her out, every little detail. She was so excited to tell me about it. I barely got a word in.

A week later I received a message from Blake. He asked me to kill some molochs. Our numbers were too low. I agreed to do my part and went out the same day. He wanted to come with me, but I didn't want to be around him and have him criticise me at every turn.

Ben had gone out to meet with some friends that day, which was perfect. I could get my duties done while he was away and not miss out on spending time with him.

It was one of the usual spots close to the shooting range; a parking garage under a large office-type building. I drove my white Volvo into the middle of the structure and could see the molochs all around me. Before even getting out of the car their squeaky noises were audible.

Two of them dared to jump on the bonnet of the car, eyeing me with their blood-red eyes. I kept the headlights on so I could see in the otherwise sombre concrete parking garage.

The two on the bonnet climbed on the wiper blades and up onto the roof of the car. Their claws scratching and clicking on the metal.

I checked there were no molochs immediately by the driver's side and opened the door just wide enough to fit the handgun through. The shots echoed loudly and their creaks and yelps broke out as soon as I started shooting.

I jumped out of the car and swung the gun around at any creature coming my way. By the time I ran out of bullets, the rest of them had disappeared behind remote and dark corners. I reloaded and looked around. Their noises had been reduced to distant cries. I was not in the mood to try and follow them into the dark shafts, not when I was alone without any back-up. All I had to do was kill some of them. Looking around, I counted twelve down. Not enough, but a start.

I was about to get into my car when I saw two of them on the ground in the beams of the headlights. There was blood seeping out of one of them. It had fed not long ago. The red liquid fled the shell of its body and poured out onto the dirty concrete. I walked over and crouched by the one oozing blood.

My thoughts drifted to my accidental ingestion of vampire blood. Would moloch blood have the same effect? Though only briefly, it had slowed down the poison from suffocating me. It had probably saved my life in the end. Caleb had had those few additional minutes to get to me.

I reached into the pool of blood and dipped two fingers into it. Then I brought the red glistening fingers to my nose. It smelled just like you would expect it to.

Lifting my two fingers closer to my face, I bared my tongue and touched the blood. Nothing happened. I sucked the blood from both of my fingers. The blood was not exactly tasty but not bad either.

I found myself dipping my fingers again into the blood and sucking it off my fingers. Would I be able to drink the moloch blood instead of needing Caleb's?

Something made me continue. Was it curiosity? Maybe it was the unusual faint taste...

I looked around. As expected, the parking structure was completely empty. No one could see what I was doing. I continued dipping my fingers into the blood as if it was a frowned-upon sweet treat.

A sense of ease spread gradually through my body. It made me feel good, closer to my human life. I breathed in deeply, letting the moloch blood mix in my stomach. Eagerly I dipped my fingers inside the dead moloch's open chest and licked my fingers. Warmth invaded my body. It felt like ecstasy; it was close to the feeling I got from Caleb. All troubles disappeared. My head started spinning. The world was circling around me.

Before it got too bad, I forced myself to crawl to the open driver's door and lifted myself up onto the seat. Closing the door behind me, I pressed the 'lock' sign on the key and heard the reassuring sound of the doors locking.

Now I could relax. All my senses were heightened. Finally, I felt like I was no longer trapped in this grey world full of darkness and terrors. I was free.

A stiff neck pulled me out of my sleep. I forced myself to move and realised my stomach was being crushed. Opening my eyes, I saw I was lying in a car, across the driver's and passenger's seats. The gear stick was digging into the soft tissue of my stomach. After stretching my limbs, I sat up on the driver's seat. I was still in the underground parking. The dead molochs were sprawled on the floor. Several pairs of glistening eyes lurked in the corners and blinked at me.

I rolled the window down and shot three bullets. There were yelps and the eyes disappeared. It was impossible to tell the time in the darkness. When I looked at my phone it told me it was just past 7am in the morning.

I clapped down the mirror above the driver's seat and inspected my face. My skin was whiter than before. Probably only a little but enough for me to notice. No blood was on my face, but I remembered very clearly having gotten high from it.

With an uneasy sense in my stomach I turned on the engine and quickly drove up the ramp and out into the open air. The sky was dark and a thick cover of clouds overhead pressed down upon the tall buildings of the city.

As soon as I had rolled out of the parking garage, my phone beeped several times. It kept pinging until I looked at it again. I had missed calls and a lot of text messages from more or less everyone I knew. I had been out all night…

'Hello?' Ben croaked in the phone.

'It's me. What's going on?'

'What's going on?! Where have you been all night?! I was so worried! I thought you had been killed!'

'I'm sorry, I'm coming home now. I... went out to kill some molochs and passed out in the car. I'm fine.'

'Fine?! You went alone without telling anyone where you were! I even called Blake!'

'You what? Damn, ok, I'll call him now. I should be home in half an hour.' I hung up before he could say anymore.

I had forgotten I had not informed anyone of what I was doing. Before dealing with Blake, I called Caleb. He was very angry with me but relieved nothing serious had happened. Wherever he was he couldn't sense that I was not telling him the whole truth. But there was no way I would admit to passing out from drinking moloch blood.

'When will I see you next?' I asked him. It was partly to estimate how long I had to detox before seeing him again.

'I'm in the human world and I don't know when I'll be back.'

'Human world? Why?' Was he looking for a new recruit? Was he replacing me?

'There is some business I need to attend to, but do not trouble yourself, Meerah. I will be back as soon as I can.' His voice lulled me.

I closed my eyes and remained in the moment until he hung up. At least he wouldn't uncover what I had done while he was off in the human world.

I had tried to reach Blake, but he had not answered his phone. When I arrived home, I saw him leaning against his truck parked right next to the front door.

'I see that you've started taking on some dangerous habits.' He eyed me with his icy eyes.

'I was in an underground parking and I passed out. Nothing happened.' I opened the glass door and he followed me into the small elevator.

'How come you passed out? Did you get bitten? Were there vampires?' Blake's eyes scanned me up and down.

'No, I just... I don't know I was exhausted and I didn't feel well. I had shot some molochs and I crawled into the car and locked the door. I was perfectly safe.'

'Do you realise that a vampire can rip the door open of a car without even breaking a sweat? Vampires know that we're killing molochs and they hunt in those places for us!'

The elevator doors opened onto the sixth floor and I walked out towards the entrance.

'I didn't know. I will be more careful next time. And why are you telling me off? You're the one who told me to go hunting!' I opened the door to my apartment and Blake followed me into the kitchen.

'I'm also the one who told you I wanted to go with you! I don't like leaving my recruits to go hunting alone even when they're approved! And look at what happened to you!'

Ben appeared from the terrace and looked surprised at Blake. He hugged me tightly.

'You scared me,' Ben mumbled into my ear and kissed my neck. 'Tell me where you're going next time.'

When I let go of Ben, I saw Blake standing with his arms crossed over his chest looking like a bull ready to charge.

'You made your point, Blake. I'll be more careful next time!' I rolled my eyes.

He snorted in derision. 'You think you can get rid of me so easily? Ben was so worried he called *me* of all people! And now you're telling me you were too tired and what? Fell asleep in your car? You couldn't drive home and sleep in your bed?! What the hell did you do down there?!' Blake's voice had gotten louder.

'Alright,' Ben interjected, matching his voice. He was standing behind me and stroking my arms. 'I'm sorry I called you. Maybe I overreacted. But she's not a helpless child. Let's just move past this.'

'Move past this? I don't think so! I want to know what you did down there! How come you passed out *for hours?* What did you do with those molochs?!'

I could feel myself getting nervous. I couldn't tell anyone what I had done! Even I was disgusted by my actions!

'Blake, just calm down. I don't really remember what happened. I killed some molochs and I felt dizzy. I wanted to wait for it to pass but I must have fallen asleep or something. But it's nothing to get upset about now. I felt something was happening and I locked myself in where I thought I was safe. I didn't know that vampires hunted molochs too. Next time I'll keep it in mind.'

'And she can handle herself. She's faced vampires before,' Ben added.

But the moment Ben had said it, I knew he had said too much.

'What?' Blake's eyes now scrutinising Ben.

'It was nothing, there was a slight mishap with a vampire, but Caleb got there on time and everything was fine.'

Ben moved away from behind me towards the fridge and took a beer out.

Blake stared at Ben without moving. It took him several seconds before he reacted and I knew he was about to boil over.

'She got bitten by a vampire?' Blake asked in a low menacing tone.

Ben opened the beer and took a sip. 'Yeah, happens to all of us.'

I stepped backwards closer to Ben and reached underneath the counter for the handgun he kept on the first shelf.

Blake closed his eyes and breathed in. When he opened his eyes again, he was furious. The muscles in his arms were pumped and the veins in his neck showed. 'SHE WAS BITTEN BY A VAMPIRE UNDER YOUR SUPERVISION?!'

'Calm down! I tried to keep her away from it but she followed me! Luckily she did-'

Ben didn't get the chance to finish. Blake raised his gun and I pulled out the one from underneath the counter. I moved in front of Ben and now we had the guns pointed at each other.

'GET OUT OF THE WAY!' he barked at me, but I didn't blink. 'This – this is exactly why I didn't want you around him! He will get you KILLED! I'm taking him to the council, NOW!'

'Put the gun down!' I raised my voice though it didn't match Blake's outcry.

'Blake, calm down-' Ben's interjected.

'SHUT THE **FUCK UP** YOU **PIECE OF SHIT**!!!!' Blake roared with force. 'I leave you out of my sight *for one month* and he gets you BITTEN BY A VAMPIRE!

'I was there with Kim! Caleb made it on time and everything was fine! Now *put the gun down!*'

'He will get you killed Ameerah! He is *dangerous!* He doesn't **deserve** you!'

'My job is to *kill* those monsters and sometimes things go wrong! You can't keep me locked up and protect me everywhere I go! Now *put the gun down!*' I barked at him.

'Blake-' Ben tried to get his attention.

A shot rang out.

I reacted by shooting at Blake.

I spun around and saw Ben going down, bleeding from his left shoulder.

Blake grabbed me from behind and smashed the gun out of my hands. I reached for his and clawed it out of his grip and threw it across the room.

He tried to overpower me, but I elbowed him in the face, breaking his nose. Blake kicked me in the stomach, crushing my intestines. I tackled him at his waist and threw him to the ground, landing on top of him. He sent me flying against the side of the couch, breaking at least two ribs. I tried to get up, but Blake was quicker. He kicked me violently. One of the broken ribs pierced through my lung. I gasped for air but got none.

Ben hoisted Blake off me, receiving a few blows meant for me. Blake was so overtaken by anger he broke Ben's already wounded shoulder in a single move by twisting Ben's arm onto his back. Ben screamed in pain and fell to his knees.

I could see them wrestling. Then my gaze fell onto a gun. It lay by the end of the couch. Sliding along the slick floor I reached for the black piece of metal. Blake pummelled Ben, ignoring me for the moment. Holding my ribcage together with my left hand, I forced myself to sit up where I had a direct line of sight and painfully lifted my right arm to take aim at Blake.

I wanted to yell 'stop', but only blood sprayed out of my mouth. I had no time to wait. Without thinking twice, I shot at Blake. The bullet pierced through his shoulder blade. With a thump he fell to the ground.

'Ben?' I asked, distressed, my voice cracking. His answer was a long howl, resembling a dying wolf.

Blake had turned on his back and managed to sit upright, leaning against the bloodstained back of the kitchen counter. With a shaking hand, I kept the gun pointed at him. Blake held still when he saw the deadly metal aimed at him. Our eyes locked.

Ben crawled away from him towards the fireplace.

'I'm done with you,' Blake stated breathing heavily. He grabbed the counter and pulled himself up.

His deep blue eyes stared at me one more time, and then he swayed towards the front door, disappearing behind the wall. I heard the elevator doors open and close again. My hand went limp. The gun fell to the ground.

With the little strength I had left, I crawled over to the fridge to get the bags of blood we needed. Ben was soaking in a pool of his own blood. Though my hands were shaking, I managed to insert the tube into Ben's arm. I let myself fall to the ground the moment the blood started transferring into him. It took me longer to build up the strength to also connect myself to my blood supply. Once I had finally done so, I reached for Ben's hand and clutched it.

I looked over to where Blake's blood tainted the living room. I had inflicted him with this pain. Why had it come to this?

That afternoon I got sick. At first it was a persistent headache, accompanied by fatigue. Later my stomach turned and I threw up several times. I spent the day in bed. Ghosts rarely got sick and if they did it was from bites from other supernatural beings. It had to be the moloch blood.

Ben wanted to call Caleb but I insisted it was not a good idea after the shootout with Blake. I considered telling Ben the truth but given my state he most likely would not have believed I had swallowed just a few drops. And I couldn't admit to dipping my fingers into the sweet red poison oozing from a dead moloch and sucking my fingers dry.

I swore to never take it ever again. All would be well and fine. No one would ever know. The sickness would pass and everything would be uneventfully dull as always.

BLOOD SPILL

My health returned to normal after a few days of headaches and nausea. I couldn't believe I had ingested moloch blood and not expect it to have any consequences.

Ben knew something was up. It felt horrible lying to him, but I didn't know what would happen if I told the truth. Drinking blood didn't seem like something one should admit to. What if Ben had to report me to the council? What if I needed to take some sort of detox to rid my body of the moloch blood?

There was no way for me to get any information on the side-effects without giving myself away at the same time. Ben eventually let it go.

A week later I was fully recovered and had started training intensely again to keep my mind occupied. I had run for several miles in the cold and sprinted all the way up the hill from the river to the apartment. Small snowflakes sprinkled down from the sky and danced in the air from the strong wind.

With the approaching winter I was also reminded it was yet another Christmas I wouldn't spend with my family. It was hard to imagine all the time I had been here already and the years to come could be crumbled up through a 'time loop' and have me return to my human life to the same evening I had been hit by the car. Would my mind even be able to process memories from so many additional years? What happened to ghosts once they were back on the other side?

I got off the elevator and walked into our apartment. Ben wasn't home and I took advantage of it to have a long bath. First, I stretched and took off my sweaty clothes. I filled the bath and mixed bath salts and bath soaks into the steaming water. Within minutes a thick layer of foam had formed on top of the water. I put a small table next to the tub and placed a bottle of exquisite red wine on it with a fitting crystal glass. On the opposite end of the tub I aligned scented candles and turned on some relaxing music. Finally, I eased myself into the hot water and enjoyed the aromatic scents around me. I closed my eyes and let my mind go to pleasant memories while I listened to gentle piano music.

There was a thump from somewhere in the apartment, followed by steps. I called out and shortly afterwards Ben stuck his head through the door of the bathroom.

'Hi my love, how is your bath?' His green eyes looked lovingly onto me.

'Good, but it would be even better if you joined.' I answered winking at him.

He approached and crouched down by my head, taking a sip from the wine. 'No, you enjoy your bath. I'll make a fire and we can watch a movie tonight.'

Ben leaned over and kissed me.

The foam had disappeared by the time I got out and my skin was wrinkled. I put on comfortable clothes and tied my hair into a high bun. With the bottle of wine in one hand and the glass in the other I walked towards the kitchen and placed them both on the kitchen counter when I saw what Ben was doing.

He had laid rose petals everywhere on the floor in the living room and a fire was burning in the fireplace, casting yellow flickers into the room. There was a fully decorated Christmas tree by the sliding doors to the terrace with Christmas lights twinkling in all colours. He turned towards me and had a present in his hands.

'This is for you.' He placed the gift in front of me on the kitchen counter.

When I opened it, I found a dark blue jewellery box. In the box was a delicate bracelet with diamonds set onto the silver chain. The diamonds were discrete but didn't lack sparkle.

'What's the occasion?' I asked as Ben fastened the bracelet around my right wrist.

'The occasion is I love you and you're beautiful.'

I threw my arms around him and held him tightly. He caressed my arms and back. We spent the evening on the couch watching a movie and cuddling.

*　*　*

Christmas came and I celebrated with Ben at our apartment. Kim had gone to see June over the holidays and Caleb was also away. It made me sad that I wouldn't see him at all. I hadn't seen him since I had been bitten by that vampire. He kept telling me he was busy doing other stuff and after a while I stopped chasing him. I missed him terribly, but he obviously had other priorities and I didn't want to beg for his attention.

Months went by with the usual training, hunting molochs and vampires, and spending time with Ben. With Kim now also seeing someone, I understood she wanted to spend her time with June so we only saw each other once a month.

As time went on, my desire to drink moloch blood had diminished and I had forgotten all about it by the time summer came around. Compared to the previous years, I wasn't under any pressure from Blake to adhere to any rigid schedule. All I had to do was keep up my killing numbers and that was easy enough. I hadn't heard from him since we had had the massive fight which had ended in injuries. I regretted shooting him but at the same time I wouldn't have let him drag Ben to the council.

My relationship with Ben was great and I enjoyed living with him. He made me laugh and cared for me. My feelings for him grew stronger and there wasn't much we didn't do together. Whenever I went out with Kim, I missed him, even if I was just out for a few hours at Santa's pub. The moment I came home I felt complete again.

Over the summer we had redecorated the apartment and gotten new furniture. The white leather couch was replaced with a beige cotton velvet one, and the glass coffee table was replaced with a vintage low table of dark wood and black iron. I got several plants and dispersed everything from small cacti to bamboo palms across the apartment. Ben got outdoor fairy lights for the balcony.

I wanted to move to a bigger apartment at first, but Ben explained the council imposed where ghosts had to live with their recruits. If we wanted to move, we would have to make an official request. We would also have to get Blake to testify that I could still fulfil my duties while living with Ben, and that wasn't going to happen.

It was towards the end of August when Ben woke me up in bed and told me he wanted to take me away for a few days but said the location was a surprise. His deep green eyes were on me while I caressed the side of his face. Sometimes I couldn't believe I had found him in this hellhole. He was the best thing to have happened to me. I considered myself very lucky.

Ben planted a kiss on my lips and then swung himself out of bed. I watched his naked body move as he walked out of the room and into the kitchen.

A few minutes later he came back into the bedroom, carrying a cup of coffee. A trail of steam swirled in the air.

'Thanks babe.' I took a sip and set the cup down on the bedside table.

He walked over to the wardrobe at the foot of the bed and picked out clothes he wanted to pack for our getaway. I was getting turned on watching him. His body was so muscular...

I climbed out of bed and walked up to him until our bodies were touching. I kissed him passionately and gestured him to come back to bed. Ben's eyes filled with excitement; he didn't need a second invitation.

Ben and I each packed a bag. Out of precaution we took some guns and ammunition. This world always had a joker card in its hand and when you least expected it, you would get hit by a wave of trouble.

I took the elevator down to Ben's car and put my bag in the back. I put two machine guns in the boot and left one on the backseat with extra ammo.

I texted Kim our plans, while I waited for Ben.

We drove out of our district and into a new one, away from the river towards the west. Things began looking unfamiliar.

Buildings flashed by, schools, offices, houses. Every now and then I would see a human or two.

We stopped at a traffic light and Ben took my hand up to his mouth and kissed the back of it. I grinned and could feel my cheeks reddening.

Suddenly, Ben's face changed. Anxiety manifested in his eyes. Seconds later, I could feel it too. There was something in the air. Something wasn't right. A knot in my stomach tightened. Ben pulled into one of the side streets. My sense of unease augmented; I felt in danger now.

'What's happening?' I asked. He had let go of my hand and was looking around, searching for something.

'Vampire.'

The panic instantly spread through me. I hadn't expected to fight a vampire suddenly. Even if I had fought them before, I always needed time to mentally prepare myself.

'I need to see who it is,' Ben answered calmly. 'It could be Jason.'

His eyes were dead, his muscles tense, like a cheetah ready to pounce. Ben was cold and calculated, just like Blake got when he was in a dangerous situation. He was in trainer-mode. Yet, I felt like *we* were the prey.

'Babe, I don't know if we have enough ammunition, we-'

Ben brutally spun the car around. His eyes flashed with insanity. *'I saw him! I saw Jason!'*

He made the car roar and raced at incredible speed towards a distant figure.

The anxiety coursed through my veins. My body was on high alert.

The vampire turned around to face us just as the car slammed into him. His body gave a sickening thud against the windshield and bounced off the metal frame of the car. The windshield splintered on impact. In the rear-view mirror I saw the vampire crash into the pavement behind us. Blinded by fury,

Ben slammed the brakes and jumped out of the still running car. The smell of burnt tyres invaded the car.

I reached onto the backseat and grabbed the machine gun. Moments later I followed Ben out of the car. I saw Jason running with astonishing speed at Ben who was emptying his clip into the vampire. It didn't slow Jason in the least.

I raised my machine gun and let the bullets rain until the two got too close together and finally slammed into one another. Ben was thrown backwards and skid along the road until he was brutally stopped by the pedestrian walkway. I started shooting again. The vampire barely stumbled from the barrage of bullets.

He turned and his eyes settled on me. In a split second he closed the gap between us and tore the machine gun from my hands. He gripped my throat and pressed my windpipe shut, while lifting me up in the air.

I had to free myself from his deadly grip. I could feel my throat swelling from the pressure. My head was about to burst. In seconds, I would pass out.

With my left hand I reached down my left leg while I pulled my ankle up. I unholstered a small gun and shot from below at the arm suffocating me. It was enough for Jason to let go with an annoyed roar. I fell on the hard concrete, gasping for air. Coughing and wriggling on the pavement I pointed the gun and fired at the vampire's heart from underneath him.

From behind me another storm of bullets hit him as well. He fell to his knees from the impacts. I unsheathed one of my trusted knives I kept at the back of my hips, hoisted myself up, and plunged the blade into his heart. Three bullets hit me from behind, sending me sprawling on top of the vampire. The back of the knife drilled into my ribcage.

I had to get away from him! I rolled to the side, but the vampire got a hold of my vest before I could get clear. With one powerful yank, he pulled me back towards himself. Instinctively, I protected my face with my arms. He sank his teeth into my left underarm. The excruciating pain immediately numbed my body. A tortured scream echoed from my throat. It felt like I was corroding from the inside.

He bent my hand backwards and aimed for my throat, breaking my wrist in the process. The paralysing pain from his bite had maxed out what I was able to feel. I only realised the bone had broken from the crack it made.

The bullets stopped. The red-eyed beast fought his way up, grabbed me by my jacket and pulled me to his face. His velvet cat-eyes stared at me thirstily. He licked his razor-sharp teeth and pulled me closer.

My breathing shuddered.

The sound of bullets pierced the air again. My ears rang, blocking all other sound. The vampire's head turned away from me. More bullets hammered it. The monster let go. We fell backwards onto the ground. Moments later Ben appeared above me, firing with a machine gun at the vampire. The empty casings rained down on me.

Ben aimed directly at Jason's head, tearing apart his face. Ben stopped when the creature hadn't moved for several seconds. A thin trail of smoke escaped his gun. He turned to me. 'You ok?'

'I was bitten,' I said, having trouble speaking. Ben checked my body and looked at the trail of blood escaping the bite wound, crisscrossing down my arm and finally dripping from my elbow to the ground.

'Fuck!' He lifted me up and supported my weight as I hobbled back to the car. I had trouble breathing. My throat ached and closed up.

'You need Caleb, fast.' Ben's voice was panicked. I could hear my heart pounding in my ears over the ringing from the gunshots.

Something wasn't right. The bad feeling in my gut momentarily dimmed the ringing in my ears. 'Ben...' I reached for his collar and grabbed it as tightly as I could. We weren't alone.

Ben looked up. He could feel it too. Abruptly he spun around, letting go of me, and started shooting. I crashed onto the concrete, hitting my head. I saw Ben firing, a shadow draping itself over him and wrestling him to the ground.

With absolute horror it dawned on me. The shadow was *another* vampire.

My heart skipped a beat, before accelerating to a point where I couldn't make out the individual beats anymore. Ben laid helplessly on the ground. The vampire bent over him. I wrestled onto my side and grabbed Ben's leg, pulling myself towards the gun. I got a hold of it and fired the entire clip at the monster. The vampire started turning towards me, but several more bullets hit him in the face. The vampire fell backwards with his face deformed by bullet holes. But where had the shots come from? The body landed on the ground next to Ben's.

Ben lay lifeless in a pool of his own blood. It couldn't be. He was alright, yes he was. He had to be! He **had** to be!

Fearing the worst, I pulled myself closer to him, powering through the pain. My vision was swimming from tears. I pushed the vampire away from Ben and placed my hands on his face. His eyes flicked towards me. He was alive! Oh thank you heaven, he was alive!

A chunk of flesh was missing from Ben's neck where the vampire had bit him. Blood was pissing from the wound. I held the gash closed as well as I could.

'Ben,' I mouthed tonelessly.

'Je... Jes...,' was all I could hear.

I understood and frantically got out his phone. With shaking and blood smeared fingers I searched for Jesper in his contacts. The ringing was so slow. Years passed between each tone.

Finally, a soft click as he answered.

'Jesper,' I gasped, not waiting for him to speak, 'BEN NEEDS YOU **NOW**! He was bitten by a vampire!' My voice was wheezy.

Ben shook beneath me and a wave of blood sputtered out of his mouth and over my hand. 'Hold on baby, 'old on. Jesper is on his way, oh-ohk?' My hands were trembling.

It was getting painful to inhale.

I got my phone out. I dialled the first speed dial, but it went straight to voicemail. 'I ne-need you. Ben is wounded... and I was... bitten- bitten by...' I gasped for air. 'Vampire...'

I tried to steady my breathing but the more I inhaled the less air reached my lungs.

I dialled the next number on speed dial. Ben's breathing was growing shallow. His eyes were half closed. Even with my hand on his neck the blood escaped my grasp. I couldn't lose him!

'I'm here, Caleb is close.' A voice answered on the phone before I said a word.

'Jesper is comin'...' I sobbed, trying to comfort us both. Tears fell from my face and mixed with the expanding lake of blood around Ben.

My throat continued to swell, crushing my windpipe further.

'Meeeaaaa...'

'Yes, I'm 'ere. 'old on. Jesper is comin'.' I managed to gurgle between the gasps of air.

A hiss made me look up from Ben. Three molochs were eyeing us hungrily from an alley inching closer. They would be a problem soon. I still had Ben's gun but no more bullets.

Tears rolled down my face as I sobbed over Ben's struggling body.

He had to make it. I had to save Ben. Jesper would come any minute now. Yes, for his trainer he would make it. He would make it here and save Ben.

Another hissing echoed. Why couldn't those pieces of shit leave us alone?!

Ben's movements stilled.

I caressed his face gently with my broken hand, inadvertently smearing blood on his cheeks. We looked into each other's eyes, just like we had this morning, lying in bed. We were back in the apartment, safe, just lovingly looking at each other, smiling and kissing.

Gunshots drowned out my sobbing. All three molochs fell dead to the ground. I turned my gaze to see the shooter but all I could see was a vague figure. The tears in my eyes made it impossible to see who it was.

'Let me see.' A calm voice surrounded me. Caleb was by my side. A slight sense of control and relief spread in me. Caleb would know what to do. He would be able to help Ben while Jesper got here.

He bowed down towards Ben and sucked blood out of his wound, spat it out, and repeated the process.

My blood-covered hands trembled. My left arm had ballooned and taken on a fiery red colour. The veins had turned a deep purple, crawling visibly over the red skin.

Caleb took out a needle and inserted it into Ben's arm. 'Meerah, hold the bag up.'

The bag shook in my hand. Caleb inserted another needle into his neck and pressed the clear liquid in. The wound bubbled. Ben breathed a little better and I could feel the relief.

'Meerah' Caleb's voice called my name. 'It's only temporary. He needs Jesper's blood'

My relief disappeared instantly. 'He's coming. I told him to come. He's coming; he's... he's... yes.'

I tried to convince myself. Tears multiplied. It was not going to end this way. No. Please.

Caleb bandaged Ben's neck as well as he could. He then turned his attention to me but I pulled my wounded arm away from him.

'Help him first!' I mouthed, barely breathing. The poison had almost completely closed off my windpipe.

'I've done everything I can for him. I need to see to your bite or you will suffocate.' He reached again for my arm and pulled it to his mouth.

The moment his lips closed around the bite the pain shot through my body like an electric shock. Caleb sucked out blood and poison, spitting it out, just like he had done with Ben. I was starting to get dizzy. The poison burned. My heart pounded. Caleb continued working on my arm.

It was getting too hard to hold on. My upper body went limp and I fell backwards. A pair of arms grabbed hold of me, keeping me upright. I looked up but all I saw was a blond shadow.

My senses were numbed. I couldn't feel anything but terrible pain. My head was not attached to my body. I had no more oxygen in my system. My breathing became an automated process without any use. I sounded like an exhausted vacuum cleaner trying to cling to life. It was too much to try and breathe in more deeply. And before I knew it, I couldn't inhale anymore.

In a sudden spasm I came back to myself, gulping in as much air as I could. I looked around, disoriented. I was lying in a street. I had pain in my back and my arm. A shadow moved in front of me and I lay against something moving. All I heard was my desperate breathing and muffled voices. Slowly the voices got clearer. The shadows took shape. Caleb held my face and looked into my eyes. '...slowly... yes... take it... yes... relax...'

My throat was still swollen but I could breathe. Everything came back to me. The vampire, Ben... *Ben!*

'Calm down!' Caleb was somewhere to my right.

I struggled to get up and fell forward onto my hands. The shock triggered a stab of pain from my left underarm all the way up to my heart. I crawled towards the body lying too stiffly on the floor, ignoring all my pains.

'My love!' I gently tried to wake him up. 'Ben!' I shouted and he opened his eyes.

'Meeaaaa...' he whispered.

Caleb was by my side, gently trying to pull me away from him.

'No!' I freed myself from his grip. 'Where is Jesper?!' I shouted at Caleb. He didn't answer. 'Where is he?!' I screamed at him again.

Caleb carefully laid his hands on my shoulders. 'He's not here.'

I looked back at Ben. There was so much blood. His neck wound had soaked the bandages and his neck had swollen up. He was suffocating.

'I'm sorry,' Caleb whispered close to my ear.

No.

This wasn't happening.

NO!

I moved back over to Ben and held his hand. He tried weakly to squeeze back. Tears rolled silently over my face, dripping onto the cold hard ground. 'You will be ok, my love.'

I caressed his arm, looking into his beautiful green eyes. He tried to say something. I leant further down to him. His breathing was loud and shallow.

The realisation of what would inevitably happen overpowered me. But I refused to believe it. I pushed the thought away with all my willpower.

Ben tried to formulate words. He squeezed my hand lightly and pulled the edges of his mouth up into a discrete smile.

He exhaled.

His grip loosened.

His eyes lost focus.

His body went limp.

'No, no, no, no, no...' I could hear myself repeat. 'Ben! Come back!'

I turned to Caleb. 'BRING HIM BACK!'

'I can't,' Caleb stated motionless.

I looked at Ben's empty eyes staring into nothing. He was gone. He was quiet. It was over.

Ben...

He was...

He was gone…

MANIPULATIONS

I woke up in a bed. I opened my eyes. Everything rushed back to my consciousness. A scream pierced through my bruised throat. He was gone. He had been torn away from me.

Caleb hurried to my side.

I didn't want him there. He had not helped him! He could have kept him alive! He could have *saved* him!

I fought my way out of the bed and pushed Caleb away, falling onto the floor. 'DON'T!!!' I cried at him. 'Stay away!!'

Caleb followed me around the bed to the other side. I continued crawling away from him, trying to escape. He kneeled down and forced his arms around me. At first, I tried to free myself, but the sadness rendered me useless. I let myself go and gripped Caleb tightly. I screamed but my sorrow wouldn't mitigate. All I could do was cry and scream.

Days passed, weeks passed, months passed, I couldn't tell and I didn't care. The world could be collapsing outside, I didn't care. The one person I cared about the most, the one person who had loved me unconditionally, had been torn from me. All I felt was emptiness. I was lost without him. Nothing mattered anymore. Nothing. No one.

Caleb sat down next to me, quietly looking into my eyes. I could feel his warmth radiating, trying to ease my pain. Every day he spent hours sitting next to me, softly caressing my arms and hair, holding me, trying to comfort me. Sometimes we would talk but it would usually end in tears.

* * *

'Meerah, you should go outside, get some air.' Caleb's voice took me out of my eternally destructive thought spiral.

I turned my head towards him in the doorframe and blinked. How much time had passed? Caleb helped me out of bed. As I left the room I had nested in, the sudden light blinded me.

The sun was low in the sky and shone directly at me. How long had it been since I had last seen the sun?

Caleb put a jacket over my shoulders and led me outside. I breathed in but no fresh air entered my lungs. He took my hand and we started walking. Wherever he took me, I didn't care.

I looked around but didn't really see anything. All I was aware of was the gentle heat emanating from Caleb's hand. The layer of snow on the ground was crusty and a few days old. It was warmer than I had expected. Or was that just in my mind?

I would have preferred a grey sky to the blue one. I still had over half a century left... I let out a snort. This hellhole knew exactly how to break you. It was playing with all our lives. We were at the mercy of this world and the council.

Caleb turned towards me. My blank expression didn't seem to satisfy his frown. He led me to a bench and sat me down next to him.

'Ameerah, my sweet child,' his intoxicatingly sweet voice lulled to me, 'I can only imagine your pain. I wish I could have saved him.' I stared at him with empty eyes. 'I will do everything I can to help you-'

'What do you mean?' I asked aggressively.

He sighed and reached for my hand. His warmth calmed me. 'I have safe-guarded you for the past few weeks, but the council is demanding a hearing with you. They want you to explain the circumstances that resulted in Ben's-'

The moment he had uttered his name I could feel my heart bursting into pieces all over again. I tried to hold in my tears, unsuccessfully. A fresh wave of warmth came from his hand, radiating through my body. 'When is the hearing?' I asked.

'In a few days.'

I breathed in deeply. 'I... I will... I can do it'

'There is something else you should know.' Caleb was visibly uncomfortable. I waited for him to spit out whatever he was afraid of saying. 'You have been accused of... dragging him down a path of revenge...'

'Who? Who is saying that?'

Caleb closed his eyes. 'His master. Jesper,' he whispered.

The anger manifested in an instant. 'How dare he?!' I jumped up and screamed. '**HE** was the one who didn't show up! **HE** let his trainer **die** and now he wants to pin this on me?!'

'Calm down,' Caleb said half-heartedly.

'I will not calm down! *HE* left him to **die**! He's **gone** because of him! JESPER killed his recruit *and* his trainer! I told you! **I told you** to take care of him! Look at what you *did-*'

Caleb's eyes stood out against his dark skin. 'Stop it!' His words were my command. 'I told you it was very complicated to get a master removed. I told you I would try and find a way, but Ben *rushed* into a situation without *thinking-*'

My lips trembled. I couldn't listen any longer. My love had done nothing wrong. He would have been fine; he could have lived...

I hid my face in my hands and sobbed.

'I'm sorry.' Caleb placed his hands on mine and gently pulled them away from my face. He looked into my eyes trying to appease my sorrow.

'I need some space,' I mumbled.

'Meerah, that's not a good idea'

'Please, Caleb. Please don't... force me. Let me-' I broke in tears.

I turned from Caleb and walked away. I just wanted to be alone with my pain. Caleb would only try to make it go away. All I had left of Ben was my pain, my pain and my memories. This shithole had taken him away from me!

Soon the sun disappeared behind the clouds and the sky formed a black curtain over the world. The temperature dropped. I pulled the jacket closer around my body and kept walking decisively nowhere.

'I didn't ask for this!' I screamed out into the world. 'How dare you take him away from me?! Why? WHY! **WHY**???

Tell me **WHY**??!! Fuck you! FUCK YOU!' I pointed at the black sky.

No response. I broke down, letting myself fall to the ground whimpering alone in the darkness.

A sound caught my attention.

I paused for a moment. Another sound. I raised myself up. A hiss.

I couldn't believe it! Those fuckers were here, *again!*

Blinded with fury I ran towards the noises. I found them draining a human corpse. They bared their teeth at me. In return, I screamed at the disgusting creatures. Two jumped towards me; one had a darker skin, the other one was missing an eye. I punched the darker skinned one in mid-air, while the other one got a hold of my arm.

I grabbed the one-eyed thing by the back of the head, pulled it away from my arm and swung it violently into the wall next to me. It slid to the ground.

The other came right for my face. I reached for it while it flew towards me and got hold of its throat and squeezed. The beast clawed at me but only managed to scratch my arms. Tears blurred my vision in the dark. I pressed as hard as I could until there was a crack and I broke its neck. My fingers were covered in moloch blood.

The remaining one-eyed moloch moved closer. Without hesitation I jumped on it, bringing my fists down in rage. I burst its jaw open. A sob escaped my throat.

You killed him; *you* monsters did this to him!

I continued to drive my fists into the beast, blood splattering all over. Organs burst and more blood seeped out. I got up and looked at the damage I had done. The moloch was beyond recognisable.

Unsatisfied, I turned back to the other moloch I had killed.

How simple. They were gone. Just like he was. I screamed at the dead corpse. No response.

I kicked the thing, again, and again. I lifted the corpse by its arm and swung it against the building, letting it smack against the bricks. The bones cracked. I couldn't stop. I kept banging the corpse against the wall, until the wall was covered in red.

Out of breath and tired, I let the corpse go. It dropped to the floor and landed in the once white snow.

It hadn't helped. It hadn't changed a thing. He was still gone. I was still alone, now covered in moloch blood. My clothes were soaked. My arms dripped with the red poison.

My eyes fell onto the human further back. His eyes were open, one of his legs broken and twisted back at a horrible angle. There were bite marks everywhere.

I kneeled down next to the body, looking at its empty eyes. They were filled with so much fear.

Why were there monsters in this world? Why did I have to be here? Why did I have to lose him? Why did we have to run into Viktor?

Silent tears rolled down my cheeks. I reached over and gently closed his eyes, leaving two dots of red blood on his lids. He looked more peaceful now. I realigned his leg and positioned his arms down by his side, angling the underarms upwards and placing his hands together over his chest.

'I'm sorry,' I whispered. 'I'm so sorry you died.' Everywhere I touched the human I left traces of moloch blood.

I walked alone in the night for hours. Somehow, I found my way to Caleb's place. I only knew it was his place because the light was on inside and I could see him looking out onto the street.

I walked the gravel pathway up to his house. Caleb stood in the entrance and looked at me, worried.

'What?' I said tonelessly and exhausted.

'You're covered in blood.' He gestured in my direction; his eyes wide open.

I looked down at myself. Sure enough, I was covered in blood. I shrugged and dragged my feet into the house and into the bathroom, leaving a trail of wet snow and blood behind me.

In the shower I watched the blood wash off my body and disappear down the drain. All traces of my anger slowly dissolved in the water, as if nothing had happened. My skin was free of any evidence.

* * *

I eyed the creatures floating towards the podium. Here we go again.

'Explain to us the circumstances leading up to the death of the trainer named Ben,' I heard in my head.

It was cold in the hall. I felt small and insignificant looking up at the motionless creatures in front of me, behind the table lifted up on the stage.

'I was with him on my way to a raid when we both felt the vampire was near. We decided to go after it. But… were surprised… another one showed up…'

I had pushed all emotions far away from my conscience. I was telling a story that had happened to someone else, a tale from a distant land.

'Where was the location of your raid with the trainer named Ben?' they questioned.

I breathed in deeply. 'I don't know. Ben was the one who planned it. I was just his back-up,' I stated.

'Do you know the name of the two vampires you killed?'
'No,' I lied.

'One of the vampires was named Jason. Have you heard that name before?'

'I don't remember,' I answered.

'Do not attempt to fool us, recruit!'

'I do remember the name Jason from my previous hearing, yes,' I admitted.

'Do you know of the personal connection the trainer named Ben had with the vampire named Jason?'

'I assume it had something to do with his recruit's death, but I don't know anything concrete about this. I've only heard rumours,' I lied again.

'Accusations have been made against you by Ben's trainer named Jesper about your relationship with Ben. He accuses you of having dragged him down a path of self-destruction and vengeance that ultimately led to his death. Do you concur?'

I looked straight ahead without blinking. 'I don't know how Jesper could come up with such a theory. I was in a relationship with Ben, but he did not talk to me about what happened to his recruit. I assume something happened involving vampires, but I don't know who might have been part of it. I couldn't have 'dragged him down' because I don't know anything. It's unfortunate Jesper feels this way, but I bear him no ill will. It must be hard for him losing his trainer.'

I was so far away from the situation it was almost as if I was outside my body, looking down at myself in my hearing. I didn't care about the outcome. I had no feelings about it or any of the people involved. It was all unimportant.

'We find it hard to believe the trainer named Ben did not share any information about his past with you.'

'He did share some things with me, but Ben was a quiet man who didn't like to talk about himself. You must know this from the times you spoke with him. If he didn't feel comfortable sharing things with me, I did not push him to do so.'

'You seem composed for someone who lost their partner in a vampire attack,' they remarked, leaning towards me.

I blinked and took my time before answering. 'I'm not composed,' I started and took a deep breath, 'I'm devastated. I feel powerless. He was a great man. And I am... deeply saddened he was taken from me.'

I had a strange feeling when speaking about him. I knew there was darkness that surrounded my heart. But it felt like my emotions were far away from me, like I was looking at them from the other side of the river and there was no bridge to connect my mind to my emotions. I knew they were there, but I couldn't *feel* them.

'Do you believe you did everything in your power to assist in the survival of the trainer named Ben?'

I looked at them. 'Yes. I was the one who called Jesper,' I added. They needed to know he had been involved. It was important to me they knew that. Why it was so important to me? I didn't know.

'Do you believe the master named Jesper did everything he could to assist in the survival of the trainer named Ben?' they continued.

I tilted my head. I knew what I wanted to say, but the words failed me. 'It is not up to me to pass judgment on Jesper.'

'Answer the question,' they said louder.

'I will not answer. It is your task to judge the actions of Jesper, not mine.'

The creatures simultaneously leant back.

A few minutes of silence passed. My eyes swung from one end of the table to the other. The creatures didn't move an inch. Like corpses.

'You are free to go,' they finally conceded.

Slowly, I turned towards the door and approached it. The hall was void of all sounds except for the clicking of my heels on the stone floor. The door creaked open and a beam of light entered the hall. I walked into the light, the wooden door swinging closed behind me. I continued down the marble hall towards the exit.

The exit door was wide open, letting in light from the sun. I stepped outside and stopped for a moment; my eyes were blinded by the sudden light. My feet carried me to my Volvo. Once inside I closed my eyes and breathed in deeply. Another day had almost passed. One day closer to seeing my family again. One day closer to leaving everything behind me.

I turned the key in the ignition and sped off down the usual route towards the one place where I could forget my troubles. With a brisk pace, I crossed the parking lot, through one door, then the next and steered towards the bar. I grabbed a whisky bottle and downed four shots in thirty seconds. Nothing changed. I downed another four and waited.

Slowly my mind numbed. Clutching the whisky bottle in one hand and the shot glass in the other, I poured myself several more shots. It wasn't long before I was drunk. The bar was filling up with cheerful and happy people. The noise annoyed me. I left.

The next best medicine involved demons. I drove to the nearest hideout but didn't have any luck. The next was also a bust. But the third one, yes, the third one was a success. With my trusted handgun by my side I walked in, shooting any moloch I could see. The dark cave fell silent except for the ringing of the gun shots that echoed in my ears. I used my phone to light up the corners. Nothing but moloch corpses.

I turned around, ready to head out, when I saw one lying by my feet. I kneeled down to it. A trail of blood trickled from its abdomen. Its head was twisted backwards at an angle that assured me its neck was broken. Its jaw was wide open; hair covered its face.

I could feel the temptation. I remembered the high I had felt when I first drank moloch blood. It was so close. Hesitantly I reached with my right index finger into the thick red liquid. I brought the finger up to my nose; there was a hint of copper. Just one taste. Who cared anyway?

I leant my head backwards and lifted the finger above my mouth and stuck out my tongue. A drop of blood fell from my finger down onto my tongue.

Like honey to a bear I couldn't resist. I plunged my finger inside my mouth and licked the red liquid off it. I dipped my index and middle finger back in the gaping hole in the monster's torso and repeated the process.

Memories of my hearing from earlier flashed back into my conscience, more and more numerously, more intensely. However, this time I was no longer detached from my feelings. The bridge had formed between my mind and my feelings.

'Come back to me,' I whispered. No answer.

Tears left my eyes and dripped onto the dead moloch by my feet. This was worse than hell. There was no escaping this! My eyes opened.

Yes, there was.

I dipped my hand into the blood and licked my fingers eagerly. The euphoria mixed with my tears and pain. The sorrow overpowered the ecstasy quickly. All I cared about was numbing the anguish I was in, but the moloch didn't have enough blood in him. And I didn't want to dig too deep into the body. Though the red velvet was my absolution, I was not about to rip open a moloch and lick off all the insides. I could get another one.

I jumped up and ran outside. Where were they? Where had they gone?

My head was spinning from the sudden movement. The alcohol still coursed through my system. I tumbled along the tall brick wall. Come on, you little fucks!

I turned a corner but nothing, only an empty street filled with parked cars. The yellow streetlight created pockets of light in the dark. A breeze picked up and a gust of wind periodically pulled at my clothes, messing up my hair.

My search continued. I had to find them. I was not done. Come on, show yourself! I wobbled further along a bend, but the streets were deserted. The houses were all dark, the humans sleeping peacefully inside. Or so I assumed. The humans were all safely on the other side of the curtain while I was here patrolling and keeping them safe.

Too quickly my thoughts became as sombre as the night. My heartbreak slowed me down. I began to sob. What would I do without him? Life was pointless without him. Where was he? Why? Why did he have to be taken away from me? Why did he go after that shitty vampire? Why did he have to…- Why?!

I broke down crying. I had not tasted enough of the red drug and grief was taking over. I sank down along the wall onto the cold ground. There was a hole in my heart, a big empty hole that would never be filled again.

I pulled my legs towards me and crossed my arms over my knees, burying my face into my cocoon. Someone please come and kill me. Someone please come and release me from my pain.

No one came. No one would help me.

I pulled my head up and stared down the alley. The tall buildings encircled me. What was I still doing here? What was the point of it all? Why? Why did I have to endure this any longer?

It had to end.

I couldn't bear it anymore.

I raised myself up and looked at the gun in my hand. It would be the easiest way out. Blake had said I couldn't kill myself but maybe it was a lie. It was too unbearable to stay in this misery, alone. Without him.

Seeing no other way out, I put the gun to my temple. I closed my eyes, sobbing uncontrollably. Please lord, let me go. Let me join him in heaven.

I was doing it. Yes, I was doing it. This was it. I inhaled deeply and steadied myself.

'No!'

Someone interrupted my beautiful moment! I opened my eyes and saw a figure running towards me. The shadow took shape and I recognised Blake.

Oh for fuck's sake!

'What are you doing here?!' I screamed at him, the gun still on my temple.

'Don't do it, Meerah, don't pull the trigger!' he pleaded, approaching me carefully. Blake stopped a few steps in front of me.

'Why? I can't kill myself anyway! Or was that a lie??' I barked at him, tears smearing across my face.

'You can't kill yourself, but there is a difference between pointing the gun at yourself and actually pulling the trigger! Please, Meerah, it must be so hard for you, but this isn't the solution! If you pull the trigger and realise it didn't solve your problems, it will be so much worse! Please, I'm begging you, put the gun down!'

Blake lifted his arms, palms stretched out towards the gun.

'No!' I screamed and backed away until I hit the wall behind me. There was no escape. 'Please,' I begged the gods. No answer. I let out a desperate scream. The gun trembled in my hand. I closed my eyes, trying to convince myself to do it.

Maybe he was lying.

'He wouldn't have wanted you to do it,' Blake whispered.

'Don't speak of him!' I shouted. No one could ever mention him again. It was too painful.

'You know I'm right,' he continued.

Damn.

I couldn't.

No, I didn't want to be here.

Let me go!

'Please, Meerah.' Blake inched his way closer.

The gun trembled in my hand.

Blake approached, his hands so close to the gun.

'Give me the gun, please,' he whispered. His hands closed around the gun. The sobs shook through me.

I wanted to.

I wanted it all to end.

But he was right. Ben wouldn't have wanted me to pull the trigger.

Images of his empty eyes staring at me invaded my mind.

I let go of the gun. Blake secured it and stashed it away before I had time to change my mind. I broke down in pain and slid back down the wall and onto the cold concrete. No escape from this hellhole. No salvation, no mercy.

Blake kneeled across from me and placed his arms around me.

I woke up with the sunrise. The house was silent, dead silent. All I could hear was my own breathing and the ticking of a clock somewhere. Sadness washed over me, but no tears reached my eyes. What would I do with myself now? Could I just pick up where I had left off? Go back to training and killing monsters as if nothing had happened?

A strange sense overcame me. A sensation that was familiar, but I couldn't remember where or when I had experienced it. I was sad about the loss I had suffered, but I was unable to feel my pain. I knew I felt sorrow and I was broken. But I was unable to connect to my emotions. Like a robot I understood the concept of loss and I knew I was suffering, but I couldn't... *feel* it.

I got out of the bed. The sunrays accompanied me into the kitchen, where I turned on the dusty coffee machine. Moments later the boiling water dripped into the pot with the black essence in it. The growling and ticking of the machine gave me a sense of normalcy. I always had a cup of coffee in the morning. Maybe if I had one every day, at some point it would start tasting of something again.

Caleb was still sleeping. I walked back to my room. It stank of sweat and stuffiness. The sheets were still moist from tortured dreams and tears. I had spent too much time in here. My five minutes mourning were over. I had to get back to it. There was no grievance leave for ghosts. There was no tolerance for human emotion in this world. But then again, we weren't humans anymore...

I picked up my phone and saw a myriad of missed calls and messages. I didn't want to read them. I deleted them all. They would all be messages of sympathy and about how they felt my pain, as if anyone knew what I was feeling!

What *was* I feeling? It was strange. Like wearing tight clothes after having just been in the sea and I could feel the sand and the salt rubbing between my skin and my clothes. I couldn't assimilate with my pain; there was a layer of salt and sand between my pain and my mind.

The only person I wanted to see was Kim. Even if she would try to make me feel better, she was the only one who would be able to talk about anything else, and I certainly didn't want to talk about *it*. There was nothing to talk about! He was gone! Nothing could be done, reversed, changed. The thought of people trying to empathise angered me. How dare someone say they knew what I felt?!

I texted Kim I wanted to see her tonight.

Someone came through the front door. I walked out of my room and looked out. Blake made his way into the living room of Caleb's house.

'What are you doing here?' I asked him, aware of what had happened last night. A peak of shame washed over me but anger quickly replaced it. I crossed my arms over my chest and leant on the doorframe.

'I wanted to check on you,' he answered quietly.

Of course you did.

Blake sat down on the sofa and I made myself walk over and sit on the armchair across from him.

My brain was thinking surprisingly clearly. 'What were you doing last night?' I asked him point-blank. Blake didn't answer.

'Were you following me?' I pushed. He looked at me but still didn't answer.

Of course he was. I shook my head in disbelief. 'Why?'

Blake sighed. 'Because I was worried about you.'

'And you wanted to make sure I wasn't going to do anything stupid?' He just couldn't help himself, could he?

'Lucky I did.' The words slipped out of his mouth. It pissed me off to hear them and I could tell it annoyed him to have said them.

'I couldn't harm myself.'

Now Blake shook his head. 'You still intended to pull the trigger!'

He shifted closer to the edge of the sofa, closer to me. 'I can't imagine the pain-'

'Don't!' I shouted. Silence followed.

'I just want to make sure you are ok,' Blake tried again.

'I'm not. And I won't *ever* be.' I got up from the armchair. 'Stop following me.'

'Ameerah' He got up as well and came up behind me. I turned to him and waited for him to speak.

'I want to us to get along. I want you to trust me again.' Blake's usually fiery blue eyes were a soft ocean blue. His voice was calm and pleading.

I looked into his eyes. He seemed genuine. The cold-hearted trainer was gone. A strand of his blond hair had fallen down onto his forehead, softening his hard features. He meant well, but I needed him to give me space.

'Let me grieve', I whispered. I turned away again and walked into the bathroom. I locked the door and could feel the familiar sensation of tears welling up.

Would I have to limit my conversations to ten minutes before the sorrow was too much and the tears would make me break down again? How could I wish my sorrow away when it was the only thing I had left of him?

I closed my eyes, but there he was again, smiling at me. The beautiful memory was destroyed, replaced with his dead face staring at me. I tried to shake the image out of my head; it was burnt into my brain.

After a day of tidying up my room, I had managed to push all my memories of him into a dark corner. Caleb's magic alleviated some of the torture. I did my best to live with the rest.

Later on, I met up with Kim at Santa's pub. The pub was almost empty. Those who were present sat quietly in their corners, either speaking in low voices or not speaking at all. I preferred this atmosphere to a cheerful crowd.

Kim took me into her arms and wouldn't let go. She must have gotten stronger. Her embrace was bone-crushing. Only a few moments sufficed and I could feel the tears rising, so I pushed her away. 'I don't want to cry again,' I whimpered before the moisture in my eyes dissipated.

'I'm so sorry, about what happened. I wish I had been there…'

'There is nothing you could have done,' I responded absently. The image of Ben dying in my arms reappeared. I blinked quickly and changed the subject. 'Please tell me about you, distract me,' I pleaded.

Kim told me about how Dominic had been making her train hard and giving her assignments on end. It had however paid off; since she and Dominic had killed an exceptionally high number of molochs over the past few months, they had shortened both their sentences by one year.

I could see the fatigue in her eyes. Her usually voluptuous black hair was dull and straw-like, her skin had taken on a slight yellow tone, but her movements were faster. Though her eyes flicked around the bar to capture all possible threats, the bags under them revealed her tiredness. She was not watchful; she was restless.

'And what about June?' I asked.

Kim smiled and her cheeks reddened. 'Yeah, she is… yeah, just really nice and so sweet and kind…'

You could clearly see on her face she was in love. Seeing her happy reminded me too much of him. 'So when are we having another girl's night with face masks?'

'Oh great idea! How about tomorrow? I can come to you,' she suggested.

'I live at Caleb's place at the moment. I don't know how he will feel about it. I would prefer your place to be honest. Blake keeps following me and wanting to 'check up on me', so if I can avoid him as well that will be great. All this tip-toeing around me is starting to get on my nerves.'

'No problem. I can get rid of Dom easily. He'll love the opportunity to go out drinking and chasing women. Actually, no; I will tell him to go kill some molochs! Maybe they'll take another year off our sentences!'

'They might have shortened your sentence but the way you're looking you might not last until the end if you keep this going.' I realised this hellhole would probably break us on many levels, not only physically.

'I know, it's not good for me. I need to have more time to relax, have you over or June.' A smile played on her lips.

I tried to mirror her smile, but mine was tainted with sadness. My mind was back with Ben.

Kim reached for my arm and stroked it. 'You should take up a hobby.'

I frowned. 'A hobby?'

Kim nodded in enthusiasm. 'Yes! You should have one, yes! Can be anything! Sport, or arts, anything really!' She finished her drink and prepared us a new one. 'Right, so, what do you like doing or are you good at?'

'Hmm… Let me think'

'What did you do when you were human?'

'I walked my dog Bruce a lot. I liked to read.'

'Maybe you should start there and see where it leads?' Her eyes sparkled.

'Alright fine!' I caved and she gave me a kiss on the cheek.

Later that night, I made it home to Caleb's, but couldn't make myself go into the house. I turned off the engine and just sat in front of his house in the darkness. I had been used to going home to Ben's and mine, and now I slept in someone else's house.

I decided to go for a walk. I got out of the car, fiercely wiping the remaining tears from my face. I tried to distract myself by thinking of how I would get back in the game. My feet carried me to the river.

I imagined being back in France, walking Bruce, feeling the wind through my short hair, worrying about little things like studies...

The night comforted me. So did the slow-moving river. I breathed in the scentless air and lay my elbows on the metal barriers alongside it. My thoughts unfurled and questioned my very existence. Everything had gotten worse since that night I died and came here. Could it get even worse? It was difficult to imagine anything that could make the situation worse, but I trusted this universe to deliver it to my doorstep in the very near future.

I wiped the fresh tears from my face and turned around to head back to Caleb's house.

A snarling. Very close. I froze. It had to be one. I ran towards the sound furiously, forgetting everything else around me. My rage blinded me.

And sure enough, there it was. The moloch was hovering over a fresh kill, eagerly emptying the human of his blood. I reached for my gun, but all I could feel was my hip. I had left it in the car! No, it would not get away this easily!

I approached the creature swiftly and quietly. It was too focused on its prey to notice me. Instinctually, I reached for its neck. The thing immediately thrashed around and tried to get a hold of my arms. In one quick movement, I twisted the neck and felt a snap. The limbs stopped moving, leaving the creature dangling from my hands. I removed my fingers from its neck, letting it fall to the ground.

As I had done too many times, I rearranged the human into a peaceful position and closed her eyes. My attention now turned to the moloch. I knew there was blood in its system. But the kill was so recent. It was probably undigested and still human blood...

No, no, I couldn't, no. As much as I liked the feeling it gave me, as much as I needed it, I would not resort to drinking human blood. I might as well just take it directly from the dead human! My eyes darted over to the body. No, no, I couldn't.

With those last thoughts I turned my back on the two dead bodies and walked determinedly back the way I had come from.

ADDITION TO THE FAMILY

I threw out all of my old things and got new furniture and decorations for my room back at Blake's. I got a bigger bed with cushions randomly thrown upon it, a big cupboard for all my clothes, and a dreamcatcher to hang above my door. I draped large pieces of orange fabric across the ceiling to make it look like I was in a tent in the Middle East. I added feathers to my hair and got several piercings in my ears.

After having recovered for a few weeks at Caleb's house, I had moved back in with Blake. Ben's place would be too painful; I had not been back since he had died. Caleb didn't want me staying at his place for fear I would be too strongly affected by our master-protégé bond, so I moved back to the only place I could go to. I had asked if I could live with Kim but they had argued that in my fragile state it was not wise. Dominic seemed to think I was a bad influence on her, and I didn't want to push my luck. We still had decades to go in this horrible world, at some point we would be allowed to move in together. For now, I simply didn't have the energy to fight over this.

I walked out of my room and into the living room. Blake was carefully cleaning his many weapons. 'What are we doing tonight?' I asked sitting down on his chair.

Blake looked up from the machine gun he had in his hand. 'You want to raid a nest?'

'If you let me go to the pub afterwards...?'

He rolled his eyes but nodded with a smile. I grabbed my book and made myself comfortable. Since moving back in with Blake I had taken up reading again, particularly fantasy books. It occupied my mind and gave me an escape from this horrible world I was trapped in.

The memories of him had dulled during the day... but they still haunted me at night.

Before going out to kill the molochs, Blake had some errands to run. I decided to go for a run while he was away. The sun was still up and the air crisp. The snow had been cleared off the main streets. About halfway into my jog, I came to think of Caleb. He had asked me to stop by when I had time to speak. I turned down a street, off my usual route, and headed for his house. It was not far.

I was not supposed to know where my master lived; Blake had explained this in the very beginning. But Ben dying had not been part of the big plan. Caleb and Blake had insisted I wasn't allowed to seek my master out and was only granted permission to come over if explicitly told so by either of them. His sway over me was still as powerful as the first time I met him.

I slowed to a walk when I arrived in front of his house. My shoes crunched under the partially snowy gravel pathway leading up to his house. The pathway curved and I looked into Caleb's living room through the window right next to his front door. There was someone inside. I slowed down and squinted to get a better look. Caleb was there, heavily gesticulating. Muffled sounds were audible through the window. The other person was standing just behind the window and I could only see his side. He was gesticulating just as much.

I couldn't make out what they said but it was clear they were having an argument. Caleb disappeared from in front of the window and the other person approached the window. He threw his hands in the air and turned around. I ducked down immediately and hid behind the bushes. Something told me I shouldn't be seeing what was going on.

After a few seconds I risked a peek and saw the man had his arms crossed over his chest, looking out onto the street. His eyes scanned the road, almost nervously. He had a mess of big curly dark hair on his head that contrasted with his thin figure. His shirt was clearly too big for him, making him look even smaller. The man turned away from the window and I immediately crawled away, below the window frame. I couldn't run back out to the street. I risked Caleb seeing me and I was not about to get caught doing dumb stuff again.

My phone vibrated at my hip, making me jump. Luckily, I had reached the corner of the house, out of Caleb's sight. Why did people always have the worst timing?

'Hello?' I whispered.

'Where are you? I thought you wanted to kill molochs?' Blake asked.

I held the phone against my chest and peeked around the corner. The front door opened. I snuck along the edge of the house towards the garden and hid there, away from Caleb and the other man.

'I am out on a run. I'm heading home now,' I whispered into the mobile phone, trying to sound out of breath.

'Ok, but don't be too long.' Blake hung up.

I pushed my phone back into my pocket. The man with the curly hair was walking swiftly away from Caleb's house. Caleb was probably still inside. I couldn't stay here, or he might sense my presence. I climbed the cold fence to the adjacent house and ran across the lawn, hiding behind the next fence. Carefully, I approached the street, on the look-out for the mysterious man, but he was nowhere to be seen. I jumped out into the street and jogged home, a little faster than usual.

'How long did you go?' Blake asked, arming himself. I had come home and just finished a quick shower.

'The usual loop. I stopped by the river for a bit and lost track of time.' I was still too good at lying.

Blake nodded. 'Ok, fine. Are you ready?'

'One minute.' I went into my room and reached into the drawer where I kept my 'combat' clothes. A minute later I came out wearing a tight black sweater and skinny jeans, topped by a sleeveless jacket. I swung the belt around my waist, where I holstered some of my guns. It clicked in the front and I strapped a machine gun around my chest.

Blake looked at me, smiling. 'You've come a long way.'

I smiled back at him and followed him out the door. We tried our best to get along and so far, we had not been fighting. He let me go out and do my thing and I obeyed him in all matters relating to molochs or vampires.

We were in the car when Blake got a call. 'Caleb I'm in the car with Ameerah,' he announced when he picked up the phone.

I had gotten used to them discussing things I was not privy to. I had learned how to pick up on stuff without them noticing, so not much was a secret.

'Really? What did he have to say?' I heard Blake ask.

I texted Kim to meet me later at Santa's pub.

'Do you believe him?' Blake asked.

I brushed my fingers through my wet hair and pulled them into a ponytail, securing my feathers with bobby pins. It might look cool on TV but fighting while your hair whips in your face, blinding you, is not ideal.

'Can you go to the council?' Blake continued.

My eyes followed the passing landscape. It was dark now and the switch between the night sky and the lights in the buildings composed the outside world. The snow was thick and winter was in full swing. It was cold and often stormy.

'Can I call you back later? We're about to pull up.' Blake made a turn and I could see movement in front of us. My senses spiked. I inhaled deeply. Yes, they are here. I pulled a beanie over my hair.

He hung up and stopped the car. 'Ready?' He turned towards me.

I nodded and climbed out of the rusty old truck.

We jumped right into exterminating the molochs. Several molochs escaped by climbing over the lower wall to my left. I swung my machine gun onto my back and ran straight towards the wall. I leaped and climbed up the wall. Sitting atop the wall I shot a few of the fleeing beasts. Still, two escaped around a corner to my left.

Running down the alley and around the corner I followed my instincts through the labyrinth of narrow pathways between the buildings. Soon I picked up on their scent and ran after them. Swinging my machine gun forward I was ready for them. The sound of rapid gunfire was amplified in front of me. The molochs came running back in my direction and I shot them before they had time to escape.

I stopped and looked around. It was deadly silent after the banging and crackling of gunshots. I approached the two dead molochs. A pool of blood spread from one of them. I could feel my desire to drink it. My last encounter with a bleeding moloch was weeks ago and I had not felt tempted, until now.

It was so close. I bent down, eyeing the blood. Self-conscious, I looked around again, but no one was there. I could hear the sounds of gunshots further away. I dipped one of my fingers into the blood and brought it up to my nose. The smell was intoxicating. Without hesitating I inserted the blood-covered finger into my mouth. The anticipation made me smile; in a few moments I would feel the effect.

'Ameerah?' I heard someone say close-by. I jumped up and hurried towards the voice. No one saw me. What was I worried about? It was nothing! No one had said anything to me about *not* drinking moloch blood. It just relieved my pain every now and again. There couldn't be any harm in that!

Don't fool yourself, a voice in my head whispered.

Go away!

I joined Blake in a courtyard between some houses. 'I'm here.'

'How many did you kill?' he asked.

'Five, I think.'

'Good,' he responded. We walked back towards the car.

'Meerah, I have to tell you something,' Blake started once we were in the car.

'What?' I asked, untroubled.

'Caleb was called to the council.' My head turned to him, panic in my eyes. 'He's fine, don't worry.' A wave of relief washed through me, but not for long. 'Caleb had to take on another recruit.'

'A new recruit?! What about me?' I squealed.

Blake turned towards me. 'Her trainer and master were both killed. She was supposed to go to someone else, but the council decided to give her to Caleb. They said that since you are field approved, you don't need your master as much and you've been here more than three years, so you don't need me so much anymore either. They decided to give her to us.'

'So… so Caleb is now her master and you're- you're her trainer now?! What about me! That's not fair! Ben just-' I had to stop. I buried my face in my hands. No, I wasn't going to cry. Don't think of him now.

'You will still remain Caleb's protégé. I know it's not the best of timing, but Caleb thinks it would be good for you to have someone you can watch out for. And, you know, I will be spending some time training her so you will have more time to see Kim.'

I didn't like the idea of sharing Caleb. Would it diminish my connection with him? Would he not love me anymore? I didn't like this.

'I want to speak to Caleb.' I sounded like a stressed child.

'I thought so. He'll be at our house when we get back.' Blake turned the ignition. 'Meerah, he didn't decide this. The council told him, and he couldn't refuse…'

I didn't care! Caleb was mine! My master. My family! How could there be someone else now? What if she was better? What if she was training harder? Where would I go then?

I hated this hellhole.

Before my anger unravelled completely, a sentiment of calmness replaced it. A strange sense of ease. It was the moloch blood. It wasn't enough to make me euphoric, but just enough to mellow my mood. It felt like I had drunk two glasses of wine and was enjoying the slight tipsiness. Everything would work out.

The effect wore off by the time we reached Blake's house. In a way it was better this way. I didn't want Caleb to sense anything peculiar. I'm sure it was alright, but I didn't want to risk feeling the immense guilt when I let him down. It was just like smoking! I did it every now and again but hid it from Caleb and Blake. If they knew they would annoy me about how unhealthy it was.

As soon as I opened the door to the apartment, I sensed him. I rushed out of my snow-covered boots and hurried up the stairs.

'My child!' he greeted me with open arms. We hugged and the electricity between us sparked. I felt so much better, so much more relaxed. 'Do not trouble yourself, my dear. You will always be my protégé and I will take care of you. I just have to take care of Holly as well now.'

I felt an immediate sting of jealousy.

'My dear, you cannot be selfish. Imagine, she has no one left anymore. She is all alone. Wouldn't you want to protect her?' He held my hand and amplified his plea through his touch.

Of course I wanted to help her, I found myself thinking.

'She needs our help, *your* help,' Caleb continued.

And I wanted to help her! Yes! I had to protect her and take her under my wing!

'Ok I will do what you say,' I agreed, surrounded by peace.

Caleb let go of my hands and I slipped out of my cloud, back into reality. 'My child, go have fun with Kim now. Enjoy your night.' His row of perfectly white teeth shone as he smiled. The warmth spread in my body.

Soon afterwards, I joined Kim at Santa's pub. It was a busy night, lots of drunk people dancing and singing, the air was stuffy and the temperature high. Kim was playing pool with some guy. Dominic was sitting in a corner with another person. I turned my attention to Kim. She was in an excellent mood while her opponent's expression was bleak. A few people were watching them. Kim was quite the entertainer. Every time she holed a ball, she would do a little dance and swing the pool stick wildly around, missing the spectators by a hair but no one seemed to mind.

My troubles dissipated as I watched them finish an intense round of pool. Maybe it would all fall back into place. Maybe this Holly girl was nice. Maybe my grief would lighten up enough for me to finish the remaining sixty-four years here without trying to kill myself again...

I chuckled at my naiveté.

Kim sunk the last ball and a thunder of cheer and laughter followed. Her opponent disappeared fairly quickly and was nowhere to be seen for the remainder of the night. After receiving the admiration of the crowd, Kim joined me at the bar. Her hair was so long the ends curled onto the bar top. Those big brown eyes of hers rested on me.

'How have you been?' she asked, with an underlying worried tone.

'I... don't...,' I responded. 'I'm trying to concentrate on other things.'

Ben was constantly on my mind. Everything reminded me of him. Out of the corner of my eye I could see the place where I had met him for the first time.

'I understand, but you know I'm here for you... if you want to talk...' she said carefully.

'Caleb is taking on another protégé.' I jumped as far away from Ben as I could.

'Really? Why? What about you?'

'Holly... something. Caleb said she needs our help and she has no one. I think Blake said her master and trainer were both killed. But I don't like it. I don't know her! And now I have to share Caleb?!' I could feel my jealousy stirring.

'That's really rare. I've heard of it happening, but I don't know anyone who had to share their master. I mean, will she have the same connection with Caleb as you? He didn't choose her in the human world. She is from someone else! I don't know...' Her eyes were staring at the air and her thoughts far away.

'I just hope she is nice and I'll get along with her. With Blake it's already difficult. I don't need another one like him.'

'But you said things were better now?' Kim countered. Her head tilted slightly, her hair playing with her arm.

'Yes, but it's always kind of like this. We fight like cats and dogs until we have an explosive blowout, then we avoid each other, and slowly get used to each other again. Everything is calm but then it starts again. We are so different and he... he just rubs me the wrong way!' I wriggled my shoulders.

'Don't make any assumptions. Maybe this Holly person is more like you and then there will be two of you against one of him.' Kim tried to comfort me, caressing my arm.

'Or she will be like him and then it's two of him and one of me,' I countered. Until I met her, I wouldn't know. She could be great, or a disaster. It stressed me not to know what she was like. I didn't like that she was suddenly entering my life without me having a vote. What if she was hungry for Caleb's approval and would do anything to make me look bad until he ousted me? What then?

Kim pulled me out of my negative train of thought before I sunk in too deep. We shared a few more drinks and exchanged about unimportant things like what kind of food we missed from our human lives.

Dominic made his way over to us. He announced he was leaving and turned around on his heels in the next second. Kim shrugged in response. It wasn't the first time he suddenly decided to up and go. We continued our conversation for a while before we were interrupted a second time.

Kim's eyes widened and she jumped out of her seat and threw herself at the girl coming our way. I recognised June from the picture Kim had shown me a while back. Her auburn hair shone in the light. She was more beautiful than in the picture. Kim kissed her and dragged her over to me.

'This is June,' she announced, barely able to contain her happiness.

'Hi!' I stretched out my hand and met hers. I couldn't help but feel blindsided and a little unlucky to have women intruding in more than one aspect of my life.

'Hello. I've heard a lot about you and thought I'd surprise Kim,' said June. She turned back to Kim and smiled at her. Kim giggled and her cheeks reddened.

'Come, sit!' She gestured to her seat and pulled another one over, so we could all sit together around the bar.

'So, what have you ladies been up to?' June asked taking a sip from Kim's drink. Kim did most of the talking while June and I took stock of each other. There was something about her... something... off.

Kim was oblivious to our stares. She was too overjoyed to see June. I tried to be friendly with June but no matter what I said, her eyes sent a different signal than her words.

'Kim dear, could you make me another drink?' June eventually asked, planting a kiss on Kim's cheek. Kim hoped off like a good soldier and moved out of earshot.

'You seem to make her very happy,' I said and smiled at June.

'I do. I'm good to her. She is in a very happy and loving relationship,' June announced a bit too territorially.

'I know. She deserves only the best-'

'I don't see her often, you know. She lives far away and then of course you two spend a lot of time together...'

'Kim is my best friend,' I added.

'I know, and that's so great!' June leaned forward. 'But... she has *me* now.' She leaned back again, playing with the empty glass.

'Here you go,' Kim interrupted, sitting back down on the barstool.

June wanted me out of the picture. I looked over at Kim. She reached over and caressed June's thigh, staring into her deep blue eyes. I didn't want to drag her into this. 'Kim, it's getting late. I think I should get back.'

'What? Already?' Kim looked sad.

'Yes, I have to talk to Caleb about... things. And I'm not leaving you alone.' I grinned at June. 'June will take good care of you.'

I lightly hugged June, only to be polite. Kim's hug was genuine, and I made sure it lasted long enough to rub it into June's face.

By the time I made it to my car, I was fuming. It wasn't my fault that Kim and I got along! And Kim was old enough to make her own decisions. If she wanted to spend time with me, June would just have to get used to it!

I reached into the glove compartment and took out my pack of cigarettes. What a bitch. The nicotine eased my annoyance.

When I got to Blake's house, the lights were already off. He rarely went to bed while I was still out. I guess he really meant it when he said I didn't need him that much anymore... What was happening to the world? New recruit, new Blake, Kim's new girlfriend? I shook my head and closed the door to my bedroom.

Nightmares haunted me until the early morning. Not feeling rested at all, I forced myself out of bed in the early morning hours. I brewed myself a coffee and stood by the window, looking out at the street. When was the last time I had seen any nature? I closed my eyes and dreamt of being in a forest, surrounded by tall, green trees, insects buzzing, birds singing, with the distant rumbling of the ocean.

When I returned to my human life, I would go back to nature. Maybe become a gardener.

Blake came down the stairs just as I left for a run. The fresh air would do me some good. Memories of my first few months as a ghost came back to me. I remembered the first times I had gone running and how much I had hated it. My physique had been terrible. And now I was fit, running easily for an hour straight. There was something freeing about it, something that helped me deal with the everyday shit that kept trying to beat me.

The white cover of snow reflected the spare light like a mirror. Low hanging clouds were clinging on to the buildings, making the world seem even smaller and depressing.

When I returned, Blake asked me to spar with him, this time with knives. He exceeded me in strength and technique, but he was patient and eager to teach me. His negative comments were also absent. It made me relax.

A knock at the door interrupted our sparring session. Blake peered out the window to see who it was.

'Meerah, we can stop here,' he told me and dabbed himself with a towel. 'She's here.'

I ran for the bathroom and locked the door behind me. It was happening. Now I would know what she looked like… my replacement.

I had to make a good impression, make her respect me.

The shower was brief, but not without a few seconds staring at the scar across my stomach. For just a few moments, I closed my eyes and was back home in France again: jumping in the pool with my parents, the sun was hot on my face, I enjoyed a glass of wine with my fresh salad dinner.

Eventually, I put on comfortable clothes and arranged my hair. I stood in front of the bathroom door, unable to open it. As long as I stayed on this side of the door, I was safe. Caleb was mine – Blake too…

The moment I opened that door, reality would set in. They were waiting on the other side. I took a deep breath and pushed down the handle. The door creaked open and a sliver of light entered the bathroom. I held the door in place for a few seconds while I gathered myself. With my eyes closed I swung the door fully open and stepped out.

Caleb was sitting in Blake's chair, talking in a quiet voice. Blake was leaning against the table with his back towards me. As I came closer, I saw a girl behind them. She was sitting on my chair, facing me. Her eyes found me. Blake looked over and Caleb got up as I approached.

'Hello', I said tonelessly, not sure what else to say. An overwhelming sense of fear from the unknown manifested itself in my gut.

'Meerah, why don't you sit down,' Caleb's voice sung to me. He reached for my hand and comforted me with his touch.

I sat down, not taking my eyes off the girl. She had a round face, narrow nose, and thin lips. Her hair was a deep red and went down past her elbows. Her eyes were brown, dark, almost black. Her skin on the other hand, was pale, making her eyes and hair stand out.

'This is Holly,' Caleb said, his hand resting on my shoulder, 'She is excited to meet you.'

We both did not smile. She eyed me with interest, while I eyed her with suspicion. I asked her straight, 'What happened to your trainer and master?'

'They died in an ambush.' She did not flinch.

'Where were you?'

'I was at home, reading. I don't like fighting.'

I snorted. 'How have you survived until now then?' Caleb's warmth intensified and my mood mellowed.

'I don't know. I've been lucky I guess.'

So was I, once upon a time…

I looked at Caleb, then to Blake. 'What should we do with her?'

Blake started, 'She will need to be trained by me for a while. She's not as advanced as I would like her to be.' He looked to Caleb.

'So what have you been doing all these years?'

'I wasn't very good at the whole fighting thing so I mostly stayed in the house.'

Are you kidding me?! I couldn't believe she had been allowed to stay home safely instead of fighting off vampires and molochs. How had they kept up their numbers? I had never had a choice. Blake had forced me! Now she would get a taste of his training. At least that was a positive.

'Where is she going to live?' I looked at Caleb.

Caleb didn't answer. He looked down at the floor and intensified the calming effect of his hand on my shoulder.

'Caleb!' I shouted.

'She will provisionally live with me,' he finally admitted.

The betrayal cut right through my chest. I jumped up and freed myself of his grip. Immediately my true emotions washed away any sense of ease he had tried to give me.

'She's staying with you?!' I repeated in disbelief. 'You kicked me out of your house so *she* could move in?!'

'That's not what happened. I found out about her after you had already moved out-'

'So you wouldn't let me live with you because our connection is too strong for me, you didn't let me move in with Kim because I'm too fragile, but now you decide to let a perfect stranger move into your house – into *my master's* house?!'

Caleb reached for my hand and closed his fingers around it before I could escape his grasp. Immediately all worries disappeared and I was happy. It was magical here.

'Calm down, my child. She is not competing with you for my attention,' Caleb reassured me.

Why had I had such an outburst? I was so protective for no reason. If she hadn't fought a lot, she would definitely not outshine me in any way.

Holly laid her hands in her lap. 'Look, I really don't want to cause any trouble. I only want to serve my sentence and leave all this behind. I'm not made to be here – I don't even know why I was chosen in the first place! I'm terrible at this!'

Her voice was innocent, just like her demeanour. She looked young. 'And the Caleb thing, you should know I can't bond with a master anymore. My master was Mark and when he was killed our connection was broken. I can't recreate that connection with anyone else again. Please don't think I'm taking Caleb away from you. I want a good relationship with him, but I can't have the same bond as you have with him.'

I was ashamed to feel relieved. He was mine and I didn't want to share him. Why did I feel so possessive?

'Alright fine. I'll make an effort,' I agreed. A moment of silence followed. 'So, you read?'

Blake and Caleb distanced themselves from us and disappeared into the kitchen.

Holly rearranged her hair. 'Yes, I love reading! Do you?'

I nodded. 'I've only recently taken it up again. What do you read?'

She talked about the books she had read recently and we drifted off to a dozen other topics. We got to know each other a bit better.

Then, Holly lowered her voice and told me about a secret library where the council kept books on the history of Idolon. She was dying to get into the library where those books were held but entry was forbidden. Guards watched all access points and only a few had managed to break in and steal a book or two. When Blake and Caleb came out of the kitchen, she stopped talking about the secret library.

That library could contain information on the effects of drinking moloch blood on ghosts. I had to find out more.

The image of a human cadaver I had come across one time when I had successfully refused to drink the moloch blood entered my mind. The molochs were the monsters killing humans, not me… A shiver went down my spine; no, I would **not** do it again!

* * *

Holly settled into her new home with Caleb and started regular training with Blake. Since Blake didn't know if she could properly defend herself against molochs and worse, she was not allowed to drive alone to our house. I picked her up and dropped her off. She had passed her field test years ago, but she had a propensity for getting injured. Her master and trainer had agreed to keep her indoors whenever possible.

Holly had been a teacher in her human life. She had been killed by a stray bullet in a drive-by shooting. Her master Mark had chosen her because she had volunteered in her community. Though it was not a typically sought-after trait in this world, her master had told her this world needed giving souls.

I thought it was a bit odd, but who was I to say who should be given a second chance? I had not been particularly sporty in my human life or had any flair for guns, but here I was running around shooting and killing. If you had asked me to go into the military in my human life, I would have laughed.

At first, Blake had trained her only during the day so he could keep an eye on me at night, but I had no problem drinking my pain away in the middle of the day, so he kept changing the schedule to try to obstruct my regular visits to Santa's pub.

Even with all of Blake's efforts, he could not keep me away for more than a few days in a row. Sometimes I would meet up with Kim at the bar, when June didn't magically become available just as we had made plans.

Kim was happy and I would not rob her of her happiness. Unfortunately, it meant I frequently drank alone. I was not in the mood for flirting or meeting anyone new. My reputation preceded me and soon, everyone left me to my alcohol.

Once Carl stumbled onto me and lingered. Drunk, he told me about himself instead of reading between the lines and leaving me alone. He hadn't killed enough demons over the last few months and the council had already warned him to improve or they would add years to his sentence. Carl blamed it all on Vladimir's death. He was oblivious to my unease at the mention of

Vladimir's name. In a way I felt sorry for him. But it was too difficult to listen to him speculate about Vladimir's death, so when Carl wobbled towards the bathroom, I left.

With the music blasting in my car, I drove to Blake's house. Instead of going inside straight away, I went for a walk, taking with me the bottle of Vodka I kept in my car. About half an hour later, I reached the river and walked along it, letting my thoughts drift into the same dark corners they did night after night. It was an unhealthy habit but getting drunk helped me sleep easier.

When it wasn't enough, I roamed the streets, looking for molochs to kill. It was my way of coping. Everything was under control.

Tonight was one of those nights. The molochs had stayed hidden for a few days and my need to hunt had increased with every passing night. I was surprised at my desire to kill. It wasn't the only thing that had changed. My nose for molochs had gotten better. My sense for danger was constantly on, like a radar always scanning my vicinity.

My phone rang. It was better to answer. If I didn't answer Blake would come looking for me.

'I'm out,' I answered in a slur.

'You're drunk again.'

'What d'you want?'

'Come home! This is not good for you!'

'Leav'me alooon'!'

'It's dangerous! You could get attacked by a vampire! Remember the car accident?! Come home, please. I'll pick you up-'

'Let'em get me, let'em come! I'm no' scared!' I screamed out in the street. No response.

Blake changed his tone. 'Why are you doing this? Why? Are you trying to get hurt?!'

'Whaa do you care?!' I continued screaming.

'I care about you!' he now screamed back through the receiver.

I didn't answer. I closed my eyes and tried to breathe steadily. The night was cold. Tiny snowflakes danced from the sky down to the ground. The river was quiet, barely moving on the surface. It was peaceful. I could almost trick myself into thinking it was a beautiful winter night, calm and comforting. But it only reminded me of what I had lost. I looked down at my left hand. What I wouldn't give to be holding Ben's hand. I closed my eyes and pictured him next to me, his warm hand holding mine, leading me back home to our place where we would lay next to each other. I could almost feel his warm arms wrapped around me. When I opened my eyes, I was alone, standing in a dark city, snow drifting around me.

I hung up on Blake. I just wanted to be by myself, reminiscing and dreaming about better days. The guilt quickly called me back home. I couldn't continue aimlessly wandering around town. Angry at Blake for telling me off and angry at myself for caving to his authority, I stomped back towards the house.

About halfway home, I heard them. There was a pack of three molochs, fighting amongst themselves. Hearing them channelled my anger towards them. Like a distant thunderstorm, it growled deep inside me and quickly made its way to the surface. Without thinking, I drew my gun and a few bullets later, the molochs were lying dead on the ground. I walked towards them. It was so easy to pull the trigger and kill. I never thought about the fact that I was ending a life. One bullet and they were free of this world...

Two of them had recently fed and blood was spilling out of their wounds. My anger left and was replaced with desire. Inadvertently, I licked my lips. I bent closer to smell the blood that dripped out. It smelled of copper and relief.

Before I knew it, I was dipping my fingers in the blood and savouring it...

DEATH OF A MASTER

I woke up abruptly. It was cold. My back was killing me. I sat up. Snow slid off my jacket onto the ground. I could smell rotting corpses. To my right were decaying moloch bodies. Immediately I began to dry heave.

I felt dirty. No, guilty. This was not good. Why couldn't I stop? I had to get rid of this... this disease before it became too difficult.

You're in too deep now, a voice whispered in my head.

I stumbled away from the corpses as fast as I could. The sky was still dark and the air crisp. A faint glow on the horizon told me the sun would be coming up soon.

Half an hour later I was home, trying to shower all my guilt away. It was just a one-time thing, a small slip-up. I wouldn't do it again. No one saw me, no one would ever know. It couldn't be that bad. I was drinking alcohol and smoking too, this was just another thing I did. No point in telling anyone.

Afterwards, still wrestling with my inner thoughts, I poured myself a cup of coffee. Blake stormed into the kitchen. 'Where were you?' he asked.

I thought about my words for a few seconds before coming up with a lie, close enough to the truth that he would believe it. 'I was on my way home and ran into molochs. I got knocked out and woke up this morning.'

'You got... knocked out? In the middle of the street?'

'Yes.' Even I could hear the uncertainty in my voice.

'So you slept outside?'

'... yeah, I guess I did.'

Blake sighed and brushed back his hair. 'I told you, I *told* you to be careful. Do you understand the danger you put yourself in?'

He tried to stay calm, but the veins in his neck and arms visibly throbbed. He stepped in front me and blocked my way out of the kitchen. 'When I talked to you, you were drunk. This is what it leads to!'

'I know what you said.'

'You can't keep doing this! What happened to Ben's recruit-'

'Don't say his name!' The tears were close, but I was able to hold them back.

Blake looked intensely into my eyes. 'It could happen to you.'

With my coffee in hand, I tried to walk past him, but he didn't let me. Blake put one hand on my shoulder and I was forced to look up into his eyes.

'You are on a very destructive path and if you keep at it, you might not pull yourself out of it.'

I didn't know what to say. I knew what I was doing, and I knew it wasn't good for me, but I could stop anytime, so where was the harm? Why was he so insistent on treating me like a child?

I fell into bed and looked up at the ceiling. I wasn't feeling well. I remembered how sick I had been at Ben's place when I had had moloch blood before. Was it happening again?

The unease in my stomach lasted for a few hours. When I eventually returned to the living room, Blake was ready to train and wouldn't take no for an answer. He challenged me to spar hand to hand. I was stronger than I thought. I was able to beat him way more than usual. Blake was annoyed, even if he tried to hide it. Who knew? After all this time I was finally his equal, even strong enough to overpower him.

'Did you take anything?' Blake inquired when we were done.

'What do you mean?'

Was it the moloch blood? The euphoria could just be one effect... What else could it do? How could I be sure? Asking Caleb was out of the question, but maybe I could research it somehow... or get to that library Holly had talked about...

The front door opened and Caleb shouted up to us, 'It's me.'

I could feel Caleb's aura building as he came up the stairs. Instinctively I hurried towards him and touched his arm. A sense of calmness and peace settled in me.

'Where is Holly?' Blake asked.

'She's at home. I need to speak to you before I go to the council,' Caleb said to Blake.

I knew from his tone it meant they wanted to discuss something privately. 'I'm going,' I said.

His row of white teeth flashed at me and I could feel a sense of satisfaction pulsing through me.

I let go of his arm and headed to shower off from the sparring session. I hated letting him go. Caleb's touch always made me feel secure and protected.

'What's going on?' Blake asked Caleb just before I closed the door.

Before I got in the shower, I looked in the mirror. The massive scar stretched across my stomach, painfully reminding me of my origins. No tears came this time, but that was almost worse.

Eventually the sun made its way back under the horizon and I had survived another day. I spent the afternoon reading while Blake quietly strummed his guitar and hummed a tune. The book wasn't able to distract me long and I found myself drifting off to my bloody thoughts regularly. While I still felt a slight dizziness, I also kept wanting to drink moloch blood again.

Just after sunset, I heard the rumbling sound of a car and then someone opened the front door. From the sensation I immediately felt, I knew it was Caleb.

'I'm back,' he announced. I embraced him and let the positive emotions invade me.

'How did it go?' Blake asked.

'Not as well as I hoped,' Caleb admitted.

I detached myself from him and walked into the kitchen. The moment I was out of sight I could hear the two of them whispering. I proceeded to make a cup of tea ignoring the secrecy going on in the living room.

'… Jesper…' The name caught my attention.

I froze and cocked my ears to hear what they were saying.

'…trying another angle. Has she said anything we could use?'

'No, she hasn't said a word about him. The few times I've tried to bring up Ben it brings her to tears.' It was Blake's voice whispering.

I pushed back the tears in my eyes. I had to find out what they were talking about.

'I need to get him to shut up. I thought taking Holly from him would appease him. How could he possibly train her when he doesn't even have a trainer? I thought he could be reasoned with.'

'Can't believe him… you had an agreement!'

'Yes, but he is ruthless. He even had the audacity to come to my house to announce he was going after her again! I'm afraid he might fool the council enough to think there is some truth to his accusations.' Caleb sighed.

He had been at Caleb's house? Jesper?

'Should we tell her?' Blake asked.

'No, not yet. I have another meeting with the council soon. I…' Caleb sighed deeply, 'I still have hope I can win the council over.'

I tried to think and then remembered; that day I had seen the thin man with curly hair arguing with Caleb.

The cup slipped from my hand and fell to the floor, exploding in a clashing sound, the hot liquid spreading.

'Meerah, are you alright?' I heard Caleb shout from the living room.

It all became so clear. The man I had seen arguing with Caleb was Jesper! He had been in my reach! I could have ended him! A sudden pain in my chest stabbed without warning.

Caleb came into the kitchen, alarmed, followed by Blake. 'Ameerah, let me help you.'

Instinctively, I pulled my gun out aiming it at Caleb's head. 'Don't get closer,' I snarled. The colour drained from Blake's face and his mouth dropped open.

'I know how you feel, my child. Let me help you.'

'*He was in your house! He was THERE! You could have stopped him!*' I screamed.

'Ameerah, I couldn't just murder him in my house. Think about it! It would have caused too many questions if he disappeared after his trainer just died.' Caleb tried to calm me.

'I saw him! I *saw* him!' The gun shook in my hand. Jesper would get away it. He was untouchable. *Caleb was doing nothing!* I had trouble breathing.

He will never be punished, a voice in my head whispered.

'What's going on?' Blake eventually found his voice.

'My child, I have my eye on Jesper. Do not trouble yourself with him, please just put the gun down.' He risked a step closer. The authority in his voice was just below a command.

Lies, lies, lies!

'NO!' I backed away, keeping the gun pointed at him.

'Wait- what?! How could she have seen a master?' Blake turned to Caleb baffled. My eyes flicked over to Caleb as well. He turned to Blake and they exchanged a look.

Blake's eyes were back on me, his jaw tight. 'Do it.'

Caleb turned to me. Suddenly, there was a cold draft around my feet, pulling me backwards. His eyes bore into me. 'Let go, Ameerah!' Then, like he had pulled the plug from an old TV, I felt myself switch off.

Caleb caught me before I hit the floor, his touch transporting me immediately into heaven. My soul detached from my body and floated up into white paradise. It was peaceful and loving where I was. My mind roamed free over the vastness of heaven.

'What's going on with her?' Blake asked in a low voice.

Only sound kept me connected to my body in the sea of whiteness. I could hear but I was unable to respond. I couldn't really feel my body. It was as if Caleb had cut the connection.

The feeling was oddly familiar.

'She must have seen Jesper,' Caleb responded, carrying me somewhere and then laying me on a comfortable surface.

'How is it possible?'

Caleb shrugged. 'It must have been an accident. Maybe she saw him when he was at my house. He doesn't have a trainer or protégé anymore; he must have thought it unnecessary to protect his identity. But she shouldn't remember now.' A hand gently caressed my face.

'Are you sure?' Blake pressed.

'Yes.' Caleb's annoyance was audible in his voice.

'I'm worried about her. She seems... off.'

Caleb sighed. 'Grief affects people differently. Let her cope in her own way for now, it's not too late to pull her out, should we need to.'

'Are you sure it's just grief? I have this feeling she's hiding something.'

I could feel the soft surface I was lying on move. 'She probably is.'

'We need to know what it is! Ben might have had an influence on her and taught her bad habits,' Blake insisted.

I could feel my body tensing at the mention of his name.

'He was never the evil man you wanted him to be. Ben confessed to her that Jesper was supposed to watch the recruit but didn't. Ben went out to look for his recruit but when he found him it was too late. That's why she is so hell-bent on getting Jesper.'

'That can't be, that's a lie! Ben wasn't there when I found his recruit-'

'He was forced to watch,' Caleb whispered. 'Somehow he managed to escape. You must have discovered the body afterwards. Since that moment he had been seeking revenge. The vampire that killed him was one of the ones that tortured his recruit.'

Blake paused. 'Why didn't you tell me all of this?' The shock was audible in his voice.

'I... I thought it would be easier for you to cope if you believed he was a bad man.'

'What's that supposed to mean?!' Blake fired at him.

'For Christ sake Blake! I know you were in love with her!' Caleb barked at him.

A moment of silence followed.

'That has nothing to do with it!'

'Tell me, why did you have such a problem with Ben if it wasn't because you wanted to be with her?'

Blake waited a few seconds before responding. 'You should have told me.'

I could feel fingers gliding along my face. 'She confided in me and I didn't want to break that trust.'

'What about *our* trust?!'

'I'm her master. And with you having feelings for her I thought it best to keep you out of anything to do with Ben.'

'I thought we were a team and now I find out you've been keeping all these secrets from me. What else have you kept from me? You... you need to leave. I don't want to talk to you.' Blake's voice sounded hurt.

'Blake-'

'No, Caleb, I thought we worked together... but apparently we don't.'

'My duty-'

'Before you were *her* master you were *mine*. But I guess you forgot that part.'

I could hear footsteps and then it went quiet.

I felt so groggy. I turned onto my other side and opened my eyes. I was in my bed, fully clothed. A pounding headache announced itself when I sat up. I shuffled out of my bedroom. Blake was working out as usual.

'What's up with you?' Blake asked me when he saw me moving like a zombie.

'Headache,' I grunted.

'You had a big night,' he concurred.

'I did?' I scratched my head. My memory was sketchy; I remembered I had been out drinking and come back here in the morning. Everything after that was blurry. I shrugged and put on a light running jacket.

'Are you going out?' Blake asked.

'Running. Why?'

'I'll come with you.' Blake ran upstairs before I had time to answer.

I felt much better after an hour of exercise outside. Blake looked out of breath, though he tried to hide it. It was unusual for him to be exhausted, especially when I wasn't... I remembered I had beaten him sparring yesterday. Was this really a possible side-effect from the moloch blood? It couldn't be... If moloch blood really did improve your physical strength, then why weren't all ghosts drinking it? It couldn't be. It had to be something else.

Holly arrived a few hours later and trained with Blake. Occasionally, I looked up from the book I was reading and observed them. She was uncoordinated and I sensed Blake was growing impatient. She was a great shot, but terrible at anything that required physical strength. In a way she reminded me of myself when I first came here. It felt like ages ago, and at the same time as if it was only yesterday.

Holly joined me when Blake finally released her.

'That was intense!' she declared and fell into the chair next to me.

I chuckled. 'Yes, he is hardcore.' I looked over at Blake, who was manipulating a machine gun.

'What are you doing tonight?' Holly asked, tying her hair up in a high bun.

'Probably going out. Do you want to come?'

'No, I'm tired tonight. Another time though.'

To be honest I was relieved she refused. I wanted to be by myself. Once again, I thought of killing molochs and drinking their blood...

No! If I was going to stop, I had to start at some point.

'Meerah can you take Holly back home?' Blake said, interrupting my thoughts.

Holly made her way to the door while I grabbed the keys. 'Fine, but you know you have a car as well. You could drop her off yourself every now and again.'

He briefly looked up from his machine gun. 'I have too much to do here.'

I looked over at Holly while I was driving. 'Can I ask you a question?'

'Sure.'

'Is something going on, between Caleb and Blake?'

'Not that I know, why?'

I shook my head. 'Blake was weird today. He was quiet and usually it means he is thinking and that normally leads to him talking to Caleb. But he didn't want to drive you so I thought maybe he was avoiding Caleb.'

'Caleb seemed preoccupied this morning,' Holly admitted.

I looked at her again inquisitively. She continued, 'Maybe I'm reading too much into it. But I thought he was a bit off, pensive.'

I felt a pinch in my heart. 'Ok, I'll speak to Caleb, but chances are he won't tell me if they are fighting. I'll need you to look out for him, alright?'

There was no way Caleb would confide in me. He was my master and I couldn't remember a time when he opened up to me about anything. He was not wired that way. There was a chance though that I might get through to Blake.

'I'm kind of happy you are counting on me,' Holly said.

'Why?' I frowned.

'Because it makes me feel more included,' she confessed.

I felt the guilt clawing at me. 'Look Holly, you are part of us now, whether I want it or not. And I just need to get used to it. It's nothing against you, it's... it's more about me. And if I'm being bitchy you have to tell me.'

Holly chuckled. 'Thanks, it means a lot to me. And I'm sorry... for your loss. You don't deserve-'

'Stop.' My voice was ice cold.

He had been far away, but now it all came rushing back like a tsunami and I couldn't hold it all back. Tears ran down my face.

'I'm so sorry-' Holly tried to comfort me.

'Stop.' I pulled the car over and got out. When I closed my eyes, I saw him right in front of me, holding me. But when I opened my eyes, my hands were empty and all I saw was the dirty ground.

I breathed in through the nose and out through the mouth. Everything slowed down. The memories inched further away, his face faded from in front of my eyes, until all I could see was my immediate surrounding.

We didn't speak again until we arrived at Caleb's house. She got out and made her way to the door. After my sudden cry, I decided not to talk to Caleb tonight. Whatever problems he had with Blake would have to wait.

The moment Holly was inside the tears came back. No one was watching and my sorrow came rushing back stronger than earlier. Would it ever be ok again? How could I continue without him?

I didn't want Caleb to sense my distress so I drove away.

I pulled into the parking lot of a nearby block of flats and let the tears flow.

After crying until my face was swollen and red, I just sat in my car, staring into the empty air. There was movement near the entrance of the block of flats, tearing me away from my thoughts of Ben. Two molochs were fighting. Without thinking I got my gun out and ran towards them.

Several bullets later they were both dead. My heart pounded all the way up to my throat. It was snowing heavily and my breath made clouds of fog when I exhaled.

I inspected the dead bodies and the urge to drink their blood surged inside me once again. I knew the effect it would have on me, the relief that was so close. I couldn't help myself.

As the poison released me from my pain, flashes appeared in front of my eyes. Memories came back. Suddenly it was all clear again. I remembered Jesper at Caleb's house; I remembered Blake and Caleb talking, then Caleb paralysing me, trying to make me forget what I had seen.

How was this possible? I thought all he could do was sense my emotions! Could he alter my memories and feelings? Make me forget? No, that couldn't be. No, the blood was playing tricks on me.

Or was it? The feeling was familiar, the missing connection, the sensation of looking into my own feelings and not being able to connect to them...

That's why I had been so calm at the hearing after Ben's death! Caleb must have altered my memories then too! How could he do this? How could he betray me like that?! All I had were my memories of Ben and he was messing with them!

I screamed at the top of my lungs. How could he?! This was the last time, the last time he would control me! I wouldn't let him get away with this! He was just like Blake, meddling in my business! Treating me like a child! What was wrong with all these men here?!

Furious, I raced back to Caleb's house. As I approached, I saw someone leaving his house. The person gesticulated backwards towards Caleb who was standing in his open front door and walked down the gravel walkway towards the street. I swerved to the side and turned off my lights. Who was that arguing with him?

I watched the person get in the car and drive away. Caleb slammed his door shut. I decided to follow the person that had just left. It wasn't Blake, but who else would come to see Caleb in the middle of the night? What the hell was going on?!

Eventually, the car stopped in an upper-class suburban area. The streetlight was patchy, and I had trouble seeing who it was. He was too tall to be a woman...

The person locked the car and walked up to the porch of a nearby house. In the darkness I couldn't see his face, but I saw a mop of curly hair bouncing in the spare light of the porch.

It was Jesper.

There was no doubt in my mind. The moment I was sure of his identity, I decided it would be his last night. I reached under the passenger seat for the knife I had taped to the underside of the seat. The knife was long and thin, a slick and quiet killer.

This was it, my one chance for justice.

Jesper lingered on the porch for a few moments. As he entered his house, he turned on the light inside and closed the door behind himself. He turned off the porchlight. Perfect for me.

I checked my watch and waited precisely two minutes before getting out of my car. Gently, I opened and closed the door without slamming it and hurried across the street to his house. The front door was locked, but there was a side gate. I took one last look around; the street was empty.

I ran on cat's feet over the lawn and jumped up onto the side gate, swung my legs over the top, and dropped back onto my feet on the other side. I tiptoed along the wall towards the back of the garden. The light in the conservatory was on and it flooded out into the snow-covered garden. Peeking around the corner into the house, I saw Jesper filling a glass of wine. There were rhythmic sounds of bass audible through the conservatory windows.

He turned towards me and I ducked behind the wall. The thrill excited me.

The light switched off. My ears perked up. I heard the regular sound of feet hitting steps and then silence. For a second time, I peeked around the corner of the house. This time the conservatory and kitchen were dark. The garden was lit from the lights on the first floor.

I crept up towards the door of the conservatory, laid my right hand on the handle and tried to press it down. It was locked. Annoyed I looked around. There had to be a spare key somewhere. Carefully, I picked up the flowerpots around the terrace one by one but found no key. There was a bigger pot with a sort of tree bursting from it. In summer it would have been blooming, but the winter had stripped it of all its greens and only the grey branches remained.

It was heavy and before I had time to look under it, the pot slipped out of my hand and came crashing down onto the terrace. It didn't fall from very high, but it was heavy enough to make a deep thumping noise.

I hurried away from the conservatory and back behind the house. Just as I had reached safety, I heard Jesper open the window. I could see from his shadow he was standing by the window and looking outside.

Sweat pearled down my forehead. This could not go wrong. I was so close. Would he see my footsteps in the snow?

Eventually, he shut the window and his shadow moved away. Then the lights were turned on again in the kitchen. I gripped the knife tighter. If he was coming outside, I had to be ready.

But nothing happened. When I looked inside once more, I saw him pour himself another glass of wine and return upstairs.

My first thought was to be relieved he would be inebriated and could easily be overpowered. Then, I thought it was a shame because he would not realise to the full extent what would happen.

I continued my search. After checking all the flowerpots, I still had no key. Angry I started looking under the garden gnomes, trying not to make too much noise, and periodically glancing up to the lit bedroom. Under one of them I found a small black plastic bag. When I touched it, I could feel the contours of a key. Finally!

I rushed to the door and inserted the key into the lock. Slowly I turned the key until I could hear the click of the latch unlocking. I opened the door without making a sound. Jesper was still upstairs. My heart was racing. It was almost time. The feeling was exhilarating. The knife in my hand felt good.

My feet made no noise as they carried me up the carpeted stairs towards Jesper. The stairs bent around a corner and I could see his back. The sense of anticipation and excitement now mixed with my anger.

'There you are,' I whispered.

Jesper jumped and turned around, spilling his wine on the cream carpet.

'Who are you?!' he squealed, squinting in my direction as I emerged from the shadows. When he recognised me, his face expressed nothing but disregard. 'What do you want?' He waited for me to reach the landing.

'You killed Ben.' I could barely recognise my own voice. It was deep and full of hatred.

'The vampire-,' Jesper tried.

'NO!' Silence followed. 'No, *you* killed him. *You* didn't show!'

There was a flicker of fear in his eyes. 'I couldn't have saved him.'

'YES! You could have SAVED him! At least have the *balls* to admit it!'

Jesper eyed me for a moment, the wine glass still in his hand. I took out my gun. Now he finally looked worried.

'I can't do this with a gun,' I stated, 'It's too impersonal.' I placed the gun on the chest of drawers in the hallway, next to the stairs. Instead, I pulled the knife higher into view; the knife that would be his end.

For a moment we stood without moving, looking at each other. I had waited all this time for justice. I had begged Caleb to intervene and nothing had happened. Now, I would deliver justice myself.

Jesper threw the wine glass at my head and jumped backwards towards his desk. I ducked and ran after him, hearing the glass splinter on the wall behind me and shards rain down onto the winding stairs. With the knife in hand I threw myself at him. Jesper spun around and fell to the floor, taking down most of the content on his desk with him.

The knife slammed into the wooden desk and stayed stuck there. In the tussle I did not see that Jesper had found a weapon. He jammed a letter opener into my calf. I let out a scream and kneed him in the nose. I let go of my knife and Jesper threw something my way. With my arms in the air shielding my face, Jesper was able to rip the letter opener from my calf and jam it back in again. I screamed, bowed down to my calf to remove the letter opener, and thrust my foot into Jesper's side. Jesper rolled to the nightstand and reached inside it.

Before I had time to pull him away, he had a gun in his hand. I reached for the mesh bin next to his desk and threw it at him. He fired but missed as the bin hit him on the forearm. I lunged behind the desk before he had time to shoot again. The bullets pierced through his wooden desk, leaving splinters on the ground. On the floor next to me lay two drawers ripped out from his desk, the contents dispersed on the floor. I saw a gun among the debris and reached for it while Jesper tried to get up.

I slid out from underneath the desk and shot at his hand holding the gun. He screamed as the bullet tore his hand open. The gun fell to the floor. I stood up and reached for my knife still stuck in the desk. He tried to run but I pulled the trigger again. A tortured echo left his lips as he held his bleeding leg.

With the knife back in my hand, I left the gun on the desk. The air was filled with the smell of blood. I could feel a familiar desire deep inside me. Jesper lay on the floor, his back against the bedframe.

'Tell the truth,' I demanded.

He didn't reply.

'Tell me the truth!'

'Alright!' he shouted back. 'Yes, I could have saved him! Are you happy now? I could have saved him, but I didn't! He put himself in danger and I was not gonna risk my life for his sorry ass!'

His eyes glistened with madness.

I bent down awkwardly, my calf making me wriggle painfully like an eel. It had looked more graceful in my mind...

'You don't deserve to be here,' I stated and slammed the knife into his left thigh. Blood spilled out of the wound while Jesper's scream bounced off the walls.

'He died because of you,' I repeated, taking the knife out of his thigh. A wave of blood spread over his jeans and dripped onto the carpet.

I couldn't believe what I was doing. Killing molochs and vampires was one thing, killing a ghost was very close to killing a human being. Why didn't I feel guilty?

'Fuck you!' Jesper screamed in my face with spittle dripping from his lower lip.

I tilted my head to the side and slowly angled the blade for a new attack, while he tried to stem the flood of blood from the wound on his thigh with his left hand. With a quick motion I hammered the knife into his right thigh. He tried to wriggle away from me but there was nowhere for him to go.

'Stop it, please,' he begged.

I could not help but smile. 'After all you have done, you will finally be judged.'

The sharp tip trailed along his trembling skin. He gasped and cried, trying to hold the blood in his body. A part of me felt pleasure seeing him like this, seconds from his death.

'Crazy bitch!' Jesper mumbled under his breath. His face was white. His hair stuck to his sweaty forehead.

The dripping blade moved up from his thigh to his stomach where I let it hover. His face distorted in anticipation. Like a snake lunging forward to catch a frog, the blade plunged to the side of his stomach. Jesper's short scream followed. It was like a symphony. I pushed the knife in further and he screamed again.

The blood spilled over my hand. His body shivered and sank down further onto the now soaked red carpet.

'Are you suffering now?' I asked. Images of Ben flashed before my eyes.

Jesper was too far gone to answer. His upper body slowly sank towards the nightstand. The knife slipped out of his stomach with the pressure of the blood escaping the wound. The copper smell was everywhere. A sea of red was spreading underneath us.

I inched closer until our noses were almost touching. The mean little shit he had been was gone. There was nothing left but a terrified little man now. His eyes were wide open, the sweat from his face dripping into his chest, mixing with the blood.

The blade firmly in my hand, I proceeded to deliver the final and fatal blow into his torso, twisting the knife up and around to ensure maximum destruction. Jesper's face distorted as the knife tore through his intestines. The pain paralysed his face in stunned shock. The last of the colour left his face, his breathing ceased, and his muscles relaxed. The distress of imminent death disappeared. All that was left was a lifeless body sprawled on the floor, blood everywhere.

My act of revenge was completed. I looked down at my blood covered hand, still gripping the knife. The tip was trembling. A drop of blood dripped down onto my thigh. Slowly I stood up and left the bedroom. I turned right into the bathroom, where I washed my hands.

There was a noise downstairs. Immediately I froze in place. Was it my imagination or was someone there?

There was a thump and then the sound of keys.

Damn.

On cat's feet, I returned back to the scene of my crime. Did I leave anything? Frantically I picked up my gun from the chest of drawers, as well as the other gun on the desk. I stuffed the bloody knife inside my jacket pocket and nestled one of the guns into the back of my jeans. The second gun I kept in my hand. Whoever was here, I might have to kill them as well.

The front door unlocked and someone entered the house. 'Jesper?' a woman's voice called out.

I had to get out!

There were two possible exits: either out the bathroom window and into the garden, or out the guest bedroom window and into the street. Or I could hide and try sneaking out through the front door but that seemed highly risky.

'Jesper?' The woman called out again, this time louder.

She would come upstairs in a few seconds. I tiptoed towards the guest bedroom, praying the floorboards under the cream carpet would not creak as I moved.

The sound of her feet coming closer to the stairs were audible as I reached for the window in the guest bedroom. The broken wine glass and spilled wine decorated the stairs; she would know something was not right.

Before I had reached the window latch, I heard the woman come up the stairs and I deviated to hide behind the open door.

A wild scream shook the house. She cried and yelped at the horror I had created. My eyes returned to the window, but I couldn't get to it without being seen. I couldn't get out.

Her cries lasted a few minutes before she managed to stumble down the stairs again. I turned the handle and opened the window, wiping at it to smear my fingerprints. She was calling someone on the phone. Clumsily, I stretched one leg out of the window, and then swung the other one over. A small roof overhung the porch, but it was steep. I hoisted myself out of the window and lowered myself as close as possible to the gutter. While I slowly slid down, my escape was marked in the snow.

Suddenly, I lost my grip; I scrapped over the screeching gutter and landed with a thud on the ground. My feet and hands hurt as I landed clumsily on all fours.

She certainly had heard me. I ran across the street and ducked under some large bushes at a neighbouring house, away from the streetlights. Indeed, the moment I reached the bushes the woman opened the front door; gun in hand, ready to shoot. I froze, not daring to breathe. My footsteps in the snow at the front of Jesper's house led out onto the street but once there, they disappeared on the cleared road. They wouldn't lead her to my hiding place.

If I had to, I would kill her too, but I preferred to only end Jesper's life. He had now paid for his sins.

She walked towards the street but turned to the right, away from me. This was my chance. Risking it all, I darted off in the opposite direction towards my car.

Now I was very glad I had parked it further away.

As much as could, I ran quietly and quickly. I had not locked the car, so I managed to open and close the driver's door in one quick motion making no sound. Before turning the ignition, I switched off the automatic headlights. I pressed the start button and the car rumbled to life.

Then there were shots fired. Close. I pressed the gas pedal so far down the wheels spun and I stayed glued in place.

More shots. I took my foot off the gas and tried again. There was snow under the tyres. I had to fight all my instincts and gently tap the gas pedal again. Finally, the wheels gripped and the car started moving. A bullet whizzed by and splintered the window behind me. I raced off, the car swerving dangerously, hoping the woman would not be able to identify the kind of car I was driving.

Only after a few minutes did I dare to turn on the headlights.

My heart was racing. It dawned on me what I had done. The drying blood formed a sticky crust on my clothes and hands. I felt horrible, but no shame in the actual act. Jesper deserved to die after what he had done. He was responsible for the deaths of his trainer and of his recruit. It was only right to end his life.

On the other hand, the fact that I had been capable of killing him scared me. I had never thought of myself as an aggressive person. And now I was a murderer. *A murderer!*

I had taken a life. A life that wasn't deserving of living, but still a life.

Ben would have understood. He would have wanted Jesper dead too. Yes… Everything was ok…

It was done now. There was no going back. Hopefully the woman had not seen me and I had not left any fingerprints or other incriminating evidence behind. Would there even be an investigation? Did the council have police to inspect a crime scene? Probably not…

I parked in front of Blake's house. Before getting out of my car I reached into the glove compartment and got out anti-bacterial wipes. My hands had left red traces of evidence everywhere on the wheel and gearstick. I cleaned it all up and stuffed the stained wipes into my pockets.

The bullet had splintered the window in the back, but it was still holding tight, with the bullet lodged firmly in the right corner. I would have to get rid of the car.

With a wipe in my hand I opened the entrance door and took off my shoes. There was blood on the soles but just like the car, I would take care of that in the morning. My clothes were stained with blood. I would have to get rid of them, burn them somewhere. Fuck. Murder was such a mess...

I was tiptoeing towards my room when the light switched on, blinding me. I held up my arm to shield my eyes.

'What the hell happened?' Blake gasped. 'Are you hurt?'

When my eyes had finally adjusted to the light, I saw Blake's shocked expression. He came closer, looking at me with his steel-blue eyes.

I followed his gaze down to my body. I was covered in blood. It was *everywhere*. My hands, arms, sweater, jeans... I couldn't believe how much blood was on me considering how much blood had been on the floor...

'Is this from molochs?' Blake asked. His suspicion was all too audible.

'No,' I admitted. How would he react when I told him whose blood this was?

'Then, what is it?' He got closer to me. His eyes were filled with fear and shock.

A phone buzzed. Blake didn't move. We stood in silence until eventually the phone stopped. Shortly after, it started again. Annoyed he took his eyes off me and walked over to his phone lying on the table. 'I can't talk right now-'

There was a moment of silence. Then, he hung up.

'Meerah,' he took a moment before continuing. 'I will ask you a question and I need you to be honest.' I could see he was tense.

Blake's voice trembled slightly. 'Did you... did you do something to... to... *Jesper?*'

It played back in front of my eyes, the knife twisting inside his body and his eyes dying. 'He deserved it.'

Blake closed his eyes and put his hands over his face. I could hear him breathe through his fingers. He sighed and brushed his hair back with his hands. 'Did you…?'

'Yes.' There was almost a smile on my lips.

He exhaled loudly and whined desperately. Blake turned away and walked towards his training station, murmuring indistinct words.

Eventually, he turned back towards me. 'Do you – do you even realise what you did?!'

'I know what I did. He deserved it.'

'Were you at least defending yourself?'

'No.'

'Jesus Christ. The council will find out about his murder, if they don't already know,' he said through the hand covering his mouth.

A sting of fear shot through me. What would happen to me? Probably torture and death…

'Meerah… *why?*'

My eyebrows drew together in anger. 'You know what he did. He killed his recruit and Ben and got away with it!' My bloody hands formed fists.

'Did anyone see you?'

'No. Not really. A woman may have seen my car, but it was dark and I had left the headlights off.'

'Right.' Blake looked down at the floor and took deep shaking breaths. He let his hands rest on his hips. 'Right, this is what will happen.' He walked up to me and looked into my eyes, 'You are going to take a shower and go to bed. I will get rid of all your clothes and hopefully nothing will lead back to you. Give me the gun you used.' He stretched out his empty left hand.

Slowly I reached into my jacket pocket and placed the blood-covered knife into his hand.

'A knife? Really? You couldn't just shoot him?' he asked sarcastically.

'He had to suffer,' I admitted in a low voice as if I was a child caught playing with my mother's expensive make-up, but secretly enjoying my mischiefs.

'Did you leave any other evidence anywhere?' Blake held the knife as if it carried diseases.

'There is a bullet in my car-'

'I'll get you a new car.'

'My shoes as well…'

'I'll take care of it. Take off your clothes.' Blake gesticulated in my direction.

I walked into the bathroom and closed the door behind me. The blood had made the fabric stiff. Once I had taken all my clothes off and piled them by the door, I laid Jesper's gun on top of it.

'Are you in the shower?' I heard Blake shout from behind the door. The shower curtain was drawn, hiding me from the door. 'Yes.'

He opened the door and took the stack of clothes I had left on the floor. 'I'll be back. Don't go outside.'

The blood washed out of my hair when the hot water rained over it. Rubbing and scrubbing every inch of my body, I made sure to erase any evidence that I had committed the horrible crime. There was probably some leftover residue of blood that might be visible under special light, just like I remembered from cop TV shows. Would the council have any of those? Would the council ask to see my naked body?

The thought made me laugh.

I stopped the shower when there was no more hot water in the pipes and my skin was wrinkled like that of an old lady. There was nothing to do but wait for Blake's return. I mixed myself a strong drink and sat down in Blake's chair by the window, staring outside. My hands trembled, though almost not visible to the naked eye. If I hadn't been looking for it, I might not have noticed the slight ripples on the surface of my drink.

The murder played back over and over in my head: the break-in through the conservatory, sneaking up the stairs, the struggle, the gun, the knife, the woman, the escape, blood everywhere. Everything was tainted with blood. Jesper deserved every single pain he felt as he died. If I had to do it all over again, I would. He had gotten away with murder for long enough. Karma is a bitch.

What would Ben think of this? Would he be happy? Would he be relieved? Proud? Ben had rarely spoken about Jesper but when he did, it was always in anger. Jesper must have inflicted him endless pain... It made me sick to imagine the torture the poor recruit had gone through by those vampires. How could a master leave their protégé behind like that? How could one continue living knowing you were responsible for the torture and death of someone else, someone who depended on you, someone you were supposed to protect? And then blame it on someone else? I hoped Jesper was in hell, burning in eternity, being cut open by thousands of knifes making him bleed to death over and over again until the sun burnt out.

It was mid-morning when Blake returned. He tossed a set of keys my way.

'Your new car,' he said. Exhausted he sat down in the chair next to me, laid his head back and closed his eyes.

'Why did you do it?'

'You mean why am I protecting you?' he rephrased, not opening his eyes.

'I killed someone and you're ok with that?'

He took his time answering. 'Protecting you from the council and being ok with your actions are two different things. And for the record...' He tilted his head my way and opened his eyes. 'I'm not ok with you killing someone, even if it was Jesper.'

Blake closed his eyes again.

'What's gonna happen to me?' I dared to ask, taking a big gulp of my drink.

'You will most certainly be called into a hearing. And when you tell them you didn't do it, I will vouch for you and say you were with me all night.'

It seemed too easy. 'And they will believe it?'

'Either they believe us or we're both dead.' Blake got back up onto his feet. 'If you feel the need to kill someone else, **don't**.' With those words he walked up the stairs and shortly afterwards, I could hear gentle snoring from his bedroom.

Why was he protecting me? Why was he risking his life? An echo of the conversation he had with Caleb came to me. Could he still be... in love? It felt strange to even think it! What now? Should I ask him about it? Obviously, I cared for him even if he drove me crazy, but I couldn't imagine being with him!

This was all too weird. I needed another drink to calm my nerves. Just as I was putting the finishing touches on it, my phone vibrated in my pocket.

'Caleb, what a nice surprise.' My voice was way too high-pitched to sound normal.

'I have just been summoned for another hearing about Jesper.'

'Oh?'

'So have you and Blake. Tell me you at least got rid of the evidence!'

I swallowed the alcohol and bile in my mouth. 'Blake took care of it.'

'God, what have you done?! I can't leave you alone for five minutes! Tell Blake I'm coming back tonight!' His anger was audible, but I couldn't sense it like I usually did. Was it the moloch blood? Where was he coming back from? The human world?

'I'm sorry,' I whispered.

'I hope you are, considering the trouble we're in now!' He hung up.

Now that the thought had entered my mind, the desire for moloch blood grew. Last night I didn't have much and I missed its liberating effect. My fury had overpowered me, robbing me of any relief or ecstasy.

I had told myself I would stop! No more! Maybe just once... *No!* What if I got caught? Would Blake bail me out for this too? I had to be careful.

The more time passed, the more nervous I got about either of them uncovering my secret. I wasn't sure they would be willing or even able to cover that up. The itch for more blood grew steadily alongside it...

When Caleb finally arrived, it was pitch black outside. He let himself fall into one of the chairs in the living room. Blake made his way towards him but kept a safe distance. He chose to lean against the table, crossing his arms over his chest.

Hesitantly, I sat down next to Caleb. The irritation and anger were palpable in the room.

'So, who would like to start?' I broke the silence.

'Tell us what happened,' Caleb instructed.

There was no need to give them any details on the actual act, so I brushed over it quickly, hoping they wouldn't see me as the murderer I was. They remained silent. When I looked down at my hands, I could still see the blood dripping off them.

'How did you recognise Jesper?' Caleb finally said.

'I had seen him before,' I said. My answer spilled out faster than my brain had time to think. Blake and Caleb threw each other a look and I knew I had said too much.

'Where did you see him before?' Blake continued.

I couldn't admit I remembered the conversation they had had when they thought I was unconscious. The only reason I remembered was because of the moloch blood! The moment that red liquid had touched my tongue all of Caleb's magical effects to cloud my mind had evaporated.

'I... I remembered seeing him...' I tried to think of an answer that would make sense.

In a quick motion Caleb laid his hand on my arm. The positive sensation overpowered me instantly. All my willpower went straight out of the window. 'Where did you see Jesper?'

'In your house. I ran by your house and wanted to talk to you, but I saw a man arguing with you and it was him,' I admitted without hesitation.

'How did you know it was him?'

'Because I heard you tell Blake that he came to your house.'

Caleb looked away from me and towards Blake. 'Could this be right?'

Blake shrugged. 'It's possible.'

Caleb let go of my arm and I was thrust out of heaven and back to reality, like a rollercoaster pulling into its final destination, coming to an abrupt stop.

'Did anyone see you?'

'A woman saw my car, but she didn't see me, no.'

Caleb sighed deeply and retreated into himself. His eyes stared at the floor; his forehead laid in wrinkles. 'The council wants to see you tomorrow,' he said without looking up.

'... Ok, I'll... be ready,' I stammered. Would I be? Could I keep it together?

Once again, within the blink of an eye Caleb closed his hands around my arms and catapulted me back into obedient heaven. But this time it was stronger than before, he had separated my soul from my body again and I was floating in a sea of whiteness.

'You shouldn't keep doing that to her,' Blake's voice echoed in the background.

'She needs to be calm at the hearing! I can't have her ramble on about injustice! One wrong word and you're both dead!'

Silence.

'I can sense something in her, something... dark,' Caleb said.

'Could be the fact that she just murdered someone,' Blake snorted.

'When will you let go of your anger towards me?' Caleb snipped at Blake.

'When you stop lying to me!' Blake barked back.

'Blake, I am sorry. I was trying to protect you.' His voice was much softer now.

Blake breathed in deeply. 'There *is* something dark in her; I see it too.'

'What do you think it is?' Caleb's hands gently stroked my arm.

'Not sure… She drinks a lot. More than once she passed out on the street-'

'Follow her again,' Caleb instructed, 'I want to know what she does.'

I drifted into a peaceful sleep.

THE BLESSING

The council meeting had gone well as far as I could tell. Though, I faintly remembered slashing Jesper's stomach open with a knife, it felt like a distant disturbing dream. Maybe the anticipation of the hearing had given me nightmares. If I had killed someone I would have remembered, therefore it had to have been a bad dream.

Blake told them I was at home the night Jesper was killed. We had trained and then watched a movie. I assumed it was correct. I couldn't remember exactly. It was all a blur. When the council asked me what movie we saw and I couldn't answer, I noticed Blake tense up. He couldn't respond since it was my turn to answer questions and any interjections from him would have looked suspicious.

'I fell asleep to be honest. I was really tired after the training with Blake.'

The council members all leant forward. When I didn't flinch, they gradually leant back again and accepted my answers. Their dark robes floated in the air as if they were made of feathers floating in the wind. Before we were free to go, the council reminded us of our duty to eliminate molochs and vampires. Apparently, there had been an increase in their numbers and not enough counterattacks from our side.

I had made plans to see Kim after the hearing. Caleb and Blake did not speak during the ride to Santa's pub. I got the feeling there was tension in the car, but I couldn't really tell. My thoughts weren't forming properly, and I felt far away from reality.

Without a word exchanged, I got out of the car and entered Santa's pub. The music was upbeat and the warm yellow light made me forget all my troubles.

Kim wasn't there yet and as usual, I didn't wait for her before getting myself a drink. The pub was not too full and there were some seating areas available. While looking for the best spot, my gaze fell onto a dark corner behind the bar, with two tall green chairs and a small table with an old candle stuck on a wine bottle. That was where I had first met Ben, many nights ago. This was where it had all started.

An odd feeling of melancholy washed over me. There was something intense I felt in the back of my mind, but I couldn't identify what it was. Logic told me it was sorrow, but I couldn't tell, I couldn't... feel.

I moved to an empty red booth, with high backs. The booth was not the most comfortable one, but it was close to the bar.

Kim came in and hurried my way. 'You have no idea how much I've been looking forward to this!'

'It's been too long!' We hugged tightly. Kim told me she was still with June and things were going well. Kim had come out to Dominic and he had met June. Apparently, it had been as much a surprise to him as it had been to me. Kim now felt free enough to be herself. She still flirted with men but would at some point mention she was gay when she got bored of them. I gently asked if June ever got jealous of her flirting, to which she replied June didn't know she flirted casually. I remembered all too well my one and only interaction with June. It surprised me she hadn't made her jealousy clear.

The pub had filled up and the bar was no longer visible from our seats. We took turns getting new drinks and avoided talking to anyone we didn't know. I told Kim about Jesper's death and the council accusing me of having something to do with it. Of course, she asked me if I had killed him and I assured her I hadn't. I was certain of it! It gave me a weird sensation knowing that Ben's master had finally gotten what he deserved.

We drifted off into conversations about our human lives and the hours flew by. All too soon Kim was tired and ready to go home, so we left the bar and said our goodbyes at her car.

Across the parking lot we saw movement. A low hiss gave them away. Kim and I instinctively drew our guns. When the three creatures appeared behind a row of bushes Kim whispered to me to take the left one and she would take care of the two others. We fired simultaneously and two of the molochs went down. Kim grazed the third one with another shot, but it escaped yelping into the bushes that lined the back of the parking lot.

'We should check if the third one is close-by,' Kim announced, already heading towards the corpses.

I followed her and felt a cold shiver down my spine when I saw the blood oozing. It was disgusting to look at. My stomach growled.

No!

'Can't see it. Lucky bastard.' Kim turned away from the dense and dark bushes. 'I'm tired, let's go.'

I stared at the molochs on the ground. As I walked away, the urge in my head got louder and louder, like an itch screaming to be scratched. I wanted blood. I needed help. I couldn't keep going like this. I knew what I had to do.

'Kim, wait.'

'What's going on?' she asked opening the door to her car.

I looked around to make sure no one was close. Just the thought of uttering the words made me nervous.

'Close the door.' I opened the passenger side and climbed into the car. She followed suit.

'Kim, I have to tell you something,' I started, anxiously checking we were still alone. The parking lot was empty. It was dark and only a few streetlamps by the entrance of Santa's pub illuminated the surrounding.

'I... I have been doing something.' I leant closer and lowered my voice, 'Kim I have been drinking moloch blood.' My voice did not feel like my own. It all seemed surreal.

'What... do you mean *drinking* moloch blood?'

'The first time was an accident but it, it made me feel good. So I did it again and it made me feel better and better. It gives you this incredible high!' I whispered trying to hold back the smile on my face. It was as if I had gotten away with murder.

'Are you serious?'

'Yes! It's better than drugs Kim; it's so good!'

'Ameerah you sound crazy! How could you do that?! It's basically human blood!'

I had hoped she would understand. Now I realised how foolish I had been. How could anyone possibly understand and endorse what I was doing?

'It's *moloch* blood! I could never drink human blood!' I exclaimed at her accusation.

'But Meerah, you can't do this! You have to stop! It's... it's...'

'What? Dangerous? Illegal?'

'Yes!'

'Where does it say that? I was never told *not* to drink moloch blood. I get Caleb's blood transferred into me when I'm hurt anyway. What's the difference?!'

Kim shook her head. 'If it's no big deal then why don't you tell Caleb and Blake about it?!' she fired back.

I knew she was right, but it was too good, I couldn't give it up. It made me feel ecstatic! It made me feel stronger! Sure, it was morally a bit in the grey area, but what wasn't in this world?

'It makes me forget,' I confessed, staring at my hands. 'Kim, it makes you so happy and you forget all your pain!'

Kim took my hands and pulled them towards her. 'I can imagine how it makes you feel, but you shouldn't keep doing it-'

'Why not?!' I interrupted, eager to change her mind.

'There is a reason why no one else does it. Honey, you don't know what it could do to you. It could be changing you! And I might not know exactly what it does, but I have a bad feeling, hun. Please.'

It had already started changing me. I had overpowered Blake in a training session after drinking blood. But wasn't being stronger a good thing?

'I know...,' was all I could say. Telling her about my superior strength would not be a strong enough argument to make her change her mind. In my heart I knew she was right, but the voice of the addict in my head told me I wasn't doing anything wrong.

'Meerah, please. Promise me you will stop.' She squeezed my hands. Her eyes pleaded with me.

'I will try,' I agreed, unsure of my willpower to keep away from it.

Kim squeezed my hand one more time and looked at me with encouraging eyes. 'Can I drop you off?'

I shook my head. 'No, I think I want to walk'

'Are you sure? It's pretty far.'

'I need some air and I want to think. It's alright. I'll be ok.' I leant over to her and we hugged tightly.

She drove off and I was left to my thoughts. The night was crisp. Pulling my hoodie up and sticking my hands into my pockets, I started to walk in the direction of Blake's house.

Even after all this time I still didn't think of it as my home. It had always been Blake's house. Maybe I would have my own place one day, when Blake could no longer argue I was too inexperienced to live on my own. With June still in the picture Kim and I weren't moving in together anytime soon. The anger I felt for June exploded in my stomach. It surprised me to feel this intensely about her.

The moonlight reflected in the still water. It was a quiet and clear night. What I wouldn't give to be walking with my trusted Bruce back in the south of France, far away from all this...

There was a distant hissing. I stopped my brisk walk and listened for the sound again. It was them. I was sure of it.

Closing my eyes and breathing calmly, it took all of my concentration not to run towards the molochs, kill them and drink their blood. I had made Kim a promise. What would it say about me if I only kept my word for one hour?

There was a breeze and it felt like Kim was whispering in my ear to walk away. Opening my eyes, I determinedly pressed on and left the noises behind me. After a short while I was alone again and no sound disturbed my peace. My mind had stayed behind with the molochs. The addict screamed at me to go back and finish them off, to satisfy my thirst.

My legs carried me faster and faster away, hoping that my brain would eventually stop. The wind picked up and blew intensely, whistling in my ears.

The bloodthirst eventually calmed. As long as I kept moving, I would be okay. It had been a bad idea to walk home. I should have just let Kim drive me. This was an unnecessary temptation.

Another noise. I stopped and turned towards it. Again, the delicious sound called me.

A fight in my head broke out. An angel and a devil sitting on each shoulder, one telling me to keep going, the other to drink blood. The fight intensified and I couldn't move. Desperately, I tried to command my legs forward, but they wouldn't budge.

I took in a deep breath, smelling a faint scent of copper in the air.

That was it.

It was over.

My legs hammered down on the pavement as I ran as quickly as I could towards the moloch, gun in hand. One bullet in its head, the second bullet in the chest.

There were more. I could hear them, smell them. My head turned and my body followed into a nearby shop. The window was broken, but I was too big to fit through the hole.

I kicked in the door. Wild hissing and yelping accompanied my entrance. The molochs fled deeper into the shop, hiding in shadowy corners. I let several bullets fly. I had to reload the gun before finishing them off. Eventually, all was quiet again.

A few seconds of silence filled the space. My hands shook as I stashed the gun away. The anticipation was unbearable.

Sinking down to my knees close to one of the corpses, the intoxicatingly sweet smell of blood danced around my nose. The copper in the air made my head spin. Eagerly I dipped my fingers into the open wound and licked off the red release. I continued for several minutes before it entered my blood stream and started working its magic. The poison spread gradually and numbed my pain, replacing it with an incredible high. My mind detached from my body and soon I was high.

A violent noise woke me up. The door from the shop had been slammed shut by a sudden gust of wind. I couldn't have been out long; the bodies of the molochs had not started decaying yet. When I got up, the movement made the moloch blood stir in my system and the high lingered in my veins. It was powerful. I knew it would take a while for me to digest the copious amount of blood I had swallowed. Though I was satisfied and happy, I also felt the guilt quickly build up. Only a few hours ago had I promised Kim I would keep away from the red poison and I had not even managed one night... Was the problem more serious than I thought?

No! If I was still standing here, still breathing, after losing Ben, then I could fight this off too. This was nothing.

The drinking has intensified since Ben died, a voice in my head countered.

The demons were everywhere! Any excuse to keep my habit going!

Annoyed I kicked one of the molochs and a wave of blood spread out from underneath the body, sticking to my shoe.

I was on my way out when I saw a shelf full of sodas. It gave me an idea. I got one off the shelf and emptied it of its sticky sugary liquid. Then, I began the gory process of filling the bottle with blood from the moloch corpses. It was a messy job.

After twenty minutes of shovelling with my hands, and occasionally licking my fingers, I had three small bottles filled.

This would be my emergency supply. I was going to do my best to still fulfil my promise to Kim. These were... just for emergencies. Nothing more. Yes, just in case...

I could hear laughing in my head as I tried to tell myself it was just an emergency supply.

You don't have to stop.

I knew I had to. Kim was right. Who knew what it would do to me? What it was *already* doing to me...

Then let's just keep going!

No!

The voices in my head were getting louder.

I opened the door out into the night. The wind had picked up and whistled by my ears. Small drops of rain spattered my face. It was colder now. My hands and clothes were covered in blood once again. The wind made me shiver and the icy rain picked up. I hurried back towards the river and rushed the rest of the way home.

A good half an hour later I reached Blake's house. Before going up I stashed my emergency bottles in the glove compartment of my car. I pressed the door handle and silently entered the house. I hoped Blake was not awake, but I seemed to always have bad luck.

I tiptoed up the staircase, but Blake was standing in the middle of the living room and he turned the light on.

When my eyes had gotten used to the brightness, I knew there was something wrong. It was as if I was wearing old contact lenses. There was something like a curtain of fog everywhere I looked. All colours were faded.

'What did you do?!'

I looked down at myself and though the colours were faded, I could clearly see the velvet red blood sticking to my clothes and hands.

Déjà-vu...

This was not the first time I had come home, my clothes soaked in blood. All my blocked memories came rushing back; the

council meeting, Caleb manipulating my mind and Jesper. *Jesper!*
It was so clear now; I had broken into his house and killed him. *I
had killed him with the knife!*

The shock made me lose my balance, forcing me to hold
on to the wall next to my bedroom, leaving red stains on it. I was
a *murderer*. Caleb had made me forget so I would be calm during
the council hearing. Blake and Caleb had protected me.

'Answer me!'

I could feel the pressure; if I slipped up it was all our
heads, not just mine. And I had gone out drinking moloch blood
again. Damn, what had I done? I had to stop. I had to.

'Molochs,' I mouthed.

'Are you sure about that?' Blake stepped closer and
grabbed me by my shoulders, forcing me to look at him.

His expression changed. 'What's going on with your
eyes?'

The steel-blue in his eyes was dampened by the curtain
of fog but I could still see them clearly stand out against the grey
contrast.

'It was molochs,' I repeated louder and turned my face
away from his.

'Look at me!' Blake reached for my chin and pulled my
head towards his.

'Back off!' I retaliated and pushed him away, making
him stumble backwards.

He brushed his hand through his hair in defiance and
pointed at me. 'There is something going on with you and I will
find out what it is!'

Another part of my memory came back. I remembered
Caleb asking Blake to follow me! Had he seen me with the
molochs? Did he know my secret?

'Did you speak to Caleb after you dropped me off at
Santa's?' I hurried to ask before he was up the stairs to his
bedroom.

Blake stopped. 'Yes… Why?'

If he had been with Caleb, he couldn't have been spying on me. 'No reason, you two were so quiet in the car. I thought there was a problem between you two.' I shrugged.

'Caleb and I are fine. Don't worry about it,' he grunted then stomped up the remaining stairs and slammed his bedroom door shut.

I knew he was worried and his way of showing it was through anger. This blood-drinking was tearing us all apart... I had to end it.

The voice in my head was still laughing.

* * *

Holly walked into the house and waved at me. She was wearing a blue shimmery top with a low-cut front, her long red hair tumbling down both sides of her shoulders, a pair of tight black jeans topped off with black high heels.

'Ok, Holly just got here. I'll come pick you up in twenty minutes. Be ready!' I warned Kim over the phone.

'Relax, I'll be ready!' Kim responded and hung up.

'Women.' I rolled my eyes. 'Let's go.' I nodded towards Holly.

Blake had gone off somewhere for the night, leaving me in charge of Holly. The council had called Caleb in for another hearing, so he was indisposed as well. Holly and I had decided to go out with Kim to celebrate our 'adult-free' time before it was back to the usual training schedule.

To my delight June was not able to join. The further I stayed away from her the better. Every time I thought about her, I got angry.

I slipped into my pumps and grabbed a gun.

'What are you doing?' Holly pointed at the gun while I stashed it into the back of my skirt.

'I always carry a gun. In this shithole you can never be too careful. Didn't Blake teach you?' I reached for two additional clips and dropped them in my handbag. The memories of Vladimir still haunted me.

'He did but I thought since we're going to the pub it won't be necessary tonight.' Holly shrugged her shoulders.

She was probably right but out of habit, I took my gun everywhere. We walked down to the brand-new BMW that Blake had procured for me after ditching the incriminating Volvo.

I switched my shoes over to flats to drive us to Kim's house. We parked in front of her apartment and waited in the car. Ten minutes later, she finally came rushing towards us in a figure-hugging dress that went down to her knees.

'We've been waiting for you,' I teased.

'I'm worth the wait.' She snapped her fingers. 'Now get us to the bar!'

Holly turned towards the backseat where Kim was sitting and waived a bottle in front of Kim's eyes. 'Pre-bar drinks?'

'What is it?'

'Rum and coke.'

'Not my usual style, but ok.' Kim took a sip from the bottle. 'That's strong!'

I looked in the rear-view mirror and saw her face distorting. A chuckle escaped my mouth. The girls were getting tipsy while I only had a few small gulps of the strong rum and coke mix. Blake had explicitly told me to watch out for Holly and I was not about to have another car accident and have to explain myself. It was one thing if she got a scratch from a moloch, a completely different one if I was the reason for Holly's broken bones.

'So, Holly should we get you a man tonight?' Kim nudged Holly.

'I don't know; I'm not into all those muscly guys, they all seem so shallow and self-absorbed.'

Kim smiled cheekily. 'You could come onboard the girl's side.' She winked at Holly and we all exploded in laughter.

Kim's phone rang and she shushed us. 'Dom I told you-' Kim stopped mid-sentence. I looked up in the rear-view mirror. I saw her face was in shock. Something wasn't right.

'Where are you?' Was Dominic in trouble? The strong, tall, Italian man? It had to be serious. Or he was making a scene...

'Ok just stay where you are,' Kim went on, 'We'll come get you. Ameerah is with me-' Kim went silent again. All colour drained from her face.

'Yes, I will... Ok... Yes – but... Yes... Understood.' She hung up and pulled herself forward on her seat. 'Meerah we need to go to this address. And we need to get Blake there too.'

My phone dinged, indicating I had received a message. Holly opened the message and put the address into the GPS.

'What's going on?'

'Dom got surprised by a pack of molochs. He barricaded himself in a room, but he doesn't know how long it will hold them off. He's badly injured and losing a lot of blood.' Her voice sounded uncharacteristically scared.

My thoughts raced for few seconds as I formulated a plan. 'Holly, dial Blake's number and give me your phone.'

'I'm calling Gordon,' Kim interjected.

'I have a bag of Caleb's blood in the back, we can use that to keep Dom going,' I said, looking into the rear-view mirror at her.

'Shit-wait! Gordon is in the human world! He might not make it back in time!' Kim held her head with both hands.

'Caleb did for me so call him.' Echoes of Jesper's betrayal played in my head.

Holly held out her phone towards me. 'Holly what's going on?' I heard on the receiving end.

'It's me. We have a problem,' I announced calmly while making a tight turn. The tyres squealed in protest.

'What?'

'Dom is hurt and pinned down by molochs. Holly is gonna text you his address. I need you to get there ASAP.'

'Is Holly with you now?'

'Yes, she's in the car'

'Fuck...' I could hear Blake taking a deep breath, 'Meerah you have to-'

'I will. Just get to the address.'

'Are you loaded?'

My eyes went over to my handbag on Holly's lap. 'Kim, how many guns do you have?' I lifted my head and looked in the mirror.

'One handgun with one extra clip,' she answered while on the phone with her master.

'Two guns, three clips' I responded to Blake. This was slim to fight off a hoard of molochs.

The car was brand new and I hadn't stocked it full of guns yet like I usually did. I glanced over to my phone and saw we were almost at the destination. It was an industrial part of the city with high-rising factory buildings looming over us.

'Holly can't fight. I know she's field approved but-' Blake started.

'I know. I'll take care of it. We're almost there, I have to go.'

'Watch your back please. I can't lose you.' His last words resonated in my head. Was he trying to tell me he was in love with me?

'Don't worry,' I responded softly and hung up. There was no time for that nonsense now.

I stopped the car and turned to Holly. Kim leant forward and we had a huddle in the car. 'Holly, I need you to get back to Kim's and get blood bags for Dom.'

'I'll text you my address,' Kim said, already typing on her phone.

'When you get back here, I want you to park away from the building and text us. Do not get out of the car!' I emphasised the last sentence while looking Holly directly in the eyes.

'Are you sure?' Her eyes were big and anxious.

'Yes! Do not leave the car. I can't be worrying about you if we need to get Dom out.' I looked at her with as much authority as I could. If she got hurt Blake would never forgive me.

'I'll do as you say.' She nodded.

I reached for my handbag and gave the two clips to Kim. Then, I handed Holly my handgun. 'Just in case.'

Holly nodded and got out of the car and hurried to the driver's side. In a quick motion I reached for the glove compartment and shoved the three bottles of moloch blood into my purse. Kim had taken Caleb's blood bag from the boot and joined me outside the car. We walked towards the factory where Dom was hiding. My BMW sped off behind us.

'I shoot and you – stay behind me.' Kim checked her gun. Her high heels were making a lot of unwanted noise.

'Fine. Did Dom say how many molochs were in there?' We approached a service entrance.

'He said more than a dozen.'

I stopped and turned to her. 'More than a dozen?! And I have no gun!'

Kim shrugged apologetically and pressed her lips into a tight line.

'Let's just get it over with.' I pointed at the door, annoyed at the situation. Kim walked towards the door, her back to me. Maybe I should have kept my gun... too late now.

Kim might be confident in her abilities with one single gun and a bleeding Dominic attracting all the molochs in a ten-mile radius, but I was not rolling the dice. I reached into my handbag and got out one of the blood bottles. As soon as I opened it, the blood called me. Kim entered the building and I followed her inside, taking a big gulp from the red liquid. Inadvertently, I made a sound of pleasure and Kim turned around. Her first reaction was shock; then it quickly changed to anger. 'What the hell are you doing?!' she whispered forcefully.

'It makes me stronger'

'It also makes you high! You said so yourself!'

'Not if I'm careful! Come on Kim, it's two of us against a hoard of molochs and I don't even have a god-damn gun!'

Kim stepped towards me and pointed at my face. 'If you fuck up, I'm leaving you here!'

Her eyes blazed with fury. With a quick movement she turned around, whipping her hair at my face and continued to walk along the hallway. I rolled my eyes and followed her deeper into the factory.

The walls and floors were white, neon lights above us turned on as we walked further inside, activated by our movements. There were numerous doors on each side, but all were locked. We listened at each of them but couldn't hear anything from the inside. If Dom was pinned down by molochs we would hear them.

The corridor turned left, and we followed it around the corner. When I looked back it was dark. The lights at the end of the hall had already switched off, obscuring the exit. This promised to be fun...

I lifted the bottle to my lips and swallowed half of the contents. Kim growled when she heard me drinking.

The hall ended at a door with a small window. Kim peered through the window. 'I see big engines downstairs. We need to go down a flight of stairs and then there are large containers and machinery on each side. Plenty of hiding places...'

'Do you think he's down there?' I leant against the door and looked at her.

'If I was a moloch I would hide down there so I'm assuming he is as well.'

'Can you hear them?'

Kim pressed her ear against the window. 'No... I hear the sound of machinery. If they are down there the machines are drowning them out.'

She nodded in my direction and I opened the door. With the gun pointed straight ahead she stepped out onto the metal stairs. Suddenly she tripped backwards and would have landed on the floor, if I hadn't caught her.

'Fucking shoes!' she swore and slipped out of her high heels, one of which was firmly stuck in the metal-grated stairs. When she ripped it out, the heel nearly came off. Angrily, she placed the shoes to the side of the door and went on barefoot. I followed her out into the lit warehouse.

We were lucky molochs could not shoot guns otherwise we would have already been dead. The stairs were in the middle of the room and high up. We were exposed from all sides. Slowly we stepped down the stairs, as quietly as possible. The further we went, the more noises we heard. Some of the rounded white metal containers were vibrating slightly and emitting a deep humming sound. I guessed there was some sort of pressure system making things rotate at a steady pace. From the clean and spartan surroundings I could not make out what kind of production this was, and to be honest I didn't care. All I wanted was to get Dom out and be done with it. We were supposed to be having a ladies night out, not sneaking around in a factory, outnumbered and outgunned.

Kim walked to the left side of the warehouse and stayed close to the wall to give us some cover. The moloch blood started taking effect, making me feel confident. I concentrated on my steps to steady myself against the high that was building inside me. If I passed out Kim would have two bodies to drag out of here...

'I can hear something,' Kim whispered over her shoulder.

I looked back to make sure no one was following us. That's when I saw it. A single moloch had climbed up the metal container and was eyeing us from above.

'Kim!' I called under my breath, tapping her on the shoulder. When she turned, I pointed at the moloch and she pulled the trigger. The sound resonated loudly in the large hall and echoed off the metal structures. We both heard the hissing and howling in the distance that seemed to come from everywhere. They knew we were there.

Kim continued to the left around a corner. The sound of rabid molochs was much louder. The corridor was dark and the light would not turn on. I looked back only to see three of them crawling closer. When I turned back towards Kim two more were in front of her. Kim shot the front two but by the time she turned backwards she only managed to shoot one out of the three following us. The others escaped behind shadowy corners.

There was a sudden banging nearby; first one, then several thumps.

'Dom,' Kim said under her breath.

He must have heard the shots. I could smell his blood before we saw him. We came to another bend to the left and came face to face with a huge heat-sealed door. A trail of blood drops led to it. Kim ran towards it and pressed her nose against the small glass in the centre of the door.

'It's Dom!' she exclaimed with relief.

Before I had time to join her, something ran into me and slammed my head against the wall. My head split with pain that set my ears ringing. I fell to the ground as the world spun. Shots echoed and mixed with the ringing in my head. Kim appeared to my right. Her dark vague outline stood over me. She bent down and said something to me, but I couldn't understand what she was saying. Slowly the ringing subsided and the pain diminished enough for me to make sense of the world. I knew I had to get up to help Kim get out of here.

'Gimme som,' I managed to say.

'What? What do you need?' Her voice sounded muffled.

'Blood!'

Kim must have thought about it because it seemed to take forever before she finally raised my head and put the bottle to my lips. Holding the bottle with both hands I let the red liquid enter my body. Kim positioned herself behind me and pulled my upper body up.

Shots pierced the air, renewing the ringing in my ears and making me cringe.

Within minutes the blood started working. The ringing disappeared, my sight cleared, and my mind sharpened.

'Meerah, are you ok now?' Kim shook me. Her arms were wrapped around my stomach, holding me upright. Her gun rested in her right hand in my lap. The molochs had been scared away by her shooting, but they were lurking behind every corner and eyeing us with hungry eyes.

'I'm alright.' I raised myself up.

'Let's get Dom... - Meerah!' Kim gasped when I turned to face her.

'What?'

'Your eyes, they look... different. Your pupils are... oval, and the red...' she trailed off, but her gaze remained fixed on me.

A moloch behind her moved and caught my attention. It jumped into the air, stretching out its claws ready to insert them into Kim's back. It opened its mouth mid-flight, showing off its long teeth.

It was as if time had slowed down; I pushed Kim aside and stretched my right hand out towards the moloch's throat. The moloch tried to change its course mid-flight, but I was too fast. My hand closed around its throat and pressed it tight before its claws reached me. An audible crack accompanied the crushing of its spine in my bare hand. I let go of the body and watched it collapse into a stack of dead limbs. When I turned around, Kim was staring at me with wide eyes. She shook her head in disbelief.

'This is where you say thank you.' I tilted my head at her, my voice filled with sarcasm.

Kim opened her mouth but couldn't seem to find the right words. 'How did you move so fast?!' she eventually said.

'What do you think? Now let's get out of here!' I walked over to Dominic's hide-out and peered inside.

He saw me at the door and slowly raised himself up from the floor. There was a pool of blood around him. I could feel my thirst stirring at the sight of all that red. 'Take care of Dom. I'll take out the molochs.' I quickly turned away from Dominic and the terrifying temptation.

Perhaps drinking blood had not been a good idea. Yet, *not* trying to calm my craving would have been even worse.

Dom opened the door and the smell of his blood invaded my nostrils. Everything around me disappeared and all I wanted was to obey my thirst. The delicious scent of his blood seduced me. I could feel myself stepping closer to the open door. The sound of his heartbeat drummed through my body. I could hear the blood being pushed through his veins, all that sweet blood...

Something bit my leg and I awoke from my trance. The molochs, also attracted by Dominic's blood, had surrounded me, tearing my mind away from my murderous intentions. I kicked the nearest one and it smashed against the white wall, leaving a bloody crater where its head impacted. Another two jumped up towards my throat. Time slowed down again and it seemed they were floating towards me at a leisurely pace. With my right hand I formed a fist and punched the closest one in the side of its face. This sent the creature tumbling into the second.

Another moloch landed on my back. I reached back and grabbed its arm, tearing the creature off my body and throwing it at two more molochs in front of me. Attracted by the blood trickling from my leg, one snuck in closer and was getting ready to sink its teeth in. That one got a kick from my bleeding foot.

Another one behind me hopped up and got a hold of my arm and bit me. I tried to shake it off, but its teeth were deep in my flesh. A second got a hold of my bleeding leg and began sucking the blood out of it. With a violent swing against the wall I crushed the skull of the moloch clinging to my arm. Two more jumped on my back. They were everywhere!

I threw myself repeatedly into the wall, squeezing the two molochs on my back. One let go but the other one sunk its claws deep into my shoulder blades. As for the one by my leg enjoying my blood, I reached for it with my left hand and twisted its neck until it snapped before it could do any more damage. Before I even had time to inhale, yet another was attacking me.

Suddenly the molochs hissed in fear and retreated, even the one with its claws in my back. Within seconds they had all disappeared, leaving me alone, holding onto the wall, out of breath, my heart racing.

My sense of danger switched into overdrive, buzzing in every cell of my body. Something much worse was coming my way. I wanted to disappear as well, run away from whatever was coming for me, but I couldn't leave Kim and Dom behind. It would mean their certain deaths.

It was silent. No more molochs hissing. Only my own breathing.

Click. Click. Click.

I jumped up and spun away from the sound. Kim's head appeared through the open door. 'Are you al-'

'Give me the last bottle.' My voice trembled.

'What's going on?' she whispered, motionless.

I knew what was coming. It could only be one thing. I hurried to Kim, my hands shaking. 'Give me the bottle.'

Finally, she disappeared from the doorway. I took a nervous look around. It had to be close. We had to hurry. There was no time to get away. I would have to hold it off long enough for Kim and Dominic to make a run for it.

'What's going on?' Kim mouthed.

I took a long chug from the bottle. 'Vampire…'

Kim's face fell. It took her a few seconds to react. 'Take the gun.'

The moloch blood inside me spread quickly. My nerves calmed. 'No. You need it. Call Blake. When he's close, take Dom and get out.'

My vision became sharper, but colours continued to fade.

'Meerah, no! You can't face it alone!' She reached for my arms and clung to them in desperation.

'If you don't get Dominic to Gordon, he will bleed to death. You need to get out of here!' Memories of Ben needlessly slipping away because Jesper refused to come flooded my mind.

'Lock the door. I'll be alright.' I pushed her back inside, where Dom was laying half-conscious.

The vampire was close, I could feel it. I took another pull from the bottle of red liquid. Tears shone in Kim's eyes.

'Don't worry, the moloch blood makes me strong.'

I tried to look as confident as possible in my own abilities.

Hesitantly, she let go of me and closed the door. Her face looked at me through the window with desperation. I gave her one last encouraging nod and turned away.

All colours were long since gone, but my senses were at their highest. I was aware of everything around me. I could feel the blood pulsing through my veins and oxygenating my cells. My heart pumped steadily. Though it was all in grey tones, everything around me was sharp and detailed. I inhaled deeply and could smell Dominic's blood spreading on the floor, Kim's perfume hovered nearby. Overpowering all of those was the distinct smell of danger approaching.

A loud bang echoed off the walls and floors. It was inside the building. I could hear footsteps.

My eyes scanned the factory for any movement, my muscles tense and ready for attack.

Slowly, a man turned the corner and eyed me with bright crimson eyes. They stood out against his dark clothing and made him look even more ferocious.

'What do we have here?' he asked playfully, tilting his head from side to side. He breathed in deeply. 'I can smell blood but... you seem unscathed.' His clothes were of different shades of grey. Slung over his shoulders was a black coat that went down to his knees with a high collar.

This was the end. I was sure of it. Suddenly I felt naked and exposed. I had no fucking weapons! I would die. This was it. The end...

In one sudden motion he reached me, towering over me, his eyes fixed on me, his prey. I threw a punch, but he caught my arm before I even touched him. With incredible force he pushed my arm backwards, making me stumble against the wall. He grabbed my other arm and pulled himself closer. He breathed in my scent and bent down to my neck. With all my strength, I thrust my knee up into his gut. He groaned in pain, folding to the side, letting go of my arms.

There was no time. I rammed into him with my shoulder and against the opposite wall. The vampire hissed with rage. He violently shoved me off. His right fist smashed into my face as his other fist slammed into the side of my hip. The impact should have broken bones but somehow, I was still in one piece. The vampire crushed my abdomen and I sank down to the floor. He continued kicking me in the stomach and face.

Eventually, he stepped back, rearranging his clothes. I crawled away, using the wall behind me to pull myself up onto my shaking legs, trying to catch my breath. When he saw me struggling, a smile appeared on his face. He approached and swung his arm to deliver another blow. The arm approached slower than it should have. Somehow, I had time to duck and jab him into his ribs. His hand shot forward and closed around my throat, lifting me up. My feet no longer touched the ground. The pressure in my head made me dizzy. I tried to claw at his hand and arm, but I could not make his grip loosen up. Flashbacks of Viktor appeared in front of my eyes.

The vampire got closer and smelled my hair, another wicked smile on his lips. His eyes were the same colour Viktor's had been. Just like mine...

I kicked my foot into his stomach. The surprising force of it made him let go and stumble backwards. I fell to the ground and gasped for air. My body moved to get up and into a somewhat descent defensive position.

The vampire eyed me with a slight air of fear. 'How are you so strong?!'

Like a lion scouting out his prey he moved in a half-circle around me, looking at me from every angle.

Then, the beast threw himself at me yelling like a crazed animal. We both went down and smacked against the hard ground. The vampire reached for my throat again, this time with both his hands. I got a hold of his wrists before he could close his fingers around my already bruised throat.

Painstakingly slowly I pulled his arms further away from my throat, my muscles shaking at the resistance, sweat pearling down my forehead. The vampire used his bodyweight to swing himself away from above me, making me lose my grip on his wrists as he wriggled his hands free. He kicked me in the stomach, pushing us in opposite directions and out of each other's reach.

How was I still unscathed? The moloch blood was fuelling me, but would my ghost-body be able to withstand the beating it was getting?

On all fours I crawled towards the vampire, he turned his back towards me to slide away. I climbed halfway on top of his back and reached around his throat. The vampire tried to get me off him and flipped over, squeezing me between the floor and his back. He pushed as much as he could into me, pressing the air out of my lungs. He threw his arms and legs around, trying to destabilise me. I was struggling to keep a hold on him. The vampire slowed down as I suffocated him. Eventually, he stilled and slumped onto the ground. But I knew if I let go there was a chance of him waking up. So I grabbed hold of his head and twisted it violently. There was an unpleasant noise. His neck was broken.

Out of breath and exhausted I wriggled out from under him and lay there motionless, trying to calm myself down.

I opened my eyes after a minute and saw a face staring down at me. Shocked, the blood in my veins froze and my heart stopped. A pair of bright red eyes glowing with hunger. It was another one! *Another fucking one!*

Before I had even time to blink, he had grabbed my leg and started pulling me along the concrete. I tried to twist out of his grip, but he held on tightly to my leg. He pulled me around the corner, past Kim and Dominic's hiding spot, and out towards the open factory floor. The rumbling sound intensified.

Holding on to my shoe, he threw me against the wall. The impact made me dizzy and I could smell blood, my own blood. The vampire walked around me, making me feel like a lost cause. I had to keep fighting, Kim and Dom were still in danger. To my left were some tools, hanging on the wall.

A smile spread across his face when he caught sight of what I was looking at. He took a hammer, pointing the nasty spiked end towards me and took a big swing. I rolled away and the hammer narrowly missed my leg. I crawled under a row of tables while he hammered after me, throwing tools and tables aside. Long metal bars rained down on the floor and my back, bruising my spine. The pain shot through my body, paralysing me long enough for him to reach me and slam the two long spikes of the hammer into the back of my right thigh.

My scream drowned out the machinery buzzing next to us. He pulled me towards him using the hammer embedded in my flesh, tearing the wound further open. My nails dug into the floor, trying to stop myself from being pulled closer but they slipped along the waxed laminated floor.

As he dragged me back my right hand gathered a handful of nails that were tossed across the floor. When he grabbed my waist and turned me towards him, I threw the nails at his face and punched him in the side. Without thinking I tore the hammer out of my thigh and slammed it as hard as I could into his abdomen. Now *he* was the one screaming in pain.

I tried to throw myself on top of him, but he pushed me away and I landed on the hard ground, just under the wall with all the tools. There were some loose metal bars not too far from me. With a big lunge I reached for one and as I rolled onto my back, I could see him running towards me. I swung as far as I could and smashed the metal bar into his head. It stopped him in his tracks, making him stumble into the wall and onto the ground. The metal bar had bent from the impact. I used it to hoist myself up onto my legs. The back of my right leg was pissing blood, making the floor around me slippery. Both my legs were now bleeding.

Before the monster had time to get up, I hit him again, bending the metal bar further. Several times I hit the vampire until his skull split open and blood and brain splattered everywhere. The metal bar made a clanking noise when I let it go and it hit the waxed floor. My hands were trembling. My clothes were covered in his blood and pieces of his brain and skull.

Limping towards Dominic and Kim's hideout, I tried to wipe the mixture of blood and sweat from my face. I knocked on the door, but Kim only opened it when I called out her name. Her face was white as paper when she saw me.

'Get Dom out now,' was all I managed to mouth.

'You look like one of them.' Her voice was barely more than a terrified whisper. I had never seen her so scared. The look she gave me was unbearable. I wanted to scratch out my own eyes just to not have to see the fear in her eyes ever again. Her fear of me.

A renewed sense of unease in my stomach alarmed me. My head tilted towards where I had just come from.

'Kim get out now,' I whispered. Without waiting for her to respond, I limped back to where I had killed the last vampire. Another one appeared.

Another one! Was this a nest?! Where were they all coming from?!

He bared his teeth in amusement at the destruction around us.

I could hear Kim trying to get Dominic up not far behind me. The vampire ran towards me, showing his long sharp teeth. In one motion I bowed down and turned, aiming my left shoulder right at him. He hit me with full force in the shoulder, but I was able to hold him off. With my right hand I boxed into his abdomen. The vampire cast me aside and moved towards Kim who was at the door, Dominic leaning heavily on her. She fired three shots at the vampire to slow him down. I threw myself at the beast and tore him away from them, landing on the ground. The vampire got up, pushing me off his back, but I got a hold of his leg and stopped him from going after Kim and Dominic. With all my willpower I clung to his leg and refused to let go.

From the corner of my eye, I saw Kim turn her back and slowly move away from the danger. Dominic was barely able to move his feet. Kim held him upright, pulling him along with her.

The vampire kicked me in the stomach, breaking some ribs. Just as he was about to set off again in pursuit of Kim and Dominic, I swung my left leg forward between his feet, making him trip and fall. I clawed at his feet and as quickly as I could, crawled up his leg towards his hips, and further up onto his back. He tried to get me off, but my strength prevailed. As he tried to get a hold of me with his left hand, I pulled at the arm as hard as I could. A crack confirmed I had disconnected it from his shoulder. I got up and grabbed a hold of the disconnected arm and pulled him backwards, towards where I had smashed the brains in of the second vampire. He reached backwards with his good arm, but I had already pulled him to where I wanted him. I let go and lunged for another one of those metal bars. When I faced him, he was on his feet. He was leaning towards me, his bad arm dangling helplessly to his left side.

I attacked by swinging the metal bar towards him, trying to hit him. He backtracked and ducked until he got a hold of the bar and snatched it out of my hands. As he pulled it out of my hands, he also pulled me towards himself and reached for my throat. But I knew they often went for the throat and I turned sideways. I twisted his broken arm again, so I was now standing behind him.

Now I swung my right arm around his neck and pressed it closed as hard as I could. He tried to scratch at me with his one arm, but it was useless. I squeezed as hard as I could. My body wanted to give in, but I used up all of my willpower to focus on killing him. My fingers were slippery with blood and sweat, and my arms trembled from the struggling vampire. It did not matter; all I focused on was saving those I loved.

Eventually his body relaxed and he stopped struggling. Drained and worn out, I let go and prayed this was the last one. This fight had taken all of me, more than I thought I had and now there was nothing left inside. My whole body shook. With my last strength I got hold of the metal bar he had taken from me and bashed his head in until his skull was a smashed pumpkin.

The sight of the three dead vampires made me convulse. How was I still alive? How had I fought all three of them off?

Then the hissing started to come back. The molochs were lurking, eyeing an easy meal. *This world was relentless!*

I could not stay here. Blake was coming. He could not see me like this. My eyes had changed. Kim had said I looked like one of them. Altogether, those were more than enough reason for me to disappear.

My right leg screamed with pain at every step from the deep tissue damage of the hammer. My purse lay in the doorway of the room Kim and Dominic had hidden in. With the help of one of the metal bars I hobbled towards it and then out the back of the factory. Blake would most likely be coming from the front of the factory, where Kim had dragged Dominic out. He could not see me like this.

THE CURSE

I shivered near uncontrollably. The rain had picked up again. I struggled against the blasting wind. I couldn't remember how long I had been walking. My head was dizzy from blood loss. Whenever I remembered the dead vampires sprawled across the factory floor, I convulsed. How had I made it out alive? I had left so much carnage. Blood, brain and bone fragments *everywhere*.

A new gust of wind pulled at my clothes, finding the tears in my jeans jacket, cooling me again. Tumbling and shaking, I fell through a door to an apartment complex. Aiming for the first door beyond the entrance, I pushed it open and inspected the surroundings. It was a basement filled with washing machines and tumble dryers. The soft rumbling made me sleepy. It was not the safest place to hide, but it would have to do. My skin was cold and sweaty. The adrenaline had left my body and my muscles protested.

One of the dryers finished its cycle and beeped twice. With the last of my energy I emptied it of its fluffy, hot duvet sheets and wrapped myself in them.

Several times I broke out of my feverish sleep with my stomach aching and contracting uncontrollably, followed by episodes of vomiting blood.

When I fully woke up, I wanted to get up and go home but I had no energy to move. All I could do was lie there and let myself be pulled back into a troubled sleep.

Several days passed, before I was able to stay awake longer than a few moments to vomit, or later dry heave. The blood attracted all kinds of unwanted animals; small insects and crawling bugs gathered to have a taste. Every time I woke up, I found more of them had appeared, crawling over me, buzzing and flying around.

It was the rat that finally forced me to get myself up and away from the tsunami of insects. I saw it run across the floor from one side of the room to the other and disappear into a hole in the wall behind one of the washing machines. It was so disgusting if I had not emptied myself previously, I would have then. It brought with it the smell of rotting food mixed with dampness.

My hunger flourished with each step I took. Or was it thirst? There was nothing I wanted more than a shower, but I knew I had to drink blood first. It was unbearable to think about all the blood I had thrown up over the last few days and still crave more of it. If I hadn't been on my way to hell before, I certainly was now.

The sun was high in the sky, the temperatures mild. What I wouldn't give to be freed of this nightmare. Tears fell from my eyes and mixed with the dirt and dried blood on my face. I smelled of death.

On my way to Blake's house, I stopped for a quick kill; it was automatic, like a reflex. It hadn't taken me more than a few minutes to locate one and finish the little creatures off. I was repulsed by the sight of the dead moloch and the blood oozing out of its neck, but my addiction threw any sense of dignity out of the window and soon my face was covered in fresh blood.

When I finally reached Blake's house, I was relieved to see his car was not parked in the driveway. Aware of how horrific I must have looked I hurried into the house and locked the bathroom door behind me. When my eyes caught my reflection in the mirror, I froze in utter shock. There was nothing human about me anymore. I couldn't recognise myself. My face was covered in dirt, tears, and fresh and dried blood. The layer of filth on my face was so thick you couldn't see my skin beneath it. I pulled one of my sleeves up. The skin underneath was white. My once deep brown eyes had been replaced with reptilian ones. Though the pupils were back to their normal shape, they looked primitive and empty. My clothes were covered in blood and dirt. It was a much worse sight than after I had butchering the molochs after Ben's death, or after I had killed Jesper. What had I become? What would Ben think if he saw me now?

New tears rolled down my cheeks barely visible on the crust on my face. Mechanically, I undressed and stepped into the shower. The water turned grey and the dirt caked under my feet while I scrubbed my skin and hair. I washed myself thoroughly with half the bottle of shampoo and conditioner.

By the time the last of the suds had washed away, the drain had gotten clogged by the dirt. My hair felt light and fresh, as if nothing had ever happened.

Wishfully, I dared a look into the mirror. The reflection resembled something more like myself again. A bit of make-up would cover the rings under my eyes and make me look more human again. Just as I got out of the bathroom, I heard Blake open the door at the bottom of the stairs. I stuffed my blood-covered clothes under my bed and swung the door to my bedroom shut behind me. I put on some comfortable clothes and a dash of make-up before reopening the door.

Blake was sitting in his usual chair, his head resting against his left hand. He sighed deeply when he saw me come out of my bedroom.

'Where have you been? I was worried about you.' He got up and approached me. Fearing he would see something different about me, I ran off into the kitchen.

'I was out. I had to think about things. Ok? The fight brought back bad memories.'

'Where did you go? You were gone for days!' His voice got louder.

'I... I... there were molochs so I ran after them and killed some, alright?!'

'You...' Blake couldn't help but chuckle. 'You ran after some molochs? That's your excuse? You couldn't come up with anything better than that during all this time that you were gone?!' He crossed his arms over his chest and stood in front of me, blocking any possible escape from the kitchen. I proceeded to make myself a coffee.

There was a moment of silence. Then he stepped closer, eyeing me with those icy blue eyes. 'You know, Kim was very vague on what happened in that warehouse and your whereabouts afterwards. All she would say was that you would be fine. Lucky for me, Dominic woke up yesterday and filled me in on some of the details,' Blake began. His eyes fixated on me, searching for any sign of hesitation. 'He didn't remember much but he did say he clearly saw you kill a vampire *with your bare hands.*'

I let a few moments pass before I confirmed it.

'When I got to the warehouse,' Blake tilted his head, 'There were *three* dead vampires.'

'Yes... and?'

Blake backed away from me and brushed through his hair in frustration. 'How do you explain this? How were you able to **kill** *three* vampires **with your bare hands**?!' He gesticulated wildly.

'I guess I got lucky. I don't know, the adrenaline, whatever.' I reached for the cup of coffee and brushed past him out of the kitchen, my head bowed down and focusing on the floor.

'Ameerah, this is not normal!' He grabbed my arm and spun me back around. Our faces were so close I felt his breath on my cheeks. His deep blue eyes scrutinised me, searching for any flicker on my face. 'Tell me the truth!'

Had my pupils really gone back to their usual shape? Suddenly I couldn't remember.

'Fine! I killed them, with my bare hands! I was scared and I knew Kim and Dom were going to die if I didn't protect them! Dominic was bleeding all over the place-' a shudder went through me as I remembered the delicious smell of his blood. I was disgusted with myself. So much so, I had to hold back dry heaves.

He let go of my arm and I backed away. I turned around and walked towards my bedroom.

'What about when Ben died?' he asked.

Just like that he opened the box I so desperately tried to keep closed. I slowly turned to look at him. Thunder stormed inside me.

'I told you not to speak of him,' I threatened in a low voice.

'You weren't this strong when Ben died. You had guns-,' Blake pushed.

I knew he was doing it on purpose, but I couldn't stop myself. I threw the hot cup of coffee at him, the liquid spilling out and splashing across his arm, as he lifted it to protect his face. I threw myself at him, hitting him and making us both fall to the floor. Blake pushed me off and into the kitchen wall. He rolled away, trying to crawl away from me, but I jumped back on top of him, pushing the air out of his lungs. Blake hit me in the face with his elbow, breaking my nose.

Blake got out from under me and got a hold of the table in the living room. He tried to lift himself up, but I lunged at him before he had time to get out of my reach. My swing was too strong and we both crashed into the leg of the table, making the table rock. Guns sprawled out onto the floor and loose bullets rained down on us.

Blake reached back towards me and got a hold of my throat, pressing my windpipe shut. I swung my right fist and connected it with his face. He let go of my throat and I fell to the side. He then kicked me, making me slide further away. I tried to roll back on all fours, as he crawled behind the table. Furious, I fought my way back closer to him and had reached his right leg, but before I had managed anything, I heard the distinct click of a handgun being cocked.

Instinctively I ducked away. Blake fired a warning shot. Again, he kicked me, this time with both feet and I crashed into the upper staircase, banging my head against the wood.

'**Ameerah!**' he screamed.

I stopped. I realised what I had done. Blake had the gun pointed at me. His eyes were full of incomprehension and disbelief.

What had I done?

'I'm sorry, I didn't mean to…,' I spoke, barely audible.

Blake shook his head. 'What's going on with you?' he asked perplexed. I could see it in his eyes; he was worried, and afraid.

He let go of the gun and pushed himself up on his feet. Without looking at me again, he walked up the stairs and into his bedroom.

How could I snap like this? I had shot him once before but that was after he had shot Ben. This was different.

I was so ashamed. Was the moloch blood affecting my mood? It had to be. Was I too far down that path to stop? What could I do now? Admit what I had gotten myself into? No, no, no, I could never admit to Blake what I had done. He wouldn't understand.

Tears were stinging in my eyes. What was going on with me?

I had to stop. For real this time. *I. Had. To. Stop.* I couldn't continue.

You're doomed, a voice whispered in my head.

Panicked, I dialled the one person who knew my secret. Kim was grateful to hear from me, but as soon as I told her what had happened since I had left the factory, everything up to and including the fight with Blake, she grew more and more concerned. Her nervousness was contagious. By the end of the call I felt even more helpless. She was surprised Blake had not seen it in my eyes.

I remembered Caleb had asked Blake to follow me. Last time I had gotten lucky, but it wouldn't happen a second time. Now more than ever he suspected something was going on.

I had to stay positive, I could do this. If I could fight molochs and vampires and survive in this shithole of a place, away from my friends and family and forced to serve sixty-some years for a crime I had not committed, torn away from my love, then I could get over my addiction to moloch blood.

To avoid temptation, I stayed inside and trained. When I wasn't training, I read or watched TV. Blake was never far and I caught him watching me all the time.

The more time passed, the more restless I got. Clearly, I was suffering from withdrawal. How long would this last? A few days? A week? Longer?

Soon, every other thought I had was about my desire to drink blood. It grew by the minute.

Blake did his best to provoke me. It only added to my stress. I couldn't bear it and only five days later, I ended up taking a long walk outside, far away from it all.

Walking always brought me some solace. I imagined I was with Bruce walking through the dried-out grass plains in southern France, the hot air caressing my skin, thunderstorms looming in the distance.

Every time I heard a noise out on the street, the thought of blood blasted through my brain like an air horn. The desire to drink completely overpowered me. Despite trying my best to stay focused on my steps, it followed me everywhere I went like my shadow. It was better to stay indoors and wait it out. But Blake would not stop poking me, trying to make me react…

The next day Holly was training with him when he accidentally cut her on her upper arm. It was not a deep wound, but deep enough to have blood spilling down her arm and dripping from her fingertips. The urge to drink was almost unbearable. I had stormed out and run for several hours. What if I had attacked her!

You are thinking just like them, I thought to myself.

You are one of us, the voice responded.

NO!

* * *

Two weeks passed but my condition did not improve. On the contrary, I could hardly concentrate. Nothing was a distraction anymore. I could not sleep. When I tried to read, I would read the same page over and over again without actually understanding anything. All I could clearly hear was Blake's heart throbbing in my ears and the whooshing of the blood circulating in his veins. It drove me crazy!

Whenever he trained with Holly, I had to leave the house. The two hearts beating rapidly made my mouth water. I could not risk being around them.

Once again, I was walking outside, trying to escape the horrible desire building in my stomach. My legs kept drumming on, but it was not enough to keep the rest of my body occupied. My mind begged me to search for molochs. It wasn't long before my ears picked up on sounds that were all too familiar. Fear rose inside me. I knew what would happen next.

NO!

I commanded my legs to walk on. I tried to make myself deaf to the welcoming sounds of molochs. But it was useless. The thirst overpowered me. I had abstained for too long; I couldn't control it anymore. I wanted it so bad. There was nothing else I could think about.

My senses searched for prey. My primal brain had taken over, completely crushing the rational human mind aside. I followed the noise. Their snarls and their scent always gave them away.

It wouldn't take me long to locate the group.

I ran as swiftly as I could towards the noise, the anticipation of the kill growing. It was as if I could taste the blood in my mouth already! Jumping over several fences, the sounds of the three molochs increased steadily. There was a beauty in their complete obliviousness to their imminent doom.

They were close now. I slowed down and let my ears guide me. Eagerly I hurried towards the small street where they were yapping at each other. Inhaling, I could smell they had fed recently. My excitement peaked.

With two quick strides I snuck up to the first one and twisted its head completely around. The body fell limply to the ground. Before the body reached the ground, the two other molochs jumped at me. One swung out its arm, but I caught it in time and ripped it out of its socket. The last one went for my thigh and sunk its teeth in. I swung the body of the second moloch against the third and both crashed to the ground.

The second moloch lunged at me, aiming with its one remaining arm for my face. Instantly, I moved to the side and got my gun out. With one bullet it was dead. The third made a run for it but a bullet later it was lying lifeless in the street. I had wanted to kill them by hand, but the urge was so strong I needed it to be over quickly.

Desperately, I leant over the nearest moloch and dug two fingers into the wound in its chest. They disappeared into my mouth and the blood quickly entered my system. I continuously dipped my index and middle finger in the red liquid spilling out of the wound and licked it off my fingers. The feeling of ecstasy built, taking me away from my pain. All connections in my brain were formed again; all of Caleb's manipulations were erased; I was myself again. The gnawing addiction stilled as I caved into it. It was peaceful and quiet in my mind.

Too soon the flow of blood from the wound slowed. I didn't want to dig around the moloch's inner organs. I crawled to the next one and scooped up the blood and let it drip into my mouth, rolling my head back and opening my mouth wide. The high was now full-on. I was almost lifted out of my own body. My senses were heightened. This was too good to ever stop, even if I wanted to. I would not be able to. And I didn't care.

Within minutes I had swallowed enough blood to satisfy my thirst. The thrill of the kill and subsequent reward fuelled my high further. It was almost too much to bear for a human body. With the back of my hand I wiped my mouth, smearing blood across my face and hands. I leaned back against the building wall and enjoyed the tingling in my veins. The pumping of the blood through my body made a rhythmic distribution of the ecstasy. The peak slowly descended into a state of complete satisfaction. Just like after orgasm, that feeling of fulfilment with a pinch of exhaustion. Though this did not feel like an orgasm, the build-up, climax and following satisfaction followed the same pattern.

When I stood up, my knees were still weak from the sudden rush of hormones. At the same time, I felt stronger and more powerful than before, as if I had absorbed energy through the blood. It made me laugh out loud. This was far better than any earthly drugs. No human or ghost could possibly experience this feeling of power and undeniable superiority accompanied with incredible satisfaction and happiness.

I breathed in the air deeply when I realised someone was watching me. I froze in place. The person was standing in front of a streetlight. Their silhouette looked like a sombre shadow. The colours in my vision had been replaced with greys.

Carefully, I took a few steps closer. Breathing in deeply I smelled the person standing a good fifty yards away; the smell was familiar.

As I came closer, I recognised the smell. I continued to approach until I was close enough to see his face. His eyes were filled with disappointment. They glistened in the streetlight with anger and sadness. After all these months my disgusting secret had been discovered. My high descended into distress.

'I'm sorry,' I muttered. The shame overtook all feelings of satisfaction.

Blake halfway rolled his eyes and I could see tears in them. 'Is this why you killed Jesper?'

I nodded. The look in his eyes cut right through my heart.

'And why you attacked me?'

Again, I nodded. My eyes were starting to sting. 'It... it started with just one drop and... and it made me feel good-' a sob rattled through me mid-sentence. 'I kept going and the feeling got better and I- I tried to stop but- but… it was too- hard'

The realisation of how much the blood had affected me suddenly hit like a train at high speed. It had been so innocent at first. All it did was make me feel good, closer to the life I had lost. Soon it had taken over. It had changed who I was…

'Why didn't you come to me?' Blake's voice broke and more tears welled up in my eyes.

'I… I… I-was ashamed,' I whispered.

Blake inhaled sharply and brushed his hand over his eyes. 'Oh Meerah this is really bad,' he admitted in a low voice.

'I'm sorry.'

Blake took me into his arms and we both cried. For a moment the world disappeared and we were the only ones there.

Something between us started vibrating. I detached myself from Blake. He reached into his jacket and answered the phone. My ears were sharp from the moloch blood and I heard the conversation.

'Let's go,' he said, trying to sound like his usual self again. Once again, this world had not given me more than a few seconds to catch my breath, before demanding my full attention again. This was a never-ending fight.

As we approached the house, I could sense Caleb's distress in the air. Even Blake seemed to feel it. He threw me a worried look.

'He knows, doesn't he?' I whispered.

He didn't answer and to be honest, he didn't need to. I was certain he knew. When we arrived at the front of the house, I could see him glued to the window. The moment he saw us, he disappeared and came running out the front door moments later.

'Caleb be careful, you might be seen!' Blake rushed towards him annoyed. He eyed the street but there was no one. Blake ushered him up the stairs and I followed.

'Children,' Caleb said, barely able to formulate words. 'Something has happened!' He reached the top of the steps and looked like he was on speed.

'I know you are worried but-' I tried to reason with him, but what could I tell him? That it would be ok? How would I know?

'Children, we have to evacuate.'

That was a bit drastic... and how would we evacuate anyway? Evacuate where? Out of this world?

Blake grabbed my arm before I could respond. 'What do you mean?' he asked Caleb.

'The witches – they will try a spell in just a few hours and... it could go wrong so we... we need to be prepared!' Caleb was completely scattered.

'What are you talking about? What witches?!'

Blake's eyes were fixed on Caleb. 'Go back to our human lives?' he asked in disbelief.

Caleb reached for Blake's shoulders. 'Yes, nothing is guaranteed but... if it goes wrong then... yes.'

My head was spinning. I stumbled backwards and let myself fall into the chair behind me. This could not be happening. Seeing my family after all this time? I could finally escape this terrible world, go back to my innocent life!

But...

'Going back home?' Blake's voice trembled.

No.

This could not be happening. Not now, not now...

'Do you think it will work? What the witches are trying to do?'

Caleb shrugged with his shoulders. 'I don't know, but they have been wrong in the past and I don't want you to miss this opportunity!' The glow and excitement in Caleb's eyes were illuminating the room.

'I can't.'

Caleb turned his gaze away from Blake to look at me. 'My child you have been waiting for this since you got here! Why would you not leave now that you have the chance?'

'She's right,' Blake concurred. 'She can't.'

Caleb sensed something was wrong. I could not bring myself to tell him.

'Look at her eyes,' Blake whispered, looking at the floor.

The closer Caleb got to me the more he frowned, trying to see something. I couldn't look at him and averted my eyes. Caleb kneeled down to eye level and reached with his hand for my chin. Tears were in my eyes and I closed them when he turned my face towards him, dragging out the inevitable.

Eventually, I opened my eyes and let him see. Faded colours had started to reappear in my sight. I knew my pupils were still cat-like.

Caleb looked at me, his face so close to mine I could see the individual pores on his forehead. His emotions spilled over into me. Wonder, anger, disappointment, hurt...

He let go and leant backwards, away from me, his eyes still inspecting me. 'Tell me what you've done.' He rose to his feet and turned his back to me.

The weight of his authority pushed down on me. I could feel myself sinking further into the chair.

'I... I have been drinking... mo-moloch blood,' I said under my breath, hoping he wouldn't hear me.

'For how long?' his voice boomed disapprovingly.

A sob shook through me. 'Several months'

'And why would you do such a horrible thing?!'

'Because it... made me feel good,' I admitted.

Caleb paused. He turned around and eyed me suspiciously. Apparently, he had not expected that response. 'It makes you... feel *good?*'he repeated.

'Yes, it makes me feel good,' I repeated.

Caleb paused again. He was puzzled, looking at the floor, thinking. 'It... it shouldn't,' he said. He folded his hands behind his back and started pacing slowly around the table, his face frowning. 'This… this is not normal…'

'Is she turning into a moloch?' Blake inquired.

Caleb looked up but not at him. Then, he shook his head and started pacing again. 'No, no, not moloch… something else…'

The confusion in my head pushed away the crying and sobbing. Was I becoming something else? That could not be! This was an addiction like drugs or alcohol! Yes, it changed me a bit but not my essential existence! People taking drugs were not transforming into goats. This was nonsense!

Eventually, Caleb stopped pacing and looked at the two of us. 'We don't have time for this. Blake, go pack your things. We need to get Holly and then get into position!'

I got up but Caleb's eyes made me stop in my tracks.

'You.' He grabbed me by my arms. 'You can't go back to the human world. It is too dangerous.'

I knew he was right but being so close and yet so far from my family was tearing me apart. 'I just stay here?'

Caleb thought about it for a moment. Then his face changed. 'No, I will take you to the woods, where the werewolves live.'

'The… the werewolves? First witches and now werewolves?'

'You will have to be careful. I think you are changing into something dark and they hunt vampires. But it is the only way. You will have to learn to deal with whatever is inside you!'

'No, no, no, Caleb, I'm not changing into a moloch! I'm just addicted that's all! Caleb I can stop!' I could feel the panic rising. The slingshot around my throat tightened.

'It's too late my child, too late to go back. We do not have a lot of time. I cannot explain everything. I will take you to the woods. You will need to learn to control your urges. I will come and visit you in a while and when you're ready, I will get you back to your family.'

I shook my head and closed my eyes. 'Caleb this is not making any sense!'

'I know.' He brushed strands of hair out of my face.

When I looked at him, I saw love mixed with sadness in his eyes. Blake was coming down the stairs now, a small backpack in his hand.

'We must go!' Caleb turned away from me and hurried down the stairs out to the car.

Numbly I walked into my bedroom and reached for my jacket and a backpack. The only items I threw into it were a few sets of clean clothes, some loose pictures of loved ones, a knife and my phone and charger. What the hell was I going to do to in the woods?!

I heard shouting outside. I assumed it was Blake and Caleb. Without looking back a second time, I hurried out of my room and left my life as a ghost behind. Every step I took I realised I was walking away from all the fighting, all the monsters, all the bad memories, only to walk into another world that was filled with other monsters and more fighting. If I had not been so stupid, I could be going home now...

The muffled voices got louder with each step closer to the front door. To think that it could have all ended now... How did Caleb know about this spell?

When I opened the door, I saw Blake and Caleb arguing aggressively.

'You do not know, boy!' Caleb shouted at him, spitting the last word out as an insult.

'Neither do you! What makes you think you could even get her out of the Territories? The wolves will hunt you too!'

'I know a witch. How else do you think I knew about this spell! Nikaya's sister told me! And when the time is right and she's able to control herself, I will ask Nikaya's sister to open a portal and let us through!'

Were those the same portals masters used to go into the human world when they were looking for new recruits? But...

why could we use them now? Why had this never come up before?

'How can you trust her?! If this spell doesn't work what makes you think she'll help you? What makes you think they wouldn't track her magic and see her opening a portal for a master and... and... whatever *she's* becoming!' Blake flailed his arms as he spoke.

Caleb sighed deeply. 'What choice do I have?'

Before Blake could answer he shook his head and saw me standing by the door. Caleb followed his gaze. A wave of love invaded my mind, numbing my anxiety.

'We don't have time to argue. We need to get Holly,' Caleb's voice sung in my head.

'Turn it off Caleb!' I tried to sound firm, but it came across as a grateful remark. The wave of affection lessened.

Blake made the engine roar and we were off to Caleb's house. I tried calling Kim, but her phone kept sending me straight to voicemail. Caleb assured me he had told Dominic and they were probably on their way out too.

'Don't be upset Ameerah. I am sure it will all work out. The werewolf territory is no more dangerous than Idolon. You'll be fine,' Caleb tried to soothe me.

'How can you be so sure?' I turned from my seat to look at him.

Caleb caressed my face with his fingertips. 'Because you will learn to control it. You might not be changing completely. I think you will survive with this sort of second person inside you. Once you are no longer a danger to yourself, I will get you back to the human world.'

I saw Blake shaking his head.

'What?' I turned to face Blake.

Blake looked at me. 'We don't know what is happening with you and I don't think promising you that everything will be alright is the right thing to do,' he stated coldly, throwing a glance at Caleb through the rear-view mirror.

Caleb's face twisted in anger. 'How dare you contradict me in front of her?! Meerah, I am sure it will be alright. Don't listen to him; he's pessimistic as always!' A wave of affection tried to drown out all anxiety in me.

'No, I'm **realistic**! Ameerah' Blake turned to look at me briefly while he was driving, 'I don't mean to scare you, but this won't be a walk in the park, do you understand? You have been drinking moloch blood and it has altered your genes. You will probably have to continue drinking blood and this will just make everything worse. If anyone can make it, you can, but you need to really work on understanding whatever is happening to you and learn to control it. And I won't be there to help you.' He turned towards me again when he spoke those last words.

Blake was worried about me. All this time he had been incredibly tough and pushed me beyond my limits, but it had been with good intentions. Now I wouldn't be able to rely on him anymore. It was just me, in a foreign land with foreign creatures, including myself.

'I won't forget you, my child.' Caleb took my hand and massaged my fingers, sensing my distress.

'Can't you come with me?' I pleaded.

Caleb's mouth tightened into a line. No, of course not. He wanted to go back to his family. I couldn't blame him. In his shoes, I would have done the same. The enormity of what lay before me overwhelmed me. What had I gotten myself into?

Blake stopped the car and Caleb jumped out to get Holly.

The colours had returned in my sight. How long would it last though? When would I need my next batch of blood? If the past was any indication, I would need to feed again by tomorrow...

'You can do this Meerah.' Blake pulled me out of my negative spiral.

'Easy for you to say,' I retorted.

'I've trained you for more than two years. I know what you are capable of. You just... you just have to trust yourself and be disciplined. Don't let your guard down.'

'Did you know there were werewolves? All these other things? Beings? Worlds?'

'I did. I was told about them a few years after I came to this world. Things didn't add up, so I asked questions...' Blake trailed off, his eyes looking emptily into the air.

'Why didn't Caleb tell *me?*'

Blake still stared into the air. 'You haven't been here long. There are a lot of things here that even I don't know.'

Caleb reappeared with Holly following after him. Light started appearing on the horizon.

We drove for a short while and when the car stopped again Caleb told me this was where I had to go. We were in front of a four-story high building with a brick underway in the shape of an arch.

'If the spell goes wrong, you will see an opening appear under the arch. That will be the gate to enter the Territories. It will be mostly forest, hills, lakes, vast grass lands. There are many small towns, but it's all very rural. It's where the werewolves live. You have to stay away from them. To a werewolf, molochs and vampires have a distinct scent and I'm guessing you will have a scent as well.' Caleb explained everything quickly, rushing the words. 'Find an abandoned house somewhere and make that your home. When you hear werewolves, climb up into the trees and hide. It will be harder for them to track you.'

'When will you come and get me?' I asked eagerly.

'I don't know my child. You will be on your own the first few months at least. But I won't forget you. I will come back for you my sweet Ameerah.' Caleb caressed my face.

'What do I do?' It felt like I was going to another planet. Everything would be completely foreign. How would I hunt with those werewolves around? I realised at that moment I had not taken a gun or any ammunition with me. The one time I really needed it...

'Drink blood, stay out of trouble and avoid the werewolves. You can do it Meerah.' Caleb smiled at me encouragingly. He hugged me tightly and I could feel the boost of positive emotions. It felt so good, but sadness inevitably followed.

Caleb let go and smiled at me one last time before getting back into the car. Holly hugged me tightly and wished me the best of luck, tears in her eyes.

Blake had gotten out and was eyeing me anxiously. At first, we looked at each other, not sure what to do. Finally, he approached me and we hugged. I breathed in his scent. Emotions overwhelmed me and a few tears left my eyes.

'Remember your training, ok?' Blake said, gently swaying me from side to side, holding me close.

'I will.'

We detached from each other, my hands falling into his. The moment went on. I kept looking into his eyes. After all this time, all the fighting and yelling, hating each other and living together, we'd reached an abrupt end. Would I ever see him again? I doubted it. This was goodbye forever. Suddenly I felt lost. He had been by my side for such a long time. I had grown used to having him. He had always protected me, in his own way.

Eventually, he inhaled deeply and turned away. When he reached the car, he turned back to look at me one last time. With a smile on his lips, he got into the car and they drove off, leaving me standing by myself, in front of the portal to the werewolves. I felt very alone. The world bore down on me.

Maybe this wouldn't happen? Oh of course it would! I always had bad luck!

I looked through the archway and only saw the inner court of the red-bricked building. Was there really going to be an opening into another world? How did Caleb know? How would I recognise the portal? This was crazy!

A few hours passed and nothing happened. I sat on the curb, waiting for… well, something. During that time, I didn't encounter a single soul. There was a weird atmosphere in the air, as if there was an imminent storm coming and the locals had deserted the city. Had everyone left? Did they all know what was coming?

My phone rang. It was Kim.

'I just saw Blake and he told me. I'm so sorry Ameerah!' Wherever she was there was lots of noise. I could hear people shouting in the background.

'I wish I had listened to you!'

There was a subtle trembling in the ground. As if a herd of elephants was approaching.

'It's happening! Ameerah I'm so sorry, but I know you will be ok. I will find you. We will get you out!' Kim screamed into the receiver over the noise.

The trembling became more and more violent. Things started falling onto the street, windows started breaking.

Then my phone cut off entirely. I tried calling Kim, but the ground moved and cracked. My phone slipped from my hands and slid out of my reach. The sky thundered without any clouds in sight, buildings started wobbling, car sirens started to howl, buildings and roads cracked open as the world was ripped apart.

I crouched on the ground, leaning against the brick wall, hoping it would protect me. The red bricks were neatly stacked and the magnificent building held.

Without any warning, all trembling ceased and a deafening quietness followed. The dust slowly settled. It had only lasted for a few minutes.

Hesitantly, I got up and looked around. I approached the archway and peered through it. And there it was.

An opening like an invisible door had been cut through the air. I could see the green grass and trees crowning over it, accompanied by the sounds of the forest.

My knees shook. This was it. I had to jump into this other world not knowing what was waiting for me on the other side. My hands gripped tighter around the straps of my almost empty backpack. What had I been thinking? I should have taken my bedcover, a lighter, guns, ammunition, blood bags, a book on how to survive in nature! Something! I had literally nothing!

I couldn't stay here. Caleb had told me to go and I trusted him. I looked around one last time and still saw no signs of life on this side of the portal. Everyone that had known had gone back to the human world. I was the only loser going into yet another world full of monsters.

With trembling limbs, I approached the opening, taking in the ocean of green. The smell of the forest invited me closer. One last deep breath in Idolon, and I stepped through the door into werewolf territory. My steps were cushioned by the grass. Carefully, I walked further into the forest, scanning the surrounding area. There were birds singing, insects chirping, rustling of leaves on the trees, creaking of branches swaying in the gentle breeze. I had forgotten all those sounds. There had been no birds or any kind of sounds of nature in Idolon. Was this the other side? Only nature? No human buildings, streets or windows?

The sun glistened between the thick canopy of leaves above me. The air smelled of wetness and tree bark. My body relaxed at the welcoming sensations the forest gave me. Maybe this wasn't so bad. All I had to do was... survive. I started walking deeper into the forest, away from the portal, in search of shelter and... food.

If you enjoyed reading this book, please consider leaving a review on Amazon, Goodreads or any other platform. Reviews really help independent authors like myself.

If you'd like to stay up to date on the sequel of When Colour Became Grey and my other works, you can follow me here;

- Instagram: aclorenzen
- Blog: aclorenzen.org
- Facebook Author page:
  https://www.facebook.com/author.aclorenzen

ACKNOWLEDGEMENTS

I'd like to thank Conor Welter, for his extensive editing and proof-reading efforts. You were able to cut through the sometimes wordy and incomprehensible twists of my phrases, and rewrite what I was trying to say in readable English. Thank you for polishing my rough story into the amazing version it is today.

I'd like to thank Hampton Lamoureux who took my rudimentary sketch and made it into a gorgeous book cover. You understood what I was trying to convey and put my words into a much better picture than I could have ever imagined. Thank you for creating this awesome cover.

And finally, thank you to Simon, who always encouraged me to keep writing. No words will ever be enough to describe all you've done for me. I couldn't have done it without you.

Printed in Great Britain
by Amazon

85209792R00180